Kovana

Book Two of
the Outsider series.

by
Aiden Phoenix

D1526982

Kovana

ISBN: 9798393251826

Cover created by Aiden Phoenix.

Table of Contents

Welcome to Collisa!

Collisa is a new world brimming with opportunities for adventure and growth. It is also brimming with chances for romance and fun. This is the story of Dare and the life he builds for himself with the women he meets and falls in love with.

As you can guess, it is a harem tale, with all that includes. Be aware that it features varied and explicit erotic scenes between multiple partners. It is intended to be enjoyed by adults. All characters involved in adult scenes are over the age of 18.

Prologue
Farming

Dare stood over the small chest stowed at the back of the crude tent, heart pounding with excitement.

This was the first chest he'd found since his unseen benefactor had reincarnated him, then brought him to this world that was so similar to the games he'd loved in his previous life on Earth. An actual treasure chest with a lock, that is, not a mere container to hold possessions.

"It could just have junk in it, or a handful of copper," he told himself, trying to keep his expectations in check.

At his side Zuri, the tiny goblin woman he'd saved from a panther and who'd since become his lover and leveling companion, looked up, thinking he was talking to her. "Chest spawns are very rare," she said, voice soft and sweet with a pleasantly high pitch, "especially outside of dungeons or mega spawn points. They always have something good."

On his other side Ilin nodded. "Besides, we had to clear a hundred or so even level kobolds a half a dozen times to reset this camp before we got lucky. And we could've easily cleared it a thousand more without seeing a chest."

It was still sometimes odd to hear the people of this world talk about game mechanics, or world mechanics he supposed, as if they were a part of daily life. Although if the terms got too technical the world system tended to fuzz them out, likely to maintain realism.

Dare nodded at the Monk's explanation, taking his word for it.

The man had recently joined them as a leveling companion, although while he was friendly and seemed to like them well enough, he didn't trust them enough to join their party. In lieu of that, they'd made an arrangement to split the experience and loot as best they could, with a wager Dare had lost against Ilin netting the Monk a small piece of his share.

Still, the arrangement had been going incredibly well, with all three of them gaining over a full level in the four days they'd been working together. In fact, Dare and Zuri were both almost to their next level after being halfway through Level 12 to begin with.

For his part Ilin was absolutely blown away by how quickly they were all getting experience. He'd expected it would take months of careful work to reach Level 15, and was eager to keep up the progress as the group traveled north to Kov, hoping to gain even more levels since the arrangement was working so well.

Dare had no arguments with that. The man might not do an equal amount of damage in the party, due to the fact that Dare and Zuri with their ranged attacks usually had one or two enemies dead before any adds reached the Monk. But he kept aggro on the enemies that did reach them, letting the ranged keep doing damage and lessening the risk of serious injury or death.

He made a good safety net in case something went wrong. And when they all *did* want to kill enemies faster, and felt comfortable with the risk, Dare would pull one or two for Ilin to kill as he Zuri focused on their own targets.

"Well, shall I do the honors?" the bald monk abruptly asked, breaking the reverent silence.

"Go for it," Dare said. "I don't know how to pick a lock." He glanced questioningly at Zuri.

His little lover laughed. "Yeah, that would go so well with my Healer abilities."

Ilin joined the laughter. "No, no Rogue-type abilities here." He stared at the lock as if sizing it up, flexing his hand and making a fist. "But I've honed my body and channeled my inner lines to where my flesh and bones can best steel if called for."

This Dare had to see. He watched intently as the Monk took a meditative position, breathing deeply in and out a few times. Then with a sharp cry for focus and power, the bald man struck the lock with the knife edge of his hand.

The cheap iron cracked and shattered, falling away, and with a triumphant grin Ilin crouched to flip open the lid.

The almost humble pile of items within the comparatively larger space would've been disappointing if not for their quality.

Item quality ranks went, in order from worst to best: Trash, Poor, Decent, Good, Journeyman, Exceptional, Master, and Fabled. Dare had never seen anything better than Good aside from a single Exceptional item, the Level 20 short bow he had his eye on and the entire reason he wanted it. And given the steep rise in stats for each quality rank, Master and Fabled were probably completely insane.

The higher quality ones, including his bow, had a chance for item bonuses that increased their power, gave extra stats, or even gave the bearer a unique ability while worn. Including the short bow he wanted.

That was why he was so excited to see the bracelet lying on a pillow of tattered kobold cloth at the top of the small pile.

It was a wide band of crudely refined and hammered silver, polished to a mirror sheen, with inexpertly cut emeralds inset all around its circumference. The quality of the workmanship was obviously barely above Trash, but the quality of the materials used to craft it, ie the silver and emeralds, were so high for this level that they bumped it up to Exceptional all on their own.

Or maybe the quality was judged on the basis of kobold crafting ability, in which case maybe it *was* exceptional.

Either way, while it had no stat bonuses and its armor bonus was modest, its item bonus increased mana regeneration by 20%. It was also locked to healing classes.

In other words, Zuri had just picked up a kickass item that would help them level faster. Granted, her mana regeneration at this level was pretty slow, so 20% was a humble gain. But it would mean ten or so more Mana Thorns a day, which would let them kill things that much faster.

Or, for that matter, a better chance she'd have the mana needed for healing in an emergency; she was keeping her reserves high enough to heal one of them up from critical injuries, which meant that mana wasn't going towards killing monsters.

The item even had a name: Den Mother's Grace.

Ilin whistled when he saw it. "That's the most valuable, high quality ugly piece of shit I've ever seen."

"I don't know, it depends on who's wearing it." Dare picked it up and slipped it onto Zuri's wrist, admiring its contrast to her smooth, avocado-green skin. "Beautiful."

His tiny lover blushed and ducked her head, tucking a lock of sleek black hair behind her pointy ear. But she looked pleased as she fingered the piece of jewelry, which fit her slim wrist surprisingly well. "Is it fair for me to have this?" she protested.

Their new companion rummaged through the chest, pulling out two gold coins. "If me and Dare each take one of these for our share, I'll call it even. We can sell the other junk loot and materials and split the profits."

Dare brightened at the sight of the gleaming coin. It was the first one he'd seen on Collisa, let alone owned; at the earlier levels he'd been scraping to gather copper, and even with their current success farming they were looking at loot items valued at a few silver at best.

The money system was fairly simple. Perhaps almost childishly so, to make it easy to do the math. Which he guessed was imposed by the world system as part of its balancing and making Collisa more user friendly.

In any case the precious metals in order of value went copper, silver, gold, truesilver, and godmetal. It took 100 of each to equal the next higher value coin, so 100 copper was equal to 1 silver, 100 silver to one gold, and so on.

That meant that Dare had technically already earned a few gold in terms of value. But this was his first *gold*. And considering it had come out of a piece of junk chest in a filthy kobold tent, it shone beautifully.

Two gold might've seemed like a lousy haul for a rare spawn world chest, even including Den Mother's Grace and the value of the rest of the stuff. But considering this was a Level 14 chest, and comparing it to the value of loot from monsters at this level, it was more than generous and he was overjoyed at it.

He tucked the coin into his pouch with a grin. "Exceptional quality short bow, here I come."

"You want to go back to Driftwain right now?" Zuri asked, taking him literally. She looked a bit reluctant at the idea; understandable, considering how the people in the small town not far south of them treated goblins.

Dare was definitely considering it, especially now that she'd suggested the idea.

Because he was almost Level 14 he'd been planning to head back to Driftwain pretty soon anyway, to sell the Level 11 longbow he was using and purchase a Level 14 recurve bow. Which he hoped would bridge the gap to his coveted Level 20 short bow.

Besides, they needed to sell all the loot they'd collected over the last few days and split the profits in any case. "I wouldn't say no to going now," he said. "It would be a good break from the grind." He rubbed between his tiny lover's shoulders. "And we could maybe visit a tavern and order a proper meal. Something cooked by professionals."

Ilin snorted. "I don't know, my friend. Your cooking is pretty good." He motioned. "But you're right, we're starting to get loaded down with loot from the absolutely insane number of monsters we've killed since teaming up."

Zuri looked between them, then grudgingly nodded. "I'll hold you to that meal."

Chuckling, Dare stooped to kiss her sharp-featured cheek, then gathered up the rest of the loot in the chest and backed out of the tent.

It only took a few more minutes to finish looting the rest of the cleared kobold camp. Most of the stuff was garbage that didn't even qualify as vendor trash, but they found a few useful things. Metal could be salvaged for scrap, and even the worst cloth could always be repurposed by tailors. And there were a few trinkets here and there that might catch a vendor's eye.

And all the tools, of course. It was the entrance camp to a mine after all.

At the thought, Dare stared at the yawning opening leading into the nearby large hill. The entrance to a Level 21 dungeon. So far no stronger enemies had emerged from there, only the weak kobold laborers pushing carts and wheelbarrows full of dirt and ore.

He wondered how far inside he'd have to go to be "in" the dungeon. And whether he'd immediately aggro enemies.

Either way, he wasn't about to poke that bear until he was at least Level 20, preferably with his Exceptional bow, and had a group of people he trusted. Although more likely they'd leave for Kov, the region capitol to the north, long before they reached that level.

They could always come back later.

Once they'd stripped the camp of every possible item of any value, they left it behind to return to their own camp in a secluded grove nearby. The kobold camp would reset when the monsters respawned, with new loot respawning as well.

Including possibly another chest . . . not likely at all, but Dare's unseen benefactor *had* told him he'd have better than average luck along with the other gifts she'd given him. Such as the body of an elite athlete, the looks of a top movie star, and apparently the intelligence of Earth's top minds. Which was a bit harder to test.

Oh, also his Adventurer's Eye, the ability to see the information of monsters and other targets around him. Stuff that no one else on Collisa had access to aside from by dangerous and exhaustive experimentation.

That was something most people didn't or couldn't do, and so every monster they saw was a terrifying unknown that could either be weak enough to kill with a few blows, or powerful enough to tear them to pieces in seconds.

Explaining why so few people decided to become adventurers and brave the wilds.

He'd also been given Fleetfoot, increasing his speed by 34%. Which affected *everything* influenced by speed, from movement to weapon attacks to evasion. Even his *reflexes*.

It was completely busted. Especially considering the fact that one of the other two options Dare had been offered along with Fleetfoot was an ability that increased his experience gains by 50%. Which on the surface seemed incredible, until you considered that with Fleetfoot he'd be able to kill enemies 34% faster, run between spawn points 34% faster, and have an easier time killing the enemies because he could usually stay out of their reach.

If anything, Fleetfoot let him level up *faster* than a flat 50% experience increase would've. And it was way more useful.

Not to mention way more *fun*. He could do stuff he hadn't been able to on Earth, like magic tricks and acrobatics and juggling. Which Zuri found endlessly entertaining, often asking him to show her another trick or do some more tumbling. Or try to work his way up to being able to juggle another ball on top of the four he could do at the moment.

As for his unseen benefactor's gifts, probably the most surprising thing she'd given him was a night of literally mind-blowing sex, when she visited him in a not-dream dream in the form of a shadow woman.

When it came to his good luck, though, Dare hadn't gotten around to trying it out yet. Although it might account for how he'd survived some of his close calls in the almost two months since coming to Collisa.

Still, it would be fun to try his hand at cards or dice or other games of chance.

Back at their camp they sorted all their loot, trying to determine whether they could carry it all to Driftwain. Ilin could carry a shocking amount with his short, lean, perfectly honed Monk body, especially with the new pack Dare had crafted for him (and sold him at a reasonable price, at his insistence).

Dare could carry a reasonable amount, although the Hunter class didn't get significant strength gains like some others and he had to rely on the universal strength abilities. Zuri, with her small size and delicate frame, could carry the least of all.

At first he was worried they wouldn't be able to take it all. But ultimately, with some inventive packing and taking advantage of Ilin's practically obscene carry capacity, they managed to load everything up.

Nothing left behind for thieves or wandering monsters to steal.

Returning to the road leading from Driftwain to Kov, they turned south to walk the couple hours to the small town.

Kovana

* * * * *

Ilin really was a great traveling companion.

On top of having proven to be a good teammate and, ultimately, a good man who treated Zuri with respect and kindness, the Monk also stood out in a crowd: his shaved head, odd mannerisms, and the flowing robes and cowled hood he wore when traveling all drew people's attention. So much so that the fact that they were traveling with a goblin who didn't look or act like a slave went mostly ignored.

Zuri quickly realized it, too, and began to relax as they made their way through Driftwain's north gate and navigated the sparse crowds on their way to the market.

The first item of business was selling their loot, of course. They'd already divvied up all the coin and the few things they wanted to keep, but that left a huge pile of low quality items they had to try to pawn off on reluctant vendors, with much haggling and moving on to try again with someone else.

Dare found himself missing Lone Ox, the village he'd appeared close to when he first came to Collisa. Part of his deal with the Mayor, when he accepted the quest to clear out the bandits plaguing the village, was that Lone Ox would purchase any and all loot Dare brought at fair prices.

He'd made the most of that benefit while he was leveling in the area, and now he realized just how useful it had been. "Maybe we should take all this south to sell there," he joked after telling Ilin about his deal with the village.

The Monk threw back his head and laughed. "You'd bankrupt the poor farmers at this point," he said, clapping him on the back. "We'll just have to do our best here."

The bald ascetic turned out to be a great haggler, so much so that they agreed he should take the lead in negotiations with vendors.

Dare didn't mind too much. He prided himself in making sharp offers and counteroffers, and knowing when the other person was going to sell or going to bail. But he tended to be aggressive and in some cases more combative than he needed to be.

Ilin, on the other hand, was warm and friendly, drawing people in despite the fact that he was a foreigner with strange customs and an odd appearance. Or maybe that was part of his charm.

It also helped that he had an almost inhuman ability to stay calm and maintain his friendly demeanor in the face of outrageous offers, insults, and even mild threats of violence. He would speak quietly and reasonably in the face of any arguments, and somehow by the end of it the deal was usually in his favor.

Even though he didn't seem to be trying to press for any advantage in the bartering; it just came to him, like he had some mystical ability to make the universe work in his favor.

Dare, on the other hand, made do with a best out of five dice throws challenge with a particularly stubborn vendor, and walked away with the prices he wanted after winning four tosses in a row before finally losing one.

Ultimately they managed to sell the loot for a few gold and a handful of silver, and divvied it all as they'd originally agreed. After some discussion they decided to meet back up in a few hours at an inn Ilin recommended for dinner. Then the Monk excused himself; he was headed to a charitable organization he'd found in his previous passage through the town, where he planned to donate his excess funds and volunteer whatever aid he could.

The man didn't try to guilt Dare and Zuri into doing some charitable work themselves, but Dare still found himself handing over a handful of silver and several pounds of meat freshly harvested that morning to feed the town's orphans.

To his surprise, Zuri asked to go with the monk. "I want to help those in need too," she said, looking equal parts nervous and determined. As if afraid Dare would be mad at her for leaving his side. But the decision fit the kindhearted goblin; from what he'd seen of her, she hadn't chosen the Healer class for personal benefit.

"I think that's a wonderful thing to do," he said, leaning down to hug her. "Have fun, and be safe."

Ilin clapped him on the shoulder, smiling warmly. "Don't worry, I'll tear the arm off anyone who tries to harm her." His tone was light, but the fact that the Monk physically could, and by temperament would, do such a thing to protect a friend lent weight to his reassurance.

Nodding, Dare made his way over to the bowyer's stall to finally get his long-anticipated new weapons.

"Looking at the short bow again?" the vendor asked, pulling the item out of the same dusty corner he'd been storing it the first time Dare visited.

No surprise; in spite of its Exceptional quality and item bonuses, the thing's durability was a sliver of red. The vendor didn't have the skill to repair it and neither did anyone else in this small town, so he couldn't give the thing away to passing adventurers. And its Level 20 requirement meant only the guards and a handful of retired adventurers in town could even use it, so the demand for it wasn't exactly insane.

That was the only reason Dare was willing to buy what otherwise would've been a cripplingly expensive bow, with the downside of only a small increase in speed to make up for a moderate decrease in damage compared other bow types.

Especially since one of the bow's Exceptional quality item bonuses was 10% extra shadow damage while Stealthed, an ability he couldn't get. At least not yet; in his experience Stealth could potentially be in the Hunter wheelhouse depending on the game. And this world seemed pretty generous with abilities.

He supposed he could ask his unseen benefactor if he really wanted to know. But why spoil the surprise?

In any case, part of his bow crafting ability tree was the ability to repair bows, which he'd debated spending a point on back when he'd got it but was now glad he had. It meant that not only could he repair his own bows in the wilds rather than needing to find a craftsman, but that he could afford to go for deals like this.

He couldn't wait to level to 20, repair that bad boy, and vaporize monsters with it.

Dare gave his coveted bow a disinterested glance and looked away. "Actually, I think you might've had a point about it being an ambitious purchase."

The vendor gave him a narrow gaze. "Says the man who by some miracle from the gods themselves has gained a level since I saw him last."

Dare ignored that, motioning to the Level 14 recurve bow. It was only Decent quality, but recurves had all around stronger stats in exchange for being more difficult to craft, and thus more expensive. "I think that's more my speed at the moment."

"Your speed?" the vendor repeated, confused. Then he dismissed the unfamiliar phrase and motioned to the short bow, looking disappointed. "We already had a soft agreement on a price for that, eh? Very reasonable if you ask me."

"Meh." Dare held out a hand for the recurve bow. "Can I see that?"

The man passed it over. "Very nice quality," he said. "Only repaired a few times, and always expertly by my own hands, so the max durability loss was minimal. And of course you can't go wrong with recurve bows. It'll serve you in good stead until you level past it." He smirked. "Which at your rate might not be long."

"It's a Decent bow," Dare said, an appraisal as well as a statement on the quality. "How much?"

The burly vendor rubbed his jaw. "25 silver."

Dare snorted. "10 silver less than you want for an Exceptional item 6 levels higher than it."

"*Now* you want to talk about the-" The man cut off, scowling. "We both know why the short bow is dirt cheap, don't use it as a bargaining chip for a completely different sale." He glowered. "Especially when you're not even interested in that bow."

"Well, I'm not completely uninterested." Dare unslung his Level 11 longbow and set it on the table. "How do you feel about package deals?"

The vendor gave him a suspicious look. "As in?"

"I give you more business by also selling you this bow I'll be replacing, and buying both that Level 20 albatross of yours *and* the recurve bow. We negotiate it all as a package deal and take a chunk off the price at the end."

"And why would I do that?"

"Because you're getting two sales and purchasing a useful item at a discount. That beats me just walking away from here with the recurve bow."

"That's a bizarre notion." The burly man scowled, then reluctantly set the short bow and recurve bow beside the long bow. "All right, show me your package."

Dare bit back a snicker; that euphemism either wasn't used here, or the man was secretly a wag with a phenomenal poker face. "All right, let's get down to brass tacks."

"Do you ever say anything understandable?" the vendor demanded.

Dare brushed that aside and settled in to haggle. It took a while, and the vendor wasn't exactly pleased by the time they agreed on the final price: 41 silver.

Ultimately Dare sold the longbow for 9 silver, and purchased the short bow and recurve both for 50. A loss on his current bow, which he expected, but a reasonable price for the other two. He was mostly pleased.

And now he was set up with awesome weapons for potentially the next 11 or so levels. Once he got the sliver of experience he needed to reach 14, that is; he'd have to use his dual knives for damage to get there.

Served him right for rushing straight to Driftwain rather than sticking around for a few hours longer.

He browsed the vendors for a bit longer and purchased a good sturdy hatchet to replace the shitty stone ones that he'd been using to gather firewood up to this point. They kept breaking and crafting them was a waste of time, so he was glad to spend a bit of silver to get around the problem.

Last of all Dare looked for a few gifts for Zuri, picking out some things he thought she'd like. Then, since he was done with business and there was still time before they met up for dinner, he went in search of quests.

The last time he and his goblin lover had been in town four days ago, they'd been so eager to leave that he hadn't even considered the possibility. But considering that a small place like Lone Ox had given him two good quests, it served to reason that there'd be at least a few here.

As it turned out there were. And they sucked.

Many games put in lame fetch quests and other time wasters, trying to pad out their gameplay hours. Especially a lot of MMOs scrambling for content. Of course that wouldn't be the motivation here, since this was a real world with similarities to a game.

The actual motivation was that most of the tasks real people had that they didn't want to do themselves involved fetching or delivering stuff. Or super dangerous stuff, which was awesome, but not much of that going on in Driftwain, apparently.

Dare accepted a quest to gather rare herbs in the area around town, since it identified those herbs for him and would increase his Foraging skill. In the future he'd also be able to gather those herbs himself and sell them for profit.

He also accepted two quests to deliver items to Kov, where he was headed anyway. Neither were on a clock, and while the rewards were only modest delivery fees the quests were only a bit out of his way.

There was also a quest from the Guard Commander to kill wolves and cougars, actual animal predators and not monsters, which were proving to be a plague on the local farmers. That made sense given the way this world was set up.

On Collisa, animals populated the same way they did on Earth. But to encourage adventurers and provide them with more enemies to level up on, the breeding and growth rate on animals was accelerated by quite a bit.

Which meant that predator populations could swiftly explode in an area and become a menace that needed to be cleared out.

Dare had already hunted a good number of wolves and cougars, and captured more in his snares. Unfortunately those didn't count to his quest, so he'd have to go get more. It was a number he should be able to get fairly easily, though, so worth his time.

The jackpot quest, however, came from the Mayor's office. A quest to curtail the growing kobold menace, before they could break free of their spawn point and begin sneaking about in the night stealing and murdering livestock and isolated townspeople.

To his amusement, it looked as if Ilin had already turned in the quest; he must've picked it up his previous trip, what was doubtless not only how he'd known about the monsters but also one of the reasons he'd been motivated to hunt them.

However, the quest was still open to him and Zuri: kill 100 kobolds and burn down their main camp. Which also explained why the reserved, ascetic Monk had gotten on a bit of a pyro streak their second day of hunting the monsters.

The reward was a Writ of Reimbursement that could be redeemed in Kov at the Guardmaster's office for 1 gold.

Since Dare was party leader he was able to accept the quest on Zuri's behalf as well. They'd both complete the quest for killing the same 100 kobolds, which was nice. Although ultimately unnecessary; by the time they got back to Driftwain for another trade run they'd probably have killed hundreds or even thousands more of the things.

Dare also accepted the quest to kill the wolves and cougars on his lover's behalf, although unfortunately none of the other quests on offer could be done by both of them.

By the time he finished running around town, if not certain he'd gotten every quest available then confident he'd gotten the ones worth picking up, and definitely all the ones he wanted to bother with finding, he was running late for dinner. He dashed to the inn Ilin had described and reached it in time to meet the Monk and Zuri at the door.

"You got both bows!" his goblin lover cried as she rushed over to inspect the recurve bow slung on his back, and the tip of the short bow sticking out of his pack. "Did you get a good deal for them?"

"Good enough." Dare leaned down to kiss her, ignoring the disgusted murmurs of passersby, then reached into his pack and pulled out a cute embroidered dress he'd purchased for her. He'd crafted her a fine ermine fur and leather outfit a few days ago, but for more formal occasions he thought she'd like to dress up a bit.

It seemed like he was right, given how she brightened like the sun and immediately searched for a secluded place to change in the inn's voiding room, leaving Dare and Ilin to find a table and settle in with mugs of beer.

The serving woman who brought the drinks smiled a bit more warmly as she looked Dare over, and after taking their orders paused to flirt a bit, asking questions about their adventuring.

Once she finally left the Monk grinned and dug an elbow into his side. "Another addition to your harem?"

Dare snorted. Friendly as the woman was, she was a good ten years his senior (or ironically about the age he'd been on Earth). That wouldn't have necessarily been a deal breaker, but she could only generously be called plain and had the worn features and short, skinny body of a life of malnourishment and hard labor.

Also, she wore her makeup caked on a bit too heavily for his taste, and judging from the ease with which she flirted he had the feeling he wasn't the only adventurer she'd invited for some fun over the years.

"Nah, she's all yours," he joked, raising his mug.

Ilin chuckled as he took his own drink. "Vow of celibacy, remember?" He paused, then added under his breath, "Thank the Seven Paragons."

Dare shook his head. "So how did your charitable work go?"

"Well." The man thumped his arm. "Your contribution was much appreciated. And Zuri was a wonder . . . none of the healers in Driftwain selected the Healer class, so she was able to offer the poor help they couldn't. Especially cleaning people who don't get many chances to bathe, to the point their filth was leading to the spread of disease."

Dare couldn't help but smile as he thought of his kindhearted goblin lover. She'd serve people in need, regardless of the fact that most would likely spit on her if they passed her on the street. "I'm glad she felt comfortable going with you. It sounds like she had a good experience."

19

Kovana

"Yeah, you lucked out with her." Ilin grinned. "I'm glad you seem to appreciate that fact."

"Absolutely." Dare jostled his companion's arm as he started to drink, making him choke. "By the way, thanks for telling me about the kobold bounty quest."

"I was getting to it!" the Monk protested, wiping his chin. "This place is right next to the town hall . . . it would've been our next stop."

Dare laughed and started to answer, then stopped and stared as Zuri appeared, making her way towards the table.

The white dress stopped at her knees, hugging her slender curves and showing her large breasts to best effect. Its light green embroidery and ruffles complemented her pale green skin. She also wore the ribbon Dare had given her, tying her hair back in a loose ponytail.

He stood as she approached, smiling broadly. "You look beautiful," he said.

She blushed a darker green, looking around at the other patrons, a few of whom were giving her hostile looks. Under their scrutiny she wilted slightly and scuttled the rest of the way, climbing up onto the seat he pulled back for her.

Dare put a supportive hand on her leg. "The serving woman took our orders, but she'll be back soon for yours."

"Anything is fine," Zuri mumbled, staring at the ground.

"Maybe, but what you want is preferred." Ilin said, sliding the little goblin the third mug they'd ordered. "Especially since it'll all cost about the same anyway. Might as well get what you like."

The serving woman came back with another round of drinks and to take Zuri's order. Her previous flirtatious look had soured at the sight of the little goblin sitting so close to Dare's side, obviously with him.

Zuri, unsurprisingly, ordered meat. And lots of it: Steak, chicken, pork, goat, mutton, and even a few cuts from monster drops.

Goblins were adapted to be mostly carnivorous, and with their sharp teeth usually ended up swallowing their food in large chunks or even whole. Which was also how she was able to so easily deep throat Dare in spite of his massive size.

20

She also ordered a large slice of cake, which he changed to ordering the entire thing in spite of the ridiculous expense. It was a celebration, after all.

The meal was relaxed, full of good food and good companionship. Although honestly, Dare couldn't help but agree with his companions' assessment that his own cooking nearly matched it.

He resolved to see what spices he could purchase so he could just make the food himself for practically free. Considering the low tech, medieval-esque society around him spices would probably be cripplingly costly, but he could at least get salt and local spices, like garlic and onions and herbs.

Although he could already get a good variety of spice herbs from his Foraging. And he was discovering more every day. Including many not found on Earth, making a variety of tastes he'd never experienced before.

Yeah, aside from the occasional gourmet meal to treat Zuri, better off making their meals themselves.

As they finished off the cake Dare looked around at his companions, smiling in contentment. This was exactly the sort of thing he'd always dreamed of, when he played his games and fantasized about really being able to live in those worlds.

A mug of beer or ale at his elbow as he sat around a crude table by the hearth in a cozy tavern, laughing with a group of friends while they rested from the dangers of the wild. Sleeping in a soft bed, luxuriating in the warmth of a beautiful woman cuddled against him after their passionate lovemaking. Looking forward to the adventures awaiting them when they set out in the morning.

And now, thanks to his unseen benefactor, he was here, able to have everything he'd dreamed of.

Chapter One
Moving On

Dare stood at the edge of the cleared kobold camp, trying to convince his stubborn Monk companion of the completely rational position that the higher level a monster was, the more valuable loot they'd drop.

Ilin had been open about wanting to stay at this camp and farm these kobolds until they were ten levels lower than him and no longer provided experience. The kobolds had a chance to drop precious metal ore, even an incredibly low chance of truesilver ore, as well as uncut semiprecious stones and gems.

Which was all well and good, but after killing thousands of the things Dare had done the math and figured out that the treasure drops were so rare they about evened out to the vendor trash monsters most commonly dropped.

Sure, the treasure drops were easier to sell, but all in all kobolds only earned them a bit more money than other monsters. And now that he and Zuri were Level 17, and Ilin was 18, the Level 13-15 monsters were giving less experience.

Which meant they had to go around to more low level monster spawn points in the area and clear those, then range even farther in search of others. Better to just keep going and find higher level spawn points to farm.

"Besides," Zuri said, taking his side of the debate, "once we turn in the quest to kill the kobolds, we can head north to Kov and turn in the Writ for a gold."

"True," Dare agreed. "Getting there is the end goal of traveling north along this road anyway." He grimaced and looked around the hilly plain they were on, with only a few groves of trees to be seen. "And honestly, I'm ready to move on and see what's out there. This place is starting to get boring."

The Monk looked at him like he was crazy. "Boring? You're talking about putting your life on the line leveling up and monster hunting, not some game of chess!" He waved around them. "You might stride up to every new spawn point we find, fearless at the prospect they might turn out to be Charcoals or even Silver Sickles and kill us all, but I'm not so suicidal."

Dare exchanged glances with Zuri. She knew about his Adventurer's Eye, which let him see the levels of enemies, as well as the attacks they'd use and some other information. It had allowed him to confidently move from spawn point to spawn point, not having to worry about getting into a fight he couldn't handle and ending up dead.

Sure, he'd had some close calls in the two months since coming to Collisa, but mostly he'd been fine. Which was more than most adventurers who literally braved the wilds could boast, not knowing if the next monster they faced would die in two hits or tear them to pieces.

The poor saps didn't even see a hit point bar for their enemy, so they had no idea of they were one hit away from killing it or it was still at 90% health.

"What if I checked every new monster myself?" Dare asked. "I'll pull it, kill it alone, and you can see about how powerful it is."

"What kind of friend would I be if I let my friend commit suicide doing something like that?" Ilin demanded.

"A friend who trusts me to know what I'm doing." Dare looked at Zuri in question.

She nodded firmly. "I want to keep getting the most experience possible. And I agree with Dare that we'll get more wealth from higher level monsters than sticking around these kobolds hoping to get a truesilver ore on every drop." She gave the Monk a keen glance. "I thought your order frowned on gambling."

The bald ascetic's face went carefully neutral, as it did when he was annoyed or trying to maintain his nearly flawless poker face. "You . . . make a compelling point," he said reluctantly.

"I hate to split our party when we've been getting along so well," Dare said. "But ever since Zuri joined me at Level 17 earlier today I've been feeling restless. I want to move on, and she agrees . . .”

He paused to check with his lover one last time, getting a firm nod of agreement, and continued. “I hope you'll come with us, but if not I think you're almost strong enough to beat four of these kobolds on your own. Or you can find someone in Driftwain to join you.”

Ilin sighed. “I suppose if it's a choice between trying to get by with someone who does half your damage on a good day, or continuing north with you for less wealth over time, the choice is pretty clear.” He waved casually and turned towards the road leading to Driftwain. “It's been a pleasure, Dare, Zuri. Take care.”

Oh. Dare was surprisingly disappointed by the man's decision; he'd come to like the Monk over the last two weeks, and trust him in a fight. The road to Kov would've been a lot safer and more enjoyable with his presence.

Their companion abruptly whirled back, grinning. “You believed me!” he said, laughing. “We haven't even divvied the loot, and you expected me to walk right to town and leave all my things in camp behind?”

Dare laughed too, embarrassed but relieved. “I didn't realize Monks played practical jokes.”

“I'm hardly one of the Seven Paragons at my age and level of enlightenment,” Ilin said. He stepped between Dare and Zuri and clapped them both on the shoulder, turning them towards camp. “Come on, let's go get packed up . . . if we're going north, let's *go*. The ground trembles under my restless feet.”

One last time they packed up their loot for the trip to Driftwain, as always overloading with junk to get every last scrap of value out of what they'd found.

“I think our leveling between here and Kov is going to be limited not by the monsters we find, but by how much loot we can carry,” Dare joked as they reached the road and started south.

Ilin chuckled. “It won't be quite so bad, there are two other towns on the road between here and the region capitol, as well as a few small villages. We should be able to regularly find vendors willing to buy our loot, and places to get a hot meal and a good mug of ale.”

The man didn't mention lodging, which was no surprise; he spent his nights sitting in meditation instead of sleeping anyway. For Dare and Zuri's part, they'd made no secret of the fact that they'd rather camp out in the wilds, ready to hunt monsters every morning, and save the cost of a room.

There were a few travelers on the road with them, who either nodded politely or gave them a wide berth as they passed. Which was understandable; few besides soldiers, guards, and adventurers leveled much past 15, and highwaymen could potentially plague any road.

These people were all trusting in the safety of the road and occasional patrols to keep them safe. Although their best hope was the goodness of strangers.

That said, the kingdom's bounty system was surprisingly effective, discouraging criminals tempted to prey on others. Even Dare and Zuri had helped clear out a bandit camp in Lone Ox a while back, saving two kidnapped farm girls and returning them to the village in the process.

He and his companions were always on the lookout for such threats, although Dare wasn't too worried. He and his goblin lover had already outrun one such highwayman, and Ilin had proved to be even faster than him over short distances, and capable of literally inhuman endurance over long hauls.

Thankfully, this close to Driftwain they didn't have to worry much about lawlessness. They safely reached the city, where the Monk agreed to sell their loot while Dare and Zuri went to turn in quests.

They all met back at Ilin's favorite inn, several gold richer (counting the Writs they'd redeem in Kov). Zuri had been eager to return to the inn with every visit, and always insisted on buying a whole cake to share with them. Which Dare could admit was a highlight for him as well.

Junk food wasn't really a thing in Collisa, at least not in these smaller villages and towns. The best he'd found was hard candy that he personally found foul tasting, and baked goods like cakes and cookies.

"You hear the rumors going around about trouble up in Bastion?" Ilin asked.

Dare shared a glance with his goblin lover, and both shook their heads. "Honestly, I've been a bit myopic since coming to this kingdom," he admitted. "Mostly focusing on leveling up and at best the goings on of the area I'm in."

"I have no idea what myopic means," Zuri said. "One of those Dare words the translation stone doesn't seem to know. But from context I've probably been the same way." She smiled a touch bitterly. "As a former slave what's happening somewhere else doesn't really seem all that relevant or important."

He wrapped a supportive arm around his lover, ignoring a few disgusted looks from other patrons. "Still, it's good to be aware of things, even if they probably won't affect us. What's the news?"

"The usual," Ilin said with a grunt as he quaffed from his mug, "chaos along the kingdom's border."

Dare took a drink from his own mug before cutting another slice off his steak. "Invasion?"

"Of a sort." The Monk gave him an odd look. "I forget things seem to work differently wherever you're from. But you know that if monster spawn points are left alone for long enough then roamers eventually break free, right?"

"Sure." Dare had seen it himself once or twice.

"Well the longer the spawn point is left alone, the faster the monsters inside become roamers, until eventually they all start spawning as roamers aside from a small core to guard the spawn point. And it stays that way until adventurers come and clear the spawns to reset it."

Zuri nodded. "Even I knew that."

Ilin grinned at her. "Well anyway outside the kingdom's borders the only people clearing the spawn points are adventurers. So if they're not active enough then eventually the monsters begin roaming everywhere, even across the border into the kingdom. Then ultimately they began banding together under the most dangerous monster spawns and forming raiding parties or even hordes, gathering up monsters from every spawn point they pass to swell their numbers."

"Shit," Dare said, shaking his head.

"Aye, it's a small problem that eventually snowballs into a huge disaster if left alone, same as many problems tend to," the bald ascetic agreed. "Even worse, the local tribes of the savage races, beast folk, and the few races of intelligent monsters all begin fleeing south away from the rampaging monsters. Regions like Bastion begin suffering famine from refugees, increased banditry, or even the intelligent races forming raiding parties of their own. In extreme cases they've even been known to unite in armies and try to conquer a region."

Dare nodded thoughtfully. "And that's the usual trouble kingdoms encounter?"

"The most common, definitely." Ilin waved vaguely off into the distance. "With that constant threat looming over a kingdom, from roaming monsters and other races raiding, they're usually reluctant to try to expand. Not to mention any other kingdom might use it as an excuse to invade *them* while they're vulnerable and the risks to them are low.

"Occasionally you'll get a warlike kingdom trying to form an empire through aggressive settlement in the wilds and conquering nearby kingdoms. And more often you'll get necromancers or demon lords or other such threats that become a threat greater than even roaming monsters and have to be snuffed out. And rarest of all you'll get open war between coalitions of kingdoms, especially against other races, that throw an entire continent into chaos. Although usually there's only one or two of those a decade, so unless they last a long time things are relatively peaceful."

Relatively peaceful?! It sounded to Dare like the entire world was almost constantly fighting at least monsters, and when they managed to sort those out then they immediately turned their sights on a neighbor.

He couldn't help but think that maybe he should've paid more attention to the outside world from the beginning, if war was that common. He didn't want to be so focused on leveling that a tidal wave of monsters or intelligent races fleeing their incursions obliterated Zuri and him before they even knew the danger.

"If there are tribes of intelligent races out in the wilds, why don't they clear the spawn points themselves?"

27

To his surprise it was Zuri who answered. "The wilds aren't like near towns and larger villages, where the monsters from the spawn points gradually get more powerful the farther away you go. There aren't enough settlements out there to cause that effect, so the spawn points tend to be more random. You can find a Level 1 spawn point next to a Level 30 one."

"Although the small tribal settlements have at least some effect," Ilin added. "Monsters around them will be low level for a few miles at least, before things get dangerously chaotic. And there seems to be a level cap of some sort in an area, where no spawn point can be more than 30 levels higher than another one within, say, twenty or so miles. And there's an effect that if the most common level spawn points in an area are left alone for long enough, they'll "convert" other spawn points into becoming an equal level, give or take 5 levels."

Interesting. So there was a natural process that turned areas gradually into the same level, and it sounded like they'd become gradually higher level as well if left alone for long enough. So while leveling in the wilds would still be dangerous, at least there were zones where adventurers could expect to not be overwhelmed by a random monster spawn point.

"We'll actually be perfect for the wilds once we get a bit higher level," Ilin said, grinning and clapping Dare on the back. "With your odd ability to sense how dangerous monsters are, we'll be able to avoid the stronger ones and clear out the weaker ones. Do good for Haraldar while also benefitting ourselves." The man grinned wider. "There's a lot of unclaimed treasure out there. Ruins waiting to be explored, dungeons waiting to be conquered. Party and raid rated world monsters as well."

Incentives to lure adventurers out into taking more risks for more rewards. Dare was definitely interested in that since he could minimize the risk.

All in good time; returning his friend's grin, he focused on finishing his food.

Fortified by a meal and dessert, they prepared to set out. Although Dare stopped by the market one last time to see if the crafted leather armor was worth the cost, and the same way he did every time he decided that it was too costly and he'd level too quickly to make it worthwhile. Besides, with Fleetfoot he almost never got hit anyway.

He'd start buying it when he was higher level, but for now he'd content himself with the trash he could craft himself; it was better than nothing.

Their business in Driftwain was finally done, so they took to the road and started north.

Ilin always seemed amused that Dare picked Zuri up and carried her so he could run quickly, a necessity since he not only had longer legs than the goblin that barely came up to his belly button, but Fleetfoot as well.

He could maintain what for others would be a sprint for basically a full day of travel, although occasionally he'd speed up to his own sprint of 25 or so miles an hour just to make Zuri laugh. She always shouted "Zoom!", too, which was absolutely adorable.

Surprisingly, or maybe not, the Monk could keep up with him. It made the travel a lot less tedious to be able to go places fast, and meant they got to new monster spawn points that much faster.

It was only a few hours to dark by the time they reached ones they hadn't already explored in their previous leveling, and after some debate agreed to clear the nearest one out before setting up camp. It was a camp of Level 17-19 Lesser Vile Imps, hideous little things which might be tough in groups but were spaced far enough apart that they should be easy enough on their own.

Unless they had some crazy ability that called adds, although none of the attacks Dare could see with his Eye indicated they would. He *did* see a ranged attack where they spat some sort of acidic balls that did Nature damage, however, which was less than ideal.

Still, it was worth seeing how easily they died. Especially since Dare had been having Zuri pelt him with her Mana Thorn spell several times a day to build up his Nature resistance. And once Ilin realized what he was doing, he asked the little Healer to do the same for him.

The two of them were now capped at their level for Nature resist, and while Dare didn't exactly want to get pelted with acid he was at least confident that he could survive it long enough for Zuri to heal him.

Although more ideally he'd dodge it, since anything that disfigured the skin couldn't be healed by her. Such as acid burns. Apparently higher level healers could heal a surprising number of things, and higher level Alchemists could make potions to restored skin. But the services of either were ruinously expensive.

Since Dare had promised he'd test each new monster they found, he went out alone to kill the first imp to prove to Ilin that it was safe. At which point he quickly realized that even if it was, it wasn't worth the effort.

Dare had expected big, slow balls of acid, but what he got instead were spitballs shot from long hollowed wooden tubes, which moved so fast that even with Fleetfoot he barely twisted aside. He had no confidence he'd be able to dodge all of them if they moved like that.

Thankfully the target he'd chosen was his level, and with his recurve bow he killed it in four hits. Which meant he ended up getting a glob of the vile stuff on his leather chestpiece, which burned through it so quickly he almost didn't manage to yank the armor off before the acid started eating into his tunic below. The hole continued smoking as he finished off the Vile Imp, burning a fist-sized patch of his armor before it petered out.

Nope.

Dare cut away the leather that had touched the acid, then scowled as he pulled the chestpiece back on and made his way over to his companions. "Fuck those guys," he said. "We could take them, but I'd rather not."

"I don't blame you," Ilin said, eyeing his damaged armor with distaste. "A mage or more support oriented class with barrier or resist spells might do fine, but we're at a disadvantage . . . some classes are more suited to some enemies."

Zuri looked forlorn. "I wish I could make barriers for us."

"Your spells are awesome enough." Dare patted her head. "Come on, we'll find something better."

They did, another spawn of undead, these ones skeletons. They had an immolate effect that lasted a couple seconds, and arrows weren't the most ideal weapon against them. But once again Zuri's Mana Thorn did extra damage, and as long as Ilin avoided the monsters while they were burning he was able to take them apart like they were stick figures with his powerful punches and kicks.

For once Dare was able to sit back and let his party members do the damage. He even took the time to gain proficiency in his dual daggers, which weren't much better suited to killing skeletons than his bow, but at least let him rank up that ability.

He'd never be as good in close combat as he was at a distance, that wasn't how is class was designed. But he could be better than he was now.

The skeletons mainly dropped cursed bones and dust, the former of which was apparently a bounty item redeemable at most temples, and the latter of which was a reagent.

After clearing the spawn point they agreed to search for more good ones in the area, although they decided it could wait til tomorrow since it was already getting dark.

So they found a safe place they set up camp, lit a fire and got some food cooking, and Dare set out his snares for the night. Then after dinner Ilin settled down to his meditation, and Dare and Zuri retired to their tent.

Zuri was all over him as soon as the entry flaps were closed, as she usually was; goblins were almost as horny as cunids, and bunny girls were so eager to get some that they went out and pretended to be trapped or injured to entice nearby travelers to come fuck them.

Dare made sweet love to the tiny goblin, not worrying about her cries of pleasure bothering their companion; in meditation the Monk wouldn't hear anything that wasn't a potential threat.

Then he fell asleep with Zuri sprawled contentedly across his chest.

* * * * *

It wasn't really accurate to say they leveled all the way to Kov.

Actually, there were only certain areas of monsters in the right range to make it worth going after them, and in their haste to move on they were soon past the area closest to Driftwain. After that the monster levels steadily increased up to 30, then decreased as they approached a village along the road until they were back to levels Dare and his companions could fight, and finally decreased all the way down to Level 1s right outside the village.

Ilin was delighted to find another kobold camp, these ones around their level range, in the second ideal area they passed through. Although it was smaller and the mine it was connected to was barely more than a few tunnels and caves in a low hill. They could even go in and fight the kobold miners and overseers; it wasn't a dungeon.

The kobolds still had a chance to drop the raw treasure, though, and the Monk prevailed upon them to stick around farming the small camp and other monsters in the area until they all gained another level. It took about three days, and Dare didn't consider the monster spawn points particularly good for experience, but it was good enough to make the effort worth it.

And it made their companion happy to get another few handfuls of gold and silver ore and several geodes that might contain semiprecious gems.

Surprisingly, even though they passed a few more ideal areas in the next few days, as the monster levels fluctuated between closely spaced towns and villages, Ilin didn't seem too interested in any of the spawn points. He really seemed to have it fixated in his mind that kobolds equaled treasure. Or maybe mines did.

"How about if we found other monsters that dig mines or tunnels?" Dare half asked, half joked as they left another ideal area behind.

"I guess it depends on what they drop," the bald ascetic said, grinning.

Although Ilin didn't seem to care much about other monsters, Dare still convinced the group to check every single spawn point around their level that they passed, and clear out a few. It usually didn't take much longer than a half hour to an hour, and often provided interesting loot.

And even though the experience was slow, since they were only picking off spawns conveniently close to the road as they passed, it was steady.

It took eight days to reach Kov. By that time Dare and Zuri both reached Level 19, and Ilin was just shy of 20. The Monk was eager to get his level, looking forward to a new combat ability: a meditative technique that would let him store secret reserves of strength, allowing him to go longer in battle.

Dare never minded a chance to get more experience, so they paused at the last good leveling area before the city to farm a few spawns of monsters, one of which looked like deer bodies with the torso and head of owls, and the other was a spindly, clawed monstrosity that could've come straight out of a nightmare.

"I'm looking forward to seeing what's waiting at Level 20, too," Dare said as they settled in to farm the deerowls.

Zuri patted his arm in mock sympathy. "I'm so sorry that your free ability for Level 15 was to not die to assassins."

He chuckled; he supposed he had groused about it one or two too many times.

His ability was called Prey's Vigilance, a passive one that gave him 100% chance to dodge an attack, then went on a minute cooldown before becoming active again. The chance dropped to 50% against the attack of an enemy coming out of Stealth.

It sounded great, a powerful defensive ability to complement the attacks he'd gotten at 5 and 10. Especially since, in that strange way of abilities on Collisa, it basically took over his body and reacted without him needing to make a conscious effort.

Actually, that was part of the problem. The dodge always moved him where he would consciously want to go, which was convenient. But what wasn't was that he couldn't choose *not* to dodge, and it didn't discriminate between attacks that were a real danger and things that weren't attacks at all.

So when Ilin moved to playfully slug his arm, he'd find himself veering away like a maniac. Which the Monk found hilarious; he'd gotten into the habit of launching sneak attacks at his full power to watch Dare dodge them.

But it would also trigger when he was trying to improve his Nature

33

resistance with Zuri, so she'd waste mana on spells he dodged. Or he'd be in a fight with a monster and Prey's Vigilance would make him dodge when it was only going to graze him with a claw, so when it clamped down on his leg with its jaws the ability was on cooldown.

If a monster attacked him a hundred times in a minute he'd evade the first, and the probability of it being his enemy's worst attack were low. It had limited application in most instances aside from when someone was trying to sneak attack, and even then it was only effective half the time against Stealth attacks.

Even worse, he had to constantly strain his vigilance since he usually relied on speed and reflexes to dodge attacks, and he couldn't afford to count on Prey's Vigilance and not be ready to consciously dodge. It was the kind of ability that could fail him when he needed it if he got dependent on it to be there.

Maybe it would've been cooler if he didn't have Fleetfoot to make his dodge so broken all the time, and sure, don't look a gift horse in the mouth blah blah blah. But Dare just would've preferred something cooler for his eagerly anticipated Level 15 ability.

But Ilin and even Zuri both thought he was crazy for undervaluing Prey's Vigilance. "It'll save you from assassins and surprise attacks!" the Monk told him the first time he groused about it.

"Half the time, if they're Stealthed," Dare shot back. "And all they have to do to beat it is give me a love tap with their fist before their main attack."

"But at least you'll know he's there then!" Zuri chimed in. "And if he wastes the attack that has a Stealth damage modifier just to exhaust your ability, that's that much damage that won't be going straight into a critical hit on you like most Stealth attacks end up being."

"Assuming I even dodge it at all," Dare grumbled, then dropped the subject; he could admit the ability had applications, but ultimately he still wasn't all that thrilled about it. And his companions never seemed thrilled about him trying to explain why he thought it wasn't that great.

As far as Zuri especially was concerned, anything that helped keep him alive was wonderful in her book.

Still, he was hoping for his Level 20 to be better. Maybe an activated movement ability like Charge or Pounce, except in reverse. Or something badass like shooting three arrows at once for triple damage (something that seemed like it wouldn't work in real life, but on this world you could light fires by clacking rocks together for half a minute, so it'd be just fine here).

As for Zuri, she'd had a choice between a defensive ability of her own, or a new healing spell. It was objectively weaker than the healing spell she already had, less effective and costing more mana. But it cast faster, and better yet didn't require water surrounding the target to cast.

Dare had actually urged her to take the defensive ability, since he prioritized her safety and didn't mind her being more of a between battles healer rather than a combat medic. And also if she was going to use her dagger to damage enemies he wanted her to be safer doing it.

But his goblin lover had adamantly insisted that she was almost never in harm's way anyway, and anything that could help keep him alive if things went wrong was worth it. Besides, she could cast the spell on herself as well, which was almost like a defensive ability.

Honestly, Dare was glad she'd made her own choice and even gone against his advice. As a former slave she had a tendency to go along with his decisions, so it was good to see her showing more independence.

It only took a few hours of farming monsters for Ilin to get his level. After sharing some congratulations they moved on towards Kov, and a few hours after that the walls of the city came into view.

Dare was pleasantly surprised.

The other towns they'd passed through were more accurately large villages, and would've been considered highway road stops on Earth. The largest one, which they'd actually just left behind that morning, had maybe several hundred people and was double the population of Driftwain.

On the other hand Kov, capitol of the Kovana region, had to have at least ten thousand people, and possibly as many as fifty, within its expansive walls. Which were thirty feet high and made of good worked stone, well maintained and with ballistae and catapults on bastions regularly dotting their length.

The gates were large and well fortified, with half a dozen Level 40 guards watching the tide of people flowing into the city. They dressed in gleaming chain and plate armor with gold and green surcoats, and seemed alert and vigilant to smugglers, criminals with a bounty, and other such unsavory sorts entering or leaving their city.

Ilin watched with disapproval as one of the guards turned away a raggedly dressed old man, rudely telling the destitute fellow that beggars were only allowed on holy days and festival days by the Region Lord's decree.

"I believe this is where we part ways, my friends," the Monk said as he watched the downtrodden old man shamble towards a ramshackle tent city raised well away from the walls. "A big city means many unfortunates in need of aid, and I'll likely be at it for a very long time."

"Won't you at least come with us to turn in our Writs?" Dare asked, at a loss at their companion's abrupt decision to leave.

"I'm afraid my personal affairs fall by the wayside when the needs of others are great." The bald ascetic hastily embraced them both, then with a final respectful bow hurried to the beggar's camp to offer his aid.

"Until we meet again, and may it be soon!" he called over his shoulder.

Dare watched him go with a sinking heart. He would've been happy to continue traveling with Ilin, who'd become a good friend in the time they'd been together. But he supposed the man had his own path to follow, and small surprise that as an ascetic it would diverge from Dare's.

Especially since he planned to visit a brothel while in Kov. Or maybe multiple brothels, particularly if he could find ones that featured women of other races; he still had his heart set on sleeping with a beautiful elf.

That is, after he'd had the talk with Zuri that he kept putting off, about whether she was okay with his dreams of being a promiscuous degenerate with a large harem. Now that he had a chance to be with all the different kinds of girls that had always drawn his eye in games, he wasn't sure he could forgive himself for not taking the opportunity.

Besides, Ilin had assured him that goblins were usually happy to share a mate. Although it was still important to see how Zuri felt about it.

He rested a hand on her shoulder. "Well, should we go take care of selling loot and other business, then find a place that sells sweets?"

She brightened. "I'm going to get fat at this rate, but I can't help myself." She abruptly flinched and looked down at her stomach, green skin paling.

"What?" Dare asked, worried. "I don't mind if you put on a few pounds." He crouched enough to reach her ass and gave it a playful squeeze. "More to love."

His goblin lover gave him a somewhat sickly smile leaned against his leg; maybe she was feeling nerves about being around people, as usual.

"Anyway," he said, quickly changing the subject, "if you love cake you'll probably also love pie."

Zuri brightened. "A different kind of sweet? I can't wait to try it." She eagerly started for the gates, and he hurried to catch up.

The guards made him pay a tax for bringing a "slave" into the city. Two silver, same as he'd needed to pay in the other towns he visited. Which Dare didn't mind as much as the fact that he couldn't defend his lover's dignity by proving she was free.

But Zuri had made it clear, as had Ilin when Dare had broached the subject, that he'd have a hard time proving he "owned" her in order to do the paperwork to set her free. And if he went to the Slave Registrar in Kov and tried to get the paperwork done without that, the most likely result would be that they'd clap him in irons as a thief and put Zuri back on the market.

Better to keep up the pretense she was his slave, for now. Almost nobody demanded to see papers, especially not for low value slaves like goblins, so it was safe to enter cities with her.

Dare didn't like it, but if the best he could do was treat her as a free person, and insist she was free to anyone who'd listen who *wouldn't* try to take her captive again, then he'd do that until he could find a better solution for his kindhearted lover.

Maybe they could eventually leave the Kingdom of Haraldar entirely, find some place where she'd be recognized as free.

After the guards passed them through, Dare took a moment to take in the sight of his first city on Collisa.

Compared to cities back on Earth, the people in the villages and towns he'd visited lived in relative squalor. But in comparison to even those, Kov was an absolute shithole. A rancid, stinking slum of crowded, poorly constructed and ramshackle structures built to a rickety height, which made the entire thing look as if it'd fall down at any moment.

It smelled of human waste, rotting garbage, and the stench of unwashed bodies that seemed to be soaked into the very stones. The road in front of him was poorly placed cobblestone, many of which were missing, and he could just imagine the jarring ride taking a wagon or horse along it would be.

Sure, it was possible this *was* an actual slum, and the rest of the region capitol was nicer. Or at least the trade and government districts would be, and of course the residential areas of the nobles and wealthy.

Dare had to do some asking around to find the people he'd gotten delivery quests for in Driftwain, as well as a couple of the other places they'd passed on the way here. It meant a lot of tiresome running around, but at least he got a better idea of the city's layout.

As well as regular achievements for discovering various districts in the city; exploring in this game gave very small experience bonuses, but you got them frequently for finding new places.

For a lower level, it was possible you might even get a level or two if you wandered far enough.

As it turned out, the south part of the city *was* the slum. The entire city was on a slight slope, with the northernmost area at the top, and he supposed the shit literally rolled downhill from the fairly large keep he could see up there.

The other districts got better (slightly) the farther north you went, with a trade district in about the center of the city, and beyond that the merchant district, then the regional government district, and finally the nobles district directly beneath the keep.

On the western edge of the city a river ran through the walls, allowing for fishermen to work their nets and a limited dock for traders using small boats to haul their cargo. That side was only a step above the slums, probably due to the stink of rotting fish, and Dare didn't see any reason to go there.

As usual, their first stop was at the trade district to sell their loot. It turned out to be a lot easier than in small towns, with some merchants even specifically dealing in junk. And Dare got to enjoy spending some more time honing his haggling skills.

Not literally, though; like with almost all social aspects of life on Collisa, there was no ability system for speech or bartering or anything else related to trade. No bump from stats or abilities for interactions with others; you either sank or swam on your own charm and social skills.

Dare abruptly snorted back a laugh.

"What's so funny?" Zuri asked, eyeing him curiously.

He shook his head. "I was just thinking that there's no ability for lovemaking, so I can't raise my proficiency and become a god between the sheets." He winked at her. "Aside from using the usual methods for improving my skills, that is."

Rather than laughing she looked aghast. "And let the ###### take over and mate for you? It would ruin the experience!" As usual, a direct reference to the world's systems or mechanics resulted in the words being fuzzed out, as if just beyond the edge of hearing or comprehension, to maintain immersion.

"I was just joking," Dare assured her quickly. "I would never want to automate any aspect of dealing with other people." He grinned playfully. "Especially the fun ones."

He finished emptying his backpack selling everything but the essentials, making roughly three gold in the deals. That business done, he started deeper into the market to check out the vendors that catered to adventurers.

After less than a hundred feet, a particularly foul stink of unwashed bodies hit his nose, almost strong enough to make him gag. He turned towards the stench, staring at a section of the market he hadn't been able to see before due to the closely packed stalls with their awnings.

Then he stopped in the middle of the street, sickened at the sight that greeted him in a way that had nothing to do with his sense of smell.

Chapter Two
Slum

It was a slave market.

Rows of platforms lined one end, where slaves of numerous races and ages were showcased and auctioned off in front of large crowds. The rest of the space was filled with cage wagons coming and going and large permanent cages to hold the slaves while they waited to be sold. The aisles between the cages were packed with more people browsing the huddled slaves, pointing out ones that caught their interest and asking questions of guards and market attendants.

The conditions could've come out of some sort of horror movie: crude wood bars bound together with ropes buried in the packed dirt of the market grounds, full of miserable men, women, and children wearing ragged tunics or even just ragged loincloths, along with chest wraps for the females.

Just like what Zuri had been wearing when Dare first met her.

The poor people had nowhere to relieve themselves aside from overflowing buckets right out in the open, with no privacy at all. Even with that dubious amenity, most of the cage floors were covered in filth, either theirs or the cages' previous occupants.

It made his blood boil, so he probably looked like a maniac as he stared at that market dealing in misery and human suffering, fists clenched and teeth grinding.

Where was Ilin to deal with this? Sure, one low level wanderer couldn't do much in the face of this booming trade, but why go to some camp of beggars to lend aid? Much as Dare pitied the poor he'd seen in that camp, at least they were free and living in reasonable conditions.

Zuri hesitantly tugged on his sleeve. "Did you want to visit the slave market?" she asked, obviously not thrilled at the idea. Not that he blamed her.

41

Dare definitely didn't. He wasn't interested in such a miserable place, at least not until he was either powerful, wealthy, or influential enough to do something about it. But he couldn't turn his back on reality, no matter how grim, and if he wanted to understand Collisa he needed to see its ugly sides too.

So he looked. Took in all the misery and cruelty and cemented it in his mind, so when he came back here with wealth and influence he'd remember his resolve to abolish this vile trade, and help these poor souls have normal lives as free people.

Noticing something, he frowned. "Why is it separated into two sections?" he asked.

"Oh, that's because the bigger section closest to us is the laborer market. The smaller section farther back is the pleasure slave market." Zuri pointed. "You can see a group being auctioned off on that block over there."

Dare looked, then immediately jerked his eyes away when he realized the females on the block were all nude, forced to humiliate themselves in front of leering buyers until one decided to purchase her.

But the brief look had been enough to see that the auctioneer had singled out a goblin slave, even smaller than Zuri and a darker green, to the front of the block to accept bids on. He'd been using a baton to compel her to turn this way and that to better showcase her assets.

Dare grit his teeth and avoided looking that way again; he didn't want to add to the poor women's humiliation.

"There were lot of goblins up there," he growled, putting a protective arm around his lover. "I guess they're popular?"

Zuri frowned. "Popular? No, more like the opposite. But because our race breeds so quickly we're common and cheap, so those with no better options buy us. Cunids are much more popular, and should be just as common since they breed almost as fast as us and are even more eager about it, not to mention they mostly produce the desired female children. But they're miserable in slavery and easily sicken and die."

Dare clenched his teeth, sick and angry and wishing he'd just dropped the subject.

He hated the thought of goblins, individuals just like his beloved Zuri, being bred for convenience because they were considered cheap and inferior. And probably terribly mistreated because of their meek natures. And those poor bunny girls, so cheerful and free-spirited, their playful roleplay in their beloved forests turned into nightmarish reality.

Struck by a sudden urge to be far away from the misery of the slave market, he took Zuri's hand and turned away. "Let's go," he said tersely, striding off down the street.

There was nothing he could do to help those poor people right now. Even if he wanted to try something reckless and stupid like trying to free them, there were dozens of high-level guards watching them like hawks. Or maybe vultures.

And even if he could free them what the hell would they do? Run and be hunted down like wild animals until they were recaptured, and treated even more harshly after that? The only other option he could think of was to purchase slaves and free them, but he didn't have the funds to buy even a single one at the moment.

"Dare?" Zuri asked timidly, squeezing his hand. "Did I say something to make you angry?"

Dare stopped and dropped into a crouch, impulsively wrapping his arms around his tiny lover and holding her protectively. Around him he heard a few people muttering about such shameful displays in public, and to take it to a private room if he wanted to fondle his slave, but he ignored them.

"Of course you didn't," he said gently. "I'm angry because of the evil of the slave markets, and the people suffering there. People who should be free to pursue their own dreams, like we are."

She looked at him with her golden eyes. But instead of her usual blank expression when he talked like this, not quite understanding the new and complex ideas he was trying to explain, her expression was sad.

"That would be a nice world," she said, patting his back before pulling away. "But it's not this one."

Dare sighed and stood, taking her small hand in his again as they continued down the street. "No. Although it could be."

They walked in heavy silence for a couple blocks before Zuri abruptly spoke up, voice so quiet he could barely hear her. "I was a pleasure slave."

Dare looked down. His lover had avoided talking about her past before, so this was a surprise. He released her hand so he could put a hand around her shoulder and hug her to him. "I'm sorry you had to live through that."

Her expression was flat as she shrugged. "Better than the breeding pens or a brothel or the arenas, safer than living in the wilds. Especially if we get a good master who gives us food."

He felt a moment's fury again at the notion that a master who gave his slaves the barest necessities was considered "good". And sadness that the options for goblins seemed to be so terrible. "Still, I wish you could've been spared such horrors."

Zuri gave him a long look. "Don't look at me with pity, Dare. I was free for most of my life and only knew the misery of slavery for a comparatively short time. And now thanks to you I'm free again. Beyond that my time in chains was outside of my control, and so there is little of me within those two years. I prefer to be seen for the time I was free, and what I've made of my life in spite of any hardships. Slavery was a terrible experience that will no doubt haunt me in my vulnerable moments, but it's in the past now and I refuse to let it taint my future."

That was . . . damn admirable. "No pity," Dare agreed, holding her closer, "only the deepest respect." He paused, then continued carefully. "Still, if you feel comfortable talking about it I'd like to know more about your life."

She hesitated, then her shoulders slumped beneath his arm and she sighed. "I suppose as mates we should be open with each other." She looked ahead, full lips pressed into a thin line. "My master's wife was barren and they wanted a child, so he bred me hoping for a human baby. It's a cheap, if socially frowned upon, method for producing offspring . . . the children are human in all respects, but even so they'd be shunned and persecuted if it was found they had goblin heritage."

Dare stared at her in horror. "That's monstrous!" he said quietly, instinctively hugging the timid goblin closer. "Inhuman, even."

Zuri shrugged again, as if resigned to it. "Anyway, my master got lucky on the first try and I gave him a human son, and they pretended my master's wife had had the baby. That wasn't such a bad life while he was breeding me and then while I nursed the baby, since they treated me very well because they wanted me to be healthy, fertile, and able to produce plenty of milk."

Her expression saddened. "But once the baby weaned they tossed me into the wilds to die. I wandered for weeks, struggling to survive, until that panther nearly killed me and you saved me."

Shaking her head, his tiny lover looked up at him and smiled fondly. "And then I realized that life could be much better than being a slave, thanks to everything you've done for me." Her smile turned into a smirk. "Especially in bed. That master who threw me out was tiny compared to you, and he didn't make me feel good like you do either."

Dare forced a sickly smile and hugged her closer again, grieving at what she'd gone through. He wished he could've spared her all of it. "It must've been awful to have your child taken from you." He hesitated, the blurted. "If we leveled and became stronger, would you want to go and get him back?"

She gave him a blank look. "Every time I start to forget how strange you think, you say something to remind me," she said. "Get him back? I never had him in the first place. That baby is my master's, Dare. Human, raised by humans." She shook her head a bit bitterly. "Besides, do you think he'd be better off being raised by a goblin mother? People would view him with the same contempt they view me. If not more."

"So we'd go someplace where people wouldn't, like among Ilin's order," he said. "Or we'd raise him ourselves in the wild."

His lover shook her head impatiently, pulling away from him. "He's better off with them," she snapped. "A real family, rather than fleeing through the wilds with strangers being hunted as kidnappers."

At his stricken look she calmed down a bit and sighed. "Besides, I had no real attachment for him. I was only allowed to see him to nurse him and watch him at night so the masters could sleep. And I knew he'd be taken from me the moment I was first bought, since my master saw no reason to keep it a secret. And honestly, I was glad knowing he'd have a better life."

Dare gave in, feeling a bit guilty. "You're right. I'm sorry, I was being stupid, not taking anyone's welfare into consideration. Especially the boy's.

Her big yellow eyes softened, and she wrapped her arms around his leg affectionately. "You were taking my welfare into consideration," she murmured. "It was misguided and ignorant, but thank you." She stepped back, voice turning brisk. "Just please don't do it again."

She started back down the street, and Dare caught up again and offered her his hand. After a moment, she took it.

"So," he asked quietly, "what about before you were a slave?" Now that she was opening up a bit, he wanted to see if he could keep her talking about herself.

Zuri frowned, obviously not happy with the topic. But she seemed eager to move on from the argument about her human son, because she didn't hesitate to answer. "I was part of a tribe to the north of here, in the Gadris Mountains. It was where I selected my Healer class and got to Level 6."

She looked at the ground again, trembling slightly. "But a few years ago slavers found our village and surrounded it. We knew that if we tried to fight we'd only lose people, so we surrendered. Everyone was separated from their families to be sold, and since I was young and fertile I went to the pleasure slave markets."

"I'm sorry that was done to you," Dare said, placing a comforting hand on her shoulder. "You probably hate humans after what you've suffered."

The goblin gave him a confused look. "I mean, no more than I would anyone who'd done something bad to me," she said timidly. "After all, our tribe had slaves of our own we'd taken."

He couldn't help but admire her understanding perspective. "Still, that makes you more reasonable than many people I've known." He laughed sourly. "Where I come from many people hate humans and consider them evil."

Zuri frowned. "Why? Are humans like that there?"

"Just the opposite. In most ways they're kind and enlightened, and have eliminated many of the common evils of the world."

"Like demon lords?" she asked.

Dare had to laugh again, although more genuinely; the battle between good and evil could be a lot more literal on Collisa. "Like slavery, for the most part."

His lover's frown deepened. "Then are there far fewer humans than the other races where you're from, and they're a mistreated because they can't defend themselves?" From her tone she could understand that position.

He shook his head. "Actually, humans are the only intelligent race that have ever existed there."

Zuri's confusion turned to outright disbelief. "So they're all humans who are kind and enlightened, and they hate their own kind and think they're evil?"

"Many of them."

"They think that way about themselves?" she pressed.

Dare sighed. "Some, maybe. Although most think they're the exception to humanity's general awfulness."

His tiny lover stared at him, clearly distressed. "Then they think that way about their families?"

"Some," Dare said again. "But no, for the most part they love their families."

"Then their friends?" she insisted. "Neighbors? The butcher down the block, the farmers in the fields? The travelers they swap tales with and the wandering bards who sing them songs?"

He grinned. "No, most would probably not consider any of those people evil. They'd admit that they're all mostly decent people doing their best to live their lives."

Zuri's eyes narrowed. "So they can't point to any human they know that's evil, but they still somehow hate your race?"

"I'm guessing they probably don't think about it that carefully. Or they think that it's everyone they don't know that's somehow like that." Dare patted her shoulder. "Although if you tried to talk about this with them, they'd probably walk away in a huff at about this point in the debate without changing their views."

Her yellow eyes looked up at him thoughtfully. "So you were raised among kindhearted humans who don't believe in slavery and want to treat each other well, but all hate their own kind? No wonder you have such strange ideas."

"Not all of us are like that," he said defensively. "Not even most of us. It's mainly just the ones who are already miserable and disillusioned and unquestioningly believe the people who are always telling them how evil the world is."

His tiny lover patted his hand. "Well, I'm glad you were able to get away from such a hateful place and still be so full of love."

Dare sighed; somehow he'd managed to present Earth in a poor light, which was the exact opposite of what he'd meant to do. "Anyway, I'm here now. We have to live with the world the way it is."

Zuri was thoughtful for a while. "So there's no slavery in your kingdom," she finally said.

"No slavery," he agreed.

His tiny lover stared down the street. "Well maybe we should go there."

"I wish we could." Dare sighed. "I came here by a, um, magical portal." That was probably even true. "I have no idea where my home is in relation to here, or how to get back." He rubbed her shoulder absently. "Besides, I'm happy here. I wouldn't mind if I could never return."

Which was good, because even though he'd never specifically asked the disembodied voice and she hadn't said anything about it, he was certain he'd never be able to go back to Earth.

"You're happy here, when it's so much worse than where you came from?" she asked slowly.

Dare chuckled. "Well like I said, my home wasn't perfect. And my life there certainly wasn't what I would've wanted." On impulse he leaned down to pick Zuri up and kissed her. "Besides, here is where I found you, my mate."

She smiled tentatively. "Well, maybe one day you can show the people of this kingdom the ways of your own."

"I hope so." He glanced around at the scowling passersby and, not wanting to draw any unpleasantness to her, only hugged her for a few more seconds before setting her back down. "Come on, let's see what we can buy you for your class."

As it turned out, the answer was not much. Apparently casters didn't get much in the way of good gear unless they bothered to enchant it, or sprang for the super expensive high quality gear with item bonuses.

In a way that was an advantage, since it meant their class was balanced at lower levels with modest gear, and they didn't need to break the bank leveling. But on the other hand he wished he could get more for her.

He did sell their Level 12 knives and replaced them with Level 19 ones. It was long past time to do that anyway, and Decent quality ones were relatively cheap at the vendor they browsed because he was improving his crafting with that pattern.

Dare also bought Zuri a sturdy pair of boots that would last longer and protect her feet better than the leather moccasins he'd crafted for her. They didn't have any item bonuses, but they had high tops and would protect her calves from snakes or small vicious animals and monsters.

Their last stop before leaving the market was to buy spices. Dare picked out a handful of ones that weren't ludicrously expensive and he couldn't Forage for himself, then had Zuri smell and taste them to see which ones she wanted.

She seemed okay with quite a few, so he spent a hefty sum buying a small wax-paper container divided into several sections with the new spices in each.

Last of all was turning in their Writs of Reimbursement at the Guardmaster's office and retrieving their gold coin each. The clerk was a bit dubious about Zuri turning in the quest, but a quest was a quest and he couldn't think of a way to refuse her. Although he did scowl as he handed over the gold.

All in all, their finances were solid. At this rate Dare would easily be able to buy his next bow after he out-leveled the Exceptional short bow.

"So," he told his goblin lover with a grin as they headed towards the merchant district, which was distinguished from the market district by having proper stores, inns, and taverns, as well as residences for the moderately wealthy. "Ready to find a place to get dinner?"

"And pie?" Zuri asked, brightening.

Dare chuckled. "Actually, we could maybe search for a bakery if you really wanted the good . . . desserts . . ." He trailed off and came to a stop in the middle of the street, staring openmouthed at the most amazing thing he'd ever seen.

It was a brothel tucked away on a side street, just outside the market district. A somewhat faded but proud place whose sign boasted the services of beautiful women of many other races. There were even cutesy but sexy stylized drawings of curvy female silhouettes with tails, horns, and other attributes humans didn't have.

In other words, the place was a dream come true for Dare.

Zuri stopped and looked back at him, brow furrowing in confusion when she saw the stupid grin on his face as he stared off down the other street. Then she came back and followed his gaze.

"Oh!" she said, brightening. "You want to hire a mate while we're in Kov?"

Dare felt himself blushing; looked like the cat (or catgirl in this case) was out of the bag. "Actually, that was a topic I've been trying to find a way to bring up. I love you, and I want to be with you, but . . ." He took a breath. "I still wish to mate with many other women."

To his surprise Zuri giggled. "Unlike every other male out there?" she asked wryly.

He couldn't help but laugh. "I guess that's true. But I actually intend to do it." He looked into her eyes. "I want to ask how you feel about that. Whether you can accept it."

She looked at him blankly; even after being able to talk to each other for so long and getting to know each other better, he still regularly earned that expression from his tiny lover. "Of course you'll have many mates and spread your seed to many wombs," she said slowly. "Like any other great man does."

Dare couldn't help but feel touched. "You think I'm a great man?"

Zuri's expression was incredulous. "Do you not, Dare? You are very clever and always seem to think of the best way to do things. Like how you found a way for us to level together even when the best I could do was stab monsters with a knife. We've both leveled more since we started together than most people manage in a decade.

"Even Ilin, who is very powerful, educated, and wise, came to look to you when we were hunting monsters." She patted his arm. "And you're also fearless, jumping into dangerous fights when needed to protect people, like me or those girls we saved from the bandits. And you're powerful and resourceful . . . when the fight is tough you manage to win with barely a scratch on you."

She mock pouted. "I almost never get to heal you of anything worse than a cut or bruise."

"You're hoping I get hurt?" he teased.

"No!" She stroked his chest fondly. "I just want to feel useful." Before he could protest that of course she was, she continued quickly. "Also you're very strong and faster than anyone I've ever seen, and you have your magic tricks and you made me laugh even when we couldn't talk and-"

His lover cut off, skin flushing darker green. "And you're very handsome," she admitted almost shyly. "The most handsome male of any race I've ever seen. I sometimes get wet just looking at your face and body."

That was interesting to know. And also made the times when he'd caught her staring at him intently a lot more sexy.

Zuri patted his chest, yellow eyes glowing with affection. "And you're kind. Kinder than I ever could've hoped to deserve. A great man inside and out . . . you'll one day be one of the highest level and most renowned heroes of our world, and I'll be honored to be your mate and share you with many other mates. The more the better, as you deserve."

Dare felt warmth spread through him. "And you'll be right there beside me, a great woman renowned for her kindness." At her look of amused disbelief he leaned down to kiss her. "I love you," he murmured.

"Get a room, you pukeskin fucking degenerate!" an older woman giving them a wide berth as she passed snapped irritably.

Scowling after her, Dare was prepared to shout something back when Zuri tugged him insistently towards the side street, murmuring reassuring words to calm him down.

"I'm glad it bothers you when other people are mean to me," she said, patting his arm. "But don't get us in trouble over it."

"I know." He took a deep breath. "Anyway she's a stupid idiot. Don't listen to her."

His goblin lover peered around the corner of the street after the rude woman, then gave him a confused look. "I can't, she's well out of earshot by now."

Dare had to chuckle, even though he was still furious at the awful things the hateful woman had said about his kindhearted lover. "I mean don't pay attention to what she says. She's not a nice person, and the things she says aren't true."

"A lot of humans call goblins pukeskins," Zuri pointed out.

He grit his teeth. "That just makes it worse." He crouched and hugged her, pulling her close. "Anyway fuck her and anyone else who's a jerk to you, because you're amazing and it's their loss they'll never get to know you."

Her eyes softened, and she hugged him back with a pleased sound. "I know you're hoping to visit the brothel, but we could also find someplace safe and private to mate if you want."

"Always," he said with a laugh. Then he sobered. "Just one more quick thing about me having a harem. I know it'll make me look like a hypocrite and an asshole, but I don't want you to have any other mates but me."

Zuri gave him that blank look again, although she also seemed offended. "Of course not, Dare. If I took other mates you could never trust that my children are yours." She stroked his cheek. "Besides, I want no other mate but you."

"Good." He leaned in and kissed her more fiercely, slipping his tongue in her mouth; she was still getting used to that, but he thought she was starting to enjoy it.

His tiny lover abruptly drew back, staring at him uncertainly. "But, um, you don't mind if I share pleasure with your other mates, do you?"

Dare blinked in surprise, then laughed outright. Mind? "As long as you let me watch," he joked.

She took him seriously. "Only if you don't want to join in."

He motioned to the brothel. "How about we start right now, then? You can pick the woman we mate with, as long as its not a race I've already mated with before."

Zuri hesitated, looking uncomfortable. "They'll probably charge extra to bed a goblin."

"Then I'll pay extra. And we'll find someone who's cool with it so she doesn't make you feel bad." Dare took her hand and they walked through the brothel's large front doors together.

The interior was fine in the way putting a pretty layer of frosting on a dry, crumbling cake was; cheap gold paint peeling away to show weathered and worm eaten wood, a few vases of sad, wilted flowers, thick fancy rugs that were worn and frayed and padded furniture that had seen better days.

The madam, elegantly clothed in a genuinely fine dress that looked incongruent in the surrounding drabness, had seen better days as well. Although she'd made a valiant attempt to hide it with artfully applied makeup and, no doubt, a tight corset.

For a moment her eyes narrowed in distaste at Dare's clothes, but then she saw his bow and knives and took in his level. Apparently even humbly dressed adventurers met her standards, because she plastered on a smile.

53

Kovana

"Welcome to the Pussy Palace, young master," she said in a sugary voice, bustling over to lead him towards a door that he assumed led to a private lounge. "We have the most beautiful beast girls, demi-humans, and exotics in Kov. Guaranteed to suit your tastes. Can I start you with some wine, brandy? Only the finest vintages here."

Or at least served in the finest bottles, repurposed from some richer place. Dare resisted the older woman's attempts to usher him through the door. "This is going to sound odd," he told her, "but I only want the services of a girl if she's not a slave and is willingly employed here."

The madam's phony smile faltered. "Pardon?"

"A free girl, willingly employed," he repeated firmly.

The older woman stared at him blankly; he was more than used to that look by now. "Young master," she said carefully. "There are many brothels in this city where you can find human women who are willingly employed. But this is a brothel boasting the services of females of other races, as well as a few tamed monster girls and one plant girl."

She gave him a careful look. "Obviously there are very few non-humans in the city who aren't slaves. You'd be hard pressed to find whores among that number."

Dare felt his heart sinking in disappointment, more for the sake of the poor women here than his own. "So your girls are all slaves?"

"Indeed."

"Well is there another brothel where I could possibly find what I'm looking for?" he asked.

The madam arched a gray eyebrow. "You wish me to direct you to my competition?"

Fair enough. Dare sighed and held up a silver coin.

She arched her eyebrow again, and he added a couple more until she finally held out her hand to take them, grimacing in distaste. "Adherents of the Outsider run a charitable institution in the slums where discarded slaves are rescued, nursed back to health, and freed. The institution endeavors to find gainful employment for the freed

54

slaves, and I believe many of the freed women elect to become prostitutes as their best option. The institution runs a brothel in the slums to ensure they're treated well."

The elegantly dressed woman sniffed derisively. "I'm sure that you'll find few good options among the castoff leavings, though. You'd be much better served with one of my girls. And I assure you that even though they're slaves, I treat them well and they're happy and eager to enjoy the company of patrons."

Dare highly doubted that, at least the last part. "Could you point me to it?"

Grimacing, the woman quickly rattled off some directions. Likely more out of eagerness to get him out of her establishment if he wasn't buying.

Once they were outside he looked at Zuri, who'd stood silently by his side the entire time. "It's a long walk back to the slums. Want to look for a bakery or good tavern on the way?"

She brightened. "Okay!"

Chapter Three
Deep Blue

Ten minutes later, they entered the slums while contentedly wolfing down the entire peach pie Zuri had purchased from a pie merchant.

Dare couldn't help but think that the little goblin was developing a bit of a sweet tooth. Then again, he usually ate just as much as her so who was he to talk?

The street the madam had directed them towards was much nicer than the surrounding ones, the houses all well made and brightly painted, with small garden plots and planters on the windowsills. Dare wondered if it was because the entire area was owned and operated by these Adherents of the Outsider, or if they'd merely chosen to put up shop in the nicest part of the slums.

Either way, the brothel the older woman had described was a sturdy structure, larger than the buildings nearby but by no means palatial. It was well built and well maintained, brightly painted in inviting colors, and somehow seemed a lot more genuine than the ridiculously named "Pussy Palace".

Dare already felt better about coming here. He glanced at Zuri, who grinned and nodded, then rapped lightly on the plain blue door.

A large, muscular minotaur whose class was Level 29 Brawler pulled it open, obviously acting as security. Dare would've thought that race would be considered monsters, but his Eye identified the hulking creature as "Bovid. Humanoid, intelligent."

Also he had a human torso and head, so he wasn't really a minotaur. It was just the dark gray, lightly furred coloring of his skin on his human portion that had momentarily thrown Dare off.

He couldn't help but idly wonder what a female of the species would look like. Probably thick and with huge tits and ass.

Maybe there was one here?

The bovid eyed him, then grunted and ponderously moved aside. Dare took Zuri's hand again and stepped past him, looking around.

The brothel's entry room was a small, plain square, painted a soothing yellow and empty of furniture aside from a desk on the far side of the small room. Obviously patrons were meant to quickly be ushered inside, for privacy or perhaps just eagerness to enjoy a prostitute.

Or maybe the big Brawler behind him was waiting to knock him out, drag him into a back room, and rob him before dumping his body in an unmarked grave.

Dare had trouble really believing that possibility, though, because behind the desk sat a petite, bookish woman in her mid 20s with auburn hair and delicate features. She looked for all the world like a librarian, or maybe the pretty girl next door, or some combination of both, and he somehow doubted she'd be involved in anything nefarious.

The girl looked up from a ledger she was scribbling in, then scrunched her cute little button nose and lowered a tiny pair of spectacles to get a better look at him. Getting a better look at the petite redhead at the same time, Dare realized she was more than just pretty; she was unquestionably beautiful.

The bookish girl perked up in sudden excitement, looking almost as if she recognized him, and quickly stood. "Welcome, D-" she began, then cut off hastily, cheeks turning pink. "Dear customer. Welcome!"

"Are you the madam?" Dare asked.

She hesitated, blushing even more deeply. Her flustered air was adorable, not to mention more than a little sexy. "Well, technically I'm High Priestess of the Outsider. But I keep the books and oversee this establishment."

Dare hadn't paid much attention to the religions of this world. Although he wondered if the deities they worshiped here showed themselves to their followers and even took an active hand in events, like they tended to in fantasy worlds.

It might be something to look into, at the very least so he didn't get on the wrong side of one at some point. But right now he had more important things on his mind.

Or more accurately one thing. "I was told I could find, um, company here?"

"Yes, we have eleven courtesans for you to choose from, all of different races," the priestess said eagerly. "If you want I can introduce you to them all so you can make a pick, I assure you they're all very lovely. But if you have a specific desire we have a goblin . . ." She hesitated and motioned to Zuri. "Although I suppose you're content with your even more beautiful lover."

"More than content," Dare said, then with a start realized this woman was the first person besides Ilin who'd called Zuri something besides his sex slave. And complimented her, on top of it.

A charitable assumption from a Priestess of an order that freed slaves, cared for them, and helped them find new lives?

The bookish woman smiled in approval. "We also have a saurid, a bovid, a mermaid-"

"You have a mermaid?" Dare cut in excitedly.

"Trissela," the priestess said, smiling fondly. "We rescued her from the sewers, where she'd been dumped by her owner. She was trapped behind a grate, almost dead from thirst and suffering from toxins and plague."

The bookish woman hesitated, as if realizing that might not be the most alluring thing to say to her client, and hastily added, "Although she's been fully healed and cleansed, of course! And you know mermaids are some of the cleanest people out there! In fact, one of her most popular services is bathing clients."

The priestess grinned with what seemed like uncharacteristic impishness. "Very sensual baths with extra enjoyable endings."

Maybe it was hasty, but at the prospect of a mermaid Dare didn't even need to hear what other women the brothel had to offer. He could always come back later and try the others. "That sounds great, I'd like her."

"Wonderful!" the woman clapped her hands, then turned towards the door to one side of her desk. "Please, come with me."

Dare paused for a moment before following, turning to Zuri. "Now's probably the time to cast Prevent Conception."

"Right." Blushing darker green, his lover quickly cast the spell on him. Then, just to be safe, on herself.

He looked at the door to find the bookish redhead watching them with a knowing smile. "Glad you're being careful," she said with a wink. "Although no need to worry, my girls have spells of their own."

She briskly opened the door and started down a hall lined with regularly spaced doors, and Dare couldn't help but admire the way her well-fitting robes hugged her slender curves as he followed.

"Do you want to mate her, Dare?" Zuri asked innocently.

"Shh!" he blurted, blushing as the brothel's bookkeeper paused to look over her shoulder at him, looking on the verge of laughing.

"Sorry, I'm not for sale," the girl said, winking again. "I'm waiting to be properly courted."

She kept going, although he couldn't help but notice that her walk had taken on more of an alluring sway, drawing his eyes to her skinny little bum and making him wonder what it would feel like to hold it with both hands and pull her sexy little body against him.

Was she hinting that he might have a shot if he went about it the right way?

Before Dare could ponder the possibility, the bookkeeper reached the door at the end of the hallway and knocked. An absolutely enchanting voice answered, too softly for him to hear the words, and the redhead poked her head in. "Trissela, you have a guest."

"Oooh, please invite him in!" the woman's slightly husky voice had a melodic quality, as if she was half singing.

Well, mermaid.

The bookish redhead stepped aside, motioning invitingly. "Please enjoy yourself, Dare-" she stuttered slightly, "c-customer."

Wait. She'd said dear customer again, right?

The question fled Dare's mind as he heard a playful splash from beyond the door, and he eagerly squeezed Zuri's hand as he led her inside. Into a room subtly lit by blue glowing crystals along the ceiling, giving the entire place the rippling, ethereal appearance of a tidal grotto.

Most of the floor had been converted into a comfortable pool, maybe a bit bigger than a public hot tub. Large, smoothly polished rocks that looked as if even the massive bovid out front would have trouble lifting them circled the pool.

Along several of the largest ones a big bed of soft, deep moss and ferns had been laid down, and seated on the edge of it with most of her tail idly swishing through the clear, sparkling water was Trissela, the mermaid courtesan.

As the bookish redhead closed the door behind Dare, he couldn't help but stand there and gape; Trissela was absolutely stunning.

She was dressed for a bath, ie not at all, allowing him to feast his eyes on her perfect body. Her human upper half had the proportions of a cheerleader, with an impossibly slender waist and unexpectedly large breasts with the palest pink nipples. Her skin was similarly the palest cream, as only someone who's lived her life under the sea could manage.

The mermaid's long, slender tail was the dark blue of the deep sea, looking sleek and smooth and with a wide delicate fin at the tip. Her vagina was located on the tail portion, a long, tightly pressed together slit with paler blue lips that looked as if it had adapted to keep out seawater. Similar to a dolphin's, although located about where he'd expect a woman's sex to be.

Was it similar enough that the asshole was also in there? That presented interesting possibilities.

The stray thought made Dare's face flush, and he realized Trissela was watching him coyly as he enjoyed the view. Something about the sparkle in her gorgeous deep blue eyes made him wonder if she knew what he'd just been imagining.

Her delicate features were soft and achingly lovely, the way some of the most beautiful women seemed to be just too perfect to actually exist in real life. Dare found himself drawn to her full lips, glistening invitingly and parted as if to welcome a kiss, and stared for a few seconds before tearing his eyes away.

Silky seafoam green hair spread out on the moss bed behind her in an elegant fan, more glossy and sleek than a human's hair as if it, too, had adapted to underwater life. That or she just took excellent care of it, in spite of living in water where it would constantly be wet. It was probably long enough to reach the part of her tail where her hips would be, and he had the urge to run his fingers through the silky strands.

"Welcome," Trissela purred, playfully splashing water his way but not quite reaching him. "Would you like to have a bath?"

"I-" Dare swallowed a frog in his throat. "Maybe just a quick rinse." His cock was already rock hard and throbbing against his pants, and he was more in the mood to experience this stunning beauty than be pampered by her with a half hour of foreplay.

"Oooh, eager to get right to the fun." The mermaid coyly teased a lock of her seafoam hair and splashed again. "Come on in, I keep the water nice and warm and perfectly balanced with minerals to revitalize our skin." Her mysterious blue eyes turned to Zuri. "Please, come in too, Z-that is, Healer."

Zuri blinked. "You know my class?"

Trissela looked a bit flustered before recovering with an easy laugh. "I'm a Cleanser. I can detect the active effects on others, and if they're harmful remove some of them." Her eyes danced. "I see you two came prepared."

Dare chuckled. The disarming mermaid had him oddly at ease, especially with Zuri here to help bolster his confidence. So he wasted no more time setting aside his possessions and stripping down.

His goblin lover hesitated a moment longer before doing the same.

The mermaid watched avidly as he removed his shirt. "Oooh," she said again, biting her lip. One slender hand with long, graceful fingers trailed up to rest on her stomach, rubbing sensuously around her cute little belly button as if she wasn't sure whether to move her hand up to her breasts or down to her slit.

"I don't think I've ever seen a more beautiful body," she continued, finally making her decision and raising her fingers to toy with a nipple. Which quickly flushed a rosy pink and stiffened to the size of an eraser head. She lifted her eyes to meet his, full lips slightly parted and glistening. "Or a more handsome face."

Dare felt his face flush at the compliment; a lifetime of being average at best on Earth, with a mostly disappointing love life, hadn't prepared him for this sort of attention. Of course she could just be saying all that, but she certainly *seemed* sincere.

Mustering his confidence, he got into the spirit of things. "It gets better," he said with a wink as he finished shucking off his pants. Then, hooking his fingers through the waistband of the undershorts Zuri had made him, he turned sideways to show just how prominent the bulge was and was satisfied to hear the courtesan's admiring gasp.

And considering her profession, she'd probably seen more than a few.

Smiling wide, Dare pulled his underwear down, taking some satisfaction in how Trissela's eyes widened greedily when his fully erect cock sprang free. "Oh Goddess, sexy," she moaned. "I've been waiting for a chance to try it."

Dare gave her a quizzical look as he stepped towards the pool. "My cock?"

"Definitely." Trissela giggled. "But I meant the common knowledge that females from even the smallest race can handle males from even the largest race." She motioned between them. "We're about the same size, but considering you're practically swinging around a bovid cock I'd say this counts."

She bit her lip again, cheeks flushing. "Maybe you'll even bottom out in me."

"Count on it." Dare looked at the tightly pressed together lips of her slit as he stroked his cock. "If I can go balls deep in you it'll be a first for me."

"With that monster I can believe it." The mermaid slipped gracefully into the water with barely a splash, floating on her back so the water lapped over her large breasts. "Come in, the water's wonderful."

He glanced at Zuri and nodded, smiling, then stepped into the pool, finding a seat/step running along the outside edge of it as if it was a usual hot tub.

Trissela hadn't been lying, the water was glorious.

Dare couldn't help the groan of enjoyment that escaped him as he settled down onto the seat until everything but his head was submerged. He hadn't enjoyed a bath or hot tub in years, even before dying and coming to Collisa. Although since his reincarnation even a hot shower had been a luxury he longed for.

The mermaid's pool was the perfect temperature, warm but not uncomfortable, and the water did indeed seem to have minerals that made it flow like silk across his skin. It was a particularly enjoyable sensation against his throbbing erection, bobbing free in the water.

Zuri joined him in the water, standing on the seat since if she sat she would've been fully submerged, and gasped in amazement. "I don't think I've ever felt anything this wonderful."

"Relaxing, isn't it?" Dare agreed, pulling his little lover to sit on his lap. She felt his erection between her legs and giggled, rubbing against him with her pussy and thighs in a way that made him groan.

"Oooh," Trissela said, pouting. "I thought you were here for me, sexy." She gave Zuri a playful grin. "Although I can't blame you for not being able to keep your hands off your beautiful girlfriend. She's really a sweetheart, isn't she?"

He was pleasantly surprised, and relieved, at the mermaid's open acceptance of his lover. He hadn't thought to tell the bookkeeper he wanted someone who Zuri could have fun with too, so he was glad it seemed to be working out.

"Although maybe I can get your attention back," the courtesan teased. With a flicker of her tail she slipped under the water and started towards him, slender back gliding just beneath the surface.

She popped up just in front of him, eyes sparkling as she stared into his. "Have you ever had an underwater blowjob?" she said in a sexy little voice. "I don't need to come up for air."

"Oh, Nature's bounty," Zuri moaned, rubbing more quickly against Dare's cock for a moment before abruptly scrambling off him to make room for the mermaid. "I need to see this."

Her response surprised him; did watching blowjobs turn her on? Considering how much she loved deep throating him herself he supposed he shouldn't be surprised.

"Well, sexy?" Trissela said in a throaty voice, licking her full, glistening lips. "You want to catch me with your giant hook? Trap me on your barbs so I can only squirm helplessly?"

"Oh hell yes," he replied with a grin.

"Goody." Smirking mischievously, she slipped beneath the water, hands on his hips as she kissed his throbbing tip, then began running a soft tongue over his length beneath the water. At the same time she curled around, her long tail slipping out of the water to wrap around his shoulders so the fin rested across his chest.

It was unexpectedly soft and smooth, with no hint of sharp edges or rough surfaces. Not skin, of course, but warm and alive and pleasant. Dare began running his hands over her tail just above the fin, as well as the fin itself, luxuriating in the feel as the mermaid continued to kiss and lick his massive manhood.

Then he gasped and involuntarily thrust his hips forward as she took him into her soft, warm mouth, the sensation of water flowing around him replaced by gentle suction and a playfully darting tongue.

"Yes!" Zuri exclaimed, leaning forward eagerly. "Did she just take you in?" He noticed that she'd leaned against the mermaid's tail to get a better view, and her small hands were stroking the smooth scales as she watched intently.

"She's . . . still taking me," Dare groaned as he felt Trissela take him deeper into her soft little mouth, struggling against the urge to thrust his hips again. Or for that matter blow his load down the mermaid's throat right then and there.

Although he did hold her head with both hands, luxuriating in the feel of her soft, almost soapy slick hair gliding through his fingers.

Trissela hadn't been lying earlier. She seemed determined to impale herself on his cock, forcing him into her small throat with a series of frantic gags and swallows that felt almost like a climaxing pussy. She kept it up as she forced her head down his shaft, moaning in pleasure as his length sank into her.

The vibrations along his cock combined with her swallowing and tight esophagus was almost too much; if it was a contest between Zuri's eagerness while deep throating and the mermaid's technique, he wasn't sure which he'd judge was better.

Not that Dare needed to make a choice; he could just accept that they were both incredible.

"I'm going to come!" he called through the water at the eager mermaid. In case she hadn't heard he also pulled her head gently towards him to signal she should be ready.

But again the courtesan showed her experience, soft hands running down to the base of his shaft. Her thumb and forefinger squeezed there in a painfully tight ring, preventing him from ejaculating until the overwhelming urge to blow his load had finally faded.

"Wow, is that something you can do?" Zuri asked in amazement. "I'm going to need to remember that."

"You sure are," Dare panted as Trissela again began pushing her head farther down his cock. "You're so sexy and your pussy's so tight, I can never hold out for long."

"Thanks," his goblin lover said with a giggle, kissing his neck while she rubbed her large breasts against Trissela's tail. "Although you don't need to make excuses . . . I know how long you can last after you push through your first time spilling your seed in my fertile little pussy."

He groaned again, not just at her sexy words but because Trissela had just reached the base of his cock, her nose buried in his pubic hair. Like a fish caught on a hook she was squirming delightfully, throat clenching and working desperately to adjust to his girth.

She began practically singing, voice box vibrating hard and sending a new surge of pleasure through him as she began to enthusiastically bob her head up and down his cock, her tight throat sliding over every inch of him from tip to base.

The beautiful mermaid never came up for air. In fact, she never even pulled her mouth off his cock to take a breath, breathing through fluttering gills on her neck instead, which allowed her to focus relentlessly on pleasuring him.

Dare lasted a couple minutes against that pleasurable assault, holding out with heroic determination, before with a groan of sheer enjoyment he grabbed Trissela's head and began fucking her throat with long, hungry thrusts.

Her singing hum increased in volume, and her tail around him thrashed eagerly as she prepared for what was coming.

Finally he pulled her to the base, grinding her perfect little nose into his pubic hair, and with a gasp of pleasure released pulse after pulse down her throat in an orgasm that seemed to last a blissful eternity.

The entire time the mermaid swallowed eagerly, lovingly milking every spurt of his seed into her slender little tummy. Even after his climax ended she pulled back until only his head was still in her mouth and sucked gently, tongue teasing his over-sensitive tip for any last drops she could collect.

Finally it was too much and Dare gently pushed Trissela's head away. "Holy shit," he told her as she surfaced, tail slipping off his shoulder as she cuddled against his chest.

The mermaid grinned at him. Her cheeks were flushed and she was breathing hard after taking his size in her small throat, but if her eyes had watered or she'd gagged any saliva or mucus, the water had washed it away, leaving her looking pristine.

"That was glorious, sexy," she purred, soft arms wrapping around him tight, pressing her luscious breasts to his chest. He could feel her nipples rubbing pleasantly against his skin.

Dare wrapped his arms around her and ran his hands down her back, luxuriating in the feel of her. At the small of her back, where her hips and ass would be, he could feel her silky skin give way to smooth, warm scales, and traced the line all the way around her waist.

Trissela made a contented noise and gently pressed her mouth to his, glistening lips sweet as honey as he eagerly kissed her back. He started to slip his tongue into her mouth in search of more of her sweet taste, but she beat him to it and met his tongue with her own, playfully teasing him.

Dare's roaming hands found their way to her slender tail where her ass would be, and while there was no particular curve there he still squeezed and pulled her close as they continued toying with each other's tongues. Her smooth tail pressed against his enduring erection, a surprisingly pleasant sensation, and he began sliding himself along it as his hands moved up to cup her breasts and tease her rubbery nipples.

Zuri had been quiet for a while, content to watch as she hugged his side, and Dare took a hand from the mermaid's breasts to hug his lover closer, groping her round little ass and making her giggle and begin kissing his neck.

Trissela heard the sound and broke off the kiss, turning to also wrap a slender arm around the little goblin and cuddle her closer to them both. "Was that fun to watch, Zuri?" she asked. "Your mate claiming my throat? Filling my little mermaid tummy with a big load of his cum?"

Zuri moaned and nodded, and with a giggle the mermaid nuzzled her sharp face. "You're so cute." Her hand joined Dare's rubbing and squeezing the goblin's soft little globes, and she kissed the other woman on the mouth.

Zuri stiffened with surprise, but then relaxed and wrapped an arm around Trissela's neck as she returned the kiss. Dare moved his hand between his lover's legs and began teasing her plump labia, and she gasped in pleasure against the mermaid's invading tongue.

Dare took the opportunity to kiss his way along Trissela's jaw, down her slender neck, around her delicate collarbone, and all over her lovely breasts. Finally he closed his lips around her nipple and sucked gently, and the mermaid moaned and began sliding her tail eagerly against his erection still pressed between them.

Trissela abruptly pulled back, gave Zuri a final affectionate peck on the lips, and shot Dare an impish grin. "Well, sexy?" she asked in a girlish, seductive voice. "We've kept our fun mostly above the waist." Her eyes danced. "Although not exactly chaste."

She pulled herself to the side of the pool and began to rise languidly out of the water, revealing smooth glistening skin and then even smoother, glistening deep blue scales. "How about we take this below the waist now?"

Dare looked greedily, waiting for his first close look at the mermaid's sex. Zuri leaned closer as well, curious, as the mermaid's long slit rose above the surface, feasting their eyes on the slightly paler blue, tightly closed rubbery lips.

It was as beautiful as the rest of her.

Trissela balanced the part of her tail that would be her ass on the side of the pool as if seated there, then began undulating that same part in front of him, as if waggling her hips. "Go ahead," she purred at them. "Explore my mermaid pussy all you like."

He didn't need a second invitation, gently reaching out to slide his fingers over those rubbery lips. After a moment Zuri's little fingers joined him, curiously touching the smooth skin.

Dare glanced up at Trissela's face to gauge her reaction, and she laughed lightly.

"That won't do much for me, I'm afraid," she murmured in a sultry voice. "Haven't you heard the saying "the mermaid party doesn't start until you're inside?" She wiggled again. "Come on, see for yourself."

Dare pushed a finger into her tightly closed slit, finding it surprisingly difficult, and then pushed in a finger from his other hand and began gently pulling her rubbery lips apart. The mermaid moaned softly as he did, and he assumed that this at least was doing something for her.

Since Trissela's pussy was on the tail part of her, he'd half expected her vagina to be fish-like as well. But inside those rubbery lips the interior was as smooth and pink as any woman he'd seen. It also looked about the same, with a prominent clit at the top, then the tiny hole of her urethra, and the pink depths of her tunnel, a little bead of her arousal slipping free of the tight opening to pool at the entrance.

Although he was right that her anatomy was similar to a dolphin's, in that below her pussy was an adorable little rosebud asshole.

Dare couldn't help but lick his lips at the sight of her beautiful sex, wondering if he could get his tongue close enough to taste the sexy mermaid.

69

"Oooh," Zuri said, gently sliding her finger along one of the rubbery blue lips just where it joined the pink flesh inside. "That little pink hole is so cute. I can't wait to see your big cock stretching it open."

Trissela giggled and took the goblin's hand, pulling it in to touch her glistening entrance. She moaned with pleasure as Zuri's little fingers explored around her delicate hole; definitely sensation there. "Go ahead and feel inside me, Zuri," she purred. "I bet your cute little hand would fit in nicely."

Dare felt his cock lurch at the thought of his goblin lover fisting the mermaid, and had to groan himself. The smell of the mermaid's arousal was sweet, but with a sharply salty tang that made his head swim.

He gently slipped his own finger in to carefully rub around the mermaid's little pearl, and she let out adorable little needy whimpers and thrashed her tail in pleasure.

Zuri had three fingers inside Trissela's pussy now, breathing fast in excitement as she stroked the beautiful seafoam-haired woman's walls. Then she abruptly pulled her hand back and looked up at Dare. "I want to play, but I want to see you inside her even more."

"Do you?" Dare teased, taking his lover's fingers and licking the mermaid's arousal off them. She tasted salty, but with a with a sweet musk that he found surprisingly refreshing. He sucked Zuri's little fingers all the way into his mouth to get it all, and Trissela giggled as she watched.

"Zuri's right," she teased, running her fingers through his hair. "If you're ready, I can't wait to get that big cock inside me. Let's see if you can navigate my twists and turns."

Zuri giggled. "Oh, he was ready right after he came. He can fuck right through orgasms."

Trissela's eyes widened, and she smiled in delight. "Really? Then I hope you've still got a couple more for me." She leaned back on one arm and, with some effort, pulled her rubbery lips aside with her fingers, waggling her hips. "Go on, sexy."

Dare didn't need a second invitation. Straddling her tail, he positioned himself near the bottom of her long slit and slowly pushed forward until he felt his tip press against her opening. Eager to feel her soft walls, he began to enter her.

"Oop!" Trissela squealed, squirming. "That's my bum hole." She giggled. "I may be as adventurous as the next maiden of the sea, but taking that monster up my ass dry is a bit much."

"Sorry!" he blurted, hastily pulling back as Zuri snickered.

"That's okay, it happens all the time . . . they're really close together." The mermaid took him in her hand and guided him to the right place, looking up at him with sparkling eyes. "Although it makes for some interesting opportunities, if you want to experiment a bit after you're all slick with my juices."

She giggled again. "And I cast Cleanse Target inside there, just in case. I'm all squeaky clean and ready to be stretched to the breaking point by that magnificent cock of yours."

"Oh!" Zuri exclaimed. "That's a great idea! I should try it." She nibbled her lip and slipped a hand between her legs. "Although I might not be able to fit him in my tiny butthole no matter how slippery I make his cock. It's not affected by the same ##### ###### that lets races of different sizes safely breed."

"Oh gods," Dare said through gritted teeth. "You two keep talking like that and I'll explode all over Trissela's opening before I can get inside."

The mermaid giggled. "You just came, you're good." She grabbed his ass and tugged insistently. "Come on, my little mermaid pussy needs you inside it."

Dare wasn't one to refuse a lady's request. Grinning in eager anticipation, he gently pushed into the warm tunnel waiting for him, his passage made easy by her copious juices.

"Oh Goddess," Trissela gasped, throwing her slender arms around his neck and pressing her full breasts to his chest. "You're stretching me so good."

He groaned in reply. Her pussy wasn't as tight as Zuri's of course (unsurprisingly), but the way her soft pink walls gripped him was a pleasure all its own. A soft embrace rather than a passionate welcome.

And she was *deep*. He pushed farther in than he could possibly go with Zuri, or even from what he remembered with the farmwife Ellui back in Lone Ox or Clover the bunny girl. And she was much more tight and pleasurable than a slime girl or the shadowy figure of his unseen benefactor.

The pleasure of penetrating a woman's depths rippled along parts of his cock that had never experienced them before, and he felt as if sweet fireworks were exploding throughout his nervous system as he went ever deeper.

"Oh Goddess, I haven't felt anything this far in since my last merman," Trissela moaned. "And he didn't come close to opening me up like you are."

Dare grunted and pushed in even deeper. Her sweet walls were beginning to curve oddly, as if trying to accommodate a different shape than him. A really odd, twisty shape. But with a bit of pushing he was able to half-bend, half straighten the walls to get a bit deeper.

And then he bottomed out in her pussy, still with an inch of his cock still outside.

Damn, would he ever find anything besides a slime girl or an animated shadow that he could go balls deep in? Still, he wasn't complaining as her entire pussy clenched around him and began rippling forcefully, sending a flood of her heavenly nectar to flow over his thighs and her tail and into the pool.

Trissela's arms around his neck tightened almost painfully as she buried her face in his shoulder, giving delicious little gasps as her climax swept over her.

"Keep going!" she panted when he paused. "Take me higher, sexy. Higher!"

Dare withdrew from her clutching walls until his head was at her entrance again. It felt strange to have the distance of her watertight pocket that made a gap of air between her rubbery lips, currently stretched around his girth with surprising tightness, and the opening to her sex. Out of curiosity he pulled out of her completely, then with effort pushed against her tightly closed slit until his cock slipped through again, ramming through the pocket and into her opening as he again penetrated her.

The mermaid squealed as he thrust deep, lovingly nuzzling his neck as she pushed herself eagerly against the massive rod penetrating her tender insides. "Faster!" she panted. "Don't ease up now!"

He didn't need a second invitation, speeding up and savoring the feeling of embedding himself deep in her soft folds and pushing against her tender core again and again.

"Come inside me," Trissela gasped, voice almost a whine as he continued to pound her little mermaid pussy. "I want to feel your seed filling me up."

"Yes, do!" Zuri urged eagerly. "Breed her like a great man should!"

Dare glanced over and saw his lover vigorously mashing her finger against her small clit as she hungrily watched him thrust into the mermaid.

The little goblin's tiny pussy was flowing with her juices, soaking the side of the pool and beginning to drip into the water to mix with a courtesan's. Her outer lips were flushed a dark green, and the interior was a tantalizing rosy pink that made him want to explore it with his tongue.

Zuri saw him looking and flushed a darker green with embarrassment, although he noticed that she began to rub faster. He smiled at her encouragingly, and with a sexy little squeak her eyes rolled back in her head and she began to climax, squirting once and then releasing copious juices around her fingers.

"Oh, Goddess," Trissela said, sugar walls twitching appreciatively around him; she'd been watching too. "That's so hot. You're adorable, Zuri. I wish I could taste you."

Dare groaned. "I'm not going to last long if you keep talking like that."

"Good!" the mermaid squealed, bucking her "hips" against him eagerly. "You can pretend you're going to make me pregnant." She kissed her way up his neck and face until her sapphire blue eyes met his. "Would you like that, sexy?" she said in her seductive girlish voice. "Putting a cute little mermaid baby inside me? Or a cute little human one? I've heard they kick so delightfully in the womb."

He groaned again, thrusting more frantically.

Trissela gasped and clutched him with desperate passion. He felt her tender walls begin convulsing around his cock again, accompanied by a gush of her sweet nectar squirting all over his cock and dripping down his thighs.

"Oooh Goddeeeess!" she squealed. "Paint me with your seed, Dare. Pump me so full it has no choice but to push its way into my womb! Imagine me with a big round belly, carrying your little mermaid baby!"

"Fuuuuck!" Dare groaned, and with a last powerful thrust grabbed the back of the mermaid's tail where her ass would be, pulled her tight against him, and with the tip of his cock pressed right against her core emptied himself inside her for what felt like an eternity.

Finally he pulled free with a groan and floated on his back in the pool, savoring the sensations he'd just experienced while slowly catching his breath from his exertions.

Trissela lay back contentedly on the side of the pool, sliding a finger between her rubbery lips. When she pulled the tip free it glistened with their combined juices, and Dare realized that the tightly closed pocket would probably hold his come in until she, what, absorbed it?

"Mmm," the seafoam-haired mermaid said, sucking her finger. "I think I wouldn't mind having your baby, Dare." She turned those big, deep blue eyes on him mischievously. "What do you think? Do you like the idea of leaving here knowing my little tummy will get all big with your baby? You won't have to take care of it or anything, you can just know that you have a mermaid child out there."

Dare did his best not to frown. "That sort of talk was hot when we were fucking, but don't make it weird."

The mermaid pouted and lay back. "*I* think it would be great," she muttered.

He shook his head and offered Zuri his hand, pulling her into the water so they could wash off. "Thank you, Trissela, that was amazing."

"Mmm, you're welcome to come back any time," she said. With a graceful flick of her tail she slipped into the pool, swimming over to give him and Zuri both tight hugs and kiss them each on the lips.

Then she fetched soap and cloths and began professionally bathing them.

It was a nice sensation, although he had a feeling her efforts would've been more sensual if he'd accepted her offer of a bath before fucking her. Still, he was content.

A few minutes later they were clean and dressed.

Trissela waved after them as they left her room, calling goodbyes and offers for them to come and play more later. Dare almost changed his mind and went back in for another round with the sexy mermaid when she reminded him he still hadn't tried her asshole, or alternating between it and her pussy right above it like they'd talked about.

Next time. Grinning like an idiot, he held Zuri's hand as they made their way down the narrow corridor towards the front, passing a dozen other doors on the way.

What delights might be waiting behind each? He was eager to find out.

The auburn-haired brothel overseer jumped to her feet when they entered the small entry room. "Done with Trissela?" she asked excitedly. "Did she have a great time?"

"Yeah, I had an incredible . . ." Dare trailed off when he realized he'd misheard her. "Sorry, did you ask if *she* had a great time?" He could see a madam asking if he'd enjoyed his visit, but what sort of brothel asked about the courtesan's good time?

The petite woman grinned at him. "Oh, I *know* you had a good time. And I don't really need to ask since I know Trissela did too." She winked. "Our walls are soundproof, but not *that* soundproof."

Zuri giggled, and he felt himself blush. "Well, I aim to please when I pay for sex," he joked. "Speaking of which, how much do I owe?" Come to think of it, he probably should've asked that beforehand.

The bookish woman looked momentarily surprised and seemed to fumble for an answer. "Oh, um, a silver?"

Dare and Zuri *both* stared at her blankly at that. "A silver?" he repeated. "I feel like I'm bargaining against myself here, but your service was great and so was Trissela, and it seems like it should definitely cost more than that."

The petite redhead looked flustered. "You haven't been to a brothel before, so how would you know?"

He snorted. "Even so, I know how much work goes into earning a silver, and have some idea of how much an hour with a *mermaid* should cost. How can you possibly stay in business with such absurdly low prices?"

Hell, he'd paid three times that much just to find out where this place *was*.

The madam, or bookkeeper or whatever, shifted uncomfortably. "It's a discount!" she blurted. "I'm sure Trissela will insist, for how well you treated her. Call it a big dick discount." Her cheeks flushed slightly.

Dare glanced at his goblin lover, wondering if there was some trick here. Were they going to send the minotaur to follow and rob them, or something like that?

He slowly reached into his coin pouch. "I should at least give Trissela a tip," he said, pulling out five silvers and setting them on the desk. "She really was incredible."

The auburn-haired woman smiled slightly at the small pile of coins. "Oh, bless your heart," she murmured. From her tone it almost sounded like she thought the gesture cute, like a child hearing his parents were having financial difficulty and giving them a handful of pennies he'd been saving up.

Come to think of it, Dare didn't actually know how much a mermaid courtesan cost. Even at a rundown place in the slums like this. Although he couldn't argue that Trissela had been far more beautiful and classy than he'd expected.

He shifted uncomfortably, realizing that in his ignorance probably anything he did would just make him look even more stupid. "Well, thank you again," he said awkwardly. "Does that take care of the business side of things?"

"Yes, yes, of course!" the woman said, hurriedly standing and circling the desk to usher him and Zuri towards the door. "Thank you so much for your patronage, Dare. It was really good to have you visit. So exciting, and not just for me."

Wow, this brothel really laid it on thick for the clients.

Or . . . maybe not. The petite auburn-haired bookkeeper paused him at the door with a hand on his arm, and after shooing the minotaur back a few paces leaned closer to him, voice an inviting whisper.

"My name is Ireni, by the way." She bit her lip, looking embarrassed. "I'd like to talk to you more, Dare. If you're in the city long maybe you can visit me." Her pale, delicate skin turned a bit pink. "And we can do other things besides talk, too."

It was hard not to be tempted by that, especially given her bashful delivery. Dare had always had a thing for redheads back on Earth, but the one relationship he'd had with one had been short and ended after a couple dates, before he'd even had a chance for a first kiss.

"Maybe I can," he agreed slowly.

"Good." Ireni took Zuri's hand and held it warmly with both of hers. "Take care, Zuri. It was nice to meet you . . . you're such a sweetheart."

"Thanks," the timid goblin said uncertainly.

The priestess straightened briskly and returned to her desk. "Until we see each other again," she said, winking. Her green eyes sparkled as she turned them back to her ledger.

The minotaur held the door for them, then unceremoniously slammed it shut after they passed through.

It wasn't until they were out on the street, the sun low on the horizon creating long shadows around them, that Dare realized he'd never told the high priestess his or Zuri's names. And there was no way she could've gotten them from Trissela, either, since they'd left the mermaid's room and gone straight to the front room, where they'd found her working at her desk.

For that matter, how the hell had the woman known he'd never been to a brothel before? Or that he had a big dick? And what was up with her basically charging him nothing?

She was a High Priestess of the Outsider, at least so she'd said. Did clerics have the ability to get information, maybe from divine sources?

Come to think of it, both Ireni and Trissela had both been far friendlier than even being part of the hospitality business could account for. And while he would've expected them to act like they were his best friend and knew everything about him as a tactic to make him feel more at ease, he had the uncomfortable sensation that the two *did* actually know something.

It made the hairs on the back of his neck stir.

"Zuri, what do you know about the Outsider?" he asked as he started down the street at a brisk walk, trying to keep the worry out of his voice.

She glanced up at him, yellow eyes gleaming. "She is the goddess of wanderers and new experiences. One of the older gods, yet she has few temples and churches and claims few followers." She shook her head. "I don't know too much about non-goblin deities, but she and her followers seem to be looked down on by worshipers of other gods. Which might explain why they're forced to operate out of the slums."

Dare's first impression was amusement; followers of one god looking down on followers of another? How very unusual.

But if it was all the gods there was likely a reason, and the entire reason he was curious was because of their unnerving experience in the brothel.

Zuri took his hand and squeezed it hard. "You're as uneasy about our encounter back there as I am, my mate?" she murmured.

Dare nodded. "They acted like they knew us, actually knew who we were and liked us. More than that, they knew stuff about us . . . did you notice they used our names, even though we never told them? Trissela would be one thing, we might've said our names at some point while we were fucking, but Ireni had no reason to know."

He rubbed at the goosebumps on his arms. "And she seemed oddly eager to get to know me better, even sleep with me."

His lover smiled at him. "Well she works at a brothel so she's probably no stranger to sex, and you *are* gifted with very appealing features." Her smile faded. "But you're right. And it's obvious Trissela is their most pricey courtesan . . . mermaids are rare away from water, and she's beautiful even for her kind. So why charge us less than they'd ask for even the cheapest goblin whore? They'd never make money like that."

"I don't know, but it gives me the heebie jeebies."

Zuri stared at him blankly. "Is that some sort of disease or curse?"

"I mean it creeped me out." Dared picked Zuri up, ignoring the startled sound she made, and set off down the street at a faster walk, taking full advantage of Fleetfoot. "Either way, we're done with our business in Kov, so maybe it's time to leave."

He kept his Adventurer's Eye ready and glanced frequently over his shoulder, ready to break into a sprint if he saw the minotaur leave the brothel and start to follow them.

Ireni was very cute and the prospect of sleeping with her was a tempting one. As was the prospect of paying Trissela another visit, and seeing what other women of other races the brothel had to offer.

But all things considered, after that unnerving experience he didn't plan to go back there. In fact, maybe they should put some serious distance between them and Kov before they got back to leveling.

Chapter Four
Level 20

Dare and Zuri both wanted a chance to say goodbye to Ilin, or as Dare hoped convince the Monk to join them heading north, so they swung by the beggar camp south of the city even though it was out of their way.

To their disappointment their friend was long gone, although the people in the camp all had glowing things to say about him. Apparently while he'd been helping the destitute he'd learned from them about some shelters and orphanages and other charitable locations in the city, and had gone in search of other places where he could lend aid.

Dare admired the man for his kindness, but wasn't in the mood to chase him down when Adherents of the Outsider in Kov seemed so uncomfortably interested in them. So he and Zuri headed into a nearby woods to find a camping spot for the night, then in the morning circled around the city and started north.

It turned out his desire to leave the region's capitol well behind meshed well with the terrain north of Kov. While they'd encountered forests and hilly plains on the way to the city, as they continued beyond it they discovered that the terrain flattened to plains stretching to the horizon in all directions. Similar to the Great Plains area where Dare had lived on Earth.

Which was all well and good, but it felt too exposed. Sure, there were plenty of dips and low rises to offer hiding places and obscure your view, but even so you could see for miles from the right vantage point.

The possibility of bandits and highwaymen made the entire area seem too exposed. Sure, there were plenty of monster spawn points in view, but Dare didn't want to risk it.

At first he intended to just keep going north until he reached new terrain, but a perusal of the map he'd earned in Lone Ox changed his mind. It showed only topology and terrain, with no names of marked towns or villages aside from Driftwain and the region capitols of Haraldar, but even so he could see that to the east of them was a large forest that stretched for hundreds of miles.

That would be a far more secluded place to level, especially since the Hunter class got bonuses inside forests. Zuri agreed with his reasoning, although she seemed bemused.

"Common knowledge for most people is to avoid forests wherever possible," she said. "Low visibility, so you can't see danger coming from far off. And lots of obstacles to keep you from being able to run away, especially against enemies better adapted to moving through underbrush. Without your Adventurer's Eye it can be really dangerous."

"That just means even less chance of encountering bandits and other threats," he said cheerfully.

"Aside from the fact that bandits risk the danger *because* other people are more likely to avoid forests," his lover pointed out. "Especially the ones who have kill on sight bounties and are desperate."

That reminded Dare that they hadn't had a chance to pick up any quests in Kov. Not that he would've been eager to return to turn them in anyway. "So, forest?" he asked.

She nodded. "As long as we're careful."

Careful turned out to be a good idea, because the farther they got from the road and the city, heading northeast across the plains towards the large forest, the more predators they encountered. As in, wandering animals that populated naturally like cougars, panthers, wolves, and wild dogs.

And eagles. Those guys were assholes. Swooping out of the sky to claw at them with attacks that took a healthy chunk off their hit points. Dare usually had just enough warning from his Adventurer's Eye to put an arrow in the diving bird, or at worst throw himself out of the way or tackle Zuri to safety.

Either way, the predators were quickly becoming a nuisance.

"What the hell is up with these things?" Dare asked after the third time his Eye warned of the approach of a cougar stalking them, forcing him to either kill it or run away. This time he chose to kill it, although with its Pounce ability it swiped a gouge into his leather leg armor first.

Zuri gave him a strange look as he got to work skinning the predator and harvesting the meat; since it was an animal and not a monster, rather than dropping loot he was allowed to harvest it "naturally" using his Hunter abilities. Including pulling out its fangs and claws as trophies or trade items.

"We should expect to see more predators away from people, where they're not being hunted to keep their numbers down," she said slowly.

"Sure," Dare agreed sourly as he worked his knife under the hide and began pulling it free a few inches at a time. Or at least his ability did, with the mechanical competence of all automated movements. "More of them, but not all over the damn place. Where I'm from predators are rare, maybe one every few miles or so. Not everywhere like here . . . they're practically another monster spawn, except they can roam."

He was just glad that the dangerous animals at least ignored campfires for the most part, although they'd had a few scares in the night.

"Why wouldn't they be common?" his lover asked. "Animals populate quickly, and unlike herbivores the carnivores have an almost infinite supply of fresh food."

It took him a moment, then understanding dawned. "They can eat monsters?"

She nodded. "Not only eat them, but get experience from killing them and level up in a way similar to ours."

Dare whistled in amazement. No wonder they were so common; it looked as if the creators of this world had managed to turn natural repopulation of predators into its own form of respawning so there'd always be plenty to hunt.

He frowned. "Hold on. If predators can level up and repopulate like crazy, then why aren't there a bunch of wolves and cougars and foxes and other carnivores all over the lower level spawn points, all of them just high enough level that they no longer get experience from those monsters? Or for that matter, why don't they all get slaughtered the moment they try to hunt a higher level monster?"

Zuri shook her head. "They seem to have an ability that lets them sense spawn points so they can avoid them, and also sense monster levels so they never take on a fight they can't handle. It's also why predators around spawn points are usually around that level or higher . . . once they get higher level, they move to the higher level monsters to hunt. The ones that don't usually get hunted by humans in the nearby settlements."

Dare rubbed his jaw. "So there might be ancient animals out there that are super high level and dangerous?"

"Of course. A few even become strong enough to reach godhood and become primal spirits or ancestral protectors." She grinned. "I've heard that some even took humanoid form and became the progenitors of beast folk, and that's how those races came about."

That was badass.

"Well, we'll just have to keep our eye out and hunt any predators we encounter," he said.

She nodded. "On the plus side, with them all coming to you we'll have plenty of leather and meat, as well as claws and teeth to sell."

Fighting off the predators was all well and good, until they got to the forest and started encountering Level 20 enemies.

None of the monster spawns between Driftwain and Kov had been Level 20 or higher. Dare had wondered why, assuming it might have to do with zones being capped to certain levels. At least until he saw his first Level 20 monster, a combination of a meerkat and a lizard.

Its increase in power was dramatic, similar to the difference between the weak Level 1 starter mobs and Level 2s. Even more, perhaps. To the point that the stronger monster spawn points were clearly differentiated from the lower level ones by a large space.

He was pleasantly surprised that usually that power increase for Level 20 wasn't simply more health and damage, the way so many games did to "increase difficulty" because they couldn't think of anything more imaginative.

So the fights in those games remained the same, just longer and more tedious. Where you were more likely to die by being ground down until you were out of stamina and mana, rather than because of a mistake or some surprise from the enemy.

Unfortunately, the power increase on Collisa was more inventive and made the enemies *way* more dangerous.

Dare was even more grateful for his Eye as he saw several different types of Level 20 and above monsters. Their power increase included things like that *all of them* had some sort of ability that would let them reach him and Zuri in some way. Either an ability similar to Pounce that let them cross the distance in moments, or increased speed, or ranged attacks, or even Snare abilities.

There were also some that had better defense against ranged attacks, or even a chance to reflect them. And of course the ones with increased health and armor were always more likely to reach him as well unless he moved.

In short, Level 20s were a pain in the ass.

The first one they faced, the meerkat lizard, not only moved quickly but shot spines out of its tail at a short range. It also had just enough health that they couldn't kill it without risk to themselves, and when he and Zuri came in range of the spines the attacks prevented them from shooting more arrows or casting more spells.

In the end Dare had to accept a few hits to his arms and legs in order to finish off the long, sinewy reptile. Thankfully the spines weren't poisonous, but he still needed healing from Zuri.

And that was one of the easier ones.

"Our own jump in strength at Level 20 better be just as good," he grumbled as she pulled a spine from his ass, drawing a yelp from him.

They got a chance to find out after four days of fighting along the edge of the forest to target Level 19 and lower monsters and animals. By this point they'd hunted monsters together long enough that their experience difference had been mitigated by the increase in experience required to level, so they usually leveled within a few monster kills of each other.

Because of that, Dare waited for Zuri to also level before checking what he'd gotten, eager as a kid at Christmas.

Only to be disappointed; no huge jump in power to make the harder monsters more manageable. Which he assumed meant that the easy mode of massacring even level monsters and a meteoric rise to high levels was about to slow down, as things got more difficult.

The creators of this world didn't want things too easy. They might even be trying to encourage adventurers to group up past Level 20 so they could handle the harder monsters.

The biggest letdown was his new ability. Not that it was bad, but since his focus was on bows and survivability anything else was lower priority.

Actually it was a choice between two abilities, the first time he'd had a chance to pick between options the way Zuri had been able to at Level 15. It was exciting, but would've been more so if the choices hadn't both been for melee attacks.

The first was Savage Claw: "Deal a double damage melee attack with hatchet, dagger, or spear. 40% chance to apply a bleed effect, critical hit applies double bleed effect 100% of the time. 30 second cooldown."

The second was Eviscerating Slash: "Inflict a gut wound that applies a major bleed effect with hatchet, dagger, or spear. 30 second cooldown."

Looking closely at both abilities, Dare decided on Savage Claw simply because it did more front-loaded damage, and most often he used melee attacks to finish off almost dead enemies.

Still, it was hard to be too excited about a melee attack when he'd been hoping for something better, like how awesome Rapid Shot had been at 10. He'd definitely use Savage Claw when monsters reached him, and be glad for it.

But what really excited him wasn't the ability itself but what came with it.

Savage Claw worked with daggers, *hatchets*, and *spears*. Previously Dare had only been able to use daggers, but at Level 20 the ability trees for hatchets and spears were unlocked. Both were superior weapons to daggers based on range, speed, damage, and versatility, and hatchets could even be dual wielded like daggers.

Dare cursed the fact that he'd just bought Level 19 daggers, but he resolved to buy a high quality spear the moment he could find a vendor selling one.

Games didn't always reflect just how good spears were, but in his opinion they were one of the strongest melee weapons in real life in terms of reach, offense, and defense. One of the oldest weapons, too, and they stood the test of time.

Also he had an ability that let him throw spears. Which could potentially do as much damage as his bow if he got his proficiency with it up to his level. He'd also need to get his melee proficiency with spears up, which would probably be a huge pain but needed to be done if he wanted to use them.

Of course, since he'd been using daggers all this time he'd basically wasted all the time spent gaining proficiency in them, aside from how they'd helped him level. But they could always be a backup weapon.

The biggest thing he got at Level 20, though, wasn't actually any ability or stat increase for that level; it was that he could finally use his Exceptional quality short bow.

Or, well, he actually *did* need to get his Level 20 proficiency in bow repair so he could repair the thing before he used it, but still.

Thanks to the fact that the short bow was 6 levels higher than his recurve bow, and also higher quality, it did a bit over *three times* as much damage. Even accounting for the fact that short bows were one of the worst in average damage and recurve were one of the best, it still did that much more.

He couldn't wait to try it. And the high speed of short bows would be a blast too, letting him have an easier time loosing arrows at enemies after they reached him.

Actually, it wasn't completely accurate to say that the biggest thing he got that level was his bow. Great as that was, there was something that he was even more excited about. And of all places it came from his cooking abilities.

Specifically, it gave him Sweet Tooth, which as the name suggested allowed him to harvest sugar beets, sugar cane, honey, and maple sap, refine them into syrups and sugars, and use them in recipes.

Neither he or Zuri had ever gotten to the point of being too exhausted to continue with lovemaking, thanks to his stupidly high stamina from the incredible body his unseen benefactor had given him, and her incredibly high fertility as a goblin.

But after he told his tiny lover he could start making her sweet treats himself, she was so overjoyed and excited that she spent the rest of the day working to see if she could push him to his limits.

She got awfully close.

Of course Dare didn't know what sugar beets or sugar cane looked like, so he couldn't start harvesting them yet. But he immediately tapped several maple trees along the forest's edge and kept his eyes out for beehives.

As for Zuri, she didn't do so bad herself for her Level 20.

First off she got upgraded versions of a few of her spells, including her big heal Water's Gift, the one that required water to cast, and Cleanse Target. Although the biggest upgrade was to Mana Thorn, allowing it to do more damage for a slightly higher mana cost.

She also got a new spell called Sheltering Embrace, a personal defense spell which raised a barrier that could absorb one hit from an enemy, and if the hit was powerful enough cause the barrier to explode and do moderate Nature damage to all enemies within 5 yards.

It had high mana cost and a 1 minute cooldown, but Dare still loved the ability for the fact that it would protect the woman he loved.

Speaking of which, like him Zuri also unlocked the ability to use new gear at Level 20.

For weapons, along with her daggers she could now use clubs, staffs, and spears. That last seemed out of place to Dare, but thinking about it a spear was pretty much the same as a staff for a lot of attacks, just with one pointy end.

A spear would be infinitely more useful for the tiny goblin than a dagger, not only doing more damage but allowing her to attack from a safer distance, as well as allowing her to better defend herself from attacks. While testing it out in sparring, Zuri unlocked block and parry abilities with the staff which she could gain proficiency in, even if as a Healer she'd never get abilities for the weapon or be particularly effective with it.

Still, it meant that the next time they reached a weapon vendor they'd want to get *two* spears. Preferably a longer one for Zuri, like a lance or javelin. Although honestly a normal sized spear would probably count for her.

Even better, not only did she unlock new weapons, but she also unlocked new armor. Specifically leather armor.

The fact that both of them now used leather armor was so exciting to Dare that he actually toyed with the idea of putting ability points into leather crafting so he could keep them equipped. Since his Leatherworking was a subclass the items he made would always be lower quality than a main class Leatherworker, but he still thought it would be worth it to save them money as they leveled and allow them to still be defended in case of trouble.

Zuri disagreed. She argued that their ability points were too precious to waste on abilities that would produce inferior results. "We can always buy armor," she reasoned. "We can't buy ability points. Also neither of us really takes any damage, so we're fine with poor or no armor for now."

"Until we're not," he protested. "Don't forget that Level 20 and higher monsters suck to fight."

She grinned at him. "Not all of them, so we'll focus on the ones we're best suited to hunting. We'll be fine with your Adventurer's Eye."

Dare wasn't sure he completely believed that. But he *did* have a lot of useful abilities he needed to get, and putting points in Leathercrafting meant he'd miss out on things that could help him survive and level faster.

They finished buying new abilities and allocating points, and Dare suggested they set up camp so he could cut and shape new leather armor for Zuri, then get it boiling to harden it. They had plenty of leather thanks to the aggressive predators, and he was eager to see her properly protected.

He also took the time to build a Trash bow with his crafting ability, then spent a while deliberately breaking and repairing it to get his repair skill proficiency high enough to finally repair his Exceptional short bow.

It took a small durability hit from being repaired, of course, but after it was at 100% its stats affected by durability were restored to what they should be, and he got to see it in all its glory.

"Need the tent for a bit so you can have some privacy with your weapon?" Zuri teased when she saw the almost awed look on his face.

Dare laughed and hefted the Exceptional weapon eagerly. "Nope, right now I want to take it out on the town." He expected her to be confused by the expression, but she seemed to get it.

He finished up Zuri's armor and had her try it on, waving aside her complaints that wearing boiled leather over leather clothes made her broil in the summer heat. "You'll get used to it," he assured her.

After tidying up the camp a bit, they went in search of something to shoot with his new bow.

Level 19 enemies, of course; Dare preferred to hunt higher level enemies that gave better loot or experience, and he might be willing to try it on the weaker Level 20s if the bow did well enough. But with the jump in monster power they both agreed that they should focus on 18-19 enemies until they reached Level 23. The point at which Level 18 monsters went from Purple, with a small reduction to experience gains, to Yellow with very poor experience gains.

They'd be better equipped to tackle Level 20s then.

The spawn point he chose to test his new bow was populated with Murder Rabbits. Yes, that was their actual name. Rabbits the size of small dogs that had vicious fangs to go with their buck teeth, and long vicious claws.

The sight of the otherwise cute fluffy bunnies with those savage teeth and claws put them square into uncanny valley territory and creeped Dare out. But even though they were fast and did high damage they had fairly low health, which made them ideal for hunting.

Also, he was sort of hoping they might drop rabbit foots that gave a bonus to luck; he'd been told by his unseen benefactor he already had

Kovana

good luck, but he wouldn't complain about improving it even more.

It might be a faint hope that a drop like that existed, but hey, why not try and see? He lifted his new bow for the first time, feeling that his movements were noticeably quicker and smoother thanks to the item's 5 agility bonus. With a grin of anticipation he sighted in on the nearest Murder Rabbit, drew, and loosed.

He one-shot it.

As in his arrow slammed into it and it hopped once, gave that awful rabbit death squeal, but even more nightmare-inducing with this monster, and keeled over.

Dare stared in a mixture of incredulity and delight. Sure, the Murder Rabbit had lower hit points, and he'd scored a critical hit on the monster's heart, which was the second highest damage behind the head itself.

Still, one fucking shot on a Blue monster within his level range.

"Let's goooo!" he shouted, pumping his fist. He spun to pull Zuri up into his arms in a hug, grinning at her like an idiot. "Did you see that? Holy shit!"

She laughed. "Sacred excrement indeed!" She kissed him firmly. "We'll easily plow through the monsters along the forest's edge at this rate, and get strong enough we can go into the woods in no time."

Joining her laughter, Dare ran over to where the monster rabbit had fallen so he could loot it. But just short of it he abruptly stopped dead, feeling his hackles rise as a feeling of unease swept over him.

"What is it?" Zuri asked when she saw his expression, looking around nervously.

"I don't know." He looked around too, command screens up so he could check the information on everything he saw.

Everything looked normal, just a spawn point full of Murder Rabbits with the edge of the woods a few hundred yards away, and the plains stretching into the distance in the other directions. The monsters in all the spawn points he could see seemed calm, ambling around like always.

There were no people, no roaming monsters or predators. Nothing but him and Zuri and a bunch of creepy rabbit monsters.

"I don't see anything, my perception circle isn't sending any alarms, and nothing looks out of place, but . . ." He shrugged. "Something's making the hair stand up on the back of my neck all of the sudden."

His tiny lover held him tighter, preparing herself in case he had to run away holding her. "You think there's something out there?" she whispered.

"Maybe." He checked his Adventurer's Eye to see if it had any information, but it didn't show anything either. He was about to close the ability when he suddenly paused, taking a closer look. "Huh."

Zuri jumped against his chest. "What?"

"My Adventurer's Eye unlocked a new ability at Level 20." He quickly read the text. "It lets me sense monster spawn points. I can feel when I'm inside one now."

"Really?" Zuri brightened. "I mean, usually we can just see the monsters in them and know, but that's still pretty amazing. It'll be useful for party and raid rated monsters that sometimes have larger spawn point areas or hide underground or in Stealth."

Dare hadn't even known that was a thing. "Good point," he said around a suddenly dry throat. "This could keep us from walking into death."

She nodded happily. "I wonder if you'll get other cool abilities for it as you level up."

"Hopefully." Dare set Zuri down and looted the Murder Rabbit, then they backed up to begin farming the spawn point.

* * * * *

There was always a tradeoff between getting less experience from lower level monsters, and being able to kill them faster.

Dare and Zuri were able to tear through the spawn points along the forest's edge as they headed north, and while the monsters fluctuated between level 15 and level 19, they all gave enough experience to make it worthwhile. Not to mention a whole ton of junk loot.

So much so, in fact, that it came as a huge relief when they found a logging camp at the forest's edge. The loggers were friendly enough, and their quartermaster was willing to buy the junk loot.

At a steep discount, unfortunately. But given the choice of getting less for it or lugging it on and missing out on more loot because their packs were already full, Dare haggled the best price he could and sold it all.

It left a sour taste in his mouth, and even more of one when the quartermaster tried to charge an arm and a leg for two Poor quality spears that were still better than their Decent quality knives.

Dare eventually told the man where he could shove his spears; the knives weren't *that* much worse.

Zuri giggled as he led the way out of the camp. "Humans have the funniest sayings."

"What would goblins say instead?" Dare asked, affectionately pulling her to his side.

She blushed darker green. "A proper woman shouldn't say." At his disappointed look she giggled again. "Probably to go gnaw his own arm off. Or something about poop. Most goblin insults are about poop. Or how weak your blood is."

Dare joined her laughter. "Good to know in case I ever need to insult one."

Beyond the logging camp they discovered that the monster levels began to drop, probably due to some town or large village nearby. Several hours after that he spotted a walled palisade several miles out on the plain, patrolled by armed guards and with people out tilling fields in the surrounding area.

He had to curse the fact that he'd just sold all their loot at a discount when there was a larger settlement not far away. Although it stood to reason that the loggers had to come from, and sell their lumber to, somewhere.

The upside to the lower level area, though, was that they could finally enter the woods without running into Level 20s; the monsters were still higher, up in the 18-19 range, but that was just what they wanted.

"Is it just me, or does it feel like unseen eyes that've been watching me for days are finally gone?" Dare asked as they got far enough into the trees for the plains to disappear from view.

Zuri shuddered. "I feel just the opposite, actually. Like there could be anything watching me from hiding just a few feet away."

"Maybe I don't feel that way because of Adventurer's Eye and Forest Perception," he replied, referring to his ability that allowed him to see more details in the woods around him and better understand their importance. "Since I have those, people seeing me from far off were the weakness. Being under cover is a relief."

"Well then I'll have to keep close to you," she said. She wasn't joking, either; she stuck by his side, often pressed against his leg, as they continued deeper into the forest.

Which might've been a good precaution, because a few minutes later Dare's Eye alerted him that he'd just entered a spawn point. "Heads up," he told his lover. "We just entered a spawn point." At her alarmed look, head darting nervously to check around them, he patted her shoulder soothingly. "Don't worry, there are no monsters around."

"And that makes it *better*?" she demanded, not slacking in her vigilance. "Since when is there a spawn point with no monsters? Does it cover a freakish large area and the monster is something huge, like a raid rated monster? Or has someone or something cleared it out already?"

Her voice became alarmed. "Or are these monsters with a Stealth ability? They could be all around us!"

Dare felt his skin crawl and hastily stepped back until the uneasy sensation of being in a spawn point faded. "I don't know, but the boundary is right here. We can just go around it."

"At a good distance," Zuri insisted.

He had no arguments with that, moving well away from the boundary before continuing into the forest.

Unfortunately, the strangeness didn't stop there. They passed three more spawn points, that or a very huge spawn point with a very twisty boundary, and all were just as empty. Eerily empty.

Dare didn't even see or sense predators, although they passed plenty of prey animals like deer and smaller game.

"There's something clearing these woods," Zuri murmured uneasily. "Maybe bandits?"

He nodded. "Maybe. Turn back, or keep going north and hope to get past whoever it is?"

"I don't know, but let's speed up."

Dare had no arguments with that, either. He picked up his lover, pack and all, and began trotting through the trees, doing his best to move quietly and with all his senses and abilities straining for any hint of danger.

They didn't encounter danger, just more cleared spawn points. For fifteen minutes, then a half hour.

Then they came in view of a large clearing up ahead, dominated by an immense pink flower in its center that looked vaguely like a tulip.

At the base of the flower, twirling merrily as she danced to the tune of unheard music, was a petite green woman.

Chapter Five
New Friend

The woman was naked as the day she was born.

Or perhaps more accurately planted, given the fact that she was the color of new-grown leaves and was connected to the giant flower by a slender stem, which extended from just above her pert little bum like a tail and stretched up to disappear inside the flower.

She'd have to stand on tiptoes to reach five feet and had the body of an elite gymnast, short and lithe and strong but also decidedly feminine in her graceful curves. Her small conical breasts were tipped by darker green nipples and she had a flat, taut tummy, narrow hips, and a small tight ass you could bounce a coin off.

Her hair was kinky, a mass of twirling curls like vine shoots, so pale green it was almost white and growing down to the small of her back in a silky wave. Dozens of small, pale pink flowers grew among her curly locks, so it looked as if she had strings of blossoms woven into her hair.

As she danced the flowing curls seemed to float in the breeze, super soft and fine, sometimes cloaking her supple body in a tantalizing way. Although the dance wasn't in any way meant to be sensual or provocative.

Aside from the fact that she was naked and beautiful, of course.

In spite of her athletic appearance her dancing was more carefree and exuberant than strictly skilled or graceful, her lovely elfin features lit up with joy and happy giggles occasionally escaping her as she twisted this way and that. At one point she tripped on her trailing vine and stumbled, nearly falling, and peals of silvery laughter rang through the clearing as she windmilled her arms to stay on her feet.

Dare was entranced.

He had to jump start his brain again with some effort to activate his Adventurer's Eye and inspect her, making sure she was as harmless as she appeared. Although it seemed impossible that such a bright, lovely young woman could be dangerous.

To his relief his Eye seemed to confirm that. "Floran, adult female. Humanoid, intelligent. Class: Photosynthesizer Level 2. Attacks: "

The beautiful green girl abruptly spotted them and brightened, waving eagerly. "Hello!" she called. "Welcome to my clearing! I'm Rosie." She beckoned. "Come on in and rest, it's perfectly safe."

Well that didn't sound suspicious at all.

Zuri had already slipped from Dare's arms and started forward, but when she saw his hesitation she smiled and also beckoned. "Don't worry, she's right. Plant girls are friendly and harmless. They make great places to set up camp next to, because monster spawn points won't appear on them and wandering monsters and predators usually avoid them."

"Exactly!" Rosie said with a giggle as Dare followed his lover into the clearing. "How fair would that be, just sitting here minding my own business and suddenly monsters are appearing all around me?" She tugged on the slender vine connecting her to her giant flower. "I can't exactly run away."

The plant girl seemed to forget the topic in an instant, turning to beam at Zuri and holding out her arms. "Hello, green sister! Come here!"

The little goblin hesitantly went over to hug the slightly taller woman, although she seemed to enjoy the embrace. "Green sister? I'm not a plant, though," she protested.

"You're something even better!" Rosie exclaimed, rocking Zuri enthusiastically in the hug as if she wanted to pick her up and spin her around. "You're a carnivore! Those are my favorite people!" She hastily glanced at Dare. "Of course I don't mind if people eat plants, as long as they're not me." She giggled naughtily. "Except under certain circumstances."

He felt his face flush and his cock twitch in his pants; not many ways to misinterpret that.

Zuri reluctantly pulled back from the hug. "Do you know why all the monster spawn points nearby have been cleared?" she asked. "Is

96

there someone dangerous around here?"

The plant girl waved that away. "Oh no, that's just a friend of mine. She would never hurt anyone." She stretched languidly, providing a very distracting view of her smooth little body and outthrust perky breasts. "Anyway, let's go up to my flower and talk some more. I love chatting with visitors."

"To your flower?" Dare asked, surprised and a bit taken off guard. "Is that okay?"

She trilled a delightfully carefree laugh. "Of course! It's my home, not the inside of my vagina."

He choked back his own laughter, resisting the urge to point out that wasn't that exactly what it was?

Zuri wasn't quite so tactful. "I thought the flower was the plant's vagina."

Rosie waved that away cheerfully as she climbed her vine, giving him a nice view of her cute little butt and plump pussy lips. "Oh warming sun no, no," she said as she pulled herself onto one of the thick petals and turned to sit with her legs dangling. "The flower houses and protects me, and I house the pistil." She pressed a finger to her delicate little pussy in case she hadn't gotten the point across.

Dare felt himself swiftly hardening as he watched her; he really wanted to pollinate that pistil.

Rosie caught him staring and snickered. "Ohhh! I know that look." She ran her hands teasingly down her sides. "You want to put your stamen in this delicate little flower."

His cock throbbed at the idea and his cheeks reddened. "You're beautiful," he said lamely.

"Thank you." She giggled. "Normally I'd love to, but I'm in a committed relationship with a butterfly girl right now, and she pollinates me so nicely."

Dare brightened at that. "There are butterfly girls too?"

The plant girl clapped her hands in delight. "Oooh, you also like those? If Enellia was here we could all pollinate together! Unfortunately she's off exploring."

"That's a shame," he said, which was a vast understatement; the idea of having a plant girl and butterfly girl together was blowing his mind, and he felt sharp disappointment that he wouldn't get that chance. And from the way Zuri was biting her lip while staring at Rosie, it was obvious she felt the same.

"It really is a shame," the plant girl said with an adorable little pout. "She doesn't dote on me nearly as much as I dote on her, but what am I supposed to do, go find someone else?"

"I'm sorry," Dare said.

Rosie waved that away with a wide smile. "I'd put up with worse for her . . . she's the most beautiful woman in the world, and she always brings me such tasty nectar. Besides, I can't exactly ask a butterfly to not flit about, that wouldn't be fair."

"Just out of curiosity, is a butterfly girl the same as a fairy?" he asked.

Zuri snickered, and the plant girl again pealed laughter.

"Of course not, silly!" Rosie said, legs drumming the side of her petal seat in her mirth. "Fairies are tiny . . . they're like the only humanoids that can't breed with other races. Which is a shame because the ones I've seen are so beautiful it's almost like they're too good for this world. And they all say such nice things about my flower."

If they were more beautiful than Rosie or Trissela, or Zuri in her own sharp-featured way, that was something Dare desperately wanted to see.

"I've heard some fairies are powerful enough to grow to a bigger size, and those can breed," Zuri offered.

"Really?" The plant girl squirmed in excitement. "I hope one of those visits me!" She hesitated. "When Enellia is here, that is. Or after she moves on."

Rosie abruptly patted her petal before rolling backwards, disappearing inside the giant cup-shaped flower. "Come on in!" she called, dropping a long loop of her vine back down for them to climb.

Dare glanced at Zuri and shrugged, then leaned his things against the base of the giant flower and began to climb. His goblin lover was right behind him, and soon he pulled himself up over one of the giant petals, which was stronger than it looked and had no trouble holding his weight.

He was surprised to find that the inside of the flower looked like a little round room, with a flat floor where the petals joined that looked spongy and incredibly comfortable. And it was dry; some pictures of plant girls he'd seen showed them basically lounging in a pool of aphrodisiac nectar. But if that was the case here he saw no sign of it.

Maybe only during certain times of the month.

Rosie reclined on one of the sloping petals with her hands behind her head, soaking in the sun. "Come on in," she said, patting the petal beside her. "You can strip down and get some sun if you want, although I know animal people can be weird about that sort of thing."

Dare was tempted, but given that the plant girl had said she was already taken he didn't want to blur any boundaries; he'd already fucked a woman without knowing she was married, and still felt guilty about it.

So he kept his clothes on and reclined on the petal across from her, Zuri cuddling up against him. The surface was velvety soft and springy beneath him, like a mattress. "This is a cozy home," he complimented their host.

"Thank you." Rosie patted her petal lovingly. "I can fold these up to make a watertight roof at night or when it rains, or in the rare times when I'm in danger like if an animal wanders by. I can stay here as long as I need to until it leaves."

"Do you need to eat?" Zuri asked, looking curiously at the plant girl's mouth.

Rosie giggled. "Of course, silly. My flower collects nutrients from the ground and the air, as well as sunlight, and that keeps me fed."

"Then you don't personally eat?" Dare asked, motioning to his own mouth.

"Oh, this?" She ran a teasing finger over her pouty little lips. "Nah, this is mostly just to make me look appealing for pollination. Although it connects to my pistil so I can be pollinated through it. Along with my other orifices."

Phoenix

"So you can get pregnant with a blowjob?" Zuri asked, expression a combination of envy and sympathy.

The plant girl giggled again. "And anal. Although it's not really that since it's not an anus. No poop or anything, just another hole for pollination." She rubbed her hands over her body. "Actually, my entire body is technically a pistil, although the semen has to go inside before I can grow a seed."

Dare's cock was throbbing again; this was a very difficult conversation to have considering the sexy little flower was taken. "Are you like other races, with an equal chance to have either a floran or a baby of whatever race the father is?" he hastily asked to distract himself.

Her brow furrowed. "How would that even work?"

He decided not to point out that it was equally confusing asking why she was adapted to get inseminated by creatures descended from animals when she was a plant. Or for that matter how any of the races could interbreed.

It worked because it did.

"Plant girls produce seeds," Rosie continued, "which float away in the breeze to land somewhere else where a new plant girl can take root and grow. The seeds grow vines first, though, so if needed they can pull themselves to some place where they'll get plenty of sunlight."

She abruptly grimaced. "Speaking of which . . . could you guys do me a favor?"

"Sure," Dare said. It seemed only fair since she'd been such a gracious host. Not to mention she was adorable and he was hoping to pollinate all her holes sometime in the future.

"As long as it's reasonable," Zuri added, politely but firmly.

"Don't worry, it's just a small thing." Rosie climbed up to the top of a petal and pointed to the east and west, then to the south. "See those saplings growing? I like to keep the ground in those spots clear to make sure I get as much sunlight as possible all year round. A few years back a bovid who liked to pollinate me was kind enough to cut down all the trees blocking my sun, and I want to make sure they don't grow back."

"That's fine," Dare said.

The plant girl obligingly lowered her vine to let him climb down, and he retrieved his hatchet and got to work chopping down the tough, springy saplings. Then he gathered them to use for crafting, since the material could be useful for certain patterns.

Maybe he'd even take another shot at making a collapsible chair that could support his weight.

"Thanks!" Rosie called, waving down at him. "I'm glad most of the travelers I meet are so nice."

He couldn't imagine anyone but a monster being mean to the adorable plant girl.

Dare climbed back up, and at their hosts's urging relaxed and enjoyed the sunlight for a while with Zuri cuddled against him. At some point she fell asleep, and he looked across the flower room to see that Rosie was also dozing.

The warm sun and comfortable, springy petal, along with his lover's soft body against him and the feel of her peaceful breaths, all lulled him down into a pleasant half-doze. Then, with the scent of flowers permeating his senses, he drifted off as well.

* * * * *

Dare woke up to the sensation of two warm, soft bodies pressed against him.

Or, more accurately, Rosie seemed to have cuddled up to Zuri at some point and gone to sleep again, and as she slept had curled around until she was pressed against him with the little goblin nestled between them.

No doubt the plant girl had cuddled with Zuri out of loneliness and a desire for warmth and affection, purely innocent. Unfortunately Dare just wasn't built to innocently hold a beautiful naked woman in his arms without thinking some very uncomfortable thoughts, if he wanted to respect her faithfulness to her butterfly girlfriend.

Rosie felt very, very soft. Like the softest petal, but with the warmth and firmness of flesh. On top of that with her so close her scent reached him clearly, like a mixture of the sweetest floral perfume and pure sex.

She must be producing more pheromones than even Zuri, and his goblin lover's arousal was enough to make his head spin. And he was pretty sure the plant girl wasn't even aroused; this was just her natural scent.

Dare bit back a groan as he struggled not to breathe, not to move, not to feel the sensation of her skin against his. While only her lower legs and one arm were really touching him, he immediately felt himself stiffen to aching arousal, his bulging erection straining in his pants as it pressed against Zuri's soft stomach.

Fuck, he needed to get out of here.

The sun had dropped low enough in the sky that the petal walls of the little flower room were now shading them, possibly prompting the plant girl's search for warmth, and Dare decided that unless they wanted to camp in Rosie's clearing they should probably move.

Camping here seemed like a risky idea at the moment.

Dare very carefully eased away from the two women and scrambled up to the top of the petal they were on. Behind him the plant girl murmured sleepily and hugged the smaller goblin closer, the embrace somehow innocent and erotic at the same time.

He quickly turned away to look out at the woods, blushing.

A moment later he heard Zuri give a startled squeak, then a few seconds later she climbed up to stand next to him, pale green skin flushed a deep green. "We should probably leave," she whispered. "My urge to mate is very strong right now."

He suppressed a chuckle. "You can just say you're horny." He glanced down at his own slowly receding erection. "But I agree, let's go. If Rosie was single and up for it I'd be all for staying as long as she liked, but . . ."

Behind them he heard a loud yawn. "Oh, are you guys leaving?" the plant girl asked, sounding disappointed.

Dare turned to see her sitting up, green eyes sleepy. Thankfully in that pose she was almost decent. "We are," he said apologetically. "We want to get a bit farther north before we set up camp."

"Oh." Rosie pouted. "You don't want to stay here? I so rarely get visitors."

"It's a kind offer, but we need to go," Zuri said firmly. "Thank you so much for your warm welcome, and we hope to see you again."

"I hope so too," the plant girl said, reluctantly seeming to accept their decision. She climbed up to stand beside Zuri, tossing down her vine for them.

Dare went down first, retrieving his gear and making sure it hadn't been disturbed. Zuri was right behind him grabbing her own gear.

Rosie soon joined them. "You know, I think I'll tell my friend about you."

"Enellia?" Zuri asked.

The plant girl giggled. "Well of course her, I tell my girlfriend everything! I mean my other friend, Pella. She comes and visits every now and then. She's the one who clears the spawn points, so she'll probably be showing up any time now."

She abruptly saddened. "The poor dear, she's so sad and lonely. I wish she'd stay with me and Enellia and be happy with us. We've asked her, but she always wants to go back to her master."

"I'd be happy to meet your friend," Dare said politely, doing his best to keep his eyes on her face as he awkwardly waved goodbye. "Until we meet again." He took Zuri's hand and started for the trees.

"Goodbye!" Rosie called after them, giving that enthusiastic wave again. "Please come back and visit lots! If Enellia's here we can all have fun, and if she's left me to go south for the winter then we can have fun without her, and you can cuddle me and keep me warm in my cosy bulb! I'll show you how sticky with nectar my little pistil can get."

Gods, please let her be up for it next time, Dare thought. If possible he definitely planned to visit the plant girl again.

He and Zuri were both quiet as they made their way through the woods, once again vigilant for any danger. The knowledge that the monster spawn points were being cleared by Rosie's friend was a relief, but it was getting close to when monsters respawned in the late afternoon, same as they respawned in the early morning exactly 12 hours apart.

Hunting some respawns would be nice, but he wasn't sure they'd have that much time if they wanted to set up camp and do their usual nightly chores, such as setting up his snares and getting any leather and meat he'd collected during the day on racks to cure for the night.

Dare's erection was slow to recede. Every time it was close to gone he'd find himself remembering Rosie's tantalizing scent, or the petal-soft feel of her skin. Honestly he wanted to go the other way and bust one out thinking of everything he could do with the plant girl, but he was a bit embarrassed about what Zuri would think.

Which is why he jumped in surprise when she abruptly spoke. "You're thinking of Rosie, aren't you?"

He chuckled sheepishly. "Are *you* thinking about her?" he teased.

She nodded happily. "She's so *soft*. Her skin was like flower petals, except warm and cuddly. And she smelled delicious, like flowers and sex. I wish I could snuggle her again."

He wished he could hug her too. "Just snuggle?"

"For a start." Zuri glanced at his crotch, then gave him an impish grin. "That's not going to go down until I take care of it, is it?"

Not if she kept talking about how the adorable plant girl felt like flower petals and smelled like sex.

Giggling, his little lover stripped off her armor, tunic, and pants, taking her panties with them, then quickly unhooked her bra to free her large breasts, leaving her nude before him. Dare eagerly tore off his own armor and tunic, then kicked off his boots and got to work on his pants.

Watching him with eyes glazed with lust, Zuri lay back on her tunic and spread her legs, revealing her tiny plump labia, glistening with her arousal. "You can imagine I'm the plant girl if you want," she said, her pleasantly high pitched voice sultry.

"Never," Dare growled. "I'd never get bored of your sexy little body." He leaned down, but rather than positioning himself above her he picked her up and lifted her over his cock as he straightened.

105

She looked at him in confusion. "Is this a new position?" she asked eagerly.

"One that you're uniquely suited for," he said with a smirk, then in a smooth motion pulled her down onto his rock hard shaft.

Zuri whimpered and squirmed with pleasure as he bottomed out inside her, fully impaled. Her arms instinctively wrapped around his waist and her legs around his ass, and he chuckled as he tried to lift her up and only managed to move her an inch or so.

"You're going to need to let go if you want this to work," he teased her.

She eagerly loosened her grip, hands resting on his chest and legs lightly brushing his thighs, and with a grin he lifted her up on his cock and then relaxed, letting gravity make her slide back down on her own.

His tiny lover moaned at the sensation, vise-like pussy quivering and clenching him eagerly. Her arousal flowed down his cock, easing her passage. "You're right, this is amazing," she panted. "Why haven't we done this before?"

Dare chuckled. "Usually you're too eager to climb on top of me, or too impatient for me to get inside you when I'm on top."

"You just thought of this, didn't you," she guessed, laughter in her voice. Which quickly turned to another moan when she bounced on his dick after bottoming out again.

"Let's just say I've seen it done but hadn't thought of doing it with you before now."

"Seen it done?" she asked, giggling. "And here I thought you weren't all that experienced with mating. Didn't you tell me you'd only mated a handful of times before coming here?"

Dare wasn't about to try to explain porn, or computers for that matter. So instead he began lifting her up and pulling her back down on his cock more quickly, as well as thrusting his hips.

Zuri went nuts, squealing with delight and raining loving kisses up and down his chest. She began undulating her hips along with him, doing her best to bounce on his shaft as her legs flailed against his thighs, struggling to help him raise and lower her.

She abruptly clung to him tightly again in a shuddering climax, tiny pussy milking him desperately, and he paused to let her ride out her peak. At least until she began squirming against him again. "Keep going," she begged. "Go even harder!"

So he did, slamming his goblin lover up and down while she whimpered and cried out in passion. Judging from the way she tensed up or went limp, nectar squirting over his crotch and thighs either way, he guessed she had at least three more orgasms.

"We need to do this more," she panted after the third one. "We could even do it while we travel, you walking around with me impaled on your spear like a trophy."

Dare laughed, imagining someone encountering them in the wilds while they were doing that. "You like this?" he teased.

"Nature's bounty, yes!"

"How about this?" He pulled her off his cock, ignoring her plaintive cry as she thrashed to try to get back on. With effort he rotated her squirming body, then pulled her back down on his shaft facing away from him, his cock mashing against her clit then rubbing hard against her g-spot as he impaled her again.

"Daaaaare!" she whined, immediately climaxing again. Her arms and legs hung limp, head lolling, as another flood poured from her depths and soaked his cock. But her vise-like pussy was anything but limp as it squeezed him nearly hard enough to push him right back out of her, in defiance of gravity.

Dare felt his balls boiling like never before as he witnessed the awesome power of her orgasm. He'd wanted to give her more of a chance to experience this position, but that was more than he could handle.

Panting blissfully, he clutched his tiny lover tight to his chest and with a last frantic thrust of his hips erupted up into her core, shooting what felt like every drop of his seed in his body inside her tiny pussy.

His legs abruptly went weak with the power of his orgasm, and he sank onto his knees and then onto his back, Zuri still impaled on his shaft. He was still hard, but didn't have the energy just yet to do anything about it.

His tiny lover seemed equally wrung out by their intense lovemaking, squirming around with him still inside her (an excruciatingly pleasurable sensation on his sensitive tip) to lay on her stomach on his chest with her arms and legs hanging over his sides.

"That-" she said between gasping breaths. "That was . . ."

"Yeah," Dare agreed, wrapping his arms around her and hugging her close.

Something brushed the edge of his awareness, and he suddenly tensed and went alert, prepared to lift Zuri off him and go for his weapons.

It was a presence hovering at the edge of his perception circle, which suggested it had to be an intelligent creature. But even as he looked in the direction of the presence it faded away.

Had it been there the entire time he was making love to Zuri? He'd been so distracted it might have been. Which, now that he thought of it, was pretty careless even if he could depend on his Adventurer's Eye to warn him.

As this current event clearly proved, it didn't warn him against intelligent enemies like bandits or highwaymen sneaking up.

"What is it?" Zuri panted, also looking around; she'd felt him tense.

"Did you get the hint of someone entering then leaving our perception circles just now?" he asked.

She shook her head. "No, but I was pretty out of it after the incredible orgasm you just gave me." She quickly climbed off him and reached for her dagger.

Dare also grabbed his weapon, although he was only wary and not alarmed; whoever it was could've attacked while they were distracted, which was a point in their favor. "Maybe it's Rosie's friend who's been clearing the spawn points, back to take out the afternoon respawns."

"Maybe." His tiny lover shivered and reached for her clothes. "Still, we should find a better spot to make camp and get a fire going."

He grabbed his own clothes and quickly dressed and shrugged on his pack, then together they hurried away through the trees in the opposite direction of the presence he'd felt.

Chapter Six
Loyal

Dare didn't sleep well.

He and Zuri hadn't bothered with keeping watch at night very often, only when it seemed like there might be danger from people. Sleep was important, so usually they relied on a secluded campsite and the fire keeping them safe from monsters and animals.

But with the potential of a presence out there, friendly or not, he'd only half dozed, keenly aware of his perception circle in case an intelligent creature intruded on it.

Nobody had, but he hadn't relaxed and truly slept until late.

Zuri must've realized he'd stayed up in the night, because she got up early and set about taking down their camp while he slept. He finally drifted awake a few hours after sunrise, when she got to work taking down the tent itself.

With a groan he dressed and crawled outside, sheepishly looking at their packed possessions. "Sorry for sleeping in," he mumbled, scrubbing a hand through his hair.

"You watched over me as I slept," his lover said with a fond smile. "I took the watch once you finally fell asleep." Her full lips thinned with disapproval. "Although you should've woken me for my shift."

Dare chuckled. "Right, we'll have more formal watch rotations from now on, if we feel like there might be enough danger to need it."

They set out northward, and quickly discovered at the next spawn point they found that the monsters were all there. As they were in the spawn point after that.

Had they moved out of the territory of the mysterious presence? That, or the monsters here were slightly lower level, 16-18, with no 19s to be seen, while he assumed the monsters farther south were 18s and 19s since they were between here and the 20s and higher.

Whoever was clearing the monsters might be trying to do the same

110

thing he and Zuri were, kill the easier 18s and 19s until they'd gotten a few more levels and felt comfortable tackling the tougher 20s and higher. But the pessimistic side of him wondered if it was because Rosie's friend (Pella had she said her name was?) was high enough level that she only got experience from Level 18s and 19s.

Which would explain how she could so quickly clear so many spawn points; Dare was just glad they were getting out of her territory, no matter how fond the plant girl seemed of her.

Or not.

They elected to not hunt the monsters, deciding to go someplace else where they wouldn't potentially be poaching someone else's monsters. But after only thirty or forty minutes of Dare trotting while holding Zuri, still moving faster than she could manage in a sprint, they reached an opening in the trees where he slowed to a stop, awed.

The clearing had a hushed and solemn feel to it, a place of reverence.

Probably because it was obviously well tended, the grass cultivated and trimmed, weeds pulled, and flowers planted in artful formations. Like a cross between a garden and a wild field of flowers.

The flowers grew thickest in the center of the small space, a single path leading through them to a clearly marked grave in their midst. The slightly elevated mound of earth was covered with the only white flowers in the clearing, making it stand out, and its headstone was a flat piece of slate that had been painstakingly, if not exactly skillfully, carved into a vaguely circular shape.

A few words were clumsily written on the front, and he had a feeling it was as much a lack of familiarity with writing as the difficulty of carving stone that accounted for the blocky, uneven letters.

"Who do you think is buried here?" Zuri asked in an awed voice, looking at the beds of blooming flowers. "Some lord or king?"

Dare shook his head. "Whoever it was is well loved . . . this garden is carefully tended. We should leave it in peace." But before departing he dropped to one knee and bowed his head respectfully towards the grave. "May you rest in peace, whoever you are, and have joy and

111

success in whatever life waits you after this one."

His lover was looking at him again in that way that suggested she was baffled by his incomprehensibly strange thoughts and actions. But after a moment she also dropped to one knee and bowed her head, out of respect for him if not the person buried in the clearing, perhaps.

"May the primal spirits shelter him or her until rebirth," she murmured.

After a properly respectful pause for silence Dare finally stood, picked Zuri up again, and gave the clearing a wide berth as they continued on.

Less than a minute later his perception circle warned him of someone waiting directly in front of them, in a place where the trees thinned and offered higher visibility. In his arms his lover stiffened as she, too, sensed the presence.

The person definitely knew they were there and had stopped, because she immediately called out, voice uncertain, almost shy. "Um, hello!" She approached cautiously, coming into view as she continued. "I'm Pella, Rosie's friend? She mentioned me?"

For a moment Dare was too busy staring in amazement to answer. The approaching woman was probably in her mid to late 20s, tall and with a powerful but curvy figure. She was wearing poorly crafted and patched leather clothing and armor that looked as if she'd pieced it together herself, without the help of a crafting ability.

But what had immediately caught his eye were her floppy ears and fluffy tail.

If she was a dog girl, as he assumed, he would have to say she most resembled the coloring of a golden retriever. Her tail, ears, and luxuriously thick hair hanging down to her waist in a simple braid were all that same shade of tawny gold, which provided an appealing contrast to her tanned skin. A farmer's tan, he assumed, given her hair.

He hastily pulled up his Eye. "Canid, adult female. Humanoid, intelligent. Class: Tracker level 28. Attacks: Find Prey, Track, Run Down, Disarm, Pummel, Tackle, Hamstring, Overpower, Subdue."

Level 28? That was a high enough level that if she'd been hostile his Eye would've shown her as Red, a fight they likely couldn't win.

Although she could still turn out to be hostile.

But the dog girl didn't *look* like she'd turn out to be hostile. Her shoulders slumped morosely and her beautiful heart-shaped face, soft features as open and expressive as a puppy's, looked forlorn. Her velvety, floppy dog ears also drooped miserably and her fluffy tail hung limp between her legs.

Her inexpertly but carefully mended fighting leathers molded to her form, and it was hard not to stare at her toned muscles and luscious curves. She looked like she'd fit in equally well as a supermodel or an MMA champion.

Zuri got tired of waiting for him to pick his jaw off the ground and called out a reply. "Hello! Yes, Rosie told us about you. It's good to meet you."

Pella approached a bit closer, looking equal parts shy and worried she'd scare them away with her higher level. "Rosie told me I should meet you, but I wasn't sure. I'm still not. I just, um, wanted to thank you for being so respectful of my master's grave. It's a rare person who shows such regard for someone they've never met and know nothing about."

Dare shifted in embarrassment at her obvious and sincere gratitude. "I was taught that people should be respected in death as well as in life. And seeing how obviously beloved he was, that his resting place was so well tended even in the middle of a dangerous woods, just made me respect him even more."

The dog girl had approached to within twelve feet now, close enough that he could see the tears glimmering in her soft brown eyes at his words. "Yes, a great man," she whispered. "And a good one. I just wished I could've been a better girl for him. He relied on me to protect him on our hunts, but I failed him."

"I'm sure you did the best you could," Zuri said kindly.

Pella shook her head dully. "I knew there were predators around who could attack at any time. But when Master ordered me to venture farther from his side than usual and Subdue a Level 21 monster, I obeyed. It was a tough job even though I was three levels higher, and I was so focused on holding the monster that I didn't realize he wasn't casting his spells to kill our target, because he was under attack himself, until it was too late."

She made a soft, plaintive whining noise. "By the time I reached him and distracted the eagle attacking him he was mortally wounded, and I couldn't even try to save him because I had to find a way to kill two enemies by myself. He was dead by the time I managed it, and I can never forgive myself for my carelessness."

To Dare it just sounded like bad luck. Or maybe poor decision making; from her description her master was a spellcaster of some sort, maybe one who'd prioritized offense over defense, and shouldn't have gotten that far from his companion if he was that vulnerable.

Then again, Dare sometimes took for granted what an advantage Fleetfoot gave him, and how much more difficult and dangerous leveling would be without it.

"Pella," he said gently, then repeated her name before she finally looked up at him. He met her gaze firmly. "You followed his commands, rushed to his defense, and stood over his body fighting to protect him. No master could ask for more."

Pella just shook her head and dropped to her knees in pure misery. "You're kind to try to comfort me, but if you had failed your lover would you so easily forgive yourself?"

Dare opened his mouth, then shut it helplessly. He searched for something to say to ease the pain of the poor woman, but she was right that perhaps there was nothing he *could* say.

Sad and lonely, Rosie had described her friend. And he could definitely see it. In his arms Zuri shifted, as if she wanted to go and give the dog girl a hug; maybe she would've, if Pella hadn't been 8 levels higher than them.

"I'm sorry for your loss," Dare said. "He must've been a very good man to earn such loyalty from a slave."

Zuri hissed softly in alarm and warning, shaking her head frantically.

Pella leapt to her feet in affront, expression surprisingly fierce. "I was *not* his slave, I was his faithful companion! You know, man's best friend? Some men like to keep hounds, but most who can afford it would much rather have a well trained dog girl. I stayed at his side when he traveled, hunted with him, cuddled with him as he read in his study, and-" she cut off, tanned cheeks flushing. "And did bedroom stuff with him. I was his good girl!"

Part of Dare was outraged at the thought of a loyal, kindhearted girl like this being treated like a cross between a dog and a sex slave by some wealthy lord. Just another example vindicating his unseen benefactor's warning about how brutal this world could be.

Even if Pella seemed like she'd been happy in the role, it was still wrong.

"I'm sorry," he said carefully. "I didn't mean to insult you or him. Where I come from there are no dog girls, so I don't know much about how you live."

The dog girl relaxed slightly, although unfortunately she went from affronted back to sad. "I don't really know how my kind lives either. From a young age professional canid trainers prepared me to be the perfect companion to a lord. Being purchased by my master and going to live with my new family was the happiest day of my life."

To Dare that sounded seriously fucked up, even for this world. Like the poor girl had been brainwashed. Or at least that her kind's penchant for loyalty had been exploited for her master's benefit.

And whatever she said it sounded exactly like slavery to him. Just a more expensive and higher status slave.

He hesitated, then blurted, "Do you need help?" It seemed ludicrous offering a higher level person help, but he sensed she did.

Pella looked surprised for a moment, then thoughtful. "No, I don't need it. But-but maybe after all this time I finally want it. And I've finally found someone who could give it to me."

He and Zuri stared at the golden blonde woman in confusion. "What did you want help with?" the goblin woman asked a bit timidly.

The dog girl shifted, looking awkward. "Well I've stayed in this woods a long time, keeping watch over Master. But deep down I know I can't stay forever, and Rosie and Enellia keep telling me he would want me to move on, but . . ." She trailed off miserably.

115

Even though the dog girl was a complete stranger, and she was so much higher level and could kill them both if she wanted, Dare's heart still went out to the grieving, lonely woman. She deserved better than to live like this.

"Pella," he said gently, "would you like to come with us?"

Zuri started in surprise in his arms. But at his questioning look, as he made sure he hadn't overstepped, she nodded her agreement. "Dare saved my life, then freed me and has treated me as a companion and a friend ever since," she told the dog girl. "You can be free with us, too, as free as you've lived for the last four years, without having to be owned by a master."

Pella's drooping ears rose slightly, and her limp tail twitched as if it wanted to wag. "Really?" she whispered. Her face, expressive as a puppy's, was hesitant, almost fearful. As if half afraid he and Zuri were actually tricking her, and soon they'd chase her away with shouts and thrown rocks. "You'd really take me?"

"You're welcome to travel with us for as long as you like," Dare said.

Her tail flicked once, shoulders straightening as some spark of spirit returned to the downtrodden woman. "You'd really do that for me? I mean, I'll be a good companion and friend. I'll help out and everything . . . I'm a good girl, I promise!"

He felt a mixture of amusement and sympathy at her almost desperate eagerness to please. "It's all right, Pella. We'd be happy to have you as a companion. You shouldn't have to be all alone out in these woods."

She bounded forward, exuberantly hugging them both. Her body was soft and warm and she smelled like leather, clean sweat, and a hint of a woman's scent. "Thank you," she said. "I'll be a good companion, loyal to the end. Just like a good dog girl should. You'll see."

Dare stood awkwardly in her embrace, unable to hug her back with his arms around Zuri. "I'd be happy to have your friendship," he said in embarrassment.

Zuri nodded. "Me too." With some effort she freed an arm from between his and Pella's two bodies and hesitantly wrapped it around the dog girl's neck.

The golden-haired woman abruptly pulled back, tail wagging eagerly. "Oh, and I've gathered so much treasure from the monsters I've hunted. I'll share it with you! Come on!"

"You don't need to-" Dare started, but Pella was already running away through the trees with the boundless energy of a puppy and the lean grace of a hunting hound. He ran after her, Fleetfoot allowing him to keep up without too much effort.

They didn't go far before reaching another clearing, one with a crude tent made of uncured hides, a fire pit, a trash pit that looked as if it had been dug beside half a dozen other already filled in pits, a clothes line, and other signs of a camp that had been there for a very long time.

The dog girl bolted right past the camp, climbing a low rise and stopping at the base of a big old oak tree. Between two thick roots was a hole large enough for him to enter in a crouch, forming a steep ramp that led down beneath the tree.

Pella turned to wave eagerly to them, then ducked into the hole. Dare exchanged looks with Zuri, shrugged, then followed their new companion down.

The hole led into a cave that looked as if it had dug by hand, crudely supported by roots in some places, and by fallen logs and crude boards that looked as if they'd been salvaged from monster camps everywhere else. The floor was uneven and the ceiling hung with wispy root tendrils, tickling his hair as he stepped off the ramp.

Then he stared in amazement.

In spite of the painstaking effort that must've gone into making this trove, it was big, stretching back over a dozen feet in all directions from the ramp leading down from the hole. Almost as if she'd started the cave with one small area under the tree, then expanded it in every direction from the entrance as she filled up what she had with loot.

Because the place was stuffed full of any possible thing of value that could be dropped from a monster or animal. Ranging from musty hides to crudely cured leather to salvaged lumber, cloth, metal, and other materials taken from camps. And vast mounds of trash loot of all descriptions, along with weapons, armor, and other gear of various qualities. Also piles of tarnished copper coins with silver and even some gold glimmering among them, and reagents and crafting materials.

This much loot had to come from thousands of monsters. Tens of thousands. More, possibly. Not just months but years of hoarding. Every single item Dare had harvested and looted since coming to Collisa would barely fill a portion of this cave.

"Pella," he said quietly as he looked around. "How long have you been out here?"

Her ears drooped and tail hung limp, shoulders slumping in sadness and guilt. "Over four years," she confessed. "I know I should've gone back to my family and told them Master was dead. But I felt so guilty about failing him, and I couldn't bear to leave his grave to grow wild or be despoiled by wild animals, and . . ."

Dare gently rested a hand on her shoulder. "It must've been terrible to be alone for so long, living with those sorts of feelings. I'm sorry you had to suffer that."

The dog girl sniffled and turned away, swiping at her eyes. "Y-you can take whatever you want," she said in a choked voice. "I don't really care about this stuff, I only gathered it because it felt wrong to just leave it on the monster corpses to despawn when they did. Master always insisted on never wasting anything, least of all time or money."

"So you've been farming monsters all this time?" Zuri asked, looking around with a hint of greed in her big yellow eyes.

Pella nodded sadly. "It was my favorite activity with Master, helping him hunt monsters and predators. He really wanted to level up and be a hero so his family would rise in the ranks of Haraldaran nobility, and we made a great team together."

She sniffled again. "With him gone it helped me feel closer to him to keep doing it, and also helped me get things I needed to survive out here. But I've out-leveled all the spawn points around here, and couldn't bear to get too far away from him, so I was slowly moving out to ones that were just barely Yellow to me so I was at least getting experience. That's how I met Rosie and Enellia."

"We don't want any of your loot," Dare told the dog girl firmly, ignoring Zuri's noise of mild protest. "You've worked hard for it, and we'll happily help you lug it all to a nearby town to sell. That way if you ever decide to part ways with us, you'll have the wealth you need to keep you going for a while."

"If that's what you want, Dare," Pella said, not seeming to care too much. "Thank you for wanting to help me." She abruptly started for the entrance to the cave. "Please excuse me, I'd like to say a last goodbye to my master before we leave."

Dare watched her leave, a bit helplessly. She obviously wanted to be alone, maybe even was overwhelmed about being around strange people after so many years of relative isolation aside from visits to a plant girl and a butterfly girl.

But he wasn't sure exactly what to do while he waited for their new companion to compose herself and say her goodbyes at her master's grave. And it was somewhat awkward that she'd left them inside her treasure trove after basically telling them to take whatever they wanted.

With a sigh he got to work sorting the loot. "We can't take this all, but we'll make some sleds out of hide, wood, and leather strips and load them down with as much as we can."

"I'll start picking out the most valuable items!" Zuri said eagerly, diving into the loot pile. She seemed to have gotten over her pique about Dare refusing Pella's offer, or maybe she thought he'd change his mind once he got a closer look at all the loot.

Or maybe she was just excited to handle this sort of wealth, separating out the treasure from the trash. He could admit he was more than a little interested to see what was there himself.

But first off he focused on the sleds, taking the thickest hides and rawhide to make leather strips from the piles, then going out to get wood for runners. He also snagged a bucket of beeswax he spotted near Pella's camp to wax the runners.

The dog girl's camp was neat and clean as things went, but had obviously been made and maintained with the sort of haphazard carelessness of someone who did what was required, but didn't prioritize comfort or aesthetics.

As if she was so focused on grieving her master and caring for his final resting place that she had no time or care for anything else, even herself. Like she'd basically put her life on hold, even in the fact that she'd kept continuing to hunt as she and her master had been doing when he fell.

It took an hour to rig up the sleds, since he didn't have any proper pattern for them. They were junk, but should allow them to carry several hundred more pounds between them. He also crafted a pack for Pella since she didn't seem to have one of her own.

By that time the golden-haired woman still hadn't returned, so he headed down into the cave to check on Zuri.

She was diving deep in junk near one earthen wall, although she'd already made a huge pile on and around the ramp of all the coins, any obvious valuables such as precious metals, gems, jewelry, and finely crafted items, and all the weapons, armor, and other gear. Near it was another pile of more valuable junk loot and other items.

His goblin lover had already almost gathered enough to fill their packs and the sleds, and she was still going strong; even with the sleds, it was going to take a dozen trips to cart all this to a vendor. And even then they'd probably end up leaving hundreds of pounds of absolute trash behind because it wasn't worth the effort.

"Dare!" she called eagerly when she spotted him, scrambling through the junk to join him at the ramp. "Look what I found!"

She moved over to a small pile tucked in against the dirt mound the ramp was built on. It was all gear he judged one of them would be able to use, and the first item she reached for was a spear. "It's Good quality, Level 20!" she said, shaking it in his face. "It's a huge upgrade for you!"

"Why not you?" Dare asked, pausing to admire the weapon.

Zuri laughed. "You'll get more use out of it. Spells are more convenient for me, and at the rate we kill things now I barely manage to use all my mana before we're done for the day anyway."

"All right, I'll see if Pella wants to sell it."

Her expression immediately soured. "Sell," she repeated flatly.

"Yes, sell," he said in a firm tone. "These are her possessions, and we can't accept the desperate offer of a lonely person in need of help. Besides, it's not like we can't afford reasonable prices."

"And meanwhile we cart her things to the vendors like mules, free of charge," his lover muttered.

Dare sighed and settled down on the side of the ramp, pulling her up into his lap and kissing her head. "I'm sorry, I made a lot of decisions without consulting you. I should've got your opinion first."

Her sulkiness vanished and she immediately shook her head. "That's your place as my leader and my mate, and you have no need to apologize for it."

"We'll have to have a long talk about that," he said. "But even if you accept me as leader of our group, we're still equals and it's your right to have a say in decisions that affect you. Next time I'll do better about that."

Zuri gave him that familiar blank look, as if he was discussing concepts so alien to her they seemed nonsensical.

Dare sighed. "How do you feel about Pella joining us?"

She shrugged. "Canids have a reputation for being loyal and hardworking, and she seems to exemplify those traits. Along with being kindhearted and generous. Also she's very beautiful and affectionate . . . she'll make a fine addition to your harem."

He made a strangled noise and stared down at her in amused shock. "What?"

"Your harem." His lover looked at his expression and hesitated. "Or do you not wish to mate her? Is she not attractive to you?"

Dare laughed helplessly. "She's very attractive, and I find myself liking her." He made his voice stern. "But no talk of harems to her. That would be for her to decide, and after years of isolation and grief I doubt she's in the proper state of mind for romance. She's our companion, and hopefully will become our friend, but anything more is a matter for a future time."

Zuri shook her head and sighed. "With all your genius and the things you seem to know, I sometimes forget you're a stranger to this land." She firmly took his face in her small hands, yellow eyes staring up at him intently. "Dare, we don't pussyfoot around and take our time when it comes to mating."

He chuckled. "I couldn't help but notice, considering how fast we ended up together."

"Fast?" She gave him a look of amused disbelief. "My mate, at first I was sure my eyes must be deceiving me when you looked at me with desire, because you never did anything and even after a week of tension between us you made me make the first move."

"Oh." Dare felt his cheeks heat. "Well there were special circumstances, and anyway my people take our time."

"Well the women of Shalin continent don't," his lover said firmly. "If we see a man who'll be a good mate and father, who we wish to spend our life with, we offer ourselves to him. No flirting or teasing or waiting until we've built up affection or even love. That comes after."

"I hope you don't mind if that seems strange to me, the same way me taking my time seems strange to you." Dare chuckled. "In my home, a woman who immediately sleeps with a man is usually doing so solely for her own enjoyment, not because she has plans for a committed relationship with him."

Zuri stiffened in his arms. "Are you saying you thought I only wished for pleasure, and had no desire or intent for commitment?" she asked in alarm.

"No," he said, although he might've hesitated a second. At her hurt look he hastily added, "But even if I did, I understand better now." He kissed her gently, then looked into her eyes again. "I can feel your love for me and fully trust your commitment."

He motioned up the ramp. "Still, no talk of harems or mating with Pella until we see how she feels about this. Some time in the future, after we've had a chance to build trust and friendship."

She sniffed to show what she thought of that and wiggled out of his embrace, giving him a narrow look. "If we're equals and I'm free to decide for myself, you have no right to tell me what I can or can't say to our new companion." At his plaintive look she sighed. "But I'll honor your request for as long as it remains reasonable. Although I think Pella won't be as patient as you. And there's something else you need to consider. Something very important."

Dare looked at her warily. "What?"

"Even if she doesn't want to be your mate, are you going to invite her to become a permanent member of our party?"

He hesitated. "I guess we'll have to see how things work out," he said. "I think she'd be a good addition, and I'd like to have her with us if that's she wants."

She nodded as if she accepted that, but her expression was still grave. "A lot of times you don't seem to know how different races think and act, so I need to warn you."

That sounded ominous. Dare gave his lover a nervous look. "About what?"

Her yellow eyes were as serious as he'd ever seen them. "I don't know if you appreciate how strong a canid's loyalty is. They take so strongly to masters because in the wild they'd have that same unwavering loyalty to an alpha. Whatever you might say about her being our equal companion, it's not going to matter to her. If you let her come with us then there's a good chance eventually she's going to start viewing you as her alpha, if you're worthy of it. Which you are."

She took his hand and squeezed it, expression grave. "Once she transfers her loyalty to you, she'll follow you for life as a faithful companion. After that, trying to make her leave or abandoning her would be as devastating as killing her. Far worse than if you'd actually killed her, or died yourself. So if you don't want her as a lifelong friend, you need to be very careful to make sure she doesn't become loyal to you."

Part of Dare found the prospect of Pella as a lifelong companion and friend very compelling. He liked her personality, he enjoyed her company, and he couldn't argue that she was adorable.

Especially when another part of him thought of having her as more than just a companion.

"As long as it's her decision, whatever she wants to do," he said firmly. "Whatever makes her happy. We'll give her a chance to start a life of her own and see what choice she makes."

Zuri sighed, although he caught a hint of a smile. "We're going to need a bigger tent," she mumbled. Before he could address that she turned and started back towards the spot she'd been working at. "Want to help me dig for treasure?"

"I'd love to," Dare said. "But first I want to make Pella some new clothes and leather armor . . . hers are handmade or looted from monsters and in poor condition, and I don't think she has any crafting or repairing abilities."

The goblin woman shook her head irritably. "And yet you insist on *buying* a spear she wants to give you," she muttered, just loud enough for him to hear.

He ignored her and began gathering up hides, leather, and other crafting material, then took it up and got a fire going so he could get some of the hides curing.

A few hours later Zuri had finished going through the loot, and Dare had finished some new clothes and armor for Pella. He'd even convinced Zuri to use some of the finer cloth they found among the looted items to make socks and underwear for the dog girl.

After using her Cleanse Target spell on the materials, of course.

Last of all they loaded up all three packs and the new sleds, starting with the most valuable items and working their way down. All in all it would probably come to dozens or even hundreds of gold, a fortune considering how much they'd earned so far in their own leveling.

And it was only scratching the surface of their new companion's trove.

At that point there was nothing left to do aside from pack up Pella's things from her camp, which was something the dog girl should do herself; Dare wasn't about to invade her privacy like that. But their new companion had yet to return from her visit to her master's grave, and Zuri was starting to get impatient after hours of waiting.

To be honest so was he. "I'll go get her," he finally said. "Stay here."

124

"Fine," his lover muttered. "I'll go check the loot again to make sure we didn't miss anything."

Shaking his head, he started back to the clearing with the garden and the grave.

Part of Dare had been afraid Pella had lost her nerve and ditched them, maybe to go stay with Rosie after all. But to his relief when he reached the clearing he saw the dog girl kneeling beside the crude gravestone, head bowed almost to the ground.

Dare respectfully entered the clearing, joining the golden-haired woman and kneeling as well. She didn't protest, and he let the silence hang between them for a few minutes before speaking quietly. "You miss him."

Pella nodded, huge tears streaming down her cheeks. "I'm a coward for not going home to tell his children, my family, he was dead. It was my duty." She shuddered with a heavy sob, curling in around herself. "But I was so ashamed for failing him. So sure they were going to be angry. I was certain they'd send me away, back to the markets to be sold to another master."

Her shoulders shook in another sob, and her voice became plaintive. "But I didn't *want* another master! I wanted *my* master!"

Dare hesitantly rested a hand on her back, and the grieving dog girl dissolved into wracking sobs and leaned against his side.

They knelt like that for long enough that Dare's knees began to hurt like hell, and he was certain they'd shatter when he tried to stand. But finally Pella's tears quieted, and after another respectful minute he gently patted her back.

"It's time to go," he murmured.

The dog girl sat up, face splotchy from crying but still somehow beautiful. "I understand," she said quietly. "I can't stay by his grave forever, can I? I tried to, for the first year or so. But eventually hunger and thirst and the cold forced me to see to my needs." Her ears drooped and her tail hung limp. "Part of me thinks I should've stayed by him anyway, let death claim me so I could be by his side again."

Dare frowned. "I'm glad you didn't. Loyalty is wonderful, and it sounds like your master deserved yours." *As far as the morals of*

125

owning a dog girl go, he silently added to himself. "But you deserve to have a long, happy life too."

Pella's ears raised slightly, and her tail twitched as if wanting to wag. "Do you really think so?" she whispered.

"Of course. You're a good girl."

Her entire body shook as if he'd just shocked her, and her face lit up for a moment. "I am?"

Dare winced. Of course, dog girl. She would crave people calling her a good girl. Now that he realized it, using the phrase felt a bit manipulative.

But her brown eyes were looking at him with such pleading that he didn't have the heart to say anything but, "Of course you are. I've only known you for a little while and I can already see it."

Pella showed him the first genuine smile he'd seen from her, as glorious as the most perfect sunrise, and her tail began to wag so hard her shapely ass moved with it. She turned back to the grave. "Thank you, Dare. Can you give me just a few more minutes of privacy with Master to say a last goodbye, and then I'll join you and Zuri?"

"Of course." Dare stood, briefly rested a hand on her shoulder, then turned and left the clearing.

Chapter Seven
Hashing Things Out

In spite of Zuri's grumbling about not accepting Pella's generosity while giving her things, as they waited for their new companion she busied herself crafting a lovely dress for the woman out of higher quality linen.

When she caught Dare watching her work she blushed a bit. "Forgive me if I think Pella is beautiful and want to make her something cute to wear," she said with forced indifference, brushing a lock of inky black hair behind one pointy ear.

"You're going to try to subtly arrange things to get her in my harem no matter what I told you, aren't you?" Dare asked wearily. She flushed an even darker green and he sighed. "Just be respectful of her feelings. Don't push her into anything."

"Assuming she wants to mate you, which any sane woman would," his tiny lover shot back, "don't you think you refusing to make love to her until you "know each other better" is *you* not being respectful of her feelings?"

He shook his head and left her to her work.

In spite of Pella's request for a few more minutes, it was closer to a half hour before she finally returned to camp. Her eyes were red and her ears and tail dropped, but when she met his eyes and offered a reserved smile he thought a weight had fallen off her shoulders.

Although there was nothing reserved about her response when he and Zuri gave her the clothes and armor they'd crafted. "You two made these for me?" She stared at the new items, eyes shining and tail wagging slowly but powerfully. "They're beautiful."

Dare chuckled. "They're Trash and Poor quality junk we made with basic crafting abilities we've put no points in."

"Still." She fingered the simple sundress Zuri had just sewn, and the tunic Dare had made. "You did this for me, even though we just met and I've already asked for so much from you."

"All you've asked for is our friendship, and it's freely given."

The dog girl abruptly straightened determinedly, holding the boiled leather chestpiece he'd crafted. "I'll be a good party member for you. You can invite me right now, or if you're worried about experience I can help by subduing monsters, especially adds, while you damage them down." Her tail wagged tentatively. "I'm very good at that!"

Dare couldn't help but be impressed by the sincere trust she showed, being willing to join his party and let him see so much of her personal information. "Let's talk a bit about grouping up. I'm a Hunter and Zuri's a Healer, and we've found ways to optimize our leveling with our damage and crowd control abilities. Tell me a bit about the Tracker class so I can think of how best to use your skills in our group."

Their new companion's tail stiffened in surprise, ears going up and eyes wide. "You know my class?"

"Oh, um . . ." Dare felt his face flush as he shared a look with Zuri. "She's shown us a lot of trust," he told his lover. "I think we might as well tell her."

"It's up to you, my mate," the goblin woman said carefully, tone indicating she thought he was being reckless.

Maybe so, but it was hard not to want to trust the open, kindhearted woman. "I was gifted with the Adventurer's Eye," he said simply.

He expected Pella to be incredulous, doubtful, or burst out laughing. But to his pleasant surprise she just looked amazed. "You were?" she blurted, tail wagging harder. "That's amazing! So you can see my abilities?"

Dare nodded and quickly listed them off, and their new companion became even more amazed. "That's right!" she said, clapping her hands as if he'd done a trick. "That's so neat! I bet that's helped you so much."

"It has," Zuri agreed, broad smile showing her sharp teeth. "But if you think that's amazing, you should see him juggle or do magic tricks."

He cleared his throat sternly before he could get sidetracked into entertaining the two women; plenty of time for that later. "So about your class?"

"Oh, right." Pella bit her lip thoughtfully, an adorable expression. "Trackers are basically what you'd expect, and masters often encourage their canid pets to pick the class so we can fulfill the role of hunting hounds. Trackers are very good at spotting signs of prey in the area, especially with my superior senses, then running them down and subduing them while someone else, my master in my case, captures or kills them."

Dare nodded thoughtfully; that fit the names of her abilities perfectly.

So she was a strong support role, one that specialized in scouting and crowd control rather than healing or protection or buffing. That could be incredibly useful, especially with the Level 20 and higher enemies usually able to get to Dare before he could kill them.

Of course, there was the question of damage; even Zuri as a Healer contributed to leveling up through doing damage rather than healing most of the time. "How about your attacks? You were able to kill two enemies close to your level at the same time, so you must do decent damage."

Her ears and tail immediately drooped again, and he regretted referencing what she'd told him about fighting over her master's body. But she answered willingly. "I do okay. I can't have a weapon equipped while using any of my abilities to subdue a monster, of course, since most of them involve grappling. Because of that my master often had me focus on my unarmed attacks, although they do a lot less damage. But if I can also use daggers, swords, spears, cudgels, lassos, bolos, and whips."

Wow, that was some exotic weaponry. "Do those last three also have crowd control utility?" Dare guessed.

"Yes!" Pella's tail got to wagging again; she really wore her heart on her sleeve. "My master had me use a lasso, which snares and has a chance to temporarily root, but has very low durability and often needs to be repaired or replaced. To apply Hamstring he had me use a long knife, and also when I was clear of the monster and had space to use it rather than my unarmed attacks."

"Are those two what you'd prefer to use?" Dare asked.

"Yes, absolutely," she said firmly. "I'm familiar with them, they're very strong in a group that already has good damage dealing, and most importantly using them is a tribute to my master. Hold on a second."

The dog girl disappeared into her camp, quickly returning with a length of sturdy rope, a dull and rusty knife, and a bag of what he assumed were her important possessions.

Dare clicked his teeth at the sight of the weapon; it was probably the highest quality of the gear they'd seen in her trove, but its durability was in the yellow, only a few notches above red. And while it was Level 20, in its condition his own knives were better.

"Here," he said, drawing his weapons and offering them hilt-first. "Can you dual wield?"

"Yes, but I'm usually too occupied with my other abilities to use more than one weapon in specific circumstances." Pella stared at his knives without reaching for them. "You'd give me your own knives?"

"Well really he'd prefer to trade them for that spear in your trove," Zuri supplied.

"Oh, that?" The dog girl shrugged. "It's too unwieldy for me to use along with my other abilities so I'd never use it myself. Take it." She showed no more hesitation taking his knives. "And thank you."

Then, to his embarrassment, she immediately began stripping down to change into her new clothes.

Dare hastily turned his back on her, feeling his cheeks heat. "I'll, um, go check the trove one last time."

As he walked away he heard Pella talking to Zuri in a quiet voice. "I'm sorry, did I offend him? Does he think my body is revolting?"

His goblin lover laughed, then spoke loudly enough for him to clearly hear. "No, he has this odd idea that not looking at a woman who clearly has no issues being naked in front of him is showing her respect."

"Oh. Has he taken a vow of celibacy?"

Thankfully Dare escaped out of earshot at that point. He hoped Zuri would heed his request about not saying anything untoward to their new companion.

Although he wouldn't mind if she cleared up that he *definitely* wasn't celibate and he certainly found Pella attractive. As long as his lover didn't do it in a way that pressured the dog girl to sleep with him, unless she felt the same way about him and wanted to. Either way it seemed inevitable it would lead to awkwardness.

Godsdamnit.

Zuri called him up a few minutes later, laughter in her voice. He emerged from the hole just in time to nearly be tackled in an enthusiastic hug from a grateful Pella, who was fully kitted out in her new gear. She looked much better in it, and seemed more cheerful as well.

"Thanks for this great stuff, and also for sorting out all my things and getting them ready to move," she said as she squeezed her full breasts against his chest and energetically rocked back and forth, tail wagging furiously.

Dare felt his face heat at the feel of her soft body against him. "You're welcome. Do you know the way to the nearby town that's making all the spawn points decrease in levels as we head north?"

The dog girl drew back, nodding. "Yep, Master used it as a staging area to hunt in these woods, so we came and went from there for a few years." Her face fell as she remembered him. "Although I haven't been back since the last time we set out, so it may have changed."

"Well it's still affecting the monster levels, so it should be big enough to find some good vendors."

"And a money changer to turn several tens of thousands of copper coins into silver," Zuri added. "Honestly for volume and weight there'd be a lot of loot that'd be better to take, but money is money and you don't have to worry about selling it."

Pella didn't seem interested in anything else from her camp, so after filling in the hole to her trove and disguising it to make sure nobody stumbled across it and stole everything, they all grabbed their packs and sleds and set out. Of course it wasn't quite that easy, since

131

they needed to adjust the loads for balance and weight, and put more wax on the runners of Zuri's sled.

But it worked well enough that as long as Dare led the way with his Forest Perception, they were able to find a path to pull the sleds through the undergrowth. Although he often had to kick aside fallen logs or put down a tarp over rough spots. And in some places they had to pick up the sleds between the three of them and carry them over larger obstacles.

"Too bad there's no river leading to our destination," he joked. "We could put everything on a raft and let the current do the work."

Unfortunately there wasn't, so they spent the rest of the day moving at a crawl as they laboriously lugged hundreds of pounds of loot, worth more gold than Dare had ever seen. By sunset they'd only gone about two-thirds of the way, at least according to Pella, so Dare called a halt beside a stream to camp for the night.

They were all sweaty and streaked with mud and grime from the day's work, so it was small surprise that Zuri immediately stripped off her clothes and made for the stream. Dare, who'd been occupied lighting a fire, quickly turned his back to the stream when Pella moved to join the goblin, again showing no hint of bashfulness about stripping nude.

It was a serious temptation to turn and sneak a peek at the beautiful dog girl, and he had a feeling she wouldn't mind if he did. But he kept to his discipline and focused on getting a meal cooked, then perfecting the design for collapsible chairs for their new companion and himself.

The temptation only grew as he listened to the girls splashing and laughing in the cool water, and he had to fight the longing to join them and bathe his own sweaty, grimy body.

"Can you wash my back, Zuri?" Pella asked.

"I can do even better," the goblin said. "Hold still and I'll cast Cleanse Target."

"Oooh, you have that spell? That would be great . . . I ran out of soap after the first month, so dunking in the water is the best I've been able to manage."

Dare listened as the dog girl stopped splashing in the stream long enough to let Zuri cast the spell, laughing with delight at the result.

"What a great bath spell!" she cried. "I love baths! I love being clean!" He heard another splash and Zuri's sudden surprised squeal, and he could imagine Pella picking up the goblin and hugging her. "Thank you! This is wonderful, thank you! It's been so long since I've felt truly clean like this. Not since my master used to give me the very best baths!"

He tried not to imagine the two naked women's bodies entwined, cursing himself as a lecher as he listened to Zuri grumble and complain until she was apparently set down. She soon joined Dare by the fire as Pella continued to splash in the water.

"Have a good bath?" Dare teased her.

"It's hard to argue with her enthusiasm," his lover grumbled. But Dare couldn't help but notice the deep green blush and pleased smile the goblin was trying to hide.

Looked as if Pella was starting to win Zuri over.

The goblin woman abruptly sniffed around him and frowned. "You need to get in the water so I can clean you, too," she grumbled. "You know I love your stink, but this is a bit much."

"Sure," he said, blushing slightly. "Once I finish making these chairs."

She giggled. "You mean once Pella's finally done and dressed?" she teased. "Are you going to strip down so she can see your sexy body and giant cock? She'll want to be your mate for sure after that."

Behind them the splashing abruptly stopped, and Dare felt his face catch fire. "Zuri, have you considered that dog girls probably have excellent hearing?"

His lover flushed deep green. "Shit, sorry Dare."

He cleared his throat loudly. "We are *very* happy to have Pella here as our companion, and that's all we expect her to be. Anything else is you making assumptions when you don't know what she wants."

"Unless what she wants is to be your mate," Zuri said, also exaggeratedly loudly.

Dare shook his head. "Damnit, Zuri, we talked about this. Don't embarrass her and make us seem like assholes." He nodded down the stream, where he'd be able to bathe out of sight of camp. "Let's go find a secluded spot, and you can clean me up."

"No need!" Pella said brightly, and he heard a final bit of splashing and then the rustle of clothing. Soon after she joined them at the fire, wearing the sundress Zuri had made her. "You guys are hilarious, by the way," she added, grinning at them. "Especially you, Dare . . . imagine a man panicking at the idea that a woman might realize he wants to mate her." She giggled. "As if we don't already know."

Zuri giggled as well, and Dare shook his head wearily. "You like steak and potatoes?" he asked, changing the subject.

"Love them!" Pella said happily. "Of course I'll like pretty much anything you offer, but any meat is especially good." She looked at what he was working on, ears pricking up in curiosity. "Making splints?"

"Nope, a collapsible chair he invented himself," Zuri said. She dug through the loot in her pack and produced the small chair he'd made for her, opening it up and sitting in it to demonstrate. "See?"

"Wow, you made that?" the dog girl asked, closely inspecting the contraption of leather straps and wooden poles. "That's really amazing."

"Something like it exists in my home," Dare said, embarrassed at the praise. "I'm just copying the design."

Zuri leaned over and patted his arm, expression proud. "He's being modest. He's a genius who's always thinking of amazing things, not just inventions but smarter ways to do things like leveling. And he knows so much about everything."

She patted him again. "And he's strong and brave and you can see how handsome he is. That's why he'd make such a good m-" she cut off at his sharp look and hastily amended, "that is, why I'm so happy to have him as my mate."

"I know, I could tell how much fun you were having last night," Pella said. At their stares she blushed slightly. "I wasn't spying on you, I just happened to hear. You weren't exactly being quiet."

Well, that confirmed it had been her presence Dare felt. He cleared his throat and got back to work on the chair.

Finally, after heavily reinforcing the design he'd used for Zuri's chair, he thought he had something that would work. Still, best to try it with someone lighter first. "Here," he told Pella, handing his prototype chair over. "I made this for you. Although be a bit careful in case it collapses . . . I'm still working on making it strong enough."

The dog girl looked at him with huge eyes. "You really made this for me?" she asked, cradling the chair.

He chuckled. "I plan to make one for myself too, but I figured I'd work my way up to my weight . . . first one for Zuri, then you, then me."

She giggled. "If that's your way of saying I'm cute and skinny I'll take it." She needed a bit of help getting the chair set up, but once it was she plopped down on it as if fully confident it would work.

To Dare's vast relief, it did. Their new companion made a pleased sound and wiggled around to get comfortable, fluffy tail sticking out the gap between the seat and the backrest and wagging gleefully. "This is great!" she said. "And I can carry it around and use it whenever I want a chair?"

"That's the idea," Dare said. At the corner of his vision he got a notification that he'd invented a new design of a collapsible chair for mid-sized humanoids, along with a small experience bonus.

The design confirmed the chair worked, and better yet it meant he could make one for himself using the ability, in a fraction of the time and effort.

He did, and soon they were all seated around the fire on their own chairs, waiting for the food to finish cooking.

"How many trips should we take to sell Pella's loot?" Dare asked as the silence stretched.

"This one is more than enough," the dog girl said, while right on top of her Zuri said, "As many as it takes to empty the place."

They both looked at him as if expecting him to make the decision, or at least provide the tie breaking vote. He shrugged. "It's Pella's stuff. If she's content with leaving it, that's fine."

His goblin lover frowned and folded her arms, but didn't argue. "Once we're done with this where will we go to level?" she asked. "Back south to where we found those Level 20s?"

"I'd like to keep putting distance between us and Kov if I can," Dare replied. "North of this town we're headed for will have Level 20 monsters too, eventually."

"You're getting away from Kov?" Pella asked cautiously, ears flattening. "Why?"

He winced and exchanged glances with Zuri. "Paranoia, mostly," she replied. "We weren't there long, but somehow we drew the attention of a religion we didn't know, who didn't know us, and we had nothing to do with."

Dare nodded. "So we agreed to get out of there before we found out what they wanted, just in case it was something bad."

"Oh, okay." The dog girl seemed to accept that.

He motioned to her. "What about you? Where do you think we should go?"

"Oh, I'm happy to go anywhere with you," Pella replied diffidently. But from the way she fidgeted he had a feeling she had a preference.

Dare gave her a stern look. "None of that. We're all equals in this group, and you have as much say as anyone."

The dog girl looked unsure of that, but finally nodded resolutely. "North, then. I'm not sure if I have the courage to talk to my family after all this time, but I owe it to them and my master . . . maybe by the time we get closer to Master's manor I'll have found that courage."

He looked at Zuri again to see if she'd press her argument, and she sighed. "North's fine." She climbed out of her chair and into his lap, cuddling him.

Dare tensed a bit, expecting the thing to creak alarmingly and then collapse beneath him. But maybe the fact that it was an official pattern now made it sturdier, or maybe he'd just done that good a job over-engineering the thing to hold enough weight. But either way it seemed fine.

"North it is," he said, kissing her head and luxuriating in the feel of her inky black hair beneath his lips. "To whatever adventures await us next."

"I like that!" Pella said, tail wagging behind her chair. "To whatever adventures await!"

* * * * *

After dinner and a bit of conversation, mostly casual stuff about monsters they'd encountered, Dare made Pella a tent and bedroll since she hadn't bothered to bring either. She claimed the ones she left behind were too bulky and bad quality anyway, and she was content to curl up by the fire for the night. Or, if he'd let her, at his and Zuri's feet at the entrance to the tent.

Dare wasn't about to let her do any such thing, for her sake as well as because it'd be impractical and uncomfortable for everyone. From the looks Zuri was giving him when Pella wasn't watching it was obvious she wanted him to invite the dog girl to sleep in their tent, which obviously also wasn't happening.

So he made the tent and bedroll. Then he left the women to prepare for bed and started to head out into the night, claiming he needed to take a leak.

Although beforehand he pulled Zuri aside to a distance he hoped was out of even a dog girl's earshot. "I need to ask you something," he said in a low voice.

She stared at him a bit uncertainly. "Okay."

Dare took a breath; this was going to sound crazy. "I know you're okay with me mating any women I encounter, but I still felt like I should tell you and make sure you're okay with it."

His lover brightened. "You mean Pella? Since you made the tent I thought you didn't-"

"No," he cut in hastily. "I'm not talking about her at the moment." He took another breath. "Let's say that, awhile ago, I may have met a woman in a dream who took the form of a shadow, and we had sex."

Zuri's look became a bit flat. As well as that "you baffle me with your outlander ways" stare he was so familiar with. "You want my approval to have sex in dreams."

"No," Dare said, blushing. "This wasn't really a dream. It was a . . . person I'm in contact with, who has helped me and who I speak to from time to time."

Her big yellow eyes widened in understanding. "Ah, the great god or spirit that gave you your gifts."

"Well yes, although I'm not sure what she is." He shifted awkwardly. "Anyway, I probably should've told you when it happened. But it's possible she'll want to do that again, and I want to make sure you don't mind."

"That I don't mind that my mate has drawn the desire of a goddess who wishes to give him her body," she said, smirking. "No, my mate, I don't mind. You are a great man and you'll have many mates. You can romance any woman you wish, whenever you wish, and I will cheer your efforts. You needn't even tell me about it if you don't want to. Especially if she's also your mate . . . she has as much right to you as I do."

Zuri cocked her head. "Although since you're bringing it up now, does that mean you're going to go mate with her?"

Dare swallowed at the prospect. "I'm not sure. I'm going to talk to her, at least. But I figured I should tell you first."

"Thank you for showing me such trust and honesty, my mate." She hugged him around the legs, then turned back towards camp. "I'll help Pella get settled, then go to bed." She looked over her shoulder coyly. "If you haven't tired yourself out with your patron spirit, and I'm still awake, perhaps we can do some mating as well."

He chuckled. "I love you, Zuri."

Her eyes softened. "And you, my mate. Always." She disappeared into the trees in the direction of the distant fire.

Dare walked a bit farther out, wary of threats as he went, then looked out into the darkness, pulling up his command screens. "I've got a question about crafting patterns."

Text appeared in front of his vision, accompanied by a pleasant woman's voice reading the words. Or perhaps she was speaking and the text was transcribing. "Good to hear from you. I was getting the feeling you were avoiding me."

He bit back a sigh. Okay, so they were doing this huh?

Yes, it was possible he might've been doing his best not to use the command screens, and when he did avoiding asking any questions and relying strictly on the interface. And maybe he'd put off this particular conversation for longer than he should've, not sure exactly what he was going to say or how he felt about his change in relationship with his benefactor after having sex with her.

"Not exactly avoiding you," he said carefully. "Just needed to get my head around the fact that the person who brought me to this world, gave me an awesome new body and incredible abilities, and is probably some sort of deity or even the power controlling the world systems, came to me in a dream as a shadow and fucked my brains out."

There was a long pause. "Still, a girl tends to take it personally when the guy doesn't call afterwards." She sounded uncertain. "I mean, I probably could've approached you differently. Maybe told you who I was first and gave you the chance to decide how you felt about me, instead of just showing up and climbing on your dick."

"There is a bit of that," Dare admitted. "Also, no offense, the entire living shadow with no prior explanation was kind of as creepy as it was hot."

"All right, well I understand if you just want to keep things professional."

He felt a bit guilty at the obvious disappointment in her voice. Whatever she was. "I wouldn't say that. I enjoyed our time together, even if I had no idea it was you at the time. And I enjoy talking to you and appreciate all your help. I *do* want more, I just needed time to process."

There was a long pause. "So you won't mind if I visit you again?" his unseen benefactor said eagerly.

Dare's cock twitched in spite of himself at the prospect. "Sure, I would like that. And you know, if you ever want to just hang out and talk, I'd like that too. So things aren't always just business between us."

She laughed. "Thank you, Dare. I would like that too." She sobered. "Speaking of business, though, you had a question?"

"Right." He rubbed his jaw. "Would there be a problem if I wanted to, say, make gunpowder?"

"Hmm. An alchemical compound of saltpeter, charcoal, and sulfur, which produces explosive force when ignited." His benefactor sounded amused. "Want to replace your bow with a gun?"

"Or at least explosive arrowheads."

Her amusement increased a notch. "Those are trickier to pull off than you'd think. Also, I'm assuming since you asked about patterns specifically, you're worried that if you were to invent gunpowder it would immediately become a pattern available to all Alchemists."

Dare chuckled. "Yeah, pretty much."

"The answer is yes, it would."

Shit. "So there's no such thing as an arms race on Collisa."

"No. And if an innovation proves too unbalancing to the system, it tends to be removed by mutual agreement of the gods." She paused significantly. "Which, as I'm sure you can guess, gunpowder certainly would."

He sort of figured that would be the case; no introducing advanced Earth technology here for his own benefit. "Well, it was worth a try."

His unseen benefactor laughed lightly. "There's always fire oil or impact shards. Although any dwarf or gnome could tell you the danger of using them in combat."

"Can't wait to find out all about them," Dare said dryly. "Thanks for the help, um . . ." He paused, realizing he didn't know her name and she'd never offered it. Maybe it was insensitive on his part to not have asked at some point, but considering he'd been inside her he felt like he should probably know it now.

"Your benefactor is fine for now," she said with a giggle. "You in a hurry to get to bed, or you want to have some interface sex?" Her voice became teasing. "After all, you did specifically clear it with Zuri. Which I appreciate, by the way . . . it's wonderful to see you being such a dear to that sweet young lady. And Pella too, for that matter.

She's a sweetheart and I'm glad you're taking good care of her."

He wasn't sure how to react to her giving her opinion about his companions like that, or what it might mean that she had an opinion about them at all. Although her endorsement seemed like it had to be a good thing.

So he stuck with the first thing she'd said. "Interface sex? As in what, talking dirty to each other?"

"Exactly." Her voice became low and throaty, oozing sex with every syllable. "I'm kissing your neck with my moist lips, hot breath sending shivers down your spine."

Dare did indeed shiver because as she spoke a warm breeze, damp with soft rain the clear sky showed no sign of, brushed teasingly over his collarbone.

Okay, so they were doing this huh? It was no shadow sex, but he'd take what he could get.

Grinning, he reached down and freed his dick. "I'm running my hands up and down your sides, your skin soft and warm beneath my fingers," he murmured, remembering the look and feel of his shadowy lover and imagining the incredible woman who might cast that shadow.

She moaned in pleasure, and he began to stroke himself as she teased and caressed him with her voice.

Chapter Eight
Going Merchant

The town of Hamalis that Pella led them to, several miles into the plains near a meandering river, was a decent size. Even so, the three of them dragging sleds full of treasure up to the gates drew a lot of attention.

Dare was irritated to find that the guards demanded not only a slave tax for Zuri but a pet tax for Pella, 2 silver in either case. Of course trying to argue that they were his free companions was useless since they didn't have papers, and he reluctantly handed the money over.

At which point the guards insisted on inspecting their possessions, poking through their packs and the sleds, and then announced there'd also be a major merchant trade tax.

This was the first time he'd been taxed for trade items, but he supposed he couldn't argue with it. Entering a place with a couple packs stuffed with trash loot was much different from bringing in up to a hundred gold worth of top quality monster drops.

After a hasty evaluation the guards announced a one gold trade tax. It was probably a gross overestimation of the value of Pella's goods, but they weren't in the mood to barter; when Dare tried to make a counter offer *their* counter offer was gripping the hilts of their swords and taking a step forward.

"One gold is fine," Pella said, digging through her pouch and producing a gold to hand over; at Dare's insistence she'd sorted out all the gold and silver from her huge pile of coins to carry in a coin pouch he made for her beneath her clothes.

A big pouch, considering she was going to be rich soon.

The guards gave them all odd looks for the fact that the dog girl had paid the tax, but with no further argument waved them through.

The pattern of drawing the attention of the townspeople continued as they dragged their sleds through the streets towards the market. So many people leaned out windows, stood in doorways, or even lined the streets to either side that it almost felt like a parade.

Although a few of the more unsavory observers had Dare watching their surroundings carefully.

The guards would likely come down hard on crime in broad daylight. But if some high level threat came after them, the guards would be as powerless as him and his companions.

It would take the town's resident adventurers, assuming this place had any, to stop the attacker. And by that point it might be too late for the three of them.

Thankfully nobody tried anything. Aside from one man who approached with a quest for cougar pelts, which Pella was able to complete on the spot from her hoard. Her reward was a set of fine silver cutlery and a skin of mead, and she insisted Dare and Zuri also take enough pelts to complete the quest; while for her the experience reward was small, for them it would give them a solid bump towards 21.

"Should we look for other quests while we're here?" Dare asked.

Pella shrugged. "That one was new, maybe because of the increase in predators in the area over the years. But I completed some others from here while I was hunting with my master."

"Any delivery ones heading north, or that have turn in points in the direction we're going?"

"None of the ones I remember. But those are usually more situational, depending on when we arrive. We can look around."

"We've been kind of shirking on quests," Zuri said. "It's usually better just to spend the time we'd waste running around on hunting monsters instead."

"But worth picking up ones if we'll be going that way anyway, or returning here," Dare said. "Which we might at some point, to sell more of Pella's treasure. Even if it's months down the line."

Neither of them had any argument with that. Although they didn't see any more quest givers by the time they entered the market square.

If their approach had been a parade, their arrival was practically a feeding frenzy. Vendors and merchants swarmed them, wanting to be the first to paw over the goods and pick out the prizes. Dare actually had to threaten a few with his new spear when they started to do just that, afraid someone might pocket a few of the most valuable items in the confusion.

With his companions' help he was able to establish some semblance of sanity, letting the vendors bid for turn order. Most of the bids involved more favorable offers on items sold to them, although some flashed silver or promised a sample of their wares.

One man even offered Dare an hour with his pleasure slave, which immediately dropped the sleazy vendor out of the running. Dare was tempted to drop the man himself, and had to remind himself that some evils would have to wait until he was in a better position to tackle them.

Finally he settled on an order for a dozen of the highest bidders and motioned forward the winner, who'd offered a flat 10% increase in payment for all items he purchased.

The man greedily picked through the packs and sleds and made a small pile of items, while the other merchants looked on to pick out what they wanted for when their turns came.

Finally it came time to haggle for the selected loot. The man proved to be surprisingly easy to barter with, offering little protest as Dare ran up prices. Dare was starting to think he'd double lucked out on letting this guy go first, and had extended his hand to shake on a deal that would net Pella 11 gold 57 silver on its own, when she abruptly growled.

As in literally rumbled in her throat.

"He's stolen from us," she said sharply.

"What?" the man blurted, replacing sudden fear with belligerent outrage. "How dare you, bitch!"

Dare scowled and started forward at the insult, but Zuri caught his arm. "Bitch is a valid term among dog people," she whispered. "They don't find it insulting."

Pella pointed at the merchant, undeterred by his protests. "He sweat more heavily on four different occasions while picking through the loot. The sweat of someone doing something dangerous. I gave him the benefit of the doubt at the time, since he could've been nervous about risky purchases. But then he sweat again when you offered to seal the deal, when he should've been triumphant."

She stepped closer to the clearly nervous merchant and sniffed. "Those two pockets," she said, pointing. "I smell our scent on items we've handled. Pocketed through sleight of hand."

Dare cursed himself for missing that; his Fleetfoot wouldn't do anything to help him spot others moving quickly or subtly, of course, but even so he felt like he should've seen something.

"Don't be absurd!" the merchant snapped, backing away. "These are vile accusations! Consider our negotiations over!" He started to turn.

"Ah ah ah," Dare said, catching his shoulder. "You've been accused of theft. Let's call the guards and let them search you." He turned to the second highest bidder. "What's the penalty for theft in Hamalis?"

"Losing your left hand," the man replied, looking somewhat smug at the plight of his competitor.

"Wait!" the thief squealed, sweat streaming down his face. "Okay okay, I'll return your loot. And I'll give you that absurdly unfair price we negotiated for the other items! Just please, overlook this!" He actually fell to his knees, hands clasped in desperation.

Dare glanced at Pella, who shrugged. "Your call, Dare."

The vendor losing his hand wouldn't net the dog girl any more gold, while this deal was hugely to her advantage. "All right, return the items and I'll overlook this."

"You'd let a thief go-" the second bidder started furiously.

Dare forestalled him with a raised hand. "Let's call it 12 gold even," he said firmly to the thief. "And return the items, *now*."

The man hastily drew a couple silver figurines, a few large chunks of gold ore, an uncut ruby, and a handful of small pearls from his pockets. Pella sniffed him carefully to be sure that was all, then

145

nodded to Dare.

Next he and the thief made the agreed upon trade and shook hands. Then Dare turned to the second bidder. "Call the guards."

Everyone stared at him in shock. "You said you'd overlook my crime!" the thief squealed, thrashing in his grip. Although whether to escape or strike him was anyone's guess; Dare easily subdued the man.

Even the second place bidder was nodding at that accusation, and several people in the crowd were muttering about oath breaking and trickery.

Dare smiled wolfishly at them all. "I did promise that, and I'll keep my promise. I'll speak no accusation against this man. However, I'm not the one who owns these items . . . I was merely negotiating on behalf of my companion."

He turned to Pella and bowed. "Miss Pella, do you wish to press charges as the aggrieved party here?"

She was smiling hesitantly, tail wagging. "I think so, yes. We can't allow thieves to get away with stealing in broad daylight, after all."

"You motherfuckers!" the thief snarled. Several in the crowd were chuckling at this unexpected turn, and the second bidder was openly guffawing. "You're just pretending it's her loot as a loophole to your own treachery."

Dare whirled on the man, expression dark. "I don't appreciate being called a liar or a swindler. I will swear before any magistrate, judge, or even the gods themselves that these items all belong to my companion. She farmed it all herself over years of hard work."

He motioned to her. "Look at her level if you don't believe me."

The guards arrived soon after, quickly taking the accused thief into their custody and closely questioning Dare, Pella, Zuri, and all the onlookers.

By the end of it they seemed satisfied, which might've had something to do with the second bidder taking the guard in charge off to one side for a few quiet words. And possibly a coin or two slipped into a pocket.

In the end the thief was escorted away to await his punishment.

The guards gave Dare and his companions a stern warning about avoiding trouble, a few of them sticking around to observe the continued bartering with narrowed eyes.

Then the second bidder eagerly stepped forward, rubbing his hands. "Well," he said with a smile. "I believe I agreed on 50 silver for the honor of second pick."

"Indeed you did," Dare said, accepting the small bag the man offered. He gave it to Zuri to count and motioned to the sleds. "Have at it."

"With my hands always in plain sight, I assure you," the merchant said, laughing. "By the way, that oaf Hadren is a known cheat and con around here. I could've warned you he was up to something with that absurd offer of his, but it was my word against his to outsiders."

He shrugged. "And, you know, loyalty to our own over outsiders, even if our own are cheats and cons. The guy's married to my friend's sister, and I don't want to piss her off. Because then she gets my friend pissed off, and he takes a swing at me next time we're at the pub, and it's all a mess. Better to let some suckers who are just passing through lose some gold instead."

That was a pretty asshole-ish thing to admit, but Dare still found himself liking the man. "Thanks for putting in a good word with the guards."

"No problem." The man waved at the loot. "I'll give you a hundred and ten gold for the lot."

Exclamations of surprise, and more than a few of disappointment and complaint, rose from the crowd. Dare narrowed his eyes. "Sight unseen?" he asked skeptically.

"Oh, I got a good look while Hadren was rummaging around pilfering items under your nose." The trader grinned. "We rely on lumber and farming here, and hauls like this are few and far between. Even if I pay more than it's strictly worth, I'll still make a profit selling it all. Supply and demand."

Dare glanced at Pella, whose tail was wagging. "He's being honest," she said. "And I like the offer."

"You heard the lady," he said, turning back to the man and offering his hand.

"I did indeed." The merchant stepped past him and instead shook a surprised Pella's hand, bowing over it. "And I thank you for helping put that weasel in his place so I didn't have to lose friends doing it myself."

He paused, giving the beautiful dog girl a smile that was more charming than strictly professional. "And if you're up for it I'd love to take you to a nice dinner to more properly thank you, and celebrate our mutually beneficial deal. I have a bottle of Lasisstan's Reserve we could decant."

Dare frowned, surprised to feel a sharp stab of jealousy towards the man. Which was ridiculous since Pella was just his companion, free to do as she wished.

But to his relief she quickly shook her head, blushing. "Thank you, but I must refuse." She shot a quick glance at Dare and just as quickly looked away, blushing harder.

His heart beat a little faster at that; was he reading too much into her answer?

"A pity, but the offer remains open if you change your mind." The merchant motioned to the sleds. "I'll need to visit the Hamalis guild hall to gather the gold to pay for all this. Shall I help you cart it there?"

"Wherever you want it to go," Pella said, still looking flustered.

"The guild hall it is." The man picked up the ropes for Pella's sled and began tugging it towards a building across the market square.

The merchant, whose name turned out to be Peren, had said gold, but at the guild hall he withdrew a truesilver and twenty gold instead. Which was honestly more convenient for carrying.

They made the final formal arrangements for the deal, emptied their packs of everything that had been intended to be sold and donned them again, and then offered Peren a few final handshakes before turning away.

"Farewell!" the man called after them. "I hope to do business with you again! And Mistress Pella, if ever you're in town again there's a prime cut of steak and a glass of top shelf brandy waiting for you!"

"He really wanted to get you someplace private and mount you," Zuri murmured as they walked away.

"I know, I can still smell his arousal," the dog girl said with a giggle.

Dare did his best not to scowl, not particularly wanting to think about Peren's arousal. "Should we see what wares we can buy?" he asked. "We need to get Zuri a spear and Pella a lasso. And it couldn't hurt to see what else is on offer."

"Sounds good," Pella said, patting the clinking pouch beneath her tunic. "Although Peren had the right idea about celebrating . . . should we get some lunch? My treat."

Zuri brightened. "Can we get cake, too? Or pie?"

"Zuri's always excited about dessert," Dare said with a laugh. "Just a tip if you ever need to get on her good side."

"I think we're already getting along okay," the dog girl said, leaning down to hug the tiny goblin. Her eyes danced. "Although I'd be interested to know how to get on *your* good side."

Zuri stood up on tiptoes to whisper something in the tall woman's floppy golden-furred ear, grinning wickedly, and they both snickered.

"Yes, that would do it," Pella agreed, blushing.

Dare had a pretty good idea what his lover had said, and was encouraged that their companion had found it funny rather than outrageous.

He was still concerned about taking things too fast with Pella, and about making sure she was able to pursue the life she wanted, whatever she chose. But he had to admit that if he was going to build a harem, Zuri would end up being an awesome wingman.

Or winggoblin.

After some asking around they found a tavern that had a reputation for excellent food. It didn't have cakes or pies, to Zuri's disappointment, but did offer sweet buns smothered in clotted cream; she was so excited to try them that she bought everyone their own whole bun before they even ordered their food.

"I'll be making stuff like this in no time," Dare assured her when

149

he saw her obvious enjoyment of the treat. It was nothing remarkable by Earth standards, but here where desserts were so rare the fluffy pastry and sweet cream tasted delicious.

"I hope so," Pella said, happily licking cream from around her mouth. "This is delicious."

Dare couldn't help but stare at the innocent display and think less than innocent thoughts about the sort of things she could do with her flat pink tongue.

The dog girl caught him looking and grinned, playfully sticking her tongue out all the way and then curling it around upside-down as if to show how limber it was, and he felt his cheeks flush.

Thankfully she took mercy on him and didn't call him out. "That was awesome how you outsmarted that thief in the square," she said, taking another bite and continuing with her mouth full. "You're more than just a pretty face, aren't you? My master used to be good with that sort of thing too, talking circles around enemies and using their own words against them, and knowing just how to handle confrontations like that."

"That's why I follow him," Zuri said, smirking at him teasingly as she took another huge bite of her bun. "That and his skill as a lover."

Dare felt his cheeks heat. "Come on, guys."

They both looked confused but obligingly started to stand. "Where are we going?" Pella asked.

He hastily waved them back to their seats. "That's an expression that means knock it off, or change the subject already. All this praise is embarrassing . . . it was the guy's own fault of being so vague."

"Still, thanks for looking out for me," the dog girl said, patting his hand. Her tail wagged happily. "I'm glad I finally chose to leave my guilt behind and join you."

Dare placed his other hand over hers. "So are we," he said with a smile. "It's good to see you happy."

The serving girl arrived with their meals, mostly various meats since it suited the preferences of both the goblin and dog girl, and they all tucked in. Although unlike with the dessert, his companions both agreed that his own cooking was better. Especially now that he had more spices to use on his dishes.

The serving girl, a short, plump brunette with a friendly round face, tried to make it clear to him with smiles and nods and even a few subtle gestures that if he wanted to follow her to someplace more secluded, she'd be up for a bit of fun.

Dare was certainly tempted, and with Zuri's approval probably would've gone for it. But with his relationship with Pella up in the air, assuming there even was anything there to speak of, he decided to ignore the invitation.

They finished eating and paid for their meal, then headed outside.

The rest of the visit to Hamalis was mostly uneventful. Zuri purchased a few more of the sweet buns and had them wrapped in waxed paper for dinner, and then they made their way back to the market.

Pella forked over a healthy chunk of her newly acquired gold to buy a Journeyman quality Level 27 long dagger, as well as several lengths of high quality rope to make lassos with. Zuri got a Good quality spear and got used to walking with it like a staff.

"This is going to be a hassle and get in the way more than a dagger does," she said with a frown.

Dare couldn't argue that, especially since he was going to have to figure out how to carry it as well as his own spear when he ran while holding the goblin woman. "We won't be complaining about them once we start using them in fights."

She nodded her agreement, although she still seemed irritated at clacking around with a weapon half again as long as she was.

As was his habit, Dare surreptitiously purchased a few gifts for his companions, including a wide sash sewn with silk flowers and matching ribbon she could weave into her braid for Pella, and a bag of hard candy that Zuri really enjoyed.

A final quick check of the small town netted them a quest to deliver a supply order to a larger town to the north called Yurin, which Pella assured them they'd probably end up visiting since it was close to the manor where her master's family lived, and in fact the town her master had been lord of, and his son after him.

Then they left Hamalis behind and headed north into the woods, searching for spawn points around their level so they could get back to hunting.

* * * * *

Dare grunted as his back slammed into a tree trunk, ending his brief flight through the air. He wasn't sure if the collision had just knocked the wind out of him or had broken ribs, all he knew was it hurt like hell.

"Sorry!" Pella shouted as the Unfettered Gorilla bellowed and beat its chest before charging across the clearing after him. "It shouldn't have been able to slip my Subdue!"

By some luck he hadn't lost his spear, and he grit his teeth as he used it to lever himself back up to his feet with all the speed he could manage, hobbling away from the approaching monster.

The lengths of thick chain hanging from the shackles on the gorilla's wrists whipped through the air like flails as it chased him. He could confirm that they hit with the power of sledgehammers, considering a hit from one had launched him ten feet and would've sent him farther if he hadn't hit a tree.

Hell, if he hadn't managed to block with his spear the blow probably would've seriously injured him; there was a deep gouge in the wood of its shaft where the chain had dug out a chunk.

Warm energy washed over his back as Zuri, hiding in the trees nearby, used her Plea to Nature spell a couple times in quick succession to heal him. He felt like he could run, but unfortunately the gorilla was now close enough that he had to dodge those flailing chains.

Then Pella tackled the monster to the ground, straddling its back and lashing down furiously with the knife he'd given her. Dare watched the high level dog girl's attacks chunk the Unfettered Gorilla's remaining health down, and in a few seconds the flurry of blows finished the monster off.

The golden-haired woman remained perched on the great ape's

corpse, expression savage, and even went so far as to spit on it. "I *won't* fail anyone else," she snarled at her kill. "You don't get to hurt my friends!"

Dare was shocked to see tears glimmering in the beautiful woman's soft brown eyes. He hastily stepped up beside her, resting a hand on her shoulder. "Hey," he said quietly. "It's okay. Nothing we couldn't handle."

"It's not okay," she snapped. "You depended on me and I let you get hurt!"

He sighed. "No, you depended on *me* to tell you its abilities, and I misjudged one. I thought the Loose Chains ability was an attack it used with those chains on its wrists, not something that let it escape crowd control effects."

And thanks for being so clear with the ability name about what it did, he added bitterly to the world system; what was the point of having Adventure's Eye if it was going to be giving out stupid, unhelpful names like "Loose Chains"?

Text scrawled across his screen, accompanied by the warm voice of his benefactor. "Thank you for your input, my lover. Name has been changed to "Escape Bonds.""

It might've been Dare's imagination, but she sounded a lot more affectionate, even flirty, ever since his Collisa version of phone sex with her. And her response also served as a reminder that she could read his thoughts.

Zuri joined him and Pella, also resting a hand on the kneeling woman's shoulder. "You did everything right," she agreed. "Sometimes things just go wrong."

"And no harm done," he added. "Zuri healed me with just a few spells." He squeezed their new companion's shoulder and stepped back, tone brisk. "Now that we know we'll treat the fights different, but let's get back to leveling now, okay?"

Part of his reason for hurrying things along was that he hoped getting back into another fight would distract the dog girl from what had just happened. And when she saw how much smoother things went in the future, she'd calm down a bit.

Pella nodded reluctantly and jumped off the ape, sheathing her knife. Although she spat on the monster one last time; the normally gentle woman was surprisingly fierce when it came to protecting them.

Dare retrieved his dropped bow and pack and turned his attention to the Unfettered Gorilla spawn point, thinking of how to do the fights if the monsters could get out of Pella's crowd control.

There were plenty of other safe options, thankfully. For one thing, the dog girl had already proven she could keep up with Dare up to a point, much faster than most humans and with more endurance.

She couldn't match his top speed like Ilin, unfortunately, but she could manage a bit over 20 miles an hour at a sprint, and keep up with his usual running pace for just as long as he could. More than enough to kite these hulking simians while Dare and Zuri damaged them down, which was probably the best alternative to her using her crowd control.

Pella had kindly offered to help them catch up to her level, staying out of the party for now and doing her best not to damage the monsters they hunted so they could get all the experience. Dare figured that if they could get up to Level 24, they'd be close enough in level that she could join the party and start sharing experience.

Just like how Zuri had caught up to him as they leveled, because lower levels didn't require as much experience to reach the next level, they would eventually catch up to their new companion as well.

"So basically I just keep its attention and run around until you kill it?" Pella asked when he explained her role.

"Unless you need to jump in and use your lasso or other crowd control," Dare told her. "Even if these things can break free of it, you'll probably be able to hold them for a short time at least. Just be careful they don't tag you with a surprise attack after they get out."

The athletic woman grinned at him. "Give me some credit. You ever seen a dog fight a bear?"

He hadn't, but he imagined that even if the dog could evade the bear's attacks for a while, eventually it didn't end well. And in spite of Pella's superficial similarity to canines in appearance and behavior, she was mostly human. Or humanoid.

And compared to animals humans were slow, weak, fragile, and had terrible senses. A canid might do better in a lot of those areas, but they were nowhere near the level of, say, a chimpanzee, which weighed half as much as an adult man and were twice as strong.

But that's what he and Zuri were for, to kill the bear before it could catch up to their friend. "Just be careful," he repeated, patting Pella on the shoulder.

Her fluffy tail wagged enthusiastically. "You got it!" she said.

Dare targeted the next gorilla and got close enough to hit it with his short bow. "Ready?" he asked his companions. At their nods he went ahead and pulled the monster.

Chapter Nine
Understanding

That night they feasted on a meal of meat from an elk Dare brought down just before dark, several tubers similar to sweet potatoes that he baked in the coals, and Zuri's sweet buns for dessert. They washed it all down with mead from their cougar pelt quest rewards, enjoying the warm glow of the fire, full bellies, and a light alcohol buzz.

Pella seemed talkative and Zuri was in the mood to indulge her, so they all settled down in their collapsible chairs and discussed everything that came to mind. Zuri told the story of how Dare had saved her and how they'd started leveling up together, and Pella of living in the woods surviving on hunting and farming monsters.

At some point Dare more fully explained Adventurer's Eye and Fleetfoot, as well as his first arrival on Collisa. Although he stuck to his story of being teleported to a spot close to Lone Ox from a different continent. He even let the girls wheedle him into describing a bit of his life on Earth, although of course without mentioning technology or being from another world.

Zuri took her turn describing growing up in her tribe's village as the daughter of the high priestess, and some of her experiences leveling up as a Healer. Then Pella told a few stories of living with her master's family and playing with his children.

The hours passed, and they emptied their skins of mead and then kept right on talking until the buzz had faded. Dare was starting to nod off and getting less interested in the conversation and more in finding his bed. He finally excused himself to take a leak, planning to bid his companions goodnight when he got back.

Only when he got back to camp, he found that Zuri had laid out their bedroll by the fire, and she was cuddled up in Pella's lap seated atop it. "Come sit down," his goblin lover invited him when she spotted him returning, patting the blankets beside the dog girl.

He got the feeling the girls might be setting him up.

But they had his bedroll, and he wasn't in the mood to go curl up in his tent without blankets while probably pissing off Zuri at the same time. Besides, it looked comfortable and after hours of conversation he was feeling a lot closer to Pella and more at ease with whatever it was she had planned.

So, feeling a bit of nervous anticipation, he made his way over and settled down next to Pella.

She immediately scooted closer and rested her head on his shoulder with a sigh of contentment, giving a further hint where this was going. Dare felt one of her velvety soft floppy ears pressed against his cheek, enjoying the pleasant sensation.

"This is nice," she murmured. "I've been alone for so long and missed being able to touch other people." She shifted to look up at him, her ear tickling his chin; in the firelight he could see flecks of gold among the soft chocolate brown of her eyes. "I hope you won't mind if I curl up at your feet, or even put my head in your lap."

Dare stiffened in surprise, although Zuri giving him a very firm look to indicate how he was supposed to answer wasn't lost on him.

He couldn't help but glance at Pella's curvy figure, briefly imagining her curled up at his feet, or her head with those adorable floppy ears and luxurious golden hair resting on his lap. It was a nice thought.

Zuri cleared her throat and jerked her head insistently, and Dare hastily blurted, "If that's what you want," in a strained voice.

The dog girl beamed, tail wagging happily, and with another contented sigh shifted to lay down on the bedroll with her head on his thigh, still cuddling Zuri in her arms. "This is nice," she said again.

She wasn't wrong. Her head felt soft on his lap, her obvious contentment giving him a warm feeling. They all settled in to watch the crackling fire, comfortable and sleepy and content.

"Would you rub my ears?" Pella abruptly asked, making him jump slightly in surprise. "That would make this perfect."

It was hard to refuse when she put it like that. Dare hesitantly rested his hand on top of her head, golden hair silky soft beneath his fingers, and then gently stroked his fingers over her left ear. The fur was fine and even softer than her hair, the ear beneath warm and floppy and just begging to be scratched.

So he did, and a little shiver went right through Pella's body as she pressed her head into his hand. "Mmm," she moaned, tail wagging. "I've missed this so much."

To his embarrassment he felt himself begin to stir in his pants, only inches from where his companion's head rested, and silently cursed the unconscious reaction. "What would you like to do, Pella?" he hastily asked to distract himself. "Would you like us to take you to a city, where you can find a profession and start a new life?"

"Will I live with you, Dare?" she asked, snuggling her head a bit higher up his thigh and turning it in a silent indication to scratch her other ear.

He cleared his throat and shifted slightly, trying to move her head a bit farther from his crotch again; this was getting intimate, and while he'd expected it and looked forward to it he still felt his cheeks heating.

After all, they hadn't kissed or expressed their feelings or anything, and now they were practically cuddling like lovers. "If you got a profession and settled in a city, I'm afraid not. I plan to travel and keep leveling up with Zuri."

"Oh, okay. That sounds fun."

Damnit! If she'd said that she wanted to do that too, he could've challenged her on it and made sure it was what she really wanted, and then gone over more options for her future. But her innocuous words were basically saying she planned to stay with him, without directly saying so.

Part of him was actually pleased at the prospect. But another part of him wondered if he'd be taking advantage of a girl who so easily gave away her loyalty. Especially after the way her master had, well, enjoyed her loyalty.

Pella fell silent, enjoying the attention he was giving her ears. But after a few minutes of silence she abruptly spoke, making him jump again. "Dare?"

"Mmm?" he said.

The dog girl's fluffy tail began to wag again. Tentatively, hopefully. "Will you call me a good girl again? Pretty please?"

Dare felt a sudden surge of guilt, seeing this scene through the dog girl's eyes given the way she'd been raised and trained. "Pella," he said gently, and with some reluctance carefully scooted out from under her head and gently lowered it to the blankets. "I consider you to be a very good person, but I get the feeling that that exact phrase was one you were conditioned to want as a sign of your master's approval. It makes me uncomfortable to say it."

She twisted to look at his grave expression, then slowly sat up again. "What exactly is happening right now?" she asked uncertainly. "We were all cozy and happy and then you got weird."

"I'm wondering the same thing," Zuri asked; she'd been cuddling with the dog girl almost as if she was asleep, but now she glared up at him as if he was ruining everything.

Dare took a breath; he didn't want to fuck this up and hurt Pella's feelings, or fail to properly express himself. "I'm going to come right out with this . . . did you two set up this situation so I'd end up mating you by the end of the night, Pella?"

Both women flushed, the goblin a deep green and the dog girl a rosy pink. "I mean, it would've been nice," Pella said hesitantly. "Although I wouldn't have minded just falling asleep snuggling together either."

"All right." He took another breath. "This is something of how my people view sex and love and relationships, so I hope you'll understand. There are many women I'd happily fuck and then walk away from, because I know sex is all either of us want out of it. In fact, I've noticed women in the towns we've visited giving me subtle cues that they'd be up for something like that, and I wouldn't mind taking them up on their offer and having some fun."

"I-I'm not sure where you're going with this, Dare," the dog girl said, ears drooping.

Fuck, he was saying this badly and probably giving her the wrong

159

idea. "Like I've told Zuri, I want to sleep with as many women as I can, and if possible have a large harem of wives and consorts."

"Okay sure," Pella said, puzzled. "That was Master's goal as well, the reason he was so determined to level."

Dare hesitated, then reached over and gently rested a hand on the golden-haired woman's knee. "The thing is, Pella, you're not a woman I just want to fuck and walk away from. Even though we haven't known each other long, I've already developed feelings for you. I want something more than that with you, more like what I have with Zuri."

"Really?" she asked, ears perking up and tail beginning to flail back and forth in sudden excitement, thumping his back. "She told me that once you're settled you want to have babies with her. Is that the same with me?"

The dog girl leaned closer, eyes shining. "Do you want me to have your puppies? Truly? My master didn't want me to have his puppies, so he regularly gave me a potion to prevent it. But I would've loved to have his puppies."

She grabbed his arm, hugging it to her firm breasts. "I'd love to have your puppies too, Dare. They'd be so adorable, and I'd love them so much. I'd take really good care of them, be a great mother, and of course a good girl for you."

Dare felt his face catch fire, and his cock immediately began to stir again. His sleepiness had vanished, and he wanted nothing more than to tear the beautiful dog girl's clothes off; the thought of seeing her toned belly round with his baby was a seriously tempting one.

Pella pressed harder against him. "And of course I want to mate you, too. Zuri can cast her spell so we don't have to worry about puppies until we're ready, and until then you can do anything you want with my soft little body."

She started guiding his hand between her legs. "We can start right n-"

Gah! If he let her keep talking he was going to lose his senses and fuck her right then.

"Pella!" he blurted, gently but firmly pulling his arm back. "Becoming my mate is a decision I want you to think about carefully.

You really didn't have a choice with your master-"

"That's not true!" the dog girl said indignantly. "I loved him and *wanted* to be his good girl in the bedroom!"

He continued in a firm tone. "He bought you, then had sex with you as his property. Even if you were okay with it, I can't be comfortable treating a person like that." He rested a hand on her shoulder. "I want you to be able to choose what you do, and I want you to be happy. Even if we did become mates, I'd still want you to be able to choose your own path. Even if we did become mates and then you eventually decided to leave me, I'd want you to be free to make that choice."

Zuri shot him a look of alarmed warning and shook her head frantically.

Pella stared at him with huge eyes, suddenly looking vulnerable and heartbroken. "Give my loyalty to you, breed with you and have puppies, and then leave?" the dog girl whispered in a horrified voice, huge tears beginning to roll down her cheeks. "Do you really think I'm such a bad girl?"

Dare bit back a curse. The last thing he'd intended was to make Pella cry. "Of course not!" he said fervently, reaching out to rub her fluffy ears. "I think you're a good girl. A great girl. Someone I'm becoming very fond of." He flailed helplessly for the words to make her understand. "I just want to do what's right for you, so you can be happy. You deserve that."

The dog girl sniffed, then gently set Zuri down and stumbled to her feet. "I need some time to think," she mumbled. "And so do you." Her tone became indignant again. "Because if you really cared about me you'd try to understand me, and you don't understand me at *all*!"

She turned and bolted off into the forest.

"Then help me understand you!" Dare shouted after her helplessly.

Pella turned back for a moment. "I've been *trying*, but you won't *listen*," she shouted, tears shining on her cheeks. "You think I'm blind or stupid or desperate and I'd carelessly give my love and loyalty to just anyone, and you have no idea how much it hurts that you see me like that!"

With a mournful wail she turned and bolted away again.

161

Dare watched her go helplessly, heart breaking at her obvious pain and cursing himself as a monster for causing it, whether he'd meant to or not.

He glanced down at Zuri to find her glaring at him. "Speaking of not listening," she growled furiously. "Didn't I tell you how devastating it would be to her if you tried to cast her aside after she'd given her loyalty to you?"

"I wasn't talking about casting her aside!" he protested. "I was talking about her being able to leave if that's what she wanted."

"You're not that stupid, my mate," his goblin lover snapped, hands on her hips. "I know you're not! Didn't I tell you canids give their loyalty for life? How could you suggest she'd want to break that loyalty and think it'd be anything but a heartbreaking insult to her?"

"It's not that simple," Dare said. "Her loyal nature has been exploited by people who want to use her. Even if her master was a good person, the people who trained her to seek approval even from someone unworthy as long as that person is her owner is something she'll have to learn to overcome, if she wants to live as a free person."

He waved after Pella. "If I just started acting like her new master while claiming she was free then I would be betraying her loyalty. And even if I treat her perfectly as an equal, if I let her begin acting towards me the same as she did to her old master, even if it's what she wants, it still wouldn't be fair to her. She's our equal, and she needs to see herself that way as much as we need to see her that way."

Zuri was giving him that baffled look again, but her brow was furrowed as if she was struggling to understand. "So you want to make sure that she can live free to her nature, instead of bound by how she was trained." She scratched a pointy ear. "That's a very delicate distinction."

Dare sighed. "I know, which is why I'm fucking it up trying to explain it to her."

She nodded thoughtfully. "All right, I'll go try to explain to her that you aren't a giant spurting asshole, you're just a well-intentioned idiot who doesn't fully understand her but has her best interests at heart."

His wonderful lover strode briskly off in the direction Pella had gone. "This will probably take a long time, so you might as well get some rest. We might not even be back tonight."

That was all well and good, but Dare wasn't going to be able to sleep while worrying about Pella.

With a sigh he began wandering around checking his snares and gathering crafting materials to make more; if he was going to be up all night he might as well use the time productively. And it would keep him from fretting.

He had a feeling it was going to be a long night, but what was worse was that thanks to him it would be a long one for the women he cared about.

* * * * *

Dare maxed his proficiency for his level in every ability he could reasonably work on at night in camp.

Then, the dark forest looming around him and his worry for Zuri and Pella deepening by the hour, he did his best to occupy himself practicing magic tricks, and working to add another ball to the four he was currently capable of juggling.

He even carved a set of dice, then endlessly rolled them as the sky lightened towards dawn. Which confirmed that his benefactor had given him good luck, based on his consistently favorable rolls.

Which was ironic, since in his old life on Earth he was so unlucky that in games where random chance was involved, he could guess what the worst possible outcome would be and a disproportionate amount of the time it would happen.

Although good luck hadn't prevented him from screwing up with Pella and hurting her.

To his immense relief, just as the sun broke over the horizon he felt her and Zuri entering his perception circle. And to his even greater relief, the moment his eyes met the dog girl's she bounded forward and threw her arms around him, driving them both to the ground where she buried her face in his chest with great shuddering sobs.

"I'm sorry, Dare," she bawled. "Zuri explained that you're trying to help me live like a canid out in the wilds, happy and free to follow my heart. None of us really know how they live, though, so we just have to do our best and treat each other like equals."

"No I'm sorry," he said, gently stroking her back. "I said the wrong things while trying to explain myself, and I feel terrible for hurting you."

She just shook her head and bawled harder, soaking his shirt with her tears.

Zuri soon joined them, wrapping her little arms around them both, and together they just lay like that for a while. After a while Dare felt his goblin lover begin breathing deeply as she fell into an exhausted slumber, and gently pulled a corner of the blanket up to shade her face from the rising sun.

It took longer before Pella's sobs abated, but her tearstained face looked surprisingly peaceful as she finally fell asleep as well; hopefully this had offered some catharsis for her.

Dare gently kissed her forehead, surprised at how the night's events had forged such a strong bond between them so quickly. He wasn't reckless enough to talk love when they'd only known each other for a short time, but he definitely had strong feelings for the openhearted dog girl.

He pulled the blanket farther over to cover all their eyes, then held Pella and Zuri tight in his arms as he allowed himself to finally drift off as well.

* * * * *

Dare awoke to the feel of a soft flat tongue licking his face.

It wasn't how he'd expected to wake up, especially since he felt like he'd only gotten a few hours of sleep. But he couldn't deny that it was a pleasant sensation. He simply lay enjoying the feeling for a while, then finally opened his eyes and smiled up at Pella.

"Good morning," he murmured quietly, aware of Zuri snuggled against his side still sleeping peacefully.

"Good morning," the beautiful dog girl whispered, eyes soft as she looked down at him. "You know, I've lived in these woods for over four years. I've learned to fend for myself and make my own decisions."

"That's good," he said hesitantly. "You've done well to survive out here, especially given your sad circumstances."

She caught his gaze and held it firmly, and he had the passing thought that the flecks of gold in her chocolate brown eyes made them even more compelling and beautiful. "So if you accept that I can make my own decisions, then you can accept that I know what I'm doing when I give my loyalty to someone?"

"I . . ." Dare hesitated. "Yes, I guess so."

Pella kept his gaze trapped by hers. "Even if I were to give my loyalty to you?"

He swallowed and slowly nodded.

The dog girl smiled a bit shyly, tanned cheeks turning pink. "I, um, might've been following you and Zuri for longer than I let on. Long enough to see the sort of people you are." She licked his cheek again, tongue soft and warm. "The kind of person *you* are."

Dare cleared his throat, but still couldn't think of anything to say.

Pella didn't seem to mind, because she had plenty to say. "You're the kind of person who can love a goblin who was a slave and work to make her free and happy. Who can befriend a plant girl in a matter of hours and leave with her willing to give you a glowing recommendation. Who can meet a strange high level dog girl out in the wild and instead of being afraid, worry about her welfare and how you can help her."

The golden blonde's lips twitched in a slight smile. "The sort of man who can admit that he wants to fuck that dog girl, but who refuses to do it unless it's what she wants and it will make her happy, not just in the moment but long term. Who wants to make sure she doesn't give her loyalty hastily when he knows the decision will affect the rest of her life."

She paused to look into his eyes for several long seconds. "And that's why I happily you my loyalty. And my body and my heart as well." She leaned down and gently licked his lips. "Will you be my mate, Dare?"

Dare swallowed, aware of the commitment he was making to her but in the moment fully willing to make it. "I would be honored," he said solemnly. "Will you be my mate, Pella?"

"With all my heart," she said fervently, with the same open enthusiasm she showed in everything.

"With all my heart," Dare agreed. He lifted his head to kiss her glistening lips, her taste sweet as honey.

Pella made a happy sound and kissed him back with surprising fierceness, her warm flat tongue pressing into his mouth in a way he could only describe as slobbery. Bringing more of the sweet taste of her saliva as her tongue fully wrapped around his with a nimbleness no human's could manage.

Then she pulled away with a happy sigh and rested her head against his shoulder, her floppy ear soft against his cheek. "I want us to be well rested the first time we breed," she murmured. "So I'm going back to sleep, my mate."

Dare's cock, which had started stirring the moment he woke up to her soft tongue exploring his face and had hardened during their kiss, now throbbed in disappointment as the beautiful dog girl closed her eyes and her breathing gradually slowed.

Well, his patience would be rewarded.

He closed his own eyes and willed his raging erection to settle, focusing his thoughts on plans for the day's leveling, and the potential problem of crafters having trouble reaching a high enough level to even make higher level items, and thus artificially increasing the cost of those items or even making them impossible to find.

Was it possible that all high level gear was reduced quality stuff made by secondary class crafters, thus making monster loot gear even more valuable? Or were there guilds and organizations out there that focused on helping their crafters level to keep their members equipped and make a profit for their coffers?

Would that mean Dare would have to put points into crafting after all, or join a guild to get access to their crafters? And what about if he managed to out-level everyone and there *were* no crafters high enough level to make things for him?

He knew to some degree crafting worked outside the constrictions of level, so lower level main class crafters could make slightly higher level gear. But that only went so far.

Well, monster loot was always an option. Especially if he could manage to kill party or raid rated monsters that probably dropped good stuff, or find world or dungeon chests that he was almost certain did.

And he *did* have great luck thanks to his benefactor.

Besides, if gear was hard to get for the most powerful people then the playing field would be level anyway, and . . .

Having successfully conquered his erection, Dare let himself sink into sleep with the pleasant sensation of Pella's saliva drying on his face and the blissful feel of two beautiful women pressed against him.

* * * * *

Dare was again awakened by Pella licking his face. Although now she added kisses, tender if also more than a little slobbery, and was rubbing her body slowly and sensuously against him.

"I wouldn't complain if I woke up to this every morning," he said with a smile, eyes still closed.

His new lover giggled. "I can make that happen, mate." She kissed him again, more aggressively this time, and playfully slipped her tongue into his mouth before pulling back. "Zuri has very sweetly offered to sleep elsewhere and give us privacy so our first time can be just us." She giggled again. "I told her I'd love to have her join us, and she promised she'd take us up on that in the future."

The beautiful dog girl ground her sex pointedly against his hip, breath quickening. "Anyway, hurry and wake up already. I can't wait to mate!"

Any lingering drowsiness vanished at that announcement, and Dare's cock woke up as quickly as he did, straining against the confines of his pants. "I'm awake," he said hastily.

He slipped his arms around her curvy athletic body as he opened his eyes and kissed her, hands moving down to grip and squeeze her round, toned ass as she humped his leg more vigorously. His fingers sank into the warm, yielding flesh and they both groaned in pleasure at the sensation.

"Want to get on your hands and knees?" he teased.

Pella giggled. "You just assume I'm into doggy?" she teased right back, although she started to rise off him.

Dare grabbed her ass and firmly pulled her back down. "No rush," he murmured against her lips as his tongue invaded her mouth.

Her soft, flat tongue nimbly wrapped around his and pushed him back into his mouth, following with a torrent of slobber that was even sweeter and fresher than before.

He eagerly swallowed the saliva as it filled his mouth, luxuriating in the taste of her; he couldn't wait to get between her legs and experience the heady flavor of her nectar.

"Gods you're delicious," he mumbled against her lips.

With a giggle she pulled her tongue back and grinned at him, eyes sparkling. "Am I?" she murmured in a sexy little voice. "Do you like your good girl slobbering all over you?"

"Oh gods yes," he said.

She giggled again and her cheeks worked, swishing eagerly. Then she clamped her lips to his to form a seal and her tongue pushed an entire flood of saliva into his mouth. It overflowed and poured down his lips as he swallowed greedily, and he grabbed the back of her head and pushed his tongue up into her soft mouth in search of more.

There was plenty more to find; she was drooling like he'd put a huge steak in front of her, and moaning in pleasure and passionately rubbing her body against him as her tongue wrapped around his and sucked him in deeper, keeping the seal formed by their lips as best she could as their combined saliva leaked out in a steady stream.

It was probably the messiest makeout session he'd ever enjoyed, and also the hottest. Dare swished and pushed some of his saliva into her mouth, and she moaned in pleasure as her throat worked, greedily swallowing it.

After that they swished their combined spit between their mouths as if playing catch, and all the while he ran his hands over her soft body and she squirmed against him as if trying to feel him against every part of her.

Somehow in the middle of their kissing and rubbing against each other they managed to shed their clothes. Dare luxuriated in the feel of his beautiful golden-haired lover's soft flesh as his exploring fingers found the pert mounds of her breasts, making perfect handfuls. Her small pointy nipples pressed against his palms as they stiffened at his touch, and he quickly began rolling the rubbery nubs between his fingers.

Pella moaned, fingers brushing his face. At first he thought it was a simple caress until he realized she was gathering up their combined saliva, then she reached down to grasp his cock.

"Gods," she gasped as she began slowly pumping it in her slick grip. "Zuri told me you were huge, but I thought that was from a goblin's perspective. I didn't realize she meant huge huge. This thing is going to stretch my little pussy wide open."

She sounded excited at the prospect, her fluffy tail thrashing eagerly.

They got back to kissing, their bare skin rubbing delightfully as they writhed against each other, seeking closer and deeper contact. Then the dog girl's squirming brought her leg over the top of his, pulling the rest of her body up with it, and Dare felt her velvety petals, slick and hot as a furnace, press against the tip of his cock.

He almost reflexively thrust, sliding into blissful warmth, then paused as his dog girl lover jumped with a soft yip of happy surprise, realizing he was pushing into her sweet little pussy.

"Oh gods, Dare!" Pella gasped, breaking the kiss and clutching him desperately. "Yes, yes, keep going!"

With a grunt of pleasure he rolled her onto her back with him on top and gently thrust the rest of the way inside her, bottoming out with inches of his cock still outside. She whimpered and squirmed, undulating her hips against him to indicate she wanted him to keep going, but he spent a moment luxuriating in the silky feel of her walls grasping him as he resumed their wet kiss.

She was so soaked with arousal he'd gone fully into her with his massive rod without the slightest resistance or sign of discomfort from her, and even as they lay there joined he could feel more of her nectar flowing around his cock to soak her thighs and the blankets beneath them.

Pella impatiently bucked her hips harder and bit his lower lip with a soft growl, making her desires clear, and he finally began to move inside her.

That was all it took. "Yeessss!" she moaned again within seconds, and he felt her squirt all over his crotch as her pussy eagerly milked his shaft in an intense climax. "Gods yes, I need this so much."

He kept up his slow thrusts to extend her peak, and then as she came down began to thrust faster. Considering how easily she'd taken him to begin with he wasn't worried about going harder than he normally might, and judging by her eager whines and how she panted in pure pleasure as she bathed his face in kisses she was more than okay with it.

After only a few minutes of his vigorous pounding she eagerly wrapped her legs around him, wildly bucking her hips. "Go ahead and come!" she gasped. "Fill me up with your love!" Her arms clutched him tightly and she buried her head in his shoulder, her entire body shaking with the intensity of her passion.

Dare groaned and took one of her floppy ears in his mouth, gently biting its silky softness as he gave a last few hard thrusts and then buried himself to her core, emptying himself directly against the entrance to her womb.

His entire body tensed tight as a spring with the intensity of his orgasm, pleasure surging through him in waves with every powerful spurt. Pella let out a deep, throaty moan at the feel of his seed spraying inside her, and her tender walls clenched down on him with desperate force as she joined him in an overwhelmingly intense shared climax.

He finally pulled out and collapsed beside her, panting as he pulled his dog girl lover close. She panted as well, fluffy tail wagging languidly as she kissed and licked his shoulder and chest, painting his hot skin lovingly with her slobber.

"It feels almost disloyal to my old master to say it, Dare," she murmured, chocolate brown eyes holding his with open adoration, "but that was the most incredible thing I've ever felt. And I'm not just saying that because it's been four years since I've had anything but plant girl and butterfly girl fingers in me."

Given his stamina, Dare's cock wasn't about to go soft after the pleasure he'd just experienced. And hearing her mention past exploits with Rosie and Enellia just made it that much stiffer. "Was?" he teased, playfully ruffling her ears. "What makes you think we're done?"

Pella looked down at his cock, still standing tall and proud, and her eyes widened. "Oooh," she cooed, reaching down to stroke him. "Look at you. Zuri mentioned you could go for hours."

She kept expertly handling his shaft as she kissed and licked her way down his chest and stomach. She buried her nose in his pubic hair for almost a minute, breathing in deeply and tail thrashing happily as she worked his shaft more enthusiastically with her long, elegant fingers.

Then the beautiful golden-haired woman reached his cock. He tensed in anticipation of what was coming, and she paused and gave him a playful look. "You seemed to love what I could do with my tongue in your mouth," she said in a husky voice. "Ready to see what else I can do with it?"

"Gods, yes," Dare groaned, gently resting a hand between her floppy ears and stroking her silky golden hair.

Giggling, she stuck out her wide, flat tongue and gave his aching shaft a long, slow lick from balls to tip. A shiver ran through his entire body at the incredible sensation, and then he bit back a gasp of amazed disbelief as her flexible tongue wrapped *around* his super sensitive tip, tightening with an intense surge of pleasure.

He groaned, bucking his hips and running his fingers through his new lover's luxurious hair. "That's incredible, Pella. *You're* incredible."

The dog girl moaned in appreciation, the vibration shivering through her tongue to his sensitive tip, and her tail wagged harder. "I love this taste," she said thickly, slobbering down his shaft in a wave of fresh lubrication.

"You mean you?" Dare teased.

Her eyes sparkled up at him lovingly. "And you. Us, together."

That was unexpectedly romantic.

Pella abruptly freed her tongue and pulled back, giggling at his disappointed look. "Don't worry, I want to spend many enjoyable hours seeing if I can get that massive thing all the way down my throat," she said playfully. Scrambling to straddle him, the beautiful woman rubbed her soft petals lovingly against his throbbing shaft. "But right now I need you inside me again."

She shifted forward until he was positioned at her entrance, teasingly rubbing herself on his sensitive tip. Then with a smooth roll of her hips she pushed herself onto his shaft and began lowering herself slowly.

The sensation of her tight pussy engulfing him was even better the second time, and Dare grit his teeth and threw his head back as he felt the tight ring of her labia stretching around his girth as they glided down his sensitive shaft. Beyond them her silky walls rippled and flexed over his skin with every twitch of her leg muscles as she strained to lower herself slowly and smoothly.

His dog girl lover bottomed out, perched there for a moment with a whimpery little sound that went straight back to his hindbrain, then with surprising suddenness eagerly began bouncing on his cock, tongue hanging out of her mouth in a happy grin as her fluffy tail wagged furiously.

Dare closed his eyes in pure bliss, gripping the beautiful woman's round ass as she moved up and down on his cock, slightly faster each time until their crotches were slapping together with a squelch that made her freely flowing arousal splash over his legs and torso. Her shapely muscular legs seemed tireless, and he worried that he was going to give out and explode in her before she was satisfied.

Pella's tight pussy seemed to hug the contours of his shaft with every motion, her big perky tits waving in his face, diamond hard nipples waving tantalizingly close to a mouth that wanted desperately to suck them.

"Call me a good girl, Dare!" she moaned breathlessly, face flushed and eyes glazed with pleasure. She grabbed his head and pulled him upwards to bury his face in the silky channel between her breasts as her hips continued to churn on top of him.

Dare hesitated. He wanted to make his sexy lover happy, but he didn't want to feel like he was patronizing her or manipulating her loyalty.

The dog girl sensed his hesitation and pushed his head back down, droplets of her sweat misting his face as she glared down at him. "Haven't I been a good girl, Dare?" she demanded. As if to demonstrate she clenched her thighs hard against his hips as she continued to ride him, making her soft pink walls clamp down on his cock even tighter.

"Yes," he groaned in a strangled voice.

She bounced up and down on him even faster, her own voice strained. "Then call me a good girl, please! And do it quick."

Dare finally moved his hands from her ass so he could pull her chest down to him, latching onto one of her nipples and sucking hard. She yipped in response, and he felt her pussy twitch appreciatively on his shaft.

"You're a good girl, Pella," he panted. "A very, very good girl."

"Yeeesssssssss!" his dog girl lover squealed through clenched teeth. He felt her nectar flood his crotch, stomach, and thighs, and her silky walls crushed his cock even more tightly in rippling contractions as she had what seemed like the mother of all orgasms.

He couldn't hold out against that sort of overwhelming sensation when he'd already been so close to the edge. Especially at the sight of Pella's beautiful expressive face twisted in pleasure above him.

With a groan he grabbed her round ass again, pulled her down against his cock while simultaneously thrusting his hips up to press his head against her cervix, and held her there as his cock began to pulse against her contracting walls.

She flopped limply down on top of his chest as he emptied himself inside her, tail wagging in weary happiness above her as she came down from her climax. "Thank you," she whispered, kissing his collarbone. "That was wonderful."

"It was," he agreed, wrapping his arms around her and hugging her close. He kissed her soft floppy ears. "You're amazing."

"Wow, you guys had fun," Zuri said as she climbed out of the tent, making them both jump in surprise. She rubbed at her hair sleepily as she took in the state of them and their bedroll. "I don't think we've ever made that big a mess together, Dare."

"There's always next time," he said, grinning as he held out an arm to his tiny lover.

She obligingly snuggled up next to him, not seeming to mind the saliva and mingled juices of his and Pella's lovemaking that covered his body. "You could've stayed," he told her.

"Oh I will next time," she said with a giggle. "But your first time should be special." She stroked his saliva-soaked chest. "Like ours was."

Pella rolled off Dare to cuddle on Zuri's other side, so she was sandwiched between them. "You guys are both the best," she said happily. "I'm so glad to be here with you."

"We're glad too," Zuri said, contentedly burying her face in the dog girl's breasts. "Even after a just few days together, I can't imagine not having you with us."

Dare let himself lay there cuddling his lovers for a few minutes, luxuriating in the blissful afterglow of the incredible sex he'd just had. But finally he pulled away and stood with a reluctant sigh.

"I'd love to lie around with you all day, but we still have leveling to do," he said briskly. "There'll be plenty of time to have more fun tonight."

The two women groaned, but they reluctantly climbed to their feet as well. "After we drag ourselves and our clothes and this bedroll to the stream so I can clean everything," his goblin lover said with a giggle.

Pella giggled too. "Get used to us having to clean up often . . . I'm kind of a messy lover, and I don't apologize for it."

"Why would you need to?" Dare said with a laugh. "It's sexy as hell." He couldn't help but pause from dressing as he watched his new lover rummaging around for her discarded clothes, admiring her luscious body in all its flushed, sweaty glory.

Then he forced his eyes away and focused on gathering his gear; if he stood around staring for much longer he wouldn't be able to stop himself from pulling the beautiful dog girl back down to the bedroll and mounting her again, and pulling Zuri into the fun for good measure. Then they'd spend the entire day not getting anything done.

Work before pleasure.

Chapter Ten
Yurin

With every level the experience required for the next level jumped up sharply. Not double, which would quickly become impossible, but enough that leveling slowed more and more as each level up required more time.

That experience jump was even more pronounced after 20, as if that had been some sort of difficulty checkpoint. Which fit with the monsters also becoming more powerful for their level.

Still, with Pella providing crowd control for Dare's stupidly high damage, and Zuri supplementing the damage with her spells, they managed to keep leveling as quickly as before. Even quicker, maybe.

As a Tracker the dog girl was perfectly suited to help them level while doing almost no damage, so they got all the experience. The main thing slowing Dare down from purely damaging down enemies before was that he had to worry about them reaching him, or bringing adds. But Pella was able to handle both of those things.

In fact with Pella constantly pulling enemies and keeping them occupied, Zuri was even able to gradually kill one after another with her slower but more efficient damage over time spell, Nature's Rebuke.

They were even able to risk hunting higher level enemies, 22s, 23s, even 24s, for the greater experience bonus.

All the party needed now was a good tank, maybe another damage dealer, and they'd be unstoppable. They could probably even risk venturing into dungeons or tackling party rated world monsters.

And so, making slow, sweeping circuits of spawn points with monsters ranging from Level 17 to 24, coming back for the respawns and then continuing on in their gradual passage north, Dare and Zuri were able to reach Level 22 in four days.

22 was also probably about the number of times they made love in

that time, Zuri joining in as promised. Pella didn't seem to have the same rampant libido as his goblin lover with her high fertility, but she made up for it with being affectionate and enthusiastic.

Also it was their honeymoon period, so to speak, and she never missed an opportunity to touch or hold him. Zuri either, for that matter.

The two women didn't seem too interested in just randomly going at it with each other, like they did with Dare. But when they were all together they definitely seemed to enjoy playing with each other, too. And outside the bedroom, or the tent they now all shared, the two women were practically inseparable.

Not that any of them were in the habit of wandering off on their own, of course. But it was nice to see his two lovers becoming so close.

By the time they reached Level 22 they were getting close enough to Yurin that the spawn points began dropping in level. With the experience also slowing down, they agreed to stop doing circuits to wait for respawns and just plow through any spawn points they found on their path to the town; they could get back to serious leveling on the other side when they continued on.

After Pella finished her business with her old master's family, that is.

Although in spite of her insistence she needed to fulfill her duty, the dog girl was obviously reluctant to confront the painful situation. To the point that when they reached the point where the monsters had dropped down to Level 11, no longer offering experience for Dare and Zuri, she still wanted to farm them as an obvious delaying tactic.

"After all they're in our path," she said cheerfully. "It'd take almost as long to go around as through, and we can get some easy loot."

That wasn't strictly accurate, but if his new lover needed more time to mentally prepare herself for an unpleasant confrontation, he figured there was no harm in indulging her.

So they began clearing the monsters, weird semi-humanoid bird creatures with the black and white coloring of magpies. And the obnoxious screeching of magpies, too.

It was a relief that pretty much all their attacks killed the things in one shot, aside from Zuri who needed two with her Mana Thorn, so they didn't have to listen to that racket much. It also didn't take long to reach their camp of half-hovel, half-nest structures.

"Treasure pile!" Pella abruptly blurted, ears perked and fluffy tail wagging eagerly as she pointed into the camp.

Sure enough, there was a pile of objects shining invitingly in the center of the haphazard collection of ramshackle dwellings, surrounded by a dozen of the birdlike monsters.

Treasure or loot piles were far more common than treasure chests, sort of a small reward for clearing out a monster spawn point. Although they usually didn't have much of value in them, usually just a lot of junk.

The objects in this one, however, had a promising glitter. And it stood to reason that if these enemies resembled magpies, and magpies liked shiny things, and treasure was shiny . . .

"Oh, now you care about treasure?" Zuri teased.

The dog girl laughed. "Now that I'm actually using it instead of shoving it in a dank hole, sure."

Dare snickered at her phrasing, although his lovers probably thought he was just laughing along. Which he was, of course.

They quickly cleared the rest of the camp, then hurried to the treasure pile to see what they got. Which as it turned out was mostly junk made of brass, copper, tin, polished iron, steel, as well as a scattering of copper coins.

"What a huge tease!" Pella said with a pout, kicking a polished brass cup halfway across the camp. "From a distance this looked like gold and silver!"

"Magpie treasure," Dare said with a chuckle as he reached down and picked up a shiny sheet of tin, which his information window identified as a mirror. "They don't care if it's diamonds or glass shards, silver or tin. As long as it's shiny they'll-"

He caught sight of his reflection in the mirror and froze.

Movie star handsome features greeted him: a v-shaped face with high cheekbones, tanned complexion, strong mouth, and an elegant aquiline nose. Piercing blue eyes, slightly tousled hair so jet black it shone with blue highlights, matched by a hint of heavy stubble along a square jaw with a cleft chin.

A face that had a charisma all its own. His face. And it surprised him every time he saw it in a surface reflective enough to give him a clear look.

"Are you okay, Dare?" Zuri asked, worriedly reaching up to rest a hand on his arm. "You look like you've seen a ghost."

Just the opposite of one, technically. "I'm fine," Dare mumbled, absently patting her hand. He pulled away and started towards the edge of camp, tucking the crude mirror under his arm. "Give me a second, okay? I just . . . I need a second."

He didn't glance back as he walked into the woods, but he could practically feel his lovers' concern as they stared after him. He didn't want them to worry, but he kept going anyway.

A ways in he found a mossy nook between two tree roots to settle down in, leaning back against the trunk of a large sycamore tree. Then he pulled out the mirror and stared at himself, trying to remember his old face.

To his dismay, the appearance he'd known for 27 years kept morphing into the handsome features he stared at now; was he forgetting what he looked like?

Looked. *Looked* like. Before Dare had been blown to smithereens and ended up here.

How long had he been on Collisa? Almost three months now, right? And yet his memories of Earth were fading as quickly as his face, like it had all been a dream. One he thought of less and less as he became more cemented in his new life.

Especially now that he had Zuri and Pella to ground him here.

"You there?" he asked his benefactor. Then he snorted. "What am I asking, of course you are."

There was a long pause, then her comforting voice. This time with no text accompanying it. "I'm here, my lover."

Dare stared at his face, finding it stranger and stranger the more closely he picked out specific details. In a way the fact that it was so aesthetically pleasing just made it feel that much more fake. Like he was an avatar in a game, not in a real body in a real world.

"Can you show me my old face?" he asked quietly.

She paused again, for longer this time. "It's possible, but not like this." She sounded sympathetic. "Next time we're together in a dream, I'll make sure you see it."

"Thank you." He tossed aside the crude mirror, thoughts still far away on Earth. "You ever ride a roller coaster?"

His benefactor/lover laughed wryly. "I'm afraid my visit to your world wasn't quite that . . . hands on."

"More like observing it from the clouds?" Dare joked.

"More like absorbing all information about the planet, humanity, and its development and innovations within a short space of time, then moving on."

Oookay. Omniscience put his benefactor more firmly in the "god" category. Or goddess, he supposed. A deity of some sort, definitely.

And in his last conversation with her she'd given him a vividly sexy description about gagging up mucus as she took his cock down her throat to the base.

"You absorb details about the Grand Canyon?" he asked.

"Of course. It's a beautiful landmark from any point of view, but with the limited perspective of a human especially powerful."

"Does Collisa have anything like that?"

"No, although we have a whirlpool that pulls ships down into an underwater tunnel, which takes them through a barrier mountain range to a different ocean that can't otherwise be accessed by water."

Dare blew out an incredulous breath. "Shit, is that even physically possible?"

She laughed again. "As possible as the phenomena you see in the night sky here." Her voice became teasing. "Most of the people on this world don't have the background in physics or astronomy to realize how strange their sky is."

He hesitated. "If I ask for more specific details about this world you're going to clam up, aren't you?"

"Actually, I'm going to disappear," his benefactor said lightly. "I only have so much time to talk to you. So until we meet again, my lover."

"Sure," he said, settling back with a sigh.

But to his surprise she spoke again, voice sober. "Your previous life was important to you. I'm glad you're holding onto it, even if details are beginning to fade. And I'm sorry the reminders of what you've lost cause you pain. I wish I could comfort you better."

"I'm just glad I have you to talk to about it. Otherwise I'm scared it'll disappear completely." Dare hesitated again. "You're going to say no if I ask for permission to tell Zuri and Pella about Earth and my life there, right?"

"Yes, I'm going to say no," his benefactor said, stern but kind. "Not because I forbid it, but because we both know how it'll be received, and what sort of explanation it'll require. Best for now if you tell them as much as you can without adding any awkward details. And if you ever feel like you're lying to them, even through omission, remember that I'm telling you to wait until a later time. For all our sakes."

"Thanks," he said sincerely. "Goodbye, Benefactor. I-" He cut off, about to tell her he loved her, but unsure if it would be honest when his feelings for the mysterious woman, if that's even what she was, were still so confused.

He cared for her, and he was certainly attracted to her. At least in the context that she'd successfully gotten him off twice now, since he'd never actually seen what she looked like and wasn't sure she even had a body.

It went without saying that he was grateful for everything she'd done for him, but was that enough to call it love?

Maybe people made too much of a big deal about the idea of "love", put it on a pedestal and gave it more weight than was realistic in life. An impossible, magical ideal that left most disappointed in their actual relationships with their partner.

Either way, he held off on saying it to her just yet.

She laughed as if she understood his thoughts, which of course she probably did. "Goodbye, Dare. I- too."

Then she was gone.

Dare retrieved the mirror and made his way back to the magpie monster camp, rejoining Zuri and Pella. They were both waiting at the edge of it rather than continuing to loot the place, obviously worried about him.

Worried enough that when they spotted him they both ran over and wrapped their arms around him.

He laughed, a bit embarrassed as he hugged them back, fielding their concerned questions. "I'm fine," he told them. He waved the mirror. "Looking at this just pulled me into some bittersweet memories."

"Did you have a mirror like it once?" Pella asked.

"No, it was more what I saw in it. Or didn't see." Dare kissed one of her floppy ears, rubbed Zuri's back, then made his voice brisk. "Come on, let's see if there's anything in the magpie rubbish pile worth taking."

The scrap metal would probably sell for something, at least, and there were one or two silver coins among the copper. A lot of the pile ended up in their packs, even if they weren't overly optimistic about its value.

Then they continued on to Yurin, ignoring the monster spawn points they passed until they reached the dubious safety of the road leading to it, and turned their wariness to potential bandits.

* * * * *

The guards at the gate were a friendly lot. Which was why it was even more noticeable when they made Dare answer a bunch of questions about his business and about his slave and pet before letting him enter the town.

Then there was the taxes. For Zuri he had to pay the usual 2 silver,

183

but for Pella they demanded 10.

"I thought the tax was the same for slaves and pets," Dare protested. It galled him to refer to his lovers as either, but he knew he had to keep up the pretense for their sake as much as his.

The lead guard looked apologetic, even smiling kindly at the dog girl. "For most, yeah. But canids are a special case in Yurin. A lot of the nobles in the area want to be the only ones who can afford to have them as pets, and the local lord's not a fan of dog girls in particular. They banded together to impose the higher tax, as well as other increased fees and disincentives."

Pella's ears drooped in barely concealed anguish, and her fluffy tail hung limp between her legs. "Lord Kinnran doesn't like dog girls?" she whispered.

Dare's heart went out to his new lover. She'd told him and Zuri that her master had been lord of the town of Yurin, which meant the new lord was most likely his son. Someone Pella would've loved as family, almost as closely as her master himself.

The guards shifted uncomfortably. "Just a bad business all around," the friendly guard muttered. "But anyway 10 silver's the tax, pay it or leave."

The dog girl dug into her coin pouch and counted out 10 silver, still looking heartbroken.

As they were waved through the gate, Zuri wrapped an arm around their new companion's narrow waist and hugged her side. "Maybe it's not as bad as it sounds," she suggested. "You know how gossip goes. Lord Kinnran could just have a lost poster out there, searching for you, and people are just assuming the worst."

Dare nodded. "We'll sort this out when we go talk to your family."

Pella's tail wagged hesitantly. "You think so?" she asked, longing in her voice. It was obvious she desperately wanted to believe her family still loved her and were willing to forgive her, even after all this time.

"I think it'll all work out fine," Zuri assured her. "Nobody could believe anything bad about a sweetheart like you." She patted the dog girl's back before hugging her again. "Tell you what, how about we go shopping in the market for stuff Dare wouldn't think to buy for girls, while he takes care of the business."

"That's fine," Dare said, grateful for a chance to help cheer up his new lover.

"Sounds great!" Pella said, cheerfully shrugging out of her loaded pack and handing it to him. Zuri did the same, leaving him with almost more weight than he could carry as the two women started off down the street, happily chatting about the things they needed.

It turned out that in spite of his best efforts he'd been falling short on his gift giving. Including things like a tail brush, which was apparently much different than a hair brush, and a scented oil used in place of deodorant.

Well, Dare certainly wasn't complaining if the girls wanted to take measures to make themselves more presentable. Honestly he should be finding ways to do that himself. Although maybe he'd let them take care of that and focus on ways to help them all be more comfortable.

The collapsible chairs were just a small start to that, although they'd need a home before he could really focus on providing them with all the comforts Earth had that Collisa generally didn't.

That, and a lot more coin and probably access to some skilled mages and craftsmen. But that was a matter for the future.

As he'd expected, the magpies' shiny metal didn't sell for much. The rest of the junk loot and items from their farming netted a tidy sum, but after the incredible haul Pella had sold in the last town it felt humble in comparison.

After Dare finished selling their stuff he headed straight for the vendors and crafters who catered to traveling adventurers, guards, and other fighters.

He had a goal for his visit to the market today. For himself and Zuri he could content himself with the leather armor he crafted, since they fought at a range and almost never took damage. But with Pella getting up close and personal with monsters, he wanted to make sure she had the best gear possible for her level.

He didn't care if she out-leveled it in a few weeks, or if it ended up being a huge hit on his finances. He could resell the gear when they replaced it with higher level stuff, but whatever it took he'd make sure his lover was as safe as possible.

That included planning fights so she almost never had to directly face a monster, but as they'd found already on multiple occasions sometimes the unexpected happened. Especially with enemies higher level than 20.

Besides, since they all wore the same armor at the moment Dare or Zuri could inherit Pella's used armor once they got high enough level. The fit would be a bit awkward, but one of the handy crafting tools on Collisa was Resizing, which let a crafter take any armor or clothing of a type they could make and alter it to fit someone else, without any more materials required.

Again, one of those mechanics that made no sense from a logical standpoint but was unquestionably handy.

So Dare found a Leathercrafter selling leather armor up to Level 30, ranging in quality from Decent to Journeyman. The man had full sets of armor up to Level 25, but after that it was more of a mixed bag of the few items he could make himself, monster loot, and items he'd purchased from traveling merchants or adventurers.

Dare found a used Level 27 leg armor and chestpiece that were Journeyman quality, but had been repaired often enough that their max durability was about to impact their stats, as would even a few hits damaging their durability. He picked them out anyway, since Pella would be out-leveling the gear soon enough and he could probably get a good deal for them.

He also found Level 28 Good quality bracers, Level 29 Decent quality boots, a Level 26 Decent quality hood as well as a Level 30 Good quality hood to replace it, and that rounded out his lover's armor set.

"How much for the lot?" Dare asked.

The craftsman looked over the assembled gear, musing. "46 gold," he finally said.

Dare laughed out loud, and not just as a haggling tactic. No armor he'd seen for his level came anywhere near that cost, and it seemed incredible that only five or six levels was enough for such a extreme jump.

Then, of course, there was the fact that he didn't have that much gold on him, including the money he carried for Zuri which of course he wasn't about to spend. The vendor was probably asking for a ridiculously high price since Dare had just haphazardly piled a bunch of stuff in front of him, without inquiring as to its quality or even asking about cost.

Rookie move, there.

"46 gold, for a set of average quality gear at best," he said with a smirk. "Half of which is monster loot, and the legs and chest are on the verge of falling to pieces with the next solid hit. If you're going to just joke around I'll go find another vendor."

"Go for it," the man said. "You'll have a hard time finding anyone else in Yurin who crafts at this level."

Dare shrugged, calling his bluff. "There's always the next town." He turned and walked away.

He got ten feet away before the Leatherworker swore softly and called after him. "All right, wanderer, if you're such an expert what do *you* consider a fair price?"

Dare made a show of reluctantly returning. "10 gold." One outrageous offer deserved another.

It was the man's turn to laugh. "I changed my mind, keep walking."

Now they were getting somewhere. Dare picked up the Level 30 Good quality hood, by far the finest piece and also the least urgent one to get now, since Pella was two levels away from even being able to use it. He set it aside and fixed the vendor with a steady glare. "10 gold."

"40," the vendor said flatly.

Dare pointedly picked up the old chestpiece and leg armor. "One good hit," he said, "and the stats on these will go down. Just admit you overreached to an insulting degree by demanding 46, and we can get to a more reasonable price."

The man ground his teeth. "30," he grated out.

The fact that he'd dropped the price so sharply confirmed that he really had been asking too much. "15."

"28."

Dare inwardly counted the money he remembered in his coin pouch. He couldn't go that high, which meant he had to keep haggling to even afford the items. "18 is as high as I go, and that's a better deal than the items deserve."

The vendor was silent for a very long time, glaring between him and the armor. "22," he finally growled. "Or you can go find another fool who values the time spent to level up crafting this high so little."

After a few moments of thought Dare leaned across the table and offered his hand. "22," he agreed. "And if I happen to be in the area when I can use that Level 30 helmet, you'll give me a good deal on it."

The man snorted but returned the handshake. "We'll see."

As the vendor bundled the armor in a square of cheap cloth Dare counted out coins for the payment. He needed to use 100 silver along with 21 gold, if that was any indication of how far he had to dip into his savings; the cost didn't quite wipe them out, but it definitely took the lion's share.

Still, he was reassured that Pella would be much safer with this gear. And at the rate they were leveling, they'd eventually reach a point where they could replace this amount of gold with a few hours of farming.

Just out of curiosity Dare searched among the vendors for anything else he or his lovers would find useful and could afford with his dwindling savings. He found a few things, including some new spices and a decent cooking pot. Which reminded him to buy the ingredients needed to make sweets with the honey and syrup he'd gathered.

A little treat for Zuri and Pella tonight; last night's game licking honey off each others' bodies had been a lot of fun, but he wanted to show them things like pancakes and cornbread.

Maybe even donuts, eventually.

Weapons were a bust, he'd already taken care of armor as much as he planned to for the moment, and trinkets that gave an item bonus could cost more than a hundred of gold *for their level*. So Dare left the market behind and went in search of quests.

He had the pleasant surprise that one quest could be turned in retroactively for monsters he'd already killed, in this case those magpies they'd wiped out on a whim. The quest had an interesting background story, in that during their mating season the territorial magpies would leave their spawn point and attack travelers from behind.

The quest giver even had a scar along the top of his head from a magpie attack.

The man was overjoyed to find the camp already cleared, and after profusely shaking Dare's hand gave him a handful of silver and a small hammered silver shot glass.

The downside of the quest was that apparently it wasn't repeatable, since as party leader he wasn't able to accept it on behalf of Zuri and Pella. Still, he was pleased with the good luck as he set out in search of more quests or his lovers, or both.

Zuri and Pella found him first, both excited. "We're renting a room at a tavern tonight!" Zuri said enigmatically, refusing to say more. Pella didn't say anything at all, just wagged her fluffy tail furiously as she watched for his reaction, practically bursting at the seams in her excitement.

They were obviously up to something that they couldn't wait for, but Dare played it casual. "Sounds comfortable," he said with a smile. "Lead on." As they started down the street he lifted the wrapped bundle of leather armor. "Oh by the way, Pella, I got a set of armor for us to share. Here."

The dog girl eagerly untied the gift, soft brown eyes widening in surprise. "This is really nice, Dare!" she burst out. "It's so much better than-" She abruptly cut off with a wince, realizing that she'd been about to diss his own crafting.

He chuckled. "Than the pieces of shit I can make? That's the point." He playfully swatted her firm bottom. "I want to make sure your beautiful skin doesn't get all torn up."

She didn't smile at his banter, shaking her head sharply. "I can't

Kovana

accept this," she said in a firm voice. "It must've cost a fortune." She tried to give him back the bundle.

Dare didn't reach to take it. "I can't use most of it for four or five levels, and it would just go to waste otherwise. So use it, please."

Pella frowned stubbornly. "I know what this is, you're pretending I'll just be holding onto this armor until you can use it, when really you got it for me."

He started to protest, then gave up with a sigh. "It's both, Pella," he said gently. "You're the one who's in the most danger facing monsters as part of our party, and we need to make sure you've got the best protection we can manage."

He took her hand, meeting her eyes with full sincerity. "And I did it for myself, because I couldn't bear to see you get hurt when we could've prevented it."

"Just take the armor," Zuri said, taking the dog girl's other hand. "I won't feel comfortable with you running around letting monsters chase you, or holding them pinned, if you aren't properly equipped."

Pella's eyes suddenly swam with tears, and she threw her arms around both of them. "Thank you," she said. "Of course I'll use the armor." Her voice became stern. "But the next set of upgrades we get are on me."

Dare laughed and returned her hug. "Deal."

The dog girl abruptly drew back, grinning from ear to ear. "Okay well enough business, let's get back to the night we have planned!" She took his arm and practically dragged him behind her down the street.

Laughing, Zuri took his other hand and joined her in urging him forward.

Dare allowed himself to be led along, having the warm, fuzzy feeling that he was going to enjoy whatever they had prepared for him. Especially since the two women pressed themselves affectionately against him the entire time. They didn't seem more than politely interested in his report about their loot sales, either, and absently accepted their share of the gold without breaking their stride.

The girls led him to a nicer inn, where a cheerful, portly innkeeper who introduced himself as Jekk ushered them to a private dining room on the second floor. The man had apparently already been paid, and a meal had been ordered as well because the table in the room was laden with an assortment of steaming dishes and delicious looking desserts.

The table could seat six, but Dare found himself pressed between his two lovers on one of the benches, Pella's wagging tail thumping his back with pleasant regularity.

Zuri poured them all wine, then raised her glass in a toast. "To our party!"

The dog girl giggled and raised her own glass. "To our threesome!" By her mischievous tone she wasn't talking about monster hunting.

Dare raised his glass and clinked theirs. "To the two most beautiful, amazing women on Collisa!"

They all drank deep, then began loading their plates. And eagerly dug in.

The food was really good. Some of the first he'd found that was much better than his own cooking. Pella mostly loaded her plate with meat, while Dare sampled a bit of all the dishes. As for Zuri, he was amused to see that she had no plans to wait for dessert; she piled half her plate with sweets and the other with meat.

"We might have to have an intervention about your sweet tooth at some point," he teased the tiny goblin, slipping a hand around her waist and playfully squeezing her side. "I'm finding more of you to love these days."

Her pale green skin went noticeably paler, and for a moment her mirth vanished.

Dare inwardly cursed his stupidity; any idiot knew you didn't say something like that to a woman, especially not your lover. "Which I think is super sexy," he hastily added, although he got the sense the save wasn't very effective.

"What the hell, Dare?" Pella asked, punching his arm with surprising force. Or maybe not, considering her proficiency in unarmed. "You don't say things like that to a lady."

191

He bit back a sigh, hoping this didn't ruin the festive mood. "Okay okay, both of you tease me about something."

"You say weird things sometimes," Zuri immediately said, seeming eager to move away from the subject of her thickening waist.

"And you're sometimes too much of a gentleman in the sack," Pella added, tail wagging playfully. "It wouldn't kill you to occasionally tackle me to the ground and slam into me like I'm a bunny girl you found trapped in a thorn bush."

Zuri giggled. "Ooh, you haven't heard the story of the first cunid he met? He was such a gentleman that she basically had to drag him by the collar to a clearing and mount him herself."

Considering *Dare* was the one who'd told her the story, when she'd asked offhand if he'd ever been with a bunny girl, her take on the account was even more embarrassing. "It wasn't exactly like that," he protested, blushing. "And what was I supposed to think when she was a complete stranger?"

"See," the goblin said with an easy laugh. "He says weird things."

Tension dissolved, they dove back into the feast and did an impressive job clearing the table. And emptying the wine bottle, for that matter.

In fact, once they were all full to the point of picking at what was left on their plates, Zuri shot Pella a pointed look and cleared her throat. "We should go get another bottle of wine, shouldn't we Pella?"

The dog girl's ears perked up in excitement and her fluffy tail went crazy, thumping against Dare like a crowd of people offering enthusiastic backslaps. "Yes, we should!"

Dare wasn't so oblivious that he didn't realize something was going on, but he played along. "I could go get it," he offered cheerfully.

"No no!" his goblin lover said, bouncing off the bench and starting for the door while snagging Pella's arm as she went. "Don't go anywhere, we'll be right back."

She wasn't wrong, although she was only half right too.

Less than half a minute later the door flew open and Pella bounded inside, face flushed with excitement and beaming with delight. She playfully held her hands behind her back, and he wondered what she had.

"Did you know they have baths here?" she said, lovely face glowing with excitement. "We had the serving girls get them ready before we started eating. Zuri's already in there!"

"That sounds nice," he said, smiling at her enthusiasm.

The dog girl's fluffy golden tail thumped from side to side, making her curvy hips wiggle alluringly with it. "It's a big tub," she hinted.

Dare chuckled; it was pretty obvious she wanted to take a bath with him, which sounded fantastic. But for now he kept playing dumb. "Sounds like it'll be pretty luxurious, then. I might get one myself."

"Oh no you won't," she said happily. She took her hands from behind her back to reveal that she was holding a . . . washcloth. "Here," she said, handing it to him.

He took it, staring at the small, soft square of cloth in bafflement. "I, um . . ."

Pella rolled her eyes. "You're usually really smart and always know what to do, but sometimes you can be so dense. Then I have to hold your hand and drag you to what you're supposed to be doing." When he still stared at her blankly she giggled and snatched the washcloth from him, flicking it at his face. "I want you to give me a bath, silly!"

Realization dawned like a brilliant sunrise, and Dare found himself grinning for a different reason.

Of course, dog girl. And she'd talked more than once about how much she loved baths, especially when her master had given her one.

Dare imagined running a soapy washcloth all over Pella's gorgeous, nude body, or better yet his soapy hands, as a prelude to whatever fun happened next. His cock immediately stiffened to rock hard. "I'd love to give you a bath," he blurted.

"Yay!" Pella squealed, throwing her arms around his neck and plopping down on his lap. He winced slightly and shifted to protect his crotch, not quite succeeding as her thigh pressed down on his bulge, and she giggled in realization.

"Oh goody, you've already got your wash tool ready to clean my insides," she said, eyes sparkling mischievously. "I bought some lubricated body-safe cleansing solution at the market earlier, so we have everything we need."

Oh gods. Dare's cock twitched in a fresh surge of excitement; his new lover was saying all the right things, to the point that he was afraid he wouldn't last to the bath.

The dog girl seemed to realize it because she hopped back up, tail wagging. "Come on," she said, grabbing his hands and tugging him insistently to his feet. "Zuri's already waiting for us . . . after you wash us then we're going to wash you! Everyone will get clean!"

She giggled naughtily. "After we all get dirty, that is."

It was good to know that Pella had thought to include Zuri. And Dare had to admit that he was also excited at the prospect of bathing his tiny goblin lover. He allowed himself to be dragged towards the door, grinning like an idiot.

But apparently he wasn't moving fast enough for the dog girl. "Come on!" she said, tugging him even more insistently. "I've gotten all muddy playing and need a good scrubbing."

He laughed. "Oh, are you a dirty girl?"

She giggled and her voice became husky. "Very dirty. Your naughty dog girl mate needs to be thoroughly cleaned, inside and out."

Grin and erection both showing in full force, Dare allowed himself to be dragged down the hall towards the waiting bath room.

This was shaping up to be the best night ever.

Chapter Eleven
Suds

The small bath room was surprisingly fancy.

It had a tiled floor which tilted very perceptibly towards a drain in one corner. It was dominated by a wooden tub large enough for two, with a table beside it loaded with soaps, scented oils, and other bath items. A set of shelves in the corner had space for them to place their clothes, as well as stacks of clean towels for their use.

Zuri's clothes were already stacked neatly on the shelf, and the little goblin was seated on a comfortable chair in the corner, legs tucked almost primly beneath her. She gave Dare a huge smile as he entered behind Pella, confirming that she'd helped plan all this.

He smiled back at her as he let his dog girl lover tug him over to stand in front of the tub.

"Dare," Pella said, staring at him expectantly, "bathing a dog girl tends to get soapy water everywhere. Don't you think you should undress?"

Dare grinned and quickly complied, stripping off his shirt. His cock sprang free of his pants as he peeled them and his underwear down, and he noticed Pella and Zuri both staring at it hungrily as he finished undressing.

The beautiful golden-haired woman took his clothes and shoved them haphazardly on the shelf, leaving him standing somewhat sheepishly as she moved over to stand beside the tub.

"Now my turn!" she said, fluffy tail wagging excitedly. She grabbed the hem of her leather shirt and began to lift it, then paused after only an inch and with a teasing smile began to sway to unheard music, undulating her hips provocatively.

Dare watched, openmouthed, as she began what could only be called a strip tease.

Pella's dance was surprisingly graceful, as if she'd done it many times. And she had perfect timing in teasingly peeling off her shirt an inch at a time, exposing her flat tummy and adorable belly button. But the sexiest part of the dance was her happy expression and eagerly wagging tail.

She was obviously enjoying herself.

Dare had another pleasant surprise when the seductive dog girl finished peeling the shirt up over her chest and tossed it aside, and he saw she'd made another purchase: underwear. And nothing functional or utilitarian like what Zuri had made for her, either.

He gaped at the thin, but tantalizingly not quite sheer, white silk bra that clung to her voluptuous breasts with a perfect fit.

Pella giggled. "Do you like my new bra?"

"I love it," he said. "But I have to say I'm looking forward to seeing you take it off even more."

Both women laughed. "All in good time," the dog girl said, reaching for the waistband of her leather pants.

Dare watched hungrily as she continued her dance while lowering the hip-hugging garment inch by inch, and was rewarded with the sight of a matching pair of white silk panties that also perfectly hugged her luscious curves.

Although he was delighted to see that the crotch of her panties was just loose enough that it had ridden up into her sweet little pussy to form a deep cameltoe he couldn't take his eyes off of.

Had she done that on purpose? If so, she'd been spot on guessing that he loved the sight of a good cameltoe. And hers was the loveliest he'd ever seen.

Pella grinned at him, eyes sparkling with satisfaction. "Would you like to feel it?"

Dare nodded eagerly and stepped forward, slipping his finger into the groove and pushing her panties deeper into her slit. The dog girl whined and pushed back against him as he explored her panty-clad lips, then abruptly giggled and leapt back.

"Let's keep going," she said in a girly, seductive voice. "I'm feeling very dirty and need to be bathed."

Dare felt a bit like a dog himself as he practically salivated while watching Pella strip off her pants in one smooth motion, then loop her thumbs into the waistband of her panties. She begin teasingly sliding them down, moving with glacial slowness to reveal her fluffy golden bush with its fuzz as soft as thistledown millimeter by agonizing millimeter.

Finally she peeled that glorious cameltoe away from her luscious lips, plump and glistening invitingly, and the white silk cloth began to slide down her legs. He could see a damp patch on the thin cloth's interior, not quite enough to soak through, and a single thin string of her arousal connected her beautiful pussy to her panties for a few inches before breaking away.

He tore his eyes from her delicate petals to her curvy hips as they shifted hypnotically, barely aware of the fact that it meant Pella was gliding seductively towards him until she made him jump by teasingly pushing the crotch of her panties into his open mouth.

"Here," she said, expressive brown eyes sparkling with mischief. "People usually don't understand why dog girls like to sniff and even lick objects around them, at least before they've been properly trained. But it's no mystery why men love to do that for objects like this, is it?"

Dare made a muffled sound of agreement, enjoying her sweet flavor on his tongue, as his lover danced back to the tub and climbed in, dunking herself in the warm water. She emerged wet and glistening and straightened at the edge of the tub, striking a sexy pose that made him want to pin her down and piston into her like a dog.

"Well, my mate?" his beautiful lover said in a sultry voice. "I'm such a dirty girl, don't you think you should wash me?"

If his cock hadn't already been hard as blue steel, it would've stiffened even more at that invitation. The sight of Pella in all her flushed, wet, naked glory had to rank among the wonders of the world, and the thought of seeing all that smooth skin lathered with soap made him pant in spite of himself.

He savored the taste of the dog girl for one final moment before reluctantly drawing the panties out of his mouth. Zuri hurried forward to take them from him and gather up the rest of Pella's clothes, giving him a playful pinch on the bottom before retreating back to her chair.

"Want to help me?" Dare asked his goblin lover.

She shook her head as she settled back in the chair with her legs propped up on either armrest, giving him a tantalizing look at her sopping wet pussy. "You should give her all your attention until she's content," she said, idly lowering a hand to tease her flushed lips. "The idea of you washing me is an appealing one, but Pella *loves* this and I don't want to lessen her enjoyment."

"Oh, you wouldn't!" the dog girl cried. "I want to have fun with you, too!"

"Later," Zuri assured her, slipping a finger into her glistening hole. "I want to watch you two play."

"Are you sure?" Dare asked. "I don't want you to feel left out."

His goblin lover looked at him with eyes shining with love. "You never make me feel left out, my mate," she whispered. "But this is Pella's moment. Our chance to make her happy."

He nodded, satisfied with that explanation. "I'll give you the same service when it's your turn," he said, feeling a bit guilty about how eagerly he turned back to Pella and approached the tub. She held that sexy pose as she waited for him, tail wagging hard enough to make her luscious hips sway, just begging to be grabbed and held against him.

Dare reached for the washcloth, dunked it in a bucket of warm water, and began to get it soapy. The entire time the dog girl watched him, grinning knowingly, and before he could approach her to begin she spoke in a girly, sultry voice. "Do you really want to use the washcloth?"

He swallowed, realizing he really didn't, and with a grin tossed it aside and grabbed the bar of soap again, lathering his hands.

Then, trembling in anticipation, he stepped forward and dropped to his knees beside the tub. Before he could even register the fact that the hard tiles of the bathroom floor were painful to kneel on, Zuri rushed forward with a folded towel and slid it beneath him.

She smiled at his grateful nod, then retreated back to her place to watch again as Dare turned back to his golden-haired lover.

As if Pella understood his intent, she lifted one graceful foot to rest on the edge of the tub so he could wash it. In that position he could look directly at her pink pussy, its plump lips slightly spread to reveal her glistening interior.

Hypnotized, Dare watched a drop of her arousal trickle from between her folds and glide down one gorgeous thigh. The dog girl cleared her throat, a bit impatiently, and with a start he turned his attention back to her foot.

He lovingly ran his hands over every inch of it, making her giggle as his fingers slipped between her toes. At her ankle he stopped, though, and had her switch feet so he could wash her other one just as tenderly.

But rather than continuing up her legs after that, he straightened and moved around behind her.

"Ooh, eager to get somewhere?" Pella asked, playfully shaking her round ass in his direction with her tail thumping happily.

"I sure am." Dare grinned as he undid the tie holding her braid, then began gently teasing it undone and freeing her golden locks to make a lustrous wave falling to the small of her back.

His dog girl lover craned her neck to look at him, giggling. "Really? My whole sexy body to play with, and you go for my hair?"

"You don't think your hair is ridiculously sexy?" He ran his soapy fingers through the thick waterfall of waves, teasing out a few small tangles. Her hair was soft and fine, and breathing in deeply the scent of sunshine and wildflowers and his lover's unique bouquet filled his mind.

Gods, she smelled good.

Pella obliged him as he dunked her hair in the bucket of warm water, then poured it over her head to douse the rest. Then he began carefully soaping her wet, heavy locks as her tail caressed his stomach with each contented wag.

Much as he enjoyed that, though, he was eager to finish. And as soon as he did he grabbed her fluffy tail and began to stroke it lovingly.

"Oooh," the dog girl moaned, tail going stiff in his hands; he'd noticed in previous lovemaking that the entire thing was an erogenous zone, same with her adorable floppy ears. And he could admit he loved the silky soft feel of it and how much of her feelings she expressed with it.

Not to mention the way she responded to his petting as he ran his hands along its entire fluffy length, whining softly in pure contentment.

Dare dunked and soaped up her tail, gave it a last playful squeeze, then moved to her beautiful hands with their long, delicate fingers. He massaged them the same way he used to get hand massages for carpal tunnel, and she made more contented noises and closed her eyes.

After lovingly running his soapy hands up and down her arms, luxuriating in every inch of her soft skin, he finally moved to her shoulders and massaged them as well. Given her obvious appreciation he decided to give her a full body massage at some point, but for now that would take too long and he was too eager to keep going. So he moved on to the rest of her curvy, athletic body.

For several minutes Dare just ran his fingers over the smooth, silky skin of her legs, sides, tummy, and back. He could feel Pella tense each time he got close to her breasts, ass, or between her legs, obviously eager for him to finally get somewhere fun.

But he patiently continued washing her everywhere else, taking great care not to so much as brush her more sensitive areas with his fingers. She probably thought he was teasing her, and maybe he was a bit, but that wasn't the real reason he was so careful.

He was saving the best for last.

When he finally got to her ass he was almost as excited as she was, and his cock throbbed as he rubbed and squeezed those perfect, firm globes with his soapy hands. Pella moaned and leaned forward to press her forehead against his as he took the time to fully enjoy her shapely backside, then squirmed eagerly as his hands slid up and around to cup the undersides of her large, perky breasts.

Her nipples stiffened almost immediately as his palms rubbed over them, but he ignored them for a moment as he continued to play with her boobs, luxuriating in their yielding firmness. When he finally turned his attention to her diamond hard nipples and began squeezing them and rolling them between his fingers, she gave a shuddering gasp and leaned forward in the tub, resting her knees on the edge as if her legs had suddenly weakened.

After another couple very enjoyable minutes Dare left her breasts behind and dropped to his knees again on the towel Zuri had laid out, focusing on the final part of the dog girl's body he hadn't washed.

Her butt crack and pussy.

Pella stared down at him, biting her lip in eager anticipation and tail flinging soapsuds everywhere as it went crazy. "My mate," she said solemnly, "every dog girl is taught that it's very important to clean thoroughly down there. I think you should take your time, maybe even longer than you spent cleaning the rest of me."

Dare's cock lurched, and he swallowed a lump in his throat. "It *is* important to maintain proper hygiene," he said hoarsely.

The beautiful dog girl giggled and spread her legs a bit wider, giving him better access to her glorious pink petals, dripping with her nectar. "Then please take good care of me."

He scooted a bit closer for better access, breathing deep of the heady scent of her arousal. He would've taken a good long lick, maybe even dived in and feasted on her delicious ambrosia, but soap from the rest of her body had dripped down.

Well, time for that later.

Dare ran his hand up and down her butt crack, firmly rubbing her little rosebud every time his fingers brushed it. She giggled and squirmed each time, and he grinned as he finally moved on to her taint, rubbing and pressing it firmly as she wiggled around some more. Then he thoroughly soaped up and massaged her plump mound with its small bush of fine golden hair.

Then, at long last, he reached his ultimate goal: his gorgeous lover's delicate little pussy.

Obviously he didn't want to get her soapy inside, so he focused on rubbing around and across her outer lips, as well as around her erect clit. Although the moment he accidentally brushed her throbbing pearl she immediately whimpered and leaned against the tub again, hands resting heavily on his shoulders for support, and he saw her pussy and asshole winking in orgasm as juices flowed from her sex to coat her thighs.

"Wow, you were really ready to go," he said with a grin.

Pella blushed furiously. "Can I help it when you've been teasing me this entire time?" she said a bit breathlessly.

"So you want me to play with your clit some more?" Dare teased.

"Goddess, yes, please!" she whined, pushing herself against his hand. "You don't have to be gentle, either."

Oh, was that so? He grinned and rubbed just to the side of his dog girl lover's bud as she came down from her climax, making his way around the sensitive nub for a few minutes. Then he rubbed her clit directly, and with another whimper she sagged against him and came again, flooding her thighs with more of her nectar.

Dare couldn't help but grin. If his beautiful lover responded this strongly to just a light touch, how hard could he make her pop off if he was a bit firmer?

"You're my messy little lover, aren't you?" Dare growled, rubbing her clit harder. "You like to make a mess everywhere when we mate, don't you?"

"I do," Pella whined. Her soapy tail stuck straight out behind her, and her athletic body quivered with the tension of holding still as he stimulated her.

"Yeah, you're my messy girl," he said, rubbing faster. "I bet if I keep doing this you'll squirt all over me, won't you girl?" She whimpered, and he mashed her clit. "*Won't you?*"

"Yeeeesssss!" she squealed, hips straining to press herself against him. "Please keep scrubbing my button even faster, Master, and I'll squirt all over you like the naughty girl I am."

Dare went from rubbing to flicking, using Fleetfoot to make his finger a blur on her quivering pearl. "Squirt for me, my good girl," he whispered.

"Eeeeeeee!" the dog girl squeaked, and a spray of love juices exploded from her beautiful little pussy, splattering over his chest and crotch.

He panted at how hot it was, literally as well as metaphorically, and kept punishing her little clit faster and faster. "You got more for me?"

"Yeeesssss!" she wailed, squirting again even harder. Then with a shivering whine she slumped against him as if the strength had gone from her legs, wrapping soapy arms around his shoulders and pressing his face to her soapy neck. He shifted his hand between her legs to help support her weight, and felt the entrances to her pussy and asshole again winking against his fingers as she gave in to an overwhelming climax.

She was so sexy that it was all he could do not to shoot his load all over the outside of the tub.

It took a few minutes before Pella finally straightened, still trembling slightly as she came down from her peak. "I think you've cleaned me thoroughly," she said, eyes sparkling. She pointed at the flagstone floor beside him. "Lay down, I want to rub my soapy body against you."

Oh hell yes.

Dare all but went limp and let gravity smash him to the floor in his eagerness to comply, catching himself at the last second and spreading out on the tiles. They were almost uncomfortably cool against his back, and he shivered slightly.

Although he knew that Pella would be warming him up soon.

The dog girl made a happy sound as she climbed out of the tub and straddled his thighs just below his crotch, then dropped forward to smother his abdomen with her large, pert breasts. His rigid cock was mashed between them, almost uncomfortably.

She began slowly rubbing her soapy body against him, the movements languid and sensuous. Dare ran his hands over her soapy back and ass, luxuriating in her, and she gave him wet slobbery kisses and licked his face as she continued her tantalizing movements.

"Do you want me to finish you like this so you can hold your next erection for longer?" she panted happily. "After all, you still need to clean me inside."

Dare groaned; did he have the stamina for all that? He desperately wanted to come inside the sexy dog girl's pussy and ass, which meant she would take at least two. But it wouldn't be fair to Zuri to not give her the same treatment, and honestly he wanted to come inside his goblin lover, too.

As if to let him know what he'd be getting, Pella shifted forward until her soapy pussy was gliding up and down his cock, lips wrapped lovingly around its underside as her hips undulated. "Hmm, my mate?" she moaned. "Do you want to come on my soapy little body? I bet you've got plenty of arrows in the quiver to shoot as many times as you need to tonight."

He grunted in pleasure, and in a sudden movement spun them around so Pella was laying facedown on the floor. Then he climbed on top of her, pushing his cock down between her lush thighs so the top pressed against the entire length of her pussy.

Between her warmth and the soapy wetness the sensation was almost as good as fucking. Especially since he'd just spent the last quarter hour or so turning himself on by touching literally every square inch of his sexy lover's body.

Dare panted as he began to thrust his cock in and out between her tightly pressed together thighs, always keeping the upper side mashed up against her pussy and sliding his tip over her clit every time.

Pella squealed and bucked back against him, clamping her powerful legs around him as tightly as she could manage to give him the best sensation. It spurred him to even more desperate thrusting, and he had to resist the urge to change his angle slightly and drive deep into his dog girl lover.

He didn't want to get soap in there. That was what her special cleaning solution was for.

Her tail thumped against his chest, flicking soapy water into his face, and he caught it and held it off to one side. That gave him a clear view of her round ass, and on impulse he pulled free of her thighs and began sliding his cock up and down her sexy crack, being sure to kiss her asshole with the tip on every stroke.

Pella moaned and pushed her ass back against him with every thrust, at the same time reaching between her legs to play with her clit. Her tail was jerking in his grip so hard he nearly lost his hold.

To prevent that he dropped down on top of her, pressing his whole body against her soapy back and legs. It mashed his cock between them, and he rubbed his body against hers as he continued to thrust between her cheeks, his dog girl lover whining and grunting at his weight atop her.

Dare groaned at the pleasurable sensation and looked up at Zuri to see how she was doing. Then he gasped in shocked delight when he saw her sprawled back in the chair, the fingers of one hand furiously working her clit while she'd somehow managed to push her entire other hand *inside* her pussy, the lips stretched wide around her wrist as she frantically jerked it forwards and backwards to fist fuck herself.

The sight combined with the incredible sensations of Pella's body were too much for him, and with a final noise of pure pleasure he lifted himself up on his elbows, releasing her tail to thump against his side, and erupted all over her round ass.

After emptying his balls on the adorable dog girl he slumped down on his side beside her and wrapped an arm around her waist, pulling her back to spoon against him. "I love you," he told her.

Pella's fluffy tail thumped happily between his legs, mostly trapped by his thighs and occasionally rubbing soapy fur against his cock and balls. She twisted around enough to kiss him, slow and warm. "I love you too," she whispered. "Thank you for letting me be with you, Dare."

After giving him a minute or two of cuddling to recover Pella squirmed free of his spooning and leapt to her feet, reaching down to offer him her hand. "Ready to keep going? We still have so much to do!"

Dare bit back a groan as he accepted a hand up, although her skin was so slippery with soap that she couldn't really get enough of a grip to actually help him. "You're going to kill me before this night is through, aren't you?" he grumbled.

The sexy dog girl giggled. "We'll at least make you pass out from pleasure. Right, Zuri?"

"Oh, totem spirits!" the tiny goblin moaned, finally pulling her hand out of her pussy and laying back limply. "Just watching is so good, I can't imagine how it'll be to take part."

Pella skipped happily over to a table by the tub that held various soaps, lotions, and other bathing items. She snatched up a bottle and turned to Dare. "Here's the lubricated cleaning solution!" she said, tail thumping the tub behind her. "Time to clean my insides!"

Even though he'd just come, Dare's cock immediately grew rock hard at that.

Zuri quickly stepped in to help rinse his cock and Pella's pussy and ass crack, making sure all the soap was gone. Then, at the golden-haired dog girl's insistence, the tiny goblin eagerly opened the bottle of lubricated cleaning solution and began rubbing it over Dare's throbbing member, then around and inside both the dog girl's holes while Pella moaned in pleasure.

The body-safe soap felt like any other lube to him, slick and smooth and slightly warm, and he briefly wondered if Pella had been cheated.

Before he could dwell on it the dog girl leaned over the tub with her hands gripping the side, giving him a clear view of her lush backside and flushed pussy lips dripping with lube and her arousal. "Please clean me thoroughly, my mate," she said in that girly, sexy voice, tail eagerly flicking back and forth like a fan.

Dare wasted no time stepping forward and lining his cock up with her sopping entrance. Then with a grateful groan he pushed inside in one smooth motion.

Pella squealed happily. "Yes, yes! Clean your dirty girl! Be sure to scrape my insides hard and don't miss a single inch!"

"Fuck," he moaned in pleasure, both from her dirty talk and her the feel of her tight, warm walls clamping around him. He pulled out and changed his angle slightly before thrusting in again, trying to do just what she asked and make sure he pushed his tip against every square inch of her sweet little tunnel.

Then he pulled out, shifted slightly, and slammed in again. And again, picking up his pace. He began pushing her head and shoulders down to get a better angle, cock scraping along her clit and g-spot as he hammered into her.

The beautiful dog girl whined and whimpered with sheer enjoyment the entire time, and it didn't take long before she collapsed against the rim of the tub with another squeal and squirted her nectar all over his crotch, walls lovingly massaging his length as she climaxed.

"You clean me so good," she moaned as she came down from her orgasm, cheek pressed to the polished wood of the tub and tail wagging limply. "But this is a bad angle to get the rest of me." She pushed off the tub, pulling off his cock at the same time, and lay down on her back on the spread out towels, raising her arms and legs toward him in invitation.

Grinning, Dare dropped down into her embrace, positioning his cock at her entrance as her legs wrapped around him. "I'm going to have to go fast cleaning the rest of your sweet little pussy," he said. "Because I don't know how much longer I can go before I have to get it all dirty again by coming."

Pella giggled. "That doesn't get it dirty, silly. That's how you finish cleaning it." With a needy whine she flexed her legs and lifted her hips, pushing herself up onto his cock with a whimper of pleasure.

"Gods," he groaned as she smoothly engulfed him until he bottomed out. "I hope you're ready to get your insides scrubbed."

"Yes, please!" she said, relaxing back and letting him take over.

Dare did, starting right off alternating between swift, hard thrusts and slower deep ones. He went faster and faster by the second, feeling his balls clench and his cock throb as he fought to hold off his orgasm for a bit longer.

Soon he was pounding into his dog girl lover while she squealed and pushed her soapy body back at him, matching his movements with her own with joyous enthusiasm. Until finally her entire body stiffened and she clung to him in a glorious climax, silky walls clamping down on him so tight she almost pushed his right out.

With a groan he managed to thrust in to her core as her pussy desperately milked him, then filled her with his seed in what felt like a dozen powerful spurts.

They both collapsed together as they came down from their orgasms, limp and beaming and nuzzling each other lovingly.

Dare would've been happy to cuddle for a while, but after less than a minute Pella began squirming in his arms and looked up at him, still panting. Her soft brown eyes were shining with love and devotion, a sight to melt any man's heart.

"Still one more hole to clean," she said with a giggle. "You're still up, right?"

He was. "Ready when you are."

"Yay!" she shouted happily, pulling free of his embrace to bend down over the tub again. Her tail was wagging almost hard enough to throw her off balance as she reached back with both hands to grab her round ass cheeks, and with effort pulled the slippery globes apart to reveal her asshole. "Please finish cleaning me. That's where I'm dirtiest, so take your time."

Dare groaned at her words, eagerly waiting for Zuri to finish spreading more of the lubricated cleaning solution on his cock with her tiny hands. As soon as she was done he crouched to kiss his little goblin lover in appreciation, then stepped forward and pressed the tip of his cock to Pella's crinkled rosebud, beginning to press.

The dog girl panted with need. "Go slow at first please, my mate," she gasped. "It's been a long time since I've had my asshole cleaned."

She wasn't lying; her little pucker was so tight that even with the lubricated solution and her copious love juices it took a few minutes of slow, careful stretching with Pella tense and quivering, tail straight out and stiff.

As hot as the idea of fucking this beautiful woman in the ass was, and much as Dare enjoyed the sensation of her tight little ring crushing his tip as he slowly pushed in deeper, he didn't want her to feel this sort of discomfort. "I'm going to stop," he said, gently patting her round bottom. "We can stretch you out with fingers to get you ready for-"

"No!" Pella growled. "It's fine. This may be the biggest thing I've ever had in me, but it's just stretching a bit. Once we get your head past the entrance I can start to adjust."

He hesitated, torn between consideration and lust. "Are you su-"

"I'm not made of glass!" She shoved herself backwards hard, letting out a soft yelp as his head finally pushed the last bit past her ring and it closed around his shaft.

They both swore simultaneously at the sensation, and then the dog girl's tail began wagging again. "There," she said, panting a bit. "Give it a minute or two, then you can start moving."

Dare ran his hands over her smooth backside, then reached between her legs and began rubbing her button, causing her to squirm in pleasure. He could feel her crushingly tight ring begin to loosen as she relaxed, and after a minute or two her tail playfully slapped his chest. "Okay, go ahead. Slowly."

He pushed forward slowly and gently, slipping deeper millimeter by pleasurable millimeter while Pella panted, gasped, and squirmed. "How you doing?" he asked, stroking her tail.

"You're so . . . huge," she moaned. "This is . . . going to be . . . glorious! Just a bit . . . more time . . . to adjust, and we'll have . . . so much fun!" His cock twitched at her words, and she giggled.

It turned out the fun started a bit sooner for Dare. He reached the place where he bottomed out in the dog girl's pussy and was able to keep right on going, her tight ring stimulating his shaft as he kept going, and going.

"Oh god, you're in deep!" Pella gasped. "How much more?"

Dare looked; the sight of his cock buried deep in her tightly stretched asshole was so sexy he felt his balls churning. "Holy shit, only an inch or so," he gasped. "I might actually be able to go balls deep."

Her tail wagged furiously. "That'll be a first for this monster, won't it?"

"Aside from the slime girls and my shadowy lover, yeah. But neither of them felt anywhere near this good." He looked up at the ceiling. "No offense, Benefactor."

His lovers both laughed at that.

Since Pella already knew about his abilities and had found out about his mysterious benefactor, there wasn't much point in holding back the fact that he'd had odd dream/not dream sex with her shadowy manifestation, and they occasionally had phone-ish sex via the system commands menu.

He was relieved that she was cool with it, and in fact cool with the idea of him having a harem in general and fucking whoever he wanted. He supposed that if canids followed an alpha system, it only made sense that harems would be common.

"Let's do it!" the dog girl said eagerly. "I can take another inch! I think!"

Dare slowly kept pushing while she continued to whine and wag her tail. Until finally, wonder of wonders, he felt his thighs press against her firm cheeks in full contact, his entire length lovingly embraced by her insides.

"Gods, Pella, I love you," he gasped.

The beautiful woman giggled and waggled her ass teasingly against his crotch. "Then show me."

Grinning, he gently pulled out all but the tip, then pushed inside again. The sensation of tight warmth made his head spin, and he relished the feel of his thighs slapping her ass again.

Going balls deep in her bowels and feeling every inch of pleasure along his length had to be the most incredible thing he'd ever felt. Dare had only tried anal once before, aside from with slime girls of course where any hole was pretty much the same, and it was an entirely different feeling.

It was incredible.

Dare felt himself reaching the tipping point after only a couple thrusts and grit his teeth, focusing on anything else to hold off his orgasm. He paused for a moment to compose himself, then withdrew and thrust in again. And again.

"Daaarrrrrre!" Pella whined as he went balls deep in her yet again, pushing for every bit of depth he could manage. He felt her asshole clench around his base and a flood of her juices flow over his balls and down her thighs, and that was as much as he could take.

With a groan he grabbed her wide, perfect hips and pulled her into him, unloading deep in her bowels.

The dog girl squealed, tail thrashing as her asshole winked around his pulsing shaft and she squirted all over his thighs.

They both collapsed to the ground, lying on their sides with Dare still holding her desperately as his cock gradually wilted inside her. "Wow," he panted.

"Wow wow," she agreed. "We need to do that again soon." She laughed ruefully. "Maybe in a week or so."

Dare laughed as well and twisted slightly to look over at Zuri, in time to catch her hastily pulling her fingers from her butt, sharp cheeks flushing dark green in embarrassment. "Goblins don't do anal?" he teased.

She blushed harder. "Our mates sate themselves how they wish." She stared at his wilting cock still buried deep in the dog girl's ass, nibbling her lip with her sharp teeth. "But I didn't realize we could enjoy it, too."

Considering the high fertility of goblins and Zuri's general horniness, it came as a bit of a surprise that her race had such a limited knowledge of sex. No kissing, no cunnilingus, no anal, generally not even much foreplay . . . did they just get straight to humping like bunnies?

He held out an arm in invitation for her to join their cuddling. "Want to give it a try?"

She looked genuinely nervous. "I don't think it's physically possible to fit that inside me. The ###### ######## that allows races of different sizes to comfortably mate and bear each other's children doesn't apply to all holes."

"She's right," Pella agreed, wiggling her butt against his crotch until his limp dick plopped out. "Otherwise that would've been a lot less fun."

"How about fingers?" Dare teased. "You seemed to do just fine with those."

His goblin lover gave an embarrassed giggle and slid off the chair. An act made easier by her copious arousal coating the polished wood. Then she almost shyly made her way over and draped herself atop them both.

"Pella?" he asked. "You want to do the honors?"

The dog girl smiled eagerly, tail wagging, but shook her head. "I think it's my turn to watch."

Zuri spoke up, sounding hesitant. "Can we do the other stuff first?" She rubbed Pella's soapy shoulder, looking at him bashfully. "I want you to bathe me just like that."

He laughed and kissed her silky black hair. "It would be my pleasure."

And it certainly was.

Dare gave her little body the same loving treatment he'd given Pella, substituting his fingers for his cock when he got to her shockingly tight little asshole. She seemed to enjoy it well enough, but she didn't orgasm from it.

After that his two lovers worked together to bathe him, showering him with affection in a way he definitely enjoyed and appreciated. Pella even dragged him down to the ground again so the two soapy women could rub themselves on him, and his goblin lover coaxed one last orgasm from him while giving him the best tit fuck he'd ever had.

When the dog girl mischievously suggested that Zuri put the lubricated cleaning solution on her hand and use the entire thing to clean his insides, ie his asshole, Dare laughingly refused. That final orgasm had finished the job of wearing him out, and while he wasn't completely opposed to the idea of being fisted by his goblin lover, especially after watching her fist herself, he didn't think he had the energy for it tonight.

So the three of them purposefully returned to the tub, where they all worked together to actually wash each other. Although not without a plenty of groping, some teasing spanks, and more than a little laughter.

"Thank you, Dare," Pella told him solemnly as they finished up and began drying each other off with the few remaining clean towels. She'd been wiping down his shoulders and stomach, but abruptly abandoned the effort and dropped the towel so she could hug him tight with her wet, naked body. She kissed him lovingly then rested her head on his shoulder, tail wagging contentedly. "This is the most wonderful time I've had in four years. I'm so happy right now."

Dare felt a surge of warmth from more than just the sexy body pressed against him and hugged her back. "I'm glad to hear that." She made a contented noise and hugged him tighter, rubbing against him, and he cleared his throat as he felt his cock stir against her stomach and pubic mound. "We just got finished washing," he reminded her.

"Right!" The dog girl snatched up the towel and finished drying him, then handed it over so he could return the favor.

They dressed to return to the room the girls had arranged for the night, passing a disgruntled looking serving girl headed towards the bath room to clean up. Dare felt a bit bad for her and gave her several silver for her efforts, which seemed to cheer her up.

Although he wondered if her mood would sour again when she saw the mess they'd made; Zuri had used her Cleanse Target spell as part of their final washing up, but it could only do so much.

The bedroom was small but comfortable, with a bed easily large enough to hold six if needed. It had a good thick comforter, but with the heat of an early summer night it wouldn't be used.

In fact, the girls prevailed on him to sleep in the nude. "It's too hot tonight, especially when we're all steamy from the bath," Pella argued.

Zuri nodded. "Besides, with three bodies in the bed it'll get even warmer."

Dare had a sneaking suspicion that wasn't their main motivation, but he certainly wasn't about to argue with the idea of snuggling up between two sexy, naked women and having the best sleep of his life.

Although as it turned out, given everyone involved the arrangement they eventually settled on was Dare and Pella cuddled up facing each other, with Zuri's tiny body snuggled between them.

They pulled a thin sheet over them, and then in the pleasant tangle of entwined limbs and last affectionate kisses, caresses, and loving words gradually settled down to sleep.

Chapter Twelve
Chased Out

Dare woke in the early morning as the room grew brighter around him.

The windows had been well placed to keep out morning sunlight but provide good light for the room the rest of the day, but with the shutters open wide to let in the night breezes it was still bright enough.

Especially for someone who'd grown accustomed to waking at dawn. A far cry from his previous life, when he'd been a night owl whenever his work schedule let him get away with it.

Zuri and Pella were still deeply asleep, faces peaceful and bodies soft as they cuddled against him. He could've stayed like that forever, but after a few minutes his growling stomach dragged him reluctantly out of bed.

He moved carefully to not disturb his lovers, hoping they'd get as much sleep as they wanted on this relaxing morning. To his relief his movements didn't wake them, although Pella did murmur softly and cuddle Zuri closer against her large breasts.

It was an adorable sight, not to mention a sexy one. Dare sort of would've liked to see what they did when they woke up, or maybe be there to enjoy it with them.

But last night's play had given him a good workout, and he was looking forward to a big breakfast; the tantalizing cooking smells wafting beneath the door from the inn's kitchens below was enough to prompt him to pull on his pants and shirt, then make his way down to the common room.

The fat innkeeper, Jekk, hurried over as he came down the stairs, eagerly dry-washing his hands. "Ah, good morning Master . . . Dare, was it?" At Dare's nod he offered a hospitable smile. "I trust you've enjoyed our amenities thus far?"

"Very much." Dare motioned towards the dozen or so dining

215

patrons scattered around the room. "Looking forward to enjoying a good breakfast as well."

"Of course." The man ushered him to a table and got him comfortably seated. "Your party seems to favor meat and, ah, dessert items?"

"Actually, I wouldn't say no to some good baked goods and dairy," Dare said; he'd mostly been subsisting on meat and foraged greens and mushrooms and things like that, and he wouldn't complain about stuff he had a hard time making himself.

The innkeeper grinned. "How about some flapjacks and maple syrup, buttered toast, and a bacon omelet complete with onions, peppers, and cheese?"

Dare's mouth immediately began watering at the prospect. "That sounds fantastic. And coffee or tea if you've got it, with milk and sugar."

The man's smile turned slightly quizzical. "Coffee's an expensive luxury item I don't keep in stock, I'm afraid, but tea we can certainly do. We'll be right out with your order." He bustled away.

Dare settled back to take in the peaceful, quiet morning atmosphere of the common room. He could admit that he wouldn't mind waking up to scenes like this every morning, although camping in the wilds had its own benefits. Especially with Zuri and Pella there with him.

A few minutes later a serving girl came around with toast and tea to start him off, informing him the rest would be out as it finished cooking. Which was a pleasant change from waiting up to a half hour until it was all ready to be brought out at once.

The young woman seemed to have a serious stick up her butt, not quite giving him the stink eye as she served him and wasting no time walking away. It caught him a bit by surprise; maybe it was a bit egotistical, but with his looks he was used to a different response.

As Dare ate he noticed a few of the other serving girls also giving him dirty looks, while the rest seemed embarrassed to even look at him. Although the world didn't seem to have gone completely upside-down, since at least a couple of them looked at him speculatively and smiled whenever he glanced their way.

He made his way to one of the smiling girls, a slender, pretty redhead a bit older than him with big green eyes, full lips, and pale cheeks that had a rosy flush from her bustling work.

"Did I do something wrong?" he asked, motioning to one of her scowling coworkers.

"No. I mean, not really." The serving girl's rosy flush turned into a genuine blush, all the more noticeable with her porcelain skin, and she looked around before answering in a low voice. "It's just that the bath room is just above the kitchens, and with the drain pipe we can usually hear anything louder than a whisper up there."

Dare felt his cheeks heat. "Oh." He hadn't considered the noise he and his lovers were making, or the bother it might cause the staff and other customers. "I'm sorry."

She waved that aside. "More than a few people who pay for a bath make love in there. It's not like we haven't heard it before." She blushed even more fiercely and bit her lip. "Although I've never heard anyone as, um, enthusiastic."

Well great. Granted, anyone who looked at him with his beautiful companions would probably assume he was fucking them. But he hadn't wanted to broadcast it to the world. "Would you apologize to the staff for me? I didn't realize we were causing a problem."

The slender redhead grinned at him. "Oh, I didn't mind. You sounded like you were having fun, and it gave us some entertainment as we worked."

Dare rolled his eyes and turned back towards his table.

Before he could go a step the serving girl caught his arm. She looked around again, scarlet with embarrassment at her daring, then leaned close. "I can come to your room if you want," she whispered, looking equal parts nervous and eager. She bit her lip again. "I want to know what you were doing that the goblin and canid seemed to love so much."

He thought of giving this slender, wide-eyed slip of a girl a bath like he'd done for his lovers, running his hands over her small breasts and cute little butt and delicate pussy, and his cock stirred in his pants.

217

"I would love-" he started to say.

The inn's sturdy front door burst open, interrupting him as two well armed guards in plate armor stormed in. Both were big and obviously strong, although one was closer to average height while the other was well over six feet tall.

Everyone sprang to their feet at their entrance, plates and cutlery clattering. More than a few patrons looked alarmed, even nervous as if they had something to hide, and Dare had to work to keep his own expression smooth.

He and his lovers hadn't done anything that would bring the guards down on them (unless of course noise complaints were a thing), but somehow he got the sinking suspicion these two men were here for them.

Especially with what the guard at the gate had said yesterday about the new Lord Kinnran not liking dog girls; maybe the nobleman had done more than simply raise taxes on canids.

"Innkeeper!" the shorter man bellowed, yanking off his helmet. "I'll speak to the innkeeper at once!"

It wasn't a suggestion, and the serving girls stared at the guard in terror. A few moments later Jekk rushed out of the kitchen, mopping at his brow. "I'm the innkeeper, my good guardsman," he said in a jovial tone, although his face was pale. "How can I assist the Watch?"

The taller guardsman spoke, voice deep and dangerous. "We've got word of an adventurer entering this establishment with stolen property, or possibly a runaway pet suspect of terrible crimes."

Dare was impressed that the innkeeper showed the professionalism, or whatever it was, to avoid so much as glancing his way. "What runaway pet?" Jekk demanded.

"A canid," the smaller guard snapped. "Tall, late 20s, golden retriever coloring. Tracker class with a level of 24 as of her disappearance four years ago. Anyone in possession of her is suspect in the disappearance of Lord Kinnran at that time, on a bounty issued by the new Lord Kinnran."

Dare had started backing towards the stairs the moment he heard the word "canid", but as the guard spoke several of the serving maids, including the girl he'd been talking to, gasped and looked his way. Which of course drew the attention of the two armed and armored men, who were obviously no fools.

Shit.

Turning, Dare used every ounce of his speed to bolt for the stairs, flying up them four at a time.

"Stop, thief!" the shorter guard yelled. Dare heard the clank of armor as the two men took up the chase.

Damn. Damnit. Shit shit *shit*. People were looking for Pella, even after all this time? And they thought anyone with her might've done something to her previous master?

How was he going to get out of this?

Sure, Dare could probably take the guards even if they were only a couple levels lower than him, especially if Pella jumped into the fray. But even if he'd been willing to fight innocent men who were just doing their duty, it would be a very bad idea.

More dangerous than the weapons the men bore, or even the authority they wielded to uphold the law and keep the peace in the name of their lord, was the fact that if you attacked a guard the system immediately flagged you as a fugitive, and if you killed one you were marked kill or capture on sight.

At that point the bounty they'd eventually put on your head was just a formality; you were effectively an exile anywhere in that region, or possibly even the entire kingdom if your crimes were severe enough. And the only hope you had was to turn yourself in, hoping you weren't killed in the process, and throw yourself at the mercy of a magistrate, judge, or local lord.

That just left the option of running.

With Fleetfoot he should be able to escape without too much trouble, although he'd have to carry Zuri to do it. But then what, a kingdom-wide manhunt?

This had gone bad faster than he could've imagined.

Dare burst into the room he shared with his lovers. To his relief Pella with her keen hearing must've heard the commotion of the guards bursting in, because she and Zuri were awake, had tossed on their tunics, and were scrambling to gather their things to flee.

"Here!" the dog girl shouted, filling his arms with the rest of their clothes, all three packs, and their weapons. "You take all this, I'll carry Zuri!" She snatched up the little goblin and bolted out the door, Dare hot on her heels.

The guards, slowed by their armor, had just reached the top of the stairs, still shouting for him to stop. Pella turned the other way and sprinted for the small back stairs the serving girls used, Dare putting himself between his lovers and the pursuing guards in case they threw any weapons.

They crashed down the narrow stairs in a bumping rush, the possessions he held smacking into walls and door frames as they spilled out into the kitchen. The cooks at the stoves spun, gawking at the sight of a dog girl carrying a goblin and a man burdened down with a bunch of clothes and packs bolting through their kitchen.

"Sorry for the trouble!" Pella shouted as she slammed her shoulder into the door leading out into the stable yard.

They tore through the small, muddy space, burst through a gate, and pelted down the street. They must've looked sufficiently odd to draw shouts and jeers from the townspeople out and about. As well as more than a little laughter, as if people thought this was all some folly by a drunken fool and his lovers.

The laughter cut off as shrill whistles sounded from the stable yard, the two guards alerting the rest of the Watch as they burst out onto the street in slow but dogged pursuit.

"What the poop-flinging tumult is going on, Dare?" Zuri demanded, peeking over the dog girl's shoulder at him with wide eyes.

"Pella's being hunted as either stolen property or a runaway who betrayed her old master, and they think I'm her accomplice," he said tersely.

"What?" the dog girl exclaimed, aghast; she must not have heard the finer details, just the general commotion. "Who's spreading those lies? Who would accuse me of being so disloyal?"

"The guard said the new Lord Kinnran issued the bounty."

Pella stopped dead for just a moment, before a fresh flurry of whistles from down a side street got her going again. "Braley thinks I hurt my master?" she asked, voice trembling. She looked devastated, voice heartbroken and forlorn, and Zuri hugged her comfortingly and patted her back.

"No idea," Dare said. "But we need to get out of here. We can worry about sorting this out once we're safe."

They continued to draw surprised stares and shouts from everyone on the street as they bolted past, which was less than ideal. But considering the guards were converging from all sides blowing those godsdamn whistles, Dare didn't really expect to escape unnoticed anyway.

Speaking of which, they'd probably get a dozen arrows in their backs if they tried to scale the wall while being so closely pursued. That only left the gates, which were sure to be guarded.

"Pella, when we get to the gate put Zuri on my back," he said. "You're going to need your hands free to Subdue the guards at the gates so we can get past them. Avoid injuring them at all costs." Even though she had a bounty on her it was technically a civil one, or however they judged that sort of thing here, so she hadn't been designated a fugitive or criminal by the system.

He wanted to keep it that way. Although just to double check he silently asked his benefactor if Pella using crowd control on the guards would be okay.

"It's fine . . . abilities that don't injure a guard aren't considered an attack," her disembodied voice said, low and urgent. "At worst she'll be considered evading justice, which you three are doing anyway."

"How do we get out of this?" Dare asked aloud, drawing concerned looks from his dog girl lover and Zuri. Neither of them seemed to have an answer.

His benefactor didn't either. Or at least not one he liked. "Baron Kinnran is the lord of this town. If you turn yourself in you'll be throwing yourself at his mercy, and he seems to have already decided Pella is guilty."

"So what, leave his territory? Maybe the region, or even the whole

221

kingdom?"

She hesitated. "I'm interfering too much. I'm going to get the others annoyed at me. Besides, holding your hand all the time it takes away the fun of watching you."

"*What*?" Dare shouted incredulously. She didn't answer.

Son of a bitch, she was leaving him to his own devices at a time like this? Sure, he knew she'd brought him to Collisa to entertain her with his exploits, and interfering whenever he ran into trouble would make things pretty boring for her.

But it seemed like her motives weren't quite as selfish these days, and he'd kind of been hoping he could count on her if things got really bad. Like they were right now. Was she really that constrained in what she could do?

"Dare, your thinking aloud is kind of freaking me out," Zuri said hesitantly. Then her voice brightened. "Or are you talking to your patron spirit? Is she telling you anything useful?"

"You're talking to your patron spirit?" Pella repeated, confused. "You mean you can contact her any time, without needing to meditate for a day or conduct an elaborate ritual or go to a sacred place or anything?"

"Any time but right now, apparently, which means we're on our own," Dare snapped. He dodged a group of weary laborers plodding down the street, tore around a corner, and a hundred yards ahead spotted the gates as they came into view.

Almost there. Better yet, thanks to the speed they were moving the guards who'd been pursuing or converging on them were all behind or to the sides, and the only guards blocking their escape at the gate were the usual ones.

Pella swung Zuri onto his back, where the little goblin clung tight around his neck, and loped ahead. She smoothly ducked the slash of the nearer guard, using Disarm to catch his wrist in some sort of pinch that caused him to drop his sword. Then she tackled the man to the ground with Overpower, leaving him momentarily stunned.

Dare reached the gate and bolted through as the dog girl Tracker leapt at the remaining female guard. The guard managed to slash

Pella's arm, but while his lover yelped in pain she didn't look hindered as she put the armored woman in a full body hold with Subdue.

Once he and Zuri were safely away from the gate Pella broke free of her hold and bolted away, leaving the other woman to laboriously drag herself to her feet and try to pursue with the other guard. The dog girl easily caught up to Dare, retrieved her gear as well as some of Zuri's, and together they bolted away at over 20 miles an hour, leaving Yurin far behind.

When he finally felt like it was safe he had them stop to heal Pella's cut, properly dress, equip their gear, and put on their packs.

"Nice to be prepared to travel fast now that the pursuit's far behind us," Pella said wryly as she tugged on the leather bracers he'd bought for her. Although her expression immediately became miserable and distressed again as the reality of their situation slammed back down on her.

Once they were ready Dare made for the woods to the east; the plains stretched in every other direction, with the Gadris Mountains to the north that formed the border between the Kovana and Bastion regions still days away. That left the forest as their best option for ducking pursuit.

Assuming anyone bothered.

He actually wasn't too worried about the guards themselves. He was more concerned that they, or Lord Kinnran, might call out whatever adventurers were stationed in the town. That, or that bounty hunters and traveling adventurers might come after them for the bounty.

Can I kill bounty hunters or other people who attack me? he silently asked his benefactor. There was no response, so he grit his teeth and spoke aloud. "Will the system flag me for fighting any bounty hunters who pursue us?"

On his back he felt Zuri shrug, while Pella shook her head. "As long as you're not caught." She hesitated. "But I don't want to hurt anyone, Dare."

"Neither do I," he assured her. "But if they're trying to kill us to collect a bounty I'll defend you, whatever it takes." At her crestfallen look he hastily added, "After we've tried every other option, including subduing them or outright running away."

The dog girl's shoulders slumped. "You don't need to worry about that. I'm causing you trouble, and you don't deserve that. I'll go back to my master's family and turn myself in, explain that you didn't have anything to do with this. Then you won't be in trouble anymore."

Dare immediately shook his head. "No, *we'll* go talk to them. And if we can't make them see reason then we'll run."

"I can't let you do that," she insisted. "You're only in trouble because of me, but you could all end up in prison or as slaves if you continue to associate with me."

"Then I'll be a slave again," Zuri said firmly. "You're my friend and my fellow mate . . . I won't abandon you."

"Neither will I?" Dare agreed. "You told me that your master's family will probably send you back to the markets to sell to another master, and there's no way I'm letting that happen."

Pella's ears drooped, puppy-like expression miserable. "Actually, even if my family believes me about what happened, after ignoring my duty all these years no master would trust me. They'll probably sell me to the breeders, or maybe a brothel."

"In that case there's no way in hell I'm letting you turn yourself over to them," he said sharply. "You're my mate and I love you. I'll gladly become an outlaw to protect you."

Zuri's face paled, but she nodded fiercely in agreement.

"You say that, but you don't understand!" their friend snapped. "It won't just be Kovana or even all of Haraldar. This bounty might follow you to other kingdoms, and even out into the wilds. You'd be a fugitive, maybe for life."

Dare smiled, ruffling her floppy ears. "Then we can all be fugitives together. A family."

"A family," Zuri agreed.

As for Pella, she looked at them with shining eyes, hope lighting up her features and tail beginning to wag. "All right," she said quietly. "As long as you swear that if we get in a situation where I can't avoid my fate, you two will save yourselves."

He willingly swore the oath, not feeling the slightest bit guilty that he could rationalize it that he'd never believe there was a situation where he couldn't do anything to help Pella avoid her fate.

Maybe Zuri was thinking along the same lines, or she was more willing to follow her friend's wishes. Either way, she also made the promise.

"Thank you." The dog girl hugged them both tightly for a few minutes, tears streaming from her eyes. Then she took a ragged breath, straightened, and motioned to the southwest. "All right, let's go to my master's estate."

* * * * *

Unsurprisingly, Lord Kinnran's estate was a sprawling patch of hilly plains with a river running through it, planted fields and pastureland stretching as far as the eye could see.

The manor itself was built on a low hill with a broad, flat top, orchards of fruit trees filling much of the space and the yard enclosed by a thick stand of shade trees. The only entrance in that natural barrier was the dirt road leading to the circular gravel drive, which led right up to the front doors of a main structure that was just big enough to be considered a mansion.

At Dare's insistence they snuck up to the manor through the orchards, and he was glad they did when they reached the barrier of shade trees surrounding the yard and he saw the horses crowded into the stable yard. Two men in the livery of the Yurin city guard watched the horses, answering the mystery of who the horses belonged to.

"Looks like the new lord, Braley did you say his name was, knows you've been spotted," he said grimly. "They're probably organizing some sort of manhunt."

Pella's ears drooped in distress. "We should go talk to him and sort this out right away." She started to leave the cover of the trees.

Dare caught her arm and pulled her back. "It's better to wait. If things go wrong I'd rather not have a dozen Level 20 guards on hand to cause us problems."

Zuri nodded. "Besides, if Baron Kinnran has a bunch of armed men around him he'll be more inclined to just order your arrest, instead of hearing you out."

The dog girl obviously wasn't happy about it, but she reluctantly settled in to wait. At his insistence they also ate a hasty lunch, in case they had to do more running in the near future.

It turned out to be a long wait, enough that they eventually ate a cold dinner as well. The guards didn't seem in any hurry to leave, and Dare had to fight the temptation to sneak up to the manor and try to listen in at one of the open windows.

The sun was low on the horizon before the guards finally emerged from the main building and sought out their horses. Nobody from the manor emerged to see them off, and they didn't seem in any particular hurry as they mounted up and rode away.

"I wonder if that means the guards aren't going to search for us," Zuri whispered.

Dare shrugged. "Maybe because they're leaving it up to the town's resident adventurers or bounty hunters."

"All the more reason to get this sorted out before they start coming after us," Pella said grimly. She started to stand.

Again he held her back. "Let's give it a while in case the guards forgot something."

"This is killing me," she muttered as she slumped back down.

He soothingly stroked her hair and tail, and in response she settled down with her head resting on his lap as he continued to comfort her. Zuri joined them, cuddling up close to the dog girl.

A half hour later Dare finally stirred, resting a hand on each of his lovers' shoulders. "Ready?" he whispered.

The women nodded, and together they rose and started quietly towards the manor.

Although there was still some time before dark, the main building's windows were already lighting up with lanterns in several of the rooms. Including most of the first floor, with bright, cheery light streaming invitingly from all the windows.

At the door Dare motioned quietly to Pella, to see if she wanted to do the honors. She nodded, took a deep breath, then caught the brass knocker in both hands and pounded it against the door hard enough to make the sound shiver through the house and across the yard.

"Coming!" a cheerful woman's voice called from within. A few moments later the door flew open and a girl in her late teens stood silhouetted in the light pouring out around her. He had a faint impression of a tall, willowy figure in a comfortable gown, with dark brown hair and somewhat mousy but pleasant features.

The young woman's eyes widened when she saw Pella, and she stood openmouthed for a few seconds. Then she squealed with joy and threw her arms around the dog girl. "Pella!" she shouted. "You're alive!"

Pella looked surprised for a moment, then tears filled her eyes and she hugged the woman back fiercely. "Mistress Ama," she said. "It's so good to see you."

Ama abruptly drew back, expression falling. "What about Father? Those guards and Braley were all saying such terrible things about you, but I didn't believe them." Her kind voice faltered. "But if you're here without him . . ."

The dog girl hung her head. "I'm sorry, Mistress. I did my best, but-"

"Get away from her, Amalisa!" a harsh voice shouted from deeper in the house.

Ama jumped guiltily. But not as much as Pella, who leapt backwards with a whimper. Dare looked past them to see a man standing on the rightmost flight of the foyer's double staircase holding a drawn dueling blade.

A tall, regal woman who was likely his wife stood behind him, hand on his shoulder. By her positioning she might've looked like she was seeking protection behind the man, but her expression suggested she was all but pushing him forward.

"I said back away," the man repeated, approaching swiftly to move between Amalisa and the door. "This bitch killed our father."

Pella whimpered again, tail drooping with obvious devastation.

"Don't be stupid, Braley," Amalisa snapped. "I never believed that," she assured the dog girl.

"No, you believed the bitch died with Father," Braley said harshly. "Because that's the *only* explanation for why she wouldn't have returned if something happened to him." He leveled his blade at Pella. "Only here she is, alive and well."

Dare stepped in front of the man, holding his spear casually but ready to swiftly bring it to bear. "You point a sword at someone, that's a threat of deadly force," he said quietly. "We've come here to sort out this misunderstanding . . . are you sure this is how you want to greet us?"

The young nobleman scowled, then seemed to notice that Dare was five levels higher than him and licked his lips. "Sort it out how? By turning the bitch over to us?"

"By explaining what happened and trusting to your wise and considered justice," Dare said. "May we enter?"

Braley scowled and seemed inclined to refuse, then glanced at Amalisa and back at his wife. "Fine. Leave your weapons at the entrance."

"As you wish. We're your guests here." Dare didn't hesitate to set his weapons and pack beside the door, motioning for his companions to do the same; he wasn't particularly worried about Braley.

The young nobleman was a Duelist, but at Level 17 his abilities weren't particularly fearsome to someone of Dare's speed. And even less so to Pella, 11 levels higher than the young man and able to fall back on her unarmed combat ability.

Not to mention that with her spells Zuri didn't need weapons to be dangerous.

Braley grudgingly led the way to a sitting room adjacent to the dining room, where several comfortable couches and chairs were arranged around a fireplace. He didn't motion for them to sit, but Dare did so anyway, settling down on the couch with Zuri seated beside him.

Pella stood beside the couch, stiff and miserable. Likewise, after Braley sat in a chair across from them his wife took a position standing behind him, a hand on his shoulder.

Amalisa acted the part of the gracious host and poured them whiskey from a fine decanter. She started to pour herself a glass as well until her brother snapped a rebuke at her. Abashed, she hurried to a chair near his and settled down, pulling her feet up underneath her in a comfortable position.

"All right," the new Lord Kinnran growled. "Let's hear your lies."

Pella started to protest, but Dare put a hand on her shoulder. Then he sat silently, staring at the man.

Braley finally shifted in obvious discomfort. "What?" he snapped.

"I'm waiting for you to apologize for insulting the integrity of myself and my companions," Dare replied. "You'll find I can be very patient."

The young lord scowled. "Are you a jester, stranger? Quit wasting my time and speak, or leave."

Dare didn't reply, holding his gaze until the man looked away.

"Brother," Amalisa said into the tense silence, "as Baron of House Kinnran it behooves you to be civil. And our guest is obviously educated and civilized. Let us greet him with the same high standards."

"Are you fucking serious?" Braley took a deep breath, with effort calming himself. "Very well, I'll give you a chance to say your piece and determine their veracity for myself."

That was probably the closest to an apology they were going to get. Dare inclined his head. "First off, let me tell you that I my companion Zuri first met Miss Pella in the woods south of here, near Hamalis. We were hunting in the woods and came upon a beautifully tended clearing, a garden of flowers and stone walkways leading to a grave befitting a king, topped by a lovingly carved headstone."

Amalisa gasped and raised both hands to her mouth. "Father's grave?" she whispered.

He smiled at her gently. "Yes. As good a resting place as any man could hope for. Created and faithfully tended all these years by Pella, who even after death refused to leave his side."

"Bullshit," Braley snapped. "An obvious ploy to reach our hearts and make us ignore your crimes."

"A claim we can easily confirm by going to your father's grave," Dare countered.

"Oh yes, please!" Amalisa said. "After so long not knowing his fate for sure, it would mean so much to be able to pray at his grave and hold a proper funeral."

Pella's head hung. "I'm so sorry I deprived you that for all these years," she said, voice heavy with shame.

"Deprived her by murdering our father," the young lord said coldly.

Dare fixed him with a steady look. "I believe we've already talked about you insulting our integrity."

"No, Dare, it's all right," Pella said, resting a hand on his shoulder. "They have a right to be angry at me, after so long not knowing."

"I know exactly-" Braley began.

Dare cut in. "Pella, I believe now's the time to tell your family what happened."

She nodded and straightened, looking equal parts sorrowful and determined as she explained the hunting trip she'd taken with her master, following his order to Subdue a monster, and him being attacked by a Level 22 eagle while she was distracted.

Tears filled the dog girl's eyes as she described her desperate attempt to save her master, standing over his body and fighting two enemies at once. Only to find him dead by the time she was able try to tend his wounds.

She also spoke without hesitation of her fear of returning home, of facing her family's grief and anger, and her decision to stay by her master's side instead.

Pella was weeping openly by the end, as was Amalisa. The young woman even tried to go to the dog girl to hug her, only to be snapped back to her seat by her brother.

Even Dare and Zuri were moved by her story, if mostly because of their love for Pella.

But through it all, Braley sat stony-faced, and if anything his wife was even more cold and condemning. As soon as the dog girl finished the aristocratic woman bent gracefully to whisper in her husband's ear.

The new Lord Kinnran nodded and stood. "I agree, we've heard enough." He rested a hand on the hilt of his sword. "It's been my experience that the loyalty of dog girls is grossly exaggerated. A more believable explanation for your disappearance is that you killed Father, or more likely conspired with these thugs you travel with to see him murdered, then fled. The only reason you've returned now is because you discovered the bounty on your head and wanted to try to con us into lifting it."

Pella stiffened. "I would've died before harming Master," she growled, not in anger or challenge but with perfect conviction. "I loved him with all my heart, and love him still. As I love you, my family."

"Enough, bitch!" Braley roared, fury twisting his features into an ugly mask. "As Baron of Yurin it's my right to judge you, and I judge you guilty of the murder of my father, Lord Devastes Kinnran."

Chapter Thirteen
Family

Terrible silence filled the room at the pronouncement.

Pella visibly shrank, not to much at the judgment itself as at the condemnation by her family. Dare's heart broke at her utterly devastated expression.

He stood, resting a protective hand on his lover's shoulder. "Lord Braley, please reconsider this hasty judgment," he said stiffly.

"I've had four years to consider this!" the young man shouted, shaking with rage. "Four years to live in grief and uncertainty, watching my family's position and my father's legacy crumble because I couldn't even confirm his death and step forward as his heir. Watching my sister weep, inconsolable."

He pointed furiously at Pella. "All because this faithless bitch betrayed my father and ran off! He gave her everything, he even let his marriage to our mother implode because he refused to set her aside to sate Mother's jealousy, and this was how she repaid him."

"No . . ." the dog girl whimpered, voice barely audible.

"You're wrong, but that's beside the point," Dare said. "There's got to be a compromise we can reach, an alternative. I could buy Pella from you."

"Why do you care?" Braley's wife demanded furiously. "What's this bitch to you? Have you stolen her and claim to be her new master?"

"Absolutely not," Dare snapped. "Pella is my friend and my companion, free and equal." He squeezed the dog girl's shoulder. "And I consider myself fortunate to have earned her trust and love, as I've offered her my love in turn. I'll do whatever it takes to protect her."

The young man laughed in disbelief. "Love? Have you been courting this pet as if she's human? That's almost as pathetic as Father ruining his marriage for her." He sneered at Pella with utter scorn.

233

"What is it about this bitch that turns men into fools? Does she have the cunt of a goddess?"

"You're one to talk, Braley," Amalisa snapped, furious as well. "Most of your bitterness is that you tried to seduce her behind Father's back, and she didn't even consider it because her loyalty to him is unshakeable. Then you tried to mount her by force and Father beat you with his own hand. You've never forgiven-"

"Shut the fuck up!" Braley screamed, whipping out his sword and pointing it at Pella. "There *is* no compromise to be had, no better alternative. This bitch murdered Father and she going to the breeding pens or a brothel. Even if she tries to run, we'll make sure she's pursued to the ends of Shalin. And we'll keep on raising the bounty until she's captured or killed."

He pointed his weapon at Dare. "And if you try to help her we'll put a bounty on you, too."

"Braley," Amalisa began helplessly.

"Silence, Amalisa!" he roared.

"I will not!" she snapped, bursting to her feet. "You're going too far! Pella's a good girl. She was Father's faithful companion for years. And she was a good friend and protector to us. To condemn her to such a terrible life when you can't be sure she's guilty is-"

"Perfectly within my rights!" the young nobleman cut in harshly. At his shoulder his wife nodded almost smugly. He gave Amalisa a glare of withering scorn as he continued. "I am Baron Kinnran, and in this house my decision is final."

He spit on Pella, a thick glob spattering against her chest, and his voice rose shrilly. "That bitch is my property! I can sell her to be bred, turn her into a whore, or drag her up to my room and fuck her traitorous ass if I so please! I could even cut her down right here and now, and no-"

This seemed like a good moment.

Dare surged forward, slipping around a surprised Braley's sword and twisting it out of his hand. "There actually is another alternative," he said coldly. "At least for us." He pressed the blade to the nobleman's throat with casual menace. "I could just kill you right now and the bounty disappears. You're Level 17 . . . you'd be dead before you could so much as try to run."

The entire room went deathly silent and still, everyone staring at him in shock and horror. Even Zuri and Pella.

Braley swallowed carefully, staring at the blade hovering below his chin. "Are you insane?" he asked hoarsely, still managing to maintain some of his bravado. "If you kill a Baron of Haraldar, you'll be hunted wherever you go in the civilized world."

"Seems more like you're the insane one," Dare said, not needing to pretend the fury in his voice. "I've already told you I love Pella and intend to do whatever it takes to protect her. And yet here you are openly threatening to rape her or send her into a miserable life of sexual servitude. And you think I would care in the moment about the consequences of killing you?"

"Dare, what are you doing?" Zuri hissed at him. "You wouldn't really murder the son of Pella's master right in front of her. That's not who you are!"

He gave her an impatient look. "I'll do what I have to for Pella."

Braley cleared his throat. "I think maybe I approached this wrong," he offered, voice shaking. "Maybe there's some agreement to be made after all."

"Too late for that." Dare shifted the sword against the man's neck, tensing.

Pella pushed the blade out of the way, slicing her own palm in the process, and stepped in front of him, ears flattened in dangerous resolve. "Put it away, Dare," she said.

He looked at her incredulously. "What are you doing?"

"I can't let you hurt my family."

"Your family!" Dare's arm visibly trembled with his fury, making the stolen blade shake. "He treated you like a pet! He plans to send you to a life of hell! Canid or not, how can you be loyal to him?"

"Because I love him, and I love my Master," she said quietly, pain in her voice. "I could never fail him, or them. Which is why I'm asking you to stop." Her voice hardened. "No, *telling* you to."

"No!" Dare snapped, injecting fury into his voice. "Even if you hate me for this, at least you'll be free to live your life. I'll accept your hatred, accept being hunted to the ends of Collisa, for your sake."

"Dare?" Zuri asked, alarmed.

He ignored her, trying to sidestep the dog girl to get at Braley again.

Pella moved forward in a surge that surprised even him, catching his sword hand. "Don't make me choose between them and you, Dare," she growled. "For the sake of my master I'll fight you, hurt you, even kill you to protect them."

Dare stared at her in devastation. "Even now?" he whispered. "After they spit on you, called you a traitor and threatened to make you suffer horrible degradation as revenge, when you've spent all this time faithfully staying by his grave?"

She met his eyes without flinching, and by the tears glimmering in her own he knew she meant it. "Even now."

He slumped, letting the sword slip from his hand and clatter to the ground. "I would've done anything for you," he said in a broken voice.

"And you think I would've let you do *this*? Let the people I love most in this world, you and them, suffer for my sake?" Pella released him and stepped back, ears drooping, tail between her legs, tears slipping down her cheeks. "It's better this way . . . I accept my fate."

Dare dropped to his knees, surprised to find tears in his own eyes. "Pella . . ." he whispered.

She pointed at the door. "Leave, Dare, and take your goblin with you. Just forget about me and go."

He nodded heavily and stumbled to his feet, taking Zuri's hand and starting for the door.

His little lover yanked her hand free, staring up at him with her huge yellow eyes shining with tears. "What did you do?" she demanded in a heartbroken voice. "What have you done to poor Pella?"

"The best I could think of to help her," Dare replied dully.

"Help her?" she turned away from him, hugging herself miserably.

236

"What did you do?"

"We'll talk about it outside."

"What makes you think I want to hear anything you say!" Zuri sobbed and sped up her shuffle towards the door.

Her pain ripped at Dare's insides, but there was nothing he could do about it right now. He quickly glanced over his shoulder.

Pella was still standing between him and her family, but now Amalisa had moved to put herself between the dog girl and her brother. As for Braley, he'd retrieved his sword and was pacing a tight circle, face purple with embarrassment and fury.

"I'll kill him," he snarled. "I'll call every guard in the region. Put a bounty of a thousand gold on his head!" He clenched the hilt of his dueling blade with white knuckles, waving it wildly. "I'll cut him down myself! Did you see what that madman did?"

"If he'd cut your throat it would be no less than you deserve, Braley Kinnran!" Amalisa snapped. "How could you threaten to do all those awful things to Pella? She was our closest friend for years, loyal and loving to us and to Father, and always a good girl for him!"

The young noblewoman swatted furiously at her brother. "You're a brute! An ogre! And yet even after everything you did to her, the unforgivable things you threatened to do, she was still willing to fight a man who obviously loved her and only wanted to protect her. I can't believe . . ."

Dare snatched up his and Zuri's things, yanked open the door, and stepped outside, leaving the conversation behind him. His goblin lover was at his heels, still glaring at him with devastated betrayal, and it was all he could do not to throw his arms around her right then and there.

Instead he slammed the door, and then just in case anyone glanced out the window kept up his slumped, defeated posture as he scuttled down the drive.

Zuri finally spoke as she caught up to him, sounding sick. "Are we really leaving Pella?" she demanded. "I can't believe you would-"

"And yet you did believe it," he whispered, winking at her. That caused her to pause for a moment in surprise, during which time he turned aside to hide in the border of shade trees where the drive met the road.

With a sigh he dropped into a crouch, irritably wiping at his eyes.

"What in the names of all the ancestors, totem spirits, and Nature itself was that?" Zuri demanded furiously. "I can't believe you would act like such a monster."

"But I did." Dare smiled at his tiny lover, relieved to see her pain replaced by anger. Odd as that was to think. "That, my beloved, was acting. Like a monster."

She stared at him blankly. "What?"

His smile had more than a little pain in it. "Unfortunately I've never been a good actor, and Pella's too honest and straightforward to ever be convincing, so we had to make it more real than I would've liked to compensate."

"What are you talking about?" Zuri demanded, confusion only fueling her anger. "What was that in there?"

Dare shook his head grimly. "Amalisa might've been on our side, but Braley and his wife were never going to show mercy on Pella as long as they thought she was the villain. So I had to become the villain so she could be the hero."

He glanced worriedly at the manor. "I just hope it works."

Because if it didn't, Pella would meekly go where they told her even if she was over 10 levels higher than them. And he'd probably have to do something drastic to help her.

Although judging by what he'd seen of Amalisa before he left, he had reason to hope. Assuming Braley had even a shred of humanity or the slightest bit of fondness for his sister.

So even odds, in other words.

His tiny lover's eyes narrowed. "So that in there with you and Pella was just pretend?" she said, hurt and furious. "In that case why didn't you tell *me*? I was torn between wanting to cry, hating your guts then hating myself for hating you, and wishing I could run away from everything and hide in a hole forever."

Phoenix

Dare gathered her into his arms and held her close, rubbing her back. She was stiff in his arms, and he deeply regretted how his deception had affected her. "I didn't even tell Pella," he admitted. "It was an idea that came to me while we were in there . . . I had to hope that with her canid senses she'd know that I didn't have a sincere intent to kill, and she'd be smart enough to figure out what I had planned. And it looks as if she did."

He just hoped Pella would be able to forgive him.

Thankfully they didn't have long to fret. After only a few minutes the front doors opened and Pella and Amalisa came out onto the porch, the dog girl carrying her gear and pack. The two women hugged for a long time, then the dog girl hurried down the drive towards them.

Dare was pretty sure Pella knew they were there in the trees, but even so he stepped out to meet her, heart in his throat. "How did it go?"

His lover's answer came in the form of a right cross to his face.

It was no love tap, either, but a full-bodied blow by a high level unarmed combat expert with a towering fury behind it.

He was lucky his nose wasn't broken, and that he didn't end up flat on his back seeing stars for that matter. Although he still stumbled back several steps, reeling.

Pella pursued him the entire way. "You're an asshole, Dare!" she snapped as she walked straight into his chest and wrapped her arms around him, burying her face in his neck. "The biggest asshole ever."

It looked as if she wasn't going to sock him again, at least for the time being.

Dare wrapped his arms around her and gently rubbed her back. "I know, and I expect you and Zuri are going to be pissed at me for a while."

She sighed, still clutching him tight. "After you left Amalisa threw her arms around me and told Lord Braley that wherever he tried to send me, he'd better send her too. And that she'd never forgive him if he didn't pardon me and cancel the bounty after I chose them over my new master. Then, when he finally relented, she insisted that true love like ours shouldn't be broken and demanded he free me to run to you."

239

"And he did?" Zuri asked, delighted but also surprised as she hugged the dog girl.

"After I gave him every coin I had to my name," Pella said, although her tail wagged tiredly. "I was happy to hand it over, and would've just as happily given him all the loot in my trove, too."

She made a joyful sound and her tail wagged harder as she scrabbled in her pouch for some pieces of parchment. "This one is his signed statement canceling any bounty he might've had on any of us as of today, the 25th of Kel."

The dog girl brought the second parchment to the fore, handling it like a priceless artifact. "And this one confirms that Braley relinquishes all claim on me, signed and sealed. I'm free!"

Dare let out a huge breath, as if a mountain had lifted off his chest, and held his lover tight. "Thank the gods," he whispered, burying his face in her hair.

"No, thank you," the dog girl said, pulling back slightly to mock glare at him. "Although you're still an asshole."

They all shared a laugh, as much to relieve the tension they'd been feeling all day as anything. "Come on," he said, wrapping an arm around each of his lovers. "Let's get out of here in case Braley changes his mind."

"How did you know it would work out that way?" Pella asked quietly as they left the last of Kinnran's fields and orchards behind. "How did you know what I would do?"

Dare chuckled. "Because I knew you were smart enough to figure out what I was doing and play along." He fondly stroked her golden hair. "And that even if you didn't figure it out, you'd still protect them to the same result. Because you're a good and loyal person."

"I would have, you know," she murmured.

"I know. And I promise that if it wasn't a charade, I would never force you to make a choice like that."

The dog girl chuckled. "Well, from now on my loyalty is to you and Zuri and anyone else who joins our harem." She glanced back somewhat sadly towards the manor glowing through the trees on the hill behind them. "I'll always love my family, especially Ama, but it's time to leave them behind. As I left behind the grave of my master . . . always in my heart, but no longer dominating my life."

Silence settled as by unspoken agreement Zuri climbed into his arms and they sped up to their usual traveling pace, heading back in the direction they'd come. "So what now?" his goblin lover asked. "Back to leveling?"

Dare nodded. "Although I think we should start making our way northward. Both to leave Kovana behind in case anyone wants to cause us trouble, and because it sounds like there'll be a lot of good opportunities in Bastion."

His companions nodded their agreement. "Not only more monsters, but quests will start popping up like mushrooms after a heavy rain in response to all the unrest," Zuri said.

Pella's fluffy tail wagged eagerly. "I've never gone farther than just beyond the border of this region. It'll be fun to visit somewhere different, explore new places and meet new people."

Dare could agree with that. Especially if those people happened to be beautiful women he could romance.

"To Bastion, then, and adventure!" he said, hugging his lovers tight.

Chapter Fourteen
Onward

Things were uncomfortable with Pella for the next few days.

Dare couldn't blame her for that; everything had turned out all right with her master's family, but even though they'd both been acting in their confrontation, there'd been a lot of truth in what they'd said and the feelings were very real.

Zuri was also a little cool towards him, angry that she'd been the only one who hadn't known what was going on, and still smarting from the awful experience it had been because of that.

He did his best to make it up to his lovers however he could, but he understood that it would probably take time for things to get back to normal. Until then he should be patient and give them space if they needed it.

So it was fair to say they were all more than eager to jump into leveling as a distraction from what had happened at the manor.

Over the next three days Dare and Zuri got enough experience to level up to 23, which turned out to be a pleasant surprise. Most of the class abilities unlocked every 5 levels, and since they were 2 levels from 25 he hadn't been expecting much.

But abilities could also unlock from getting enough proficiency in an ability tree, or from putting enough points in a specific ability. That latter was what happened here when Dare put his first point for Level 23 into Bows 5, unlocked at that level, and a new ability unlocked along with it.

"Eagle Eye: Passively increase visual acuity by 10%. Visual increases improve range and accuracy with a bow by 5% and critical hit chance by 2%."

That sounded awesome and he immediately put his next point into it. At which point he was delighted to see his vision sharpen as if he'd just put on a pair of glasses, something he'd needed for driving back on

Earth. He could not only see a farther distance, but see things in sharper definition as well.

Since Dare's vision had already been insanely good, courtesy of the incredible body his benefactor had given him, it felt as if he actually *did* have the vision of an eagle.

Zuri got a rank 10 ability at 23 as well, for her school of nature magic. Attuned to Nature: Passively increase damage and healing from Nature spells by 5%. As long as only Nature spells have been cast within the last hour or more, increase mana regeneration by 10%. Gain passive Minor Life Sense, which allows you to detect the presence of living things within 15 yards. Less effective against Stealthed targets.

15 yards was inside their perception circles for this level, and with it worse against Stealth it seemed of limited use. But he assumed the point was that it would let his lover see enemies, particularly animal predators and intelligent ambushers, who were in hiding.

As for the Nature restriction, at the moment all of Zuri's spells were in that school. Which made him wonder if there were spells she could've gotten that weren't, or if it applied to spells she could get in the future.

Now that they were within 5 levels of Pella, Dare suggested she join their party. It would slow down their leveling a bit, and Pella would get comparatively less for her level, but it was only fair.

The dog girl happily agreed to the idea, cocking her head eagerly as if waiting for him to invite her right then and there. He hesitated, though. "I won't look at your personal information," he promised.

She gave him an odd look. "You should. That knowledge will help you lead the party and ensure our success. Besides, I don't mind . . . you already know pretty much everything about me." She giggled, blushing slightly. "Including what I feel like inside my pussy and butt, and how my juices taste."

Dare's cock twitched at the reminder; the women had been cuddling him every night like usual, but given their raw feelings they hadn't offered further intimacy, and he hadn't asked for it. A state he hoped would be resolved soon.

Although more important was his desire to earn their forgiveness.

He quickly invited his dog girl lover to the party, perusing only her most pertinent details. Although he couldn't help but notice that she'd been pregnant once before and it had been terminated in the first trimester.

No doubt at her master's insistence, not wanting the embarrassment and inconvenience of a child with his pet.

Dare felt the same shame he'd felt when he'd seen Zuri's information when she first joined his party, and he quickly closed the dog girl's details screen. "Now it's my turn," he said. "Both of you leave the party and then each of you invite me so you can see my details. It's only fair."

"You don't have t-" Zuri protested.

"Yes, I do." Dare rested a gentle hand on her shoulder. "You don't need to let Pella see your details if you don't want her to, and same goes for you with Zuri, Pella. But I want both of you to see my past, who I am. You've shown me that trust, and you deserve the same."

He wasn't worried about them finding out about Earth or that he'd only been on this world for a few months; when he first invited Zuri his benefactor had assured him she'd fabricated an artificial past for him on Collisa. One as close to accurate to his old life as possible without giving away that he was from another world or there was anything unusual about him.

A moment later he jumped at an insistent brassy noise, the text "Zuri has invited you to her party!" floating in front of him. He quickly accepted.

His goblin lover seemed reluctant to look at his details, but at his urging she finally stared off into space as she read. Then she shrugged and dissolved their party. "Nothing there I wasn't expecting."

Pella also invited him, read through his information, then giggled. "You spent most of the last several years doing low paying manual labor moving things around in a warehouse?" she asked. "That doesn't seem like you at all."

She was actually referring to his hazardous work in a chemical plant, although the jobs were similar enough to fit. Still, she wasn't wrong; the more Dare looked at his old life from the lens of his new

244

one, the more he had to agree.

"What can I say," he said with a smile. "Some in my old home say that no matter where you go, you remain the same. But since coming here I've become a whole new person."

Literally as well as figuratively.

"I'm glad I got to meet that person," the beautiful golden-haired woman said, resting a hand on his arm. Then she briskly disbanded the party and looked at him eagerly. "All right, invite us and let's get leveling again! I can't wait for you guys to catch up to me and all of us to fight powerful monsters together!"

Dare formed their party again and they got back to leveling. They were fighting Level 24-26 enemies at the moment, comfortably between his and Zuri's and Pella's levels. Although their steady northward progress had brought them only a few hours away from the Gadris Mountains, which separated Kovana and Bastion, and things changed dramatically within them.

"My tribe had our home in the Gadris Mountains, at least before we were enslaved," Zuri said as they made their way to the next monster spawn point. She saddened for a moment, no doubt thinking of her people and their home, then made an effort to shake off the gloom. "It can be a dangerous place. Perhaps it's the constantly shifting elevations messing with spawn points, or just the nature of mountains, but the monsters within them vary in level much more than in other terrains."

Pella nodded. "And the farther in you go, the quicker they rise in level until they can become truly terrifying. Also animal predators are all over the place in level from one valley to the next." She shuddered. "My master took me hunting not far from here once. After a narrow escape with a level 27 grizzly we never went back."

Dare inspected the mountain range. They weren't quite as tall as the Rocky Mountains back home, but they looked more rugged as if they'd formed more recently. A lot of stark peaks of pale stone, with grass and trees struggling to conquer their lower slopes.

It was breathtaking. Maybe most of all because while he'd seen most of the most majestic landmarks on Earth, this one was entirely new to him. It made him want to explore those peaks and valleys and see what secrets they hid.

"Are there safe paths through?" he asked his companions.

They both nodded. "Of course," Zuri said. "But mountains are also a haven for tribes of non-humans and intelligent monsters, like my own tribe. They might attack any road we use. And of course there'll be more danger of roaming monsters unless powerful adventurers have been through recently."

He looked towards the mountains looming to the north. "Any roads near here?"

"Not for a day's travel at least," Pella replied. "The main road going from Yurin to Jarn's Holdout in Bastion."

That was a bit out of the way, but not terrible. Dare was about to suggest making for it when Zuri cleared her throat. "There's a ravine held by several goblin tribes not far east of here," she offered. "The presence of so many settlements keeps the monster spawn points low level in the nearby area, and the low level monsters don't interest the predators so they tend to go elsewhere. As for roaming monsters, we don't see them often and the goblins can usually band together to take them out."

That was promising. Especially since it would be a safer route if Braley Kinnran decided to be an asshole after all and tried to send people after them. "Will the tribes attack us?" he asked.

She hesitated. "Maybe. I can speak on our behalf, and our levels might dissuade them. Although if worst comes to worst there's always running."

Dare snorted, but he was intrigued. Thus far he'd only seen human settlements, and he wanted to see if free goblins in the wild were as savage and primitive as the people he'd met accused them of being.

After meeting Zuri he doubted it, but then again she'd said before that her tribe was different from most, even trading with nearby human villages on occasion.

At least until the slavers came for them.

"You up for traveling through goblin lands?" he asked Pella.

246

She hesitated, then grinned at him. "You should know by now I'm up for anything," she said with a wink. "And Zuri's right that there's always running . . . not to insult goblins, but there's a reason you carry her around when we travel."

Zuri laughed in agreement at that; with her short legs she had to sprint to match their casual lope, and while she had surprising endurance she wasn't built for speed. The same would apply to other goblins.

"All right, let's hunt our way in that direction," Dare said. "We'll set up camp just short of the mountains and set out through the goblin ravine in the morning."

* * * * *

Dare wasn't sure what he'd done right to get back on the girls' good sides. Maybe it was letting them be party leaders and see his information, or showing trust in Zuri by agreeing to her suggestion to visit the goblins.

Either way, as they settled into the tent that night Pella slipped out of his arms and disappeared beneath the covers. After some wiggling around he felt her bury her face in his crotch and did his best not to jump in surprise at her unexpected friskiness.

"Hello," he said with a laugh.

"Hi," she said, voice muffled by leather as she kissed his quickly stiffening cock through his pants. "Just lay back, I want a treat." She began running her soft, elegant hands along his thighs, over his stomach, and finally around his hips to firmly squeeze his ass.

Dare complied, rolling to lie flat on his back; he definitely wasn't going to complain about whatever she had planned.

Especially when Zuri said, "So do I!" and dove beneath the covers as well.

Within seconds his lovers had teased his now fully erect cock out and were kissing and stroking along its length. Then Dare's back arched with a gasp of surprise and pleasure as he felt the dog girl's soft, flat tongue wrap around the tip of his cock with its usual nimbleness, squeezing it as her saliva flowed down his shaft to coat his lovers' hands as they continued to jerk him off.

The blankets shifted vigorously as Pella's tail thumped back and forth; she was obviously pleased by his response. And even more so when, her tongue still wrapped around his tip, her soft lips wrapped around it and her tongue both, sliding down together as she took him into her mouth.

Dare's hips once again twitched as her tongue with her lips pressed tightly against it continued to work their way down his shaft until his tip was teasing the back of her throat, making her gag once and then begin swallowing rapidly.

A flood of slobber escaped her mouth and soaked his crotch, and then with a soft whimper of determination she accepted him into her throat.

The pleasure was so intense he couldn't articulate words, so he just made noises of enjoyment as he pushed the covers down so he could watch his lovers work, resting a hand on each of their heads. He gently stroked their silky hair and Pella's soft floppy ears as they continued to stimulate him with their mouths and hands, and at his touch they both redoubled their efforts.

Zuri's head was eventually pushed out of the way as the dog girl took him deeper and deeper into her tight throat, so his goblin lover moved between his legs and began licking and sucking on his balls instead.

"Gods, you two," he panted, holding onto their heads as they worked intently. "You're incredible."

Pella hummed contentedly at the praise, raising his pleasure to a new peak, and as his hips twitched at the sensation she seemed to realize he liked it and kept on humming, the vibrations shivering up and down his shaft.

Dare saw a bluish purple glow shining faintly from beneath the covers, and with a start realized Zuri had used Pella's saliva as the base to cast Cleanse Target on his nether region. He realized why a moment later when the goblin's small, soft tongue began teasing and pushing against his asshole, while her hands began gently fondling his balls and the few inches of his shaft not buried in Pella's throat.

He could only withstand a few seconds of that before all the incredible sensations combined to overwhelm him. He desperately thrust his hips upward, holding that position with his back arched and legs straining as he exploded down his dog girl lover's tight esophagus.

He felt a bit bad about not having time to warn her, but to his relief Pella didn't seem to mind. Her contented humming turned into a muffled but clearly delighted sound, and she began eagerly swallowing spurt after spurt of his seed as he emptied his balls inside her.

The beautiful woman finally pulled herself off his cock with a gasp, catching a final spurt on her lips. She and Zuri immediately got to work cleaning him with their tongues, gentle around his hyper sensitive tip, and their combined efforts kept him hard.

That seemed to be the goblin woman's plan, because before long she turned her attention to his tip, licking it lightly with her small soft tongue. Then she took him into her mouth and began expertly taking him down her throat without the slightest hesitation.

"Gods yes," Dare said, stroking her silky hair. "A bit farther, you're almost there."

"Almost . . . you can fit all of him down your throat?" Pella asked in obvious disbelief, pausing her efforts on his cock to look at the small woman.

Zuri's shoulders shook in mirth, and Dare laughed. "Watch her," he said mischievously. "With her teeth she's used to swallowing food in huge chunks or even whole." The tiny goblin made a noise of happy agreement.

The dog girl gasped as Zuri buried her sharp nose in his pubic hair, swallowing around her gag reflex as her lips reached his base. Even in the dim lighting from the fire outside he could see her throat bulging from his massive girth.

It was ridiculously sexy.

Zuri wasted no time beginning to bob up and down on his shaft, tongue working over its base along the entire length. While she didn't produce nearly as much drool as the dog girl, a small amount still flowed constantly from her mouth.

For her part Pella got over her surprise at Zuri's deep throating skills and took the tiny goblin's place between Dare's legs, her soft flat tongue wrapping around his balls one after the other and lovingly caressing them.

The sensation was incredible.

The women seemed determined to finish him off just as quickly this time as the first, and in spite of his best efforts he soon felt his balls churning with another powerful climax. "Here it comes," he warned Zuri.

She began humming loudly in approval, engulfing his shaft in intense vibrations, and with a gasp he grabbed her head with both hands, pulling her even tighter against his crotch as he twitched his hips and emptied a full load of come down her throat.

The tiny goblin rode out his entire orgasm, waiting until he began going limp in her throat before finally pulling free. Then both women again cleaned his shaft and Zuri gently tucked him back into his pants and tied the laces.

"I love you two," Dare said, wrapping his arms around his lovers as they moved up to cuddle against his sides, Pella dragging the blanket up with her to cover them all.

"I love you too," Zuri said. Or more likely she'd also said "two".

"And I love both of you," Pella said, covers shifting as her tail thumped happily against them. She leaned across him and gently kissed the small goblin, then lifted her head and pressed her lips to his as well. Zuri soon joined her, all three of them sharing a soft, intimate kiss.

Then they settled down to sleep.

* * * * *

The goblin ravine was eerily abandoned as they made their way up it, Dare straining with his improved eyesight to see any danger and paying close attention to his Adventurer's Eye. Pella prowled a bit ahead of them, her keener senses also alert for a threat.

They passed what was obviously the entrance to goblin territory, marked by crudely carved totems festooned by animal skulls and bones, and Zuri stared at the grisly decorations with clear worry.

"Something is wrong here," she said quietly.

Even though he wasn't sure what she was seeing, he was inclined to agree. "Do goblins usually set guards at the entrance to their territory?"

She shook her head. "No, they usually have these warning totems far out from their village, so there's plenty of time for scouts or hunters to send word of an attack." She pointed. "But see those spots where it looks as if skulls and bones have been removed?"

Now that Dare looked closer, he could see the patches where something was obviously missing. "I see them."

"Those were probably the remains of humans and other intelligent creatures." Zuri's jaw tightened. "When the slavers took my village, they made a point of taking those skulls and bones down and giving them a proper burial." She looked away with a haunted expression. "And punishing us for their deaths, even though most of those remains came from people who'd attacked us."

He crouched to wrap an arm around her shoulders, comforting her. "You think slavers hit the tribes here?"

"It's the most likely explanation. Our tribe was one of those closest to human settlements, and I doubt the slavers would've stopped with us. Especially when they were able to take us without a fight." The little goblin looked hopeful for a second. "Although maybe the tribes in this ravine learned of our situation and fled deeper into the mountains, and the slavers found nothing here."

It was a good hope, but it was dashed several hundred yards up the twisting ravine.

There was a goblin village hugging the slope to the left, surrounded by spiked barricades meant to make use of the steep terrain to slow and redirect attackers. And it was obvious there had been an attack, because many of the barricades had been broken or removed, and most of the crudely made straw-roofed stone and mud huts had been torched, items strewn on the ground about them and trampled as if they'd been looted first.

Even more telling, a large mound at the base of the slope was obviously a mass grave that had to hold at least a dozen bodies.

Zuri looked sick as she took in the scene, and Dare picked her up and walked a bit faster. Not just to spare her a prolonged exposure to the distressing view but in case the people who'd attacked this tribe were still lurking around and might pose a threat.

"It'll take us half a day to get through this ravine," his lover said hoarsely into his ear. "Can we go at our usual traveling pace and leave this terrible place behind?"

He exchanged looks with Pella, who nodded. "Of course," he said and broke into his usual ground-eating run. The dog girl flashed ahead, scouting in case of trouble.

They passed by three more villages as they continued up the ravine. Two showed clear signs of having been abandoned while the third, in the broad pass across the summit and by far the largest, looked like the site of an even larger battle.

There were two burial mounds outside this village; Dare assumed the fallen from the attackers were interred in the smaller, more carefully dug one. And while a few of the huts close to their side of the pass had been torched, most had been left untouched.

A pitched battle where the slavers won, but the surviving goblins had fled and the slavers had hurried to bury their dead and loot the village before pursuing?

They slowed as they passed through the place, weapons ready. Dare did his best not to see the splashes of blood at the entrances to some of the huts, and the possessions strewn about and trampled into the ground. Including what were clearly dolls and wooden balls and other toys children might play with.

Zuri looked at one little doll, made of rags and straw and covered in blood, then stumbled away and was noisily sick.

Pella looked pale as well at the signs of carnage, and Dare found himself swallowing down bile once or twice as well.

There was little he could do to fix the savagery of this world at the moment. Maybe when he was higher level, or had made more friends and gained more influence to make real changes. But at the moment all he could do was witness it and resolve to be better than what he saw around them.

252

Zuri soon rejoined them, wan but expression determined. "Let's get out of here," she growled, holding out her arms for Dare to pick her up.

Even though it might have been a bit risky, they sped up to a run again. Anything to put the tragic scene behind them.

The downhill path through the ravine leading down into Bastion was smoother and easier, and they passed signs of more abandoned villages. At the fourth Pella returned from scouting to report, expression confused but wary.

"There's no sign it's been looted," she said. "And no sign of a battle. The slavers must've either given up at this point and gone home, or they met enough resistance they were turned back."

Dare immediately set Zuri down and they readied their weapons. "Circle around or go through?" he asked.

As it turned out the question was moot, because moments later the slopes ahead churned as dozens of goblins rose into view, bristling with spears and crude bows. At the same time a dozen larger goblins bearing clubs, stone axes, and makeshift swords rose from a ditch near the path, moving to block their way forward.

It looked as if the slavers had been turned back.

Chapter Fifteen
Fight

Dare's first instinct was to flee, but as he snatched Zuri up and turned back he felt the ground beneath his feet rumbling, and watched as a small landslide of stones and dirt filled the path behind them.

Fuck.

Dare set his lover back down and warily unslung his bow, nocking an arrow. Most of the goblins ahead were lower level, around 10 or lower on average with only the big warriors blocking the path above Level 15.

Even the biggest, best equipped, and most ornately dressed goblin in the center of that group was only Level 19, and judging by the dozens of necklaces of precious stones and carved bones adorning his chest, he was most likely the chieftain or war leader.

Going by levels it would've seemed like an easy fight, but numbers and positioning gave the goblins the overwhelming advantage. Sure, maybe he and his companions could account for a couple dozen if it was a matter of life and death, but in the end they'd be overrun.

And in any case he had no desire to harm these goblins who were just trying to defend their territory, and had already suffered so much.

Running up and around the landslide was probably their best bet, but Dare couldn't help but feel like the fact that he had the daughter of a goblin High Priestess in his party might give them a chance of talking their way through this.

"Want to try diplomacy?" he asked Zuri. "Let them know we're just passing through and don't want to cause them any trouble."

"It's worth a try," she said doubtfully. She slipped out of his arms, stepped forward, and raised her voice. "Hail, Chieftain. I am Ge'welu, daughter of Ee'wena of the Swiftclaw tribe. I and my companions are peaceful travelers wishing to pass through this ravine to human lands."

The biggest goblin stepped forward, threateningly raising his

254

sword as he bellowed something in a voice that, while still having a goblin's high pitch, was far deeper than Zuri's. "I am Gar'u'wek, Chieftain of the combined Avenging Wolf tribe," she translated. "You and your companions must throw down your weapons and submit to chains, daughter of Ee'wena. I will treat you and the canid well as my mates, and not beat the human too harshly."

"Hard to do any of that after I tear his head off," Pella growled, ears flat and teeth bared.

Dare nodded in agreement. "How about you remind Gar of our level differences, and assure him that even if he might win a fight with us, we'll tear a swath through dozens of his people first." He hefted his bow. "And I'll drop him first no matter what happens, that's a promise."

Zuri exchanged a few phrases with the large goblin, who blanched and quickly went from paler to much darker green during the brief conversation, looking equal parts fearful, angry, and defiantly dignified.

She turned back with a slight smile. "Gar'u'wek has had a change of heart. He magnanimously offers us passage through his territory. He'll withdraw his warriors to a safe distance up the slopes to ensure there is no trouble."

"That's very reasonable of him," Dare said, light tone masking his intense relief that they'd found a peaceful solution; he was still sometimes haunted by the carnage his fight with the bandits, much as they'd needed to be stopped, and he had no desire to kill anyone else if there was an alternative.

Gar added something else, eyes gleaming as he looked at Zuri in a way Dare didn't like at all. She listened to the chieftain and immediately made an odd face that looked like a combination between anger and amusement.

"What did he say?" Dare asked her.

She turned to him with a grimace. "He asked how much you want for me . . . he greatly desires me for a mate."

The large goblin said something else and Zuri turned back to him. "That doesn't make it better!" she snapped. At Dare's curious look she blushed. "He said I'm the most beautiful female he's ever seen, and I would be the treasure of his harem and give him many children."

Dare chuckled. "He's not lying, you're breathtaking and I certainly treasure you. And I'm looking forward to having many children with you." He slipped an arm around his gorgeous lover's shoulders and leaned down to kiss the top of her head. "Just out of curiosity, does he really think having you as a mate could work out when you're 4 levels higher than him?"

"It has in the past," she said slowly. "Although yes, most women are drawn to a high level, powerful man, and catching the desires of a higher level woman are more difficult."

"Will you two stop joking around and tell the chieftain that of course there's no way Zuri's going anywhere?" Pella snapped. She seemed offended by the very offer.

Dare was irked too, of course, but he had no fears that Zuri would be tempted by the prospect of becoming this chieftain's mate, even if it meant being able to live among her people again.

"Right." Zuri turned to the chieftain. "I'm a free woman and the mate of this human. I reject your offer."

The large goblin shrugged, looking disappointed but not about to challenge three higher level adventurers on the point. Then he babbled something else.

Zuri cocked her head. "That's interesting."

"What is it?" Pella asked.

"There's a Level 21 party rated world monster farther down this ravine, in the mountains a few valleys over. It's not a roamer but its territory is steadily expanding, to the point it's threatening to block the Avenging Wolf tribe's retreat in the face of further slaver attacks. It might even threaten them directly if its territory grows too great. They're hoping we might be tempted to kill it for its loot and experience."

Dare felt a surge of excitement at the prospect of fighting his first party rated monster, but at the same time he was a bit worried about trying that sort of fight with only three people. Especially since they didn't have a real tank.

"How do they know the level?" he asked.

His companions shot him a blank look. "The same way people usually do," Pella said. "The dread sense we feel when a Silver Sickle is nearby."

Ah. So if the goblins had access to people of all levels up to 15, they could test the dread sense to figure out at what level their testers wouldn't feel that dread of close proximity to an enemy 11 or more levels above them.

A simple solution. Although one that would be dangerous to test in the wilds with roaming monsters and animal predators running around everywhere.

So, Level 21. "Are we tempted to try fighting this thing?" he asked his companions.

"You guys are 2 levels higher than it and I'm 7 levels higher," Pella said, looking thoughtful. "At even levels it would usually be a party of between four and eight people going after it, depending on class synergy, how well equipped they are, and how well they work together."

Zuri nodded. "It's worth taking a look at it. Dare can check to see how tough it is and what abilities it has, and we can decide once we know more."

They all seemed to agree with that. The two women looked ready to leave right then and there, but Dare paused, considering the tribe. It looked large enough to spare a reward for a task like this. "If it's a threat to the village and they're hoping we'll clear it out, maybe they'd be willing to offer some incentives."

Zuri translated, and the chieftain quickly replied, causing her to grimace. "He says he'd be willing to give you two laborers or one nubile maiden as slaves." The large goblin barked something else out with a loud laugh, and her expression further soured. "Also he's offering three nubile maidens for me, according to him an offer you'd be a fool to refuse."

Dare shouldn't have been surprised, but he was still aghast. "Is it common practice for your leaders to sell their own followers into slavery?"

"Many, perhaps. And the rest of the tribe usually goes along as long as it's not them facing that fate. I am proud to say my mother did not act that way." His lover hesitated sheepishly. "Although that was mostly because we had slaves of our own to trade in the stead of tribe members."

Dare shook his head in disbelief; even after learning so much about the cruelty of this world that his benefactor had warned him about, he could still be caught by surprise.

Zuri gave him a somewhat shamed look at his expression, as if she felt she personally were responsible for the condition of the world. "Few share your feelings against slavery. I myself didn't, at least not before I became a slave myself and saw the other end of the whip."

He gently squeezed her shoulder. "I have a hard time believing you were ever anything but kind."

She blushed. "Thank you, but I'll admit I was more selfish in my youth."

The goblin chieftain stared at Zuri in bafflement, since of course he could hear everything she'd said. Dare quickly spoke before the large goblin could ask if all three of them were touched in the head. "Tell him no trading people. If he's got any treasure or valuable items to offer we'll consider it."

The chieftain pondered that for a short time, then answered. "He's he'll give us six small pieces of gold ore and a handful of cut and polished semiprecious stones," Zuri said. "That or two dozen hides."

The hides might be more valuable, but the treasure was much more portable. "All right. Let's hear more about this monster."

According to the chieftain's description, it sounded like some sort of chimera. One with lion and serpent heads, an eagle's body and wings, and the four legs and paws of a lion, roughly twice the height of a man. It could fly, although thus far it hadn't flown near the goblin village.

Dare hadn't fought many large monsters before and didn't relish the prospect, but he hoped it would look tougher than its stats bore out. That, and at least some of Pella's crowd control abilities would work against a massive enemy without weapons or humanoid-ish limbs.

258

"Okay, tell the chieftain we have a deal," Dare told Zuri. "Is there some way to formalize it?"

"None that would matter much to our kind," she replied. "They either honor it or get punished." That seemed to be as much for the chieftain as him, and the large goblin obviously didn't look pleased about it.

That exchange seemed to be enough for the world system, because he got a notification. "Quest accepted. Displaced and Endangered: Slay the party rated monster menacing the Avenging Wolf tribe."

Judging by his companions' expressions, they'd gotten the quest as well. "All right, let's go!" Pella said, tail wagging. "This will be the first party rated world monster I've ever fought. I can't wait to see what it drops!"

Yeah, it would be Dare's first also, and most likely Zuri's as well. Although he wasn't sure whether to be excited or nervous.

At Gar's insistent barked orders the goblins of his tribe all retreated up the slopes to the ridges to either side. The chieftain remained on the path with only two other goblins, either bodyguards or lieutenants, and personally accompanied them through the territory his new, enlarged tribe had claimed.

Dare made it a point to walk between Zuri and the large goblin, and noticed Pella doing the same. That put him close enough to Gar to have to breathe in his unwashed stink, so overpowering and alien that he had to struggle to keep impassive as it washed over him. If anything, the other two goblins smelled even worse.

Considering that even at her most sweaty and dusty, Zuri never smelled worse than any other woman he'd spent time around, he could only assume that either goblin males had a particularly potent stench, or their hygiene was just that poor.

Understandable maybe, if they were refugees recently chased from their homes. But even so it was unpleasant.

Thankfully they soon reached the edge of the Avenging Wolf's territory and left the three goblins behind. Gar gave them a few last instructions about finding the chimera, and from Zuri's reaction made a last proposition to her that she pointedly ignored.

Then Dare and his companions were on their way, climbing the lefthand slope at a trot to find the monster. Thirty minutes later they crested a final ridge two valleys over and came in view of the creature's den, an overhang halfway up the far slope where the chimera was currently sleeping.

No description could adequately prepare him for the sight.

Twice the height of a man was all well and good, but it didn't give any hints about the sheer *size* of the monster in front of him. It was about as large as an elephant, but with the lean grace of a predator. Not to mention four sets of wicked claws and two dangerous heads, one of which was likely poisonous.

And the damn thing could fly.

Even curled up with its lion head tucked beneath one paw and its serpent head tucked beneath its tail, the creature radiated menace. Dare almost didn't want to tangle with it based on its appearance alone.

He wasn't the only one. "Shit," Zuri muttered in awe. "That thing could swallow me whole with either mouth."

Pella shivered. "That doesn't look like something to fuck with when we've only got three people," she agreed. "We're not *that* much higher level."

Dare had a feeling they were right. Still, he motioned down the slope. "I'm going to sneak up close enough to look at it with my Eye. Stay here, and be ready to run if it wakes up."

The two women didn't seem happy with that idea, but they grudgingly settled down to watch as he began picking his way down the slope.

Please don't let this get me or my lovers killed, he thought as he crept closer and closer to where he'd be twice the distance of his perception circle to the monster, where he could use his Adventurer's Eye. He held his bow with an arrow nocked, although it was a futile gesture since if the chimera woke up he planned to turn tail and run back to his companions, then get the hell out of there with them.

At one point the monster shifted in its sleep and he almost shit his pants. But after a few moments it settled down again, and he let himself breathe as he continued.

Phoenix

Finally Dare reached the spot where his Eye could activate, letting him take his first real look at the party rated monster:

"Escaped Monstrosity. Monster, Party Rated. Level 21. Attacks: Dive Bomb, Swipe, Pounce, Take Flight, Savage Bite, Venomous Bite, Wing Sweep, Dust Cloud, Pin."

Its health was ten times what the average monster of that level normally had, and its other stats he could see were similarly beefy. But it had no magical attacks, which was a relief. And many of its abilities seemed to be intended for crowd control, closing the distance, or escape.

Still, this would be risky. Incredibly risky. Especially since Zuri didn't have a spell that cured poison. Which seemed like something a Healer should have, but maybe she wasn't high enough level yet.

Dare made his way back up to his companions and reported what he'd found. "We have the advantage that it's sleeping, which will allow us to get in a strong first strike and make some preparations. But it's going to be hard." He paused. "I do have one idea, though."

He took out one of his arrows and a long length of the light, strong rawhide cord he was able to make. "If we can get Zuri's Nature's Curse effect on it, slowing it down and giving a chance to paralyze, as well as a one time stun for emergencies, then me and Pella might be fast enough to work around it and get our other crowd control effects like Hamstring going."

"I need its blood to cast Nature's Sympathy and invoke Nature's Curse," his goblin lover pointed out. She looked at the arrow and cord with narrowed eyes. "Don't tell me you're planning to shoot it, yank the arrow back with that cord, then give me the blood from the arrowhead."

"Would that even work?" Pella asked, frowning.

"We can test it." Dare looked around at them. "What do you think? Me and Zuri have abilities that will let us survive one attack, and Pella has high evasion. Between Nature's Curse and Hamstring we should be able to kite the thing, and if it rises into the air we have ranged attacks."

His companions looked at each other. "I'm willing to try if you two want to," Zuri said. "But I'd be just as happy to walk away."

"Party and raid rated monsters give a lot more experience along with better loot, and also progress towards prestigious achievements," Pella said. "But most of all we have a quest for it, and the goblins are depending on us to kill it."

"True," the goblin woman said reluctantly, swayed but still not liking the prospect. "But they can always move."

Dare mulled it over. "I'd like to do this," he finally said. "I want to try my hand at a party rated monster and see just what we'd be dealing with in future fights. Pella's higher level will give us an advantage, and health equivalent to 10 monsters isn't insurmountable . . . with all of us going all out we should be able to kill it before it can pose a serious threat."

He nodded to Zuri. "But we're all equal here, and we're a team. If even one of us feels uncomfortable with this, we'll move on."

She rested a hand on her belly with an expression as if she had an upset stomach. "I'll do it," she said. "As long as you both promise to be careful."

"And the same for you," Dare said, resting a hand on her shoulder. "Don't worry, we'll protect each other. We're a strong team and we've faced dangerous fights before."

That seemed to be that. He looked around for any further questions and comments, then took a breath and squared his shoulders. "All right, let's kill this thing."

* * * * *

With everyone in agreement, Dare headed back the way they'd come so he could test out whether it was possible to shoot an arrow with a cord attached to it.

As it turned out it was, although it halved the arrow's range and he had to shoot it at an awkward higher angle to account for the added weight and drop. Also it penetrated the tussock he aimed for with far less force than an arrow at that range usually would.

It helped if he threw the cord as far as he could before loosing the arrow, but even so he was going to have to get a lot closer to the

Escaped Monstrosity than he felt comfortable with. Probably reducing the number of arrows he could shoot at it before it closed the distance to him.

Yanking the arrow back was also a challenge. He couldn't manage to make it fly all the way back to him with one tug, which meant he had to either run the rest of the way to grab the arrow or pull in the slack on the cord for another tug. Testing both, he found that the former was actually faster.

Although better all around was to have Pella throw the extra length of cord before he shot, then run and retrieve the arrow when he yanked it back and throw it to Zuri. That freed Dare to continue to shoot the chimera, and put the Tracker a bit closer to the monster so she could intercept it with her crowd control abilities.

They prepared everything and got into position, and he turned to Zuri. "All right, you know what to do?"

She nodded determinedly, although her skin was a bit pale. "Cast the first Mana Thorn, and you'll loose your arrow at the same time. Then keep on casting Mana Thorn until Pella throws me the blood so I can cast Nature's Curse. Cast it and go back to Mana Thorn until either the chimera is dead, it attacks me and I have to defend myself, or someone gets hurt and I need to switch to Plea to Nature."

"Right." Dare turned to Pella. "You?"

Her tail wagged in excitement. "Keep it occupied and use whatever crowd control abilities I can that work on it. When I can, do damage to it with my knife or unarmed attacks. If I can't draw its attention and my abilities don't work, focus on doing damage to it as quickly as possible, or in an emergency get between it and its target."

He nodded in satisfaction. "Good. As for me, I'll focus on doing as much damage as possible. If Pella can't hold its attention for some reason I'll try to fill that role myself. In an emergency I'll put myself between it and its target."

With a final deep breath, he fitted the arrow with the cord tied to it to his bowstring, then activated Rapid Shot.

Dare had never used that ability for this purpose before, mostly because he hadn't needed to. But for this fight he activated it before

263

pulling the enemy, just so he could start combat holding four arrows in his bow hand. That would save the time it would otherwise take to draw each of those arrows from his quiver, a small but significant advantage.

He waited the minute it took for the cooldown to finish and the ability became active again, then nodded to Zuri. "All right, start casting."

She nodded back, looking a bit pale, and began casting her first Mana Thorn. Just as she finished Dare loosed his own arrow, and both attacks flew through the air to strike the chimera in the neck of its lion head.

"Pull, Pella!" he shouted, and the dog girl drew in the slack on the cord and yanked on the arrow as hard as she could, sending it flying back towards her.

That effectively began the fight, and he had to admit it started off great.

Dare had never encountered a sleeping monster before, and of course it would've been a surprise to catch any animal unawares napping, especially the more dangerous predators. But apparently you got a benefit from attacking a sleeping monster, or maybe just the Escaped Monstrosity itself.

The chimera bellowed in pain as the arrow and spell connected, but rather than immediately surging to its feet and charging them it stirred slowly, as if groggy.

Jackpot. "Burn phase!" Dare shouted, quickly loosing the four arrows in his hand. Then he activated Rapid Shot to put four more arrows in his bow hand and loosed those at 50% increased speed.

Zuri and Pella had no idea what that term meant, of course. But the little goblin was casting Mana Thorn as fast as she could, and Pella was desperately yanking the cord tied to his first arrow to bring it back to her.

The chimera continued to bellow as the arrows and spells rained down on it, its health swiftly dropping as they focused on doing maximum damage. Then it shook itself violently and bounded to its feet, whirling towards them.

At which point it used Pounce, tamping its paws and crouching low, then throwing itself at them with its wings flapping furiously.

In the terrifying way of that ability, it crossed the considerable distance far faster than it should've. Pella just had time to snatch up the bloody arrow and hurl it at Zuri before Dare yelled, "Scatter!" and leapt to his right. She followed suit, leaping to her left.

They managed to get out of the chimera's way just before it landed hard enough to make the ground quake beneath them. It swiftly pivoted to swipe at Dare with a paw as big as his head.

The damn thing was fast. So fast, in fact, that Prey's Vigilance activated to throw him out of the way of the attack before it could rip his head off.

He cursed inwardly and activated Roll and Shoot, throwing himself ten feet to the side as the towering monster snapped its lion head down where he'd just been. The longer, more sinuous serpent head followed his movement, and he had to throw himself awkwardly in a more conventional roll to escape the second attack, even his best speed with Fleetfoot barely saving him.

The arrow that he'd automatically nocked with Roll and Shoot fumbled out of his fingers, leaving him to claw for another one from his quiver as he sprinted away, the monster darting after him with far greater speed than anything of that size should've been capable of.

Son of a bitch, this fight was going to hell in a hand basket. He'd already used up both of his defensive abilities in his first brush with this behemoth, and it was still right on his tail.

Then the Escaped Monstrosity bellowed loud enough to make Dare's ears ring, and he turned in time to see it slowing down as if it had just stepped into quicksand. Its information screen gained the status effects "Nature's Curse" and "Hamstring", confirming Zuri and Pella had both managed to do their part slowing it down.

The chimera was either smart or at least cunning, because it seemed to realize it could no longer catch Dare with its speed alone. It whirled towards Pella, and although he was terrified for his dog girl lover after facing the wrath of the party rated monster, he focused on his part of things and began raining arrows down on their enemy's back.

Out of the corner of his eye he spotted Pella darting away to a safe distance, her long lasso flicking out to catch one of the monster's paws as she attempted to hold it. That turned out to be a mistake as the chimera yanked with such power that she was forced to either let go of the rope, or be yanked back towards the two wide open jaws bearing down on her.

She let go and darted away again.

The Escaped Monstrosity roared in frustration, but rather than giving chase its wings began beating furiously, kicking billows of dust into the air with its Dust Cloud ability. Even though the huge creature couldn't have gone anywhere in the relatively small area covered by the obscuring dust, Dare still saw that more than half of his arrows began missing. As indicated by the monster's health bar not moving when it should've taken a hit.

That was annoying, but actually not the worst thing in the world. Missing half the time meant he still hit half the time, and as long as the chimera was sitting there in its Dust Cloud it wasn't attacking them.

Which obviously meant . . . "Get ready for it to-" he started to shout.

The huge creature threw itself into the air with a bellow, far faster than even a smaller bird should've been able to take off as it used its Take Flight ability. Since it had no ranged attacks there was only one thing it could really do now, so as Dare continued his barrage of arrows he once again shouted.

"Get ready for it to Dive Bomb one of us! Also its Pounce will be coming off cooldown any second now, so watch out for that too." Even as he spoke the chimera wheeled with impossible speed and shot towards the ground.

Straight at Zuri.

The little goblin screamed in terror and hastily threw her Sheltering Embrace barrier in front of her. Just in time as the giant monster landed full on top of her with all four claws, an attack that would've crushed her without her protective spell and still bore her to the ground, buried beneath the horrific weight of its paws.

The damage dealt was far more than was necessary to overload the mana barrier, and it exploded beneath the chimera in a spray of glittering green shards of Nature magic.

And holy shit, physics was a bitch to the Escaped Monstrosity. So much so that if it hadn't currently been trying to crush Zuri, Dare almost would've pitied the monster for how badly it had been screwed by circumstances.

He'd seen the Sheltering Embrace barrier explode before for "moderate damage" to enemies. As in, as much as two or three Mana Thorns would do, depending on how many of the shards spraying out in all directions hit a target.

However, he'd loved fireworks as much as the next curious kid out there, and thankfully had heard the oft-repeated and very important warning about firecrackers: if you held it in your open palm it wouldn't do much more than maybe sting your skin a bit, but if you closed your fist around it the explosion would blow your hand off.

The detonating barrier blew the chimera's hands off.

The force of the blast threw the beast off a dazed Zuri, shredding its four paws and most of its lower legs into tattered flesh and ragged shards of bone. A full *quarter* of its health bar vanished in an eyeblink, taking it from about half life to less than a quarter.

It also gained four simultaneous snare effects from its legs becoming unusable, and probably would've become rooted if it hadn't had its wings. Losing use of its legs also disabled its Pounce and Swipe abilities. And finally, apparently taking that much damage all at once applied a Dazed effect that slowed its movement and attack speed by 50%.

In other words, the Escaped Monstrosity was royally fucked.

"Holy shit!" Dare shouted as the monster flapped with the desperate awkwardness of a mortally wounded chicken, giving a very shocked and shaken looking Zuri the time to turn and bolt to safety.

He was so amazed by what he'd just seen that it took him a few seconds to remember to keep doing damage on his stricken enemy. Although he couldn't help but keep shouting as he activated Rapid Shot, finally off cooldown, and resumed his barrage.

"Holy shit, Zuri! You completely wrecked that fucker!"

The trembling goblin responded with a plaintive whimper as she reached a safe distance and began casting Mana Thorns at the chimera again.

Monsters had the ability to heal, even from major status effects like this that should've killed or at least permanently crippled them. And no doubt the chimera would've eventually regained the use of its legs and all the abilities associated with them, given enough time.

But it didn't have time. The huge monster's Dive Bomb ability was still on cooldown, and with its Dazed status effect it flapped through the air with almost comical slowness, making for where Pella had retrieved her lasso and waited for its arrival.

The dog girl lashed out with the weapon as soon as it was in range, expertly slamming the knot at the end of the loop one of the eyes on the lion head. It screeched in agony, juddering in midair and flopping down into an awkward crash.

Pella pounced in and began slashing at the throat of its lion head with her long knife, keeping that head between her and the hissing serpent head as it tried to bite at her.

By this point the Escaped Monstrosity was almost dead, and between the higher level dog girl's slashing knife, Dare's relentless arrows, and Zuri's stinging Zaps they swiftly burned down the last of its health.

Pella finished the monster off by burying her knife into the lion's closer eye, and with a defeated bellow from both of its mouths it thrashed one final time and went still.

Text appeared in the corner of Dare's vision. "Party rated monster Escaped Monstrosity defeated. 10,000 bonus experience awarded."

"Completed 1/10 towards Achievement Protector of Bastion: Slay 10 party rated monsters in the region of Bastion."

"Objective Completed for Quest Displaced and Endangered. Return to Chieftain Gar'u'wek for your reward."

"Trophies gained: Chimera head x2. Loot body to acquire."

Chapter Sixteen
Bastion

They were alive.

The adrenaline and terror of the fight was swiftly shifting to giddy exhilaration as Dare realized it was over and they were all okay, with no injuries he was aware of. Given how it had started, and how close it had been at times, he didn't think they'd ever been in this much danger.

But they were alive, and they'd won. Not just won, they'd kicked that big bastard's ass.

"That. Was. Epic!" Dare shouted into the sudden silence of the fight's end. He began laughing wildly, pumping his fists in the air. "Holy shit that was epic . . . we're total badasses!"

He rushed over to where Zuri lay prone on the ground staring up at the sky, still visibly trembling. "Are you okay?" he asked, gently running his hands over her limbs to check for injuries while looking at her pupils for signs of concussion.

"I'm fine," she mumbled, although her eyes were wide and he could feel her heartbeat thundering. "But wh-what just happened?"

Dare laughed and gathered his little lover up in his arms, hugging her gently. "What happened is that your barrier's detonation is basically an explosion, and if the force of an explosion has no escape it will destroy whatever's closing it in."

Zuri stared at him in dazed blankness. "I have no idea what you just said."

"Neither do I," Pella said, dropping down across from Dare and hugging them both tightly. "But however you did that, Zuri, it was amazing! It completely turned the fight around."

"Basically if your barrier explodes while you're completely covered by an enemy, it'll do a lot more damage," Dare said. Then he gave up on explaining since his companions didn't seem to be in the mindset to care at the moment.

"Did you guys get all that stuff too?" the dog girl continued, tail wagging eagerly. "All the experience, and the progress towards an achievement, and the trophies?"

"I got it." He leaned down and kissed Zuri gently, rubbing her back. "Feeling up to going and seeing what the monster dropped?"

Her dazed expression sharpened into keen focus at that. "Yes!" she said, scrambling out of his arms and starting towards the dead monster. "If it was going to be such a pain I want to see what we got out of it."

Aside from the trophy heads (which conveniently the Hunter class had the ability to taxidermy to prepare them to be mounted), the chimera dropped a few hundred body feathers, dozens of large flight feathers, and a dozen lion claws.

It also dropped a few dozen cuts of something called Experimental Meat, which would probably be the first things they left behind if they had to; combined with the loot they already had, the Escaped Monstrosity's loot was massively overloading them to the point where they'd need to make sleds again to haul it away.

Especially the trophies.

They had even more loot to haul away when they investigated the chimera's nest. Not only were the remains of a dozen animals scattered around, offering loot in the form of claws, teeth, and horns, but the monster had apparently had a bit of a magpie streak and collected shiny things.

Or who knew, maybe all party rated world monsters collected loot.

Either way, there was probably 5,000 or so copper, around 500 silver, and maybe 80 gold in the pile. There were also a few worked gems, a few hunks of semiprecious stones and geodes that had apparently been ripped from the rocky peaks of the mountains, and a giant chunk of quartz that probably weighed more than all of them put together and definitely wouldn't be going anywhere.

Best of all there was a small pile of gear, apparently taken off the bodies of adventurers. Or more likely naturally spawning with the monster, supported by the fact that all the items were Level 20-22.

Unfortunately, most of it was low quality and almost none of it was useful to them. There was a Good quality leather chestpiece that

Dare insisted Zuri take, and a Journeyman quality short sword Pella could've used but was worse than her long knife.

The prize of the lot was obviously an Exceptional quality pair of plate leggings that gave bonuses to strength and damage reduction, and would no doubt fetch a fantastic price since unfortunately none of them could use the things.

All in all it was a tidy haul. They couldn't be sure how much most of it was worth, but Dare guessed that they'd get at least 100 gold off all of it. Combined with the pile of coin and and the quest reward from the goblins they should easily clear 200 gold off this monster.

Not a bad haul for a fight that lasted about five minutes; they should definitely hunt more party rated monsters in the future, and if possible join a raid for raid rated ones as well.

Dare used scraps of leather from the animal remains and wood from nearby trees to craft a couple sleds, then they loaded everything on and got to the laborious task of hauling it back to the goblin ravine. And it *was* laborious, since the trip that had taken a half hour dragged out to hours, taking so long that the sun was sinking low on the horizon by the time they reached the ridge overlooking the path below.

He pointed north to where the ridge formed a peak. "Let's camp up there, where we'll have a more defensible position in case the goblins attack after all."

His companions looked eager at the prospect, worn out by the laborious trek. Although Zuri paused and looked uncertainly up the ravine. "Think that'll be a good defensible position if Gar'u'wek and his people attack?"

"It should be," he said. "Steep approaches from only a couple directions, and the advantage of high ground." He grinned and playfully ruffled her soft, inky black hair. "Besides, if they swarm us with numbers you can just explode your Sheltering Embrace and shred them."

His goblin lover shuddered, likely remembering being smothered beneath the chimera's paws. "That was a fluke. I've never even heard of anything like it happening, and doubt it will happen again."

Dare rubbed his jaw thoughtfully. "Maybe," he said. "Although I think we could reproduce the effect. Maybe even weaponize it."

"That would be amazing!" Pella said, grinning and wrapping her arms around Zuri's shoulders, tail wagging. "Zuri can be our secret weapon!"

The goblin woman smiled tentatively. "You really think it could work?" she asked, obviously excited by the prospect in spite of her nervousness.

"It could, although I'll have to give it some thought." Dare reluctantly hefted the rope leads to the sled he was dragging and motioned towards the peak. "Anyway, it's an idea for another time. Let's get up there and set up camp."

They worked their way the final hundred or so yards, then gratefully let the sleds slide to a stop and set down their heavy packs. "We should haul this stuff right to Jarn's Holdout," Pella said as she massaged her shoulders where she'd held the leads connecting to her sled. "It'd be a shame to sell the trophies, but we don't have a residence of our own and I don't want to haul a over a hundred pounds of giant monster heads, even *after* you taxidermy them, around everywhere we go."

She had a point. Dare didn't have much use for trophies himself, and he wasn't sure he enjoyed the idea of having a bunch of dead animal heads snarling down on him from the walls of his living room. But if the things afforded some sort of status on Collisa he might have to endure them.

Maybe they could mount the trophies in a parlor he never used or something. Once they actually had a house.

On the subject of the heads, once Dare had started their dinner cooking he got to work preserving them. It took longer than he expected, but thankfully it was the ability doing the work so he didn't have to figure out any complicated process.

The taxidermy job was further extended because he had to pause halfway through, Pella alerting them that goblins were approaching. "It's Gar and his two bodyguards," she said.

They gathered their weapons, just in case, then Dare borrowed Zuri's translation stone and carried the two heads down to meet the goblins. "Proof we've slain the monster," he called as the goblins stopped a cautious distance away.

"So I see." Gar looked pleased. "You've done a great deed for the Avenging Wolf tribe." He withdrew a small cloth bag and handed it to one of his bodyguards, motioning for the brute (for a goblin at least) to go give it to Dare.

The bodyguard hesitated, looking nervous, and the chieftain grunted irritably and shoved at the smaller goblin's back until he reluctantly stumbled forward and delivered the reward.

Dare set down the trophies and accepted the bag, dumping it into his palm and sifting through the chunks of gold ore and crudely cut semiprecious stones. It was a meager haul, worth maybe 10 gold at best, but he wasn't complaining.

The expected text appeared at the corner of his vision. "Quest completed: Displaced and Endangered. 5,000 experience awarded."

He tucked the ore and stones into his belt pouch, then tossed the bag back at the retreating bodyguard; it hadn't looked particularly clean. "This concludes our business, then?"

"Unless you want to trade your goblin breeder?" Gar asked hopefully.

Dare scowled. "No, and stop asking. I'm beginning to grow angry on behalf of my mate."

The chieftain hastily raised his hands. "As you wish, adventurer. Thank you again for your service to the goblin tribe. You're welcome to travel through our territory at any time, and we welcome trade with you and your companions. We may need your help in the future as well, for generous rewards." He motioned to his bodyguards and quickly retreated with them at his heels.

Dare watched him go, then shook his head, retrieved his trophies, and headed back up to camp. "Let's set a careful watch tonight, just in case," he said.

Zuri nodded. "We won favor with the Avenging Wolf tribe, and they may be more friendly to us as long as we continue to show our strength. But they seem the sort of goblins who'll exploit any weakness they see."

"Goblins aren't alone in that," he said.

She gave him a half amused, half sad look. "I never suggested they were."

Dare wrapped his arms around her, feeling a bit guilty at his insensitivity; she'd know that truth as well as anyone.

He got back to work preserving the heads, and his companions returned to their own evening tasks, the air cold and fresh and the sky brilliant at this altitude as the sun set and darkness settled around them.

* * * * *

Dare expected the cold wind at the peak to warm as they descended down into the Bastion region and began picking their way along the base of the foothills west towards Jarn's Holdout.

And it did, to an extent. But unless he was remembering wrong, there hadn't been such a strong wind blowing from the north in Kovana. Which he supposed made sense because the Gadris Mountains would block that wind, keeping the region to the south more mild.

Either way, it was the beginning of summer and he found himself appreciating the warmth provided by his leather armor, and the thick, fur-lined, hooded leather cloaks he'd made for all of them. Especially as they worked up a sweat hauling the sleds and the north wind cut deeper.

Thankfully they had a reprieve when they found a path running in the valley between the foothills and the mountains, which offered some shelter from the wind. It also gave them a smooth surface for the sleds, speeding their progress.

"At this pace we should reach Jarn's Holdout in a couple days," Pella said. She had her hood down, long golden braid swinging free down her back, and the chill breeze had given her cheeks a rosy flush.

She looked breathtaking, and Dare just wanted to wrap his arms around her and warm her lips with his own.

"What do we know about the town, and Bastion in general?" he asked.

Zuri, huddled in her cloak with her head bowed and hood pulled low against the cold, briefly looked up at him. "My people traded here sometimes, and I've visited a time or two," she said. "Bastion's a wilder land than Kovana, and lots of adventurers pass through Jarn's Holdout on their way into the region. It should be a good place to find crafters and vendors."

Pella nodded. "I visited the town every year or so with my master. They have really good fried potatoes."

They both stared at her. "That's your takeaway from your visits?" Dare asked, amused.

She blushed. "We usually came by carriage and went straight to Baron Haldin's house. So we didn't explore around the town much, aside from brief carriage tours and stuff like that."

He assumed Haldin was lord of Jarn's Holdout. "Did you hear much about the state of the town? Crime, how adventurers and non-humans are treated, that sort of thing?"

The dog girl shrugged. "I don't know, I usually tuned out a lot of the conversation and just curled up at my master's feet or with my head in his lap. But he seemed to feel like this place was a bit wilder than Yurin, which is why he didn't want to go out as often. Especially not with me."

Dare grit his teeth at the glimpse of his companion's life as a pet; she'd deserved so much better. Freedom, and dignity, and respect.

"Well more adventurers and commerce will likely draw more thieves and other lawless sorts as well," he said. "We'll have to stay vigilant."

Zuri nodded. "Honestly, I'm glad we usually just stay in towns long enough to do our business and then leave again. I don't have many good memories of towns from my life before meeting you."

He rested a hand on her head. "Well when we do get a house, it'll have to be a manor out on our own land. I think we'd all be more comfortable there."

"As long as it's safe for our children, right?" his goblin lover asked, looking up at him intently.

275

"Of course. Safer than a village, and all to ourselves."

"That sounds fun!" Pella said, tail wagging beneath her cloak. "But hopefully we'll still visit towns. I like meeting new people."

"As long as we keep leveling we'll always have loot that needs selling," Dare assured her. "Which means fun visits to town to sell, buy, and find good inns where we can have delicious meals and tasty desserts."

"And desserts that will store for a few days that we can take with us!" Zuri added eagerly.

"And baths!" the dog girl said, grinning knowingly at him as he perked up at the very suggestion.

His goblin lover also noticed his response and laughed outright. "And a brothel so we can have some fun with Dare."

Pella brightened. "Maybe another mermaid!" she said. Zuri had told her about visiting Trissela in Kov, and the idea of being given a bath by an expert like a mermaid had immediately enchanted the dog girl.

The prospect of something to look forward to in town put some pep in all their steps, and the day passed quickly as they made good time, giving spawn points a wide berth and only occasionally having to fight off low level predators.

Since they were already loaded down Dare stopped setting out snares at night, although he continued foraging for spices and cooking ingredients. He also kept hunting game they passed so they could have some fresh meat for dinner, and dried meat for the next day's travel.

In fact, they had a pleasant surprise the second day in finding a grazing animal similar to a cow, except maybe half the size and fierce enough that it could fight off predators. Its meat was as good as prime cuts of beef, some of the best he'd had on Collisa, and they all feasted that day and the next.

Even the jerky he made with it was good.

"You have to hunt us one of these whenever you see a herd," Zuri said as they finished off the last of it. "I want more. *More*."

"Easy, girl," Pella said, laughing. "You usually only get this excited about cake."

Dare grinned. "Or pie."

Zuri blushed more than their teasing warranted. "I'm just craving food like this, that's all," she said defensively.

Pella was right about how long the trip would take. They got their first view of Jarn's Holdout just after noon on the second day after entering Bastion, and all cheered the prospect of not having to pull the stupid sleds and carry overloaded packs at a snail's pace for much longer.

"And I can get back to cuddling in yours or Pella's arms while we run around," Zuri said. She held up her arms as if wanting to be cuddled right then, and with a laugh Dare picked her up and held her close as he inspected the town.

Jarn's Holdout matched both its own name and the entry point to a region called Bastion. It was crammed snugly into a ravine between two cliffs, rugged mountains to the north and south making it the only easy way through the Gadris range.

Guard towers had been built at the junction where the cliffs spilled out into the valley beyond, a high curtain wall stretching between them and blocking their view of the town within. Although from their high vantage point they could see the slate roofs of a few two and three-storey buildings.

It was a serious fortification against a real threat, and Dare turned his gaze north to the region Jarn's Holdout had once protected Kovana from.

As far as he could see, Bastion looked to be plains dotted with patches of forestland, as well as a few lines of tall hills with forested slopes and sprawling meadows that came close to qualifying as mountains themselves. There were a few tiny ribbons of rivers sparkling in the distance, and almost out of sight was a larger expanse of deep blue that had to be a good-sized lake.

It *did* look like a wilder land than Kovana, rugged and full of promise and opportunity. Dare liked the idea of getting lost in those hills and forests and diving in that sparking lake.

Kovana

Pella made a contented noise and cuddled up to his side, nuzzling his cheek with her silky soft, floppy ears. "What?" he asked with a laugh, wrapping an arm around her waist.

She beamed up at him, lovely brown eyes shining. "You just smell so content and happy. You love this life, don't you?"

Dare thought with amusement that she didn't realize how close to dead on she was. He loved this life he'd been given since coming here from Earth.

"I do," he agreed, kissing her ear and then Zuri's cheek. "I love exploring. I love hunting monsters and leveling up. I love meeting new people and haggling in markets and eating in inns. I love campfires and nights cuddling in our tent and the beauty of this world."

He hugged them both fiercely, staring out at the new land. "And most of all I love that I can share all of it with you. I love you both more than words can say."

To his surprise Zuri sniffled and buried her face in his neck.

He and Pella both stared at her in surprise. "You okay,?" he asked, rubbing her back.

She laughed in embarrassment and looked between them, cheeks going darker green. "Sorry, that was just so beautiful, Dare."

"It was," the dog girl agreed, patting Zuri's back as well. Then she grinned playfully and slapped Dare's butt, making him jump. "But if we're done admiring the scenery we should keep going. I want to get to Jarn's Holdout and finish off all our business so we can have a good meal and maybe a bath!"

They all laughed, and Dare kissed Zuri one more time before setting her down and getting back to work pulling the sled.

❋ ❋ ❋ ❋ ❋

The guards at the gate were all Level 30.

That was a surprise, but maybe not too much of one. The guards in Kovana had mostly been there to keep the peace and stop criminals, which meant they mostly dealt with lower level people while leaving higher level people and monster threats to resident adventurers.

But the guards here would also be serving as a first line of defense against monster incursions, bandit attacks, and trouble with the wild tribes of other races. They needed to be strong enough to handle the danger.

Although most likely there were still resident adventurers or elite soldiers for the bigger problems.

The second surprise came after waiting in the small line in front of the gate until the guards finally called them forward. "Adventurers?" the tall, sturdily built woman asked, looking them over. They nodded and she grunted. "Planning to hunt monsters in Bastion?"

"As many as we can," Dare said, wondering if the region's governor required a license or some BS like that to hunt monsters.

But as it turned out, the opposite was the case. The guard grunted again and motioned them through the gates.

"No taxes?" Dare asked, surprised.

"Not for adventurers or anyone else who plans to hunt monsters in Bastion." She grinned. "Anything to encourage them to ply their trade here." She nodded towards Zuri and Pella. "You won't get any hassle about slaves or pets, either."

"Actually they're my free companions," he corrected.

"That's fine," the guard said, surprising him. She waved them through again. "Welcome to Jarn's Holdout."

The buildings inside the wall were surprisingly crowded, struggling to fit between the cliffs closing in on either side. That led to narrow streets, most of which were the bare stone of the ravine, which had been rutted and pitted by long use until the few wagons in view jolted violently as they rolled along.

The worst part about the cramped space and apparent lack of water, though, was the filth. Alleys reeking of sewage, garbage being kicked around by passersby along streets covered with grime that stuck to your shoes, and dingy walls.

"I can see why Lord Kinnran was so eager to get off these streets," Dare said, wrinkling his nose.

"It gets better farther in," Pella said, not seeming to mind the smell and in fact turning her head curiously from side to side, seeming to have to resist the urge to explore.

Zuri nodded, looking decidedly more queasy at the stench. "The ravine widens into a valley, and there's an underground river they dug down to that provides fresh water and a way to dispose of garbage and sewage."

"The market even has a grassy green," Pella added. "My master took me there for a picnic with Baron Haldin once. We should do that too!"

"Sounds fun," Dare said, dodging a group of surly dwarves.

There were a surprising number of people out and about. But unlike towns in Kovana that were mostly humans and slaves, there were a lot more members of other races in view.

He saw goblins, of course, and canids, and dwarves, and bovids. He spotted one or two orcs, and some sort of scaly creature that might've been a humanoid reptilian or dragonkin. He even spotted a couple of elves huddled close together and looking down their noses at everyone else, although to his disappointment neither one was a woman. And in one private garden built behind an inn down an alley, he saw what looked like a floran flower peeking up over a fence.

Many of those he saw were obviously slaves, but many others looked as if they might be free. Most of the latter group were even armed and armored, with high enough levels to suggest they hadn't spent their lives scratching at the dirt in a village.

Dare looked around eagerly at the variety of other races, wishing he could talk to them all and find out more about them. He wanted to know how they differed from how those races had been portrayed on Earth, and if there were races here that hadn't even been dreamed of by people in his old home.

In contrast to his own interest, he noticed that most people didn't give him and his companions more than a passing glance, aside from Pella and Zuri earning a few admiring looks. It was a refreshing change from the curious and often hostile scrutiny they'd gotten in towns in Kovana.

He was liking Bastion more and more.

The market turned out to be busier than expected, with all the vendors they'd end up using already crowded. It turned out this really was a haven for adventurers and other sorts looking for opportunities in the north.

Dare looked around, grimacing. "How about we split up? I'll take the loot like feathers, claws, fangs, antlers, and hides to vendors who'd buy them. And the trophies of course. You two see if you can find buyers for the Exceptional plate leggings, the Journeyman short sword, and the other stuff."

His companions agreed, and after a bit of redistributing the sleds they set out.

There were plenty of people who'd have use of his items. Leatherworkers, Tailors, and probably the other crafters too. As well as Jewelers, Apothecaries and Alchemists, and curio dealers. Hell, even housewives wanting to make pillows with the feathers.

He had to chase off ragged urchins creeping around the sled on two different occasions as he made his way through the market, and once nearly broke the hand of a pickpocket before sending him scurrying away. This place definitely was more chaotic; not that there weren't plenty of guards, but they couldn't be everywhere looking at everything.

He'd just have to be careful. And hopefully the girls would be just as vigilant. Not that he needed to worry on that count, since Pella could probably smell out a thief at 10 yards.

Dare visited a butcher first, since they'd have a good idea of what to do with animal remains that weren't meat. The man was friendly enough, especially when he saw the two chimera heads and Dare briefly described his fight with the giant monster.

The butcher willingly directed him to a few vendors who he seemed to respect, who'd probably be interested in his items and should offer good prices. "Tell them old Yaradan sent you," the man added with a chuckle. "It should help."

"Thanks." Dare offered a firm handshake, then dragged his sled off.

His first stop was a Leatherworker, where he was able to unload all his hides, along with most of the claws and teeth, which the man planned to use for ornamentation and things like buckles and buttons. After some haggling he was able to net 7 gold, 23 silver, which wasn't fantastic but he hadn't hoped for much from those particular items.

He also checked the armor while he was there, and saw some pieces tempting enough to come back and take a closer look at once he was done selling his items.

Before moving on he asked the Leatherworker about good places to sell the rest of his loot. The man's recommendations were similar to the butcher's; they must've either run in the same social circles or were both offering the best options.

Either way it was a good sign.

Dare stopped by a Woodcarver and was able to unload his antlers and the rest of his claws and teeth, again netting only a modest sum. Then he stopped by a tailor and had a pleasant surprise; the large flight feathers were prized, and even the smaller body feathers were deemed high quality.

All in all he made over 15 gold from them, and he was so pleased at the prices that he didn't even haggle too aggressively.

That just left the trophies, and it was there that the selling got tricky.

All the vendors he'd spoken to agreed that he'd probably be able to unload them in the market. But they were the highest value of his haul, and a vanity item only a few would be interested in. So if he wanted to get the best price out of them he should skip the vendors and go straight to the end buyer.

The noblemen and wealthy merchants.

There was an exclusive hunting lodge in the nicer part of the town, and while Dare had no hope of getting in himself, he had some hope that he might be able to convince them to see if any of their patrons were interested in the trophies.

After all, freakishly large lion and serpent heads that were the product of some madman's experiments (going by the lore implied by the name Escaped Monstrosity) would look good on some young lord's or knight's wall.

The hunting lodge looked fancier than you'd expect for a place where hunters would gather to speak of their exploits or take jobs. Then again, this was obviously a place for wealthy men to lounge. More of a gentlemen's club than a common laborers' hall.

A pair of footman stood attendance at the door to the lodge, dressed in fancy livery and bearing halberds. They looked decidedly unimpressed by Dare's display of the trophies and coldly bid him to be off.

"No one in there would be interested in the trophies of a slain monster the size of an elephant?" he tried one last time.

Their response was a coordinated step forward, hands shifting on the hafts of their polearms.

Well fine then. Dispirited, Dare made his way back to the market, heading for a novelty vendor he'd been recommended to as a potential buyer for trophies. Maybe if he was higher level or had fancier clothes, it would be a different story. But at the moment he wasn't exactly high society, and he wasn't about to humiliate himself going door to door until someone called the guards on him to run him off.

He'd take the price cut with a vendor.

"Holy shit, that's the biggest lion's head I've ever seen!" a bright, playful woman's voice said from off to one side as he entered the market.

Dare jumped slightly and turned at the unexpected greeting, fixing on a polite smile in spite of his mood. Then his smile became more genuine when he saw who was talking to him.

Chapter Seventeen
Mercenary

A catgirl.

A genuine, soft velvety ears atop her head and long sleek tail rising cutely like a question mark behind her catgirl. She even had her hands up close to her chest in forward-facing fists like little cat paws, apparently an affectation of excitement as she stared at the trophies sitting on the sled, tail lashing eagerly.

She was probably his age or a few years older. It was hard to get a good impression of her figure since she was wearing heavy chain armor, and had a shield slung on her back and a sword belted at her waist, but she barely came up to Dare's shoulder and looked as if she had a slender strength rather than bulk.

Her adorable face belied her martial appearance, though, round and friendly with big pale orange eyes, a cute button nose, and a pouty little rosebud mouth. Her flawless skin was pale as cream, and her ears and tail were a pale orange. Even her sleek, well cared for hair, pulled up in pigtails and hanging halfway down her back, had that same orange color.

Her orange and cream coloring made him think of those orange dream popsicles he'd loved as a kid, and he couldn't help but stare, enchanted.

As had become second nature, he checked her with his Adventurer's Eye. "Felid, adult female. Humanoid, intelligent. Class: Flanker Level 17."

Dare uncomfortably became aware he'd been staring when the woman cleared her throat, smirking at him. "Well? Cat got your tongue?" she teased.

"No, but that sounds like it might be fun," he blurted, then immediately felt like an ass.

But to his relief she just laughed and batted at his shoulder. "Whoa, easy there tiger."

"Sorry," he said, feeling his cheeks flush. "I've never met a catgirl before." And he could honestly say that they were up there behind elves in terms of women he'd dreamed of meeting. Especially a cute one like her.

"No worries. An stupidly handsome awkward man lugging around a huge trophy can get away with a lot." Still smirking, she held out a chainmail-gauntleted hand. "I'm Linia."

"Dare," he said, returning her surprisingly firm grip. "Pleasure to meet you, Linia."

"Sister!" a younger voice called, and a catgirl with similar if lighter orange coloring ran up to Linia. She was probably in her early teens, only Level 3, and wore basic leather armor and had a bow slung over her back and a dagger at her hip. Dare's Eye confirmed that she was a ranged class, specifically Archer.

Behind the girl came a handful of other armed and armored people, ranging from 15 to 18 in level. An eclectic group that included different races:

A scarred and grizzled older male felid was the strongest as a Level 18 Quickblade. There was also a hulking, muscular male orc with rusty reddish-brown skin wearing a slave collar, whose class was called by the straightforward name Breaker and who wore only breeches and had a battleaxe slung on his thickly muscled back. And finally a human man and woman in robes wielding spears who were a Spellwarder and Lightgiver, respectively, and looked similar enough to be siblings.

"Hey guys," Linia said as the group gathered around her to shoot cautious looks at Dare and inspect the chimera heads. "This is Dare. We were just talking about his trophies."

The grizzled felid whistled in admiration as he inspected them. "Must've been quite the battle. You take those monsters out?"

"It, actually," Dare said. "A Level 21 party rated chimera called an Escaped Monstrosity, about the size of an elephant."

"A what?" the catgirl teenager asked, little nose furrowed in an expression she had to know was adorable.

She kind of reminded Dare of his kid sister, and he felt a moment of sorrow thinking of how he'd never see Holly again, and wondering how she was dealing with his death back on Earth.

"An elephant," the older felid replied curtly. "A large gray creature of the southern continents. About the height of an ogre, but much bigger since it stands on four legs."

The young catgirl stared at the heads with wide eyes. "And you killed it?" she asked in admiration, holding her forward-facing fists up in front of her in a similar catgirl pose to her sister's. "How big was your party?"

"Three people," Dare said.

Linia and the human woman snorted, and the orc made a noise of clear disbelief. "All your level?" he rumbled; if he was a slave he certainly didn't sound or act like it, and none of his companions called him out.

"We have a 28 Tracker." Dare looked around. "We split up to sell loot, but they're around here somewhere. I'll introduce you when I see them." He motioned to Linia's group. "Are you a party?"

"At times," the male human said. "We're members of a mercenary company."

"Marshal's Irregulars," his maybe-sister added, and as one the entire group, even the young teenager, clapped a fist to their chest in salute.

Dare looked at them in new interest. He hadn't encountered any mercenaries on Collisa before now, but as a general rule in games they tended to range from lovable rogues to a tight-knit brotherhood to the scum of the earth. Historically tending more often to that last one in the real world, which made him wonder if they'd be like that here, where things were just as real as Earth.

However, at the moment these mercenaries seemed friendly enough.

"I'm Felicia, by the way," the young catgirl said, crouching to more closely inspect the lion head. "So how did the fight go?"

"The most intense minutes of my life," Dare said honestly. "We caught it napping and were able to make some preparations, but even so it nearly snapped my head off twice within the first few seconds of the fight."

"Oh?" the orc grunted. "What preparations did you make?"

Dare saw no reason not to tell the group, so he described the fight from start to finish. Although he downplayed the effectiveness of Zuri's Sheltering Embrace detonating; he didn't want that particular secret getting out, and they probably wouldn't have believed him anyway.

Also he was vague on their classes and specific abilities, just as a matter of principle.

"So you relied on mobility and trading the monster's attention between party members to get out of it unscathed," the grizzled felid concluded, idly scratching an ear that had a good-sized chunk torn out of it. "You won't always get away with tactics like that against a party rated monster."

"We won't," Dare agreed. "Thankfully it worked out this time."

Felicia leaned down to stroke the lion head's mane, ignoring her older sister's sharp words of rebuke about not asking first. "Was it scary?"

He grimaced, thinking of those few moments when the chimera almost had him, and chuckled wryly. "Almost shit my pants at times. But it's important to keep your cool and do your job in the fight even when things go wrong. Especially then, actually."

The young catgirl nodded thoughtfully at his advice. Then she brightened, motioning to his bow then patting her own. "Thanks, it's good to get the perspective of an experienced Archer." She paused. "Or are you a Marksman?"

"Hunter, actually," he said.

Felicia's expression became carefully neutral. "Oh. How . . . rustic."

Dare had to grin. "Rustic, huh?"

"Shh, little sis, don't be rude," Linia said, cheeks flushing with embarrassment as she pushed the young teenager behind her back, like she was trying to hide her; it looked like even on another world some things were the same.

"I'm not being rude!" Felicia protested, darting this way and that to try to get out from behind her sister as she snuck Dare indignant peeks. "It's just who picks Hunter? Archers and Marksmen are both better for combat, and also party and raid tactics. What's Hunter better for, shooting rabbits?"

From Dare's perusal of the different ranged classes there was some truth to that. Although a lot of it depended on how you spent your ability points, since the classes all had similar trees for the bow and melee weapons.

Linia was looking at him apologetically, and he smiled to show he didn't mind her kid sister's pestering as he answered. "Me and my companions spend a lot of time out in the wilds. With my class I'm able to craft clothes, tents, bedrolls, and other items we need to live comfortably. I can also hunt and trap plenty of meat, and forage greens, mushrooms, valuable spices, and other cooking ingredients. I can also make my own bow, which was helpful for starting out, and repair my bow as well. So with all that we've been able to save money on food and shelter, supplement our income, and spend more time out in the wilds focused on hunting monsters instead of trying to survive."

He motioned at the trophies. "And as you can see, I can still hold my own in a fight."

The older felid chuckled, seeming to approve of the impromptu life lesson to the young catgirl. "Well said, Hunter. Many forget that there's more to a life than doing damage and providing utility to your party in a fight. All the classes have practical value and people who are best suited for them."

Felicia pouted, seeming to realize her companion was speaking pretty much directly at her. "Okay sure, that's great." She finally darted out from behind Linia, drawing an exasperated noise from her older sister, and hurried around the sled to stand near Dare. "Can I see your bow?"

"Okay, that's it," Linia snapped, starting to strip off her chainmail armor. "Recruit Felicia Melarawn, you will assist me in removing my armor and convey it back to our camp, where you will thoroughly clean it. That is an order."

The young teenager gaped in outrage. "You can't order me around just because I'm your page. That's not fair!"

Dare couldn't help but think that was exactly what a page's job was. Although it had to suck to serve your older sibling; he certainly would've hated it.

"Orders are orders, Felicia," the older felid said, laughing outright and clapping the girl on the back. "Come on. I'll give you a hand with it."

Dare felt a presence at his side and turned to see Pella, who was looking at the group of mercenaries with wary curiosity. "Hey cutie," he said, slipping an arm around her waist.

"Hi," she said, absently kissing his cheek as she kept up her cautious scrutiny. "New friends?"

"I'd say so," he replied.

He couldn't help but notice that Linia was looking a bit put out by his intimacy with the dog girl. She scowled as she continued peeling off her heavy armor, revealing heavy, sweat-stained linen padding beneath. And also wafting the clean scent of her sweat and a distinctly feminine scent over to him.

Even after walking around in armor she smelled good, and as she finished removing her chainmail and got to work on her padding, revealing a light form-fitting tunic and pants beneath, he saw that she had a slender but strong figure with small breasts and narrow hips, but even so some distinctly feminine curves he wanted to run his hands over.

Or in short, she had the lean beauty and grace of a cat in a woman's form.

He hoped the catgirl didn't think he wasn't interested just because he was with Pella, and wondered how to convey to her that he was open to having fun with her, too.

He decided to go with the open approach and simply winked at her while grinning wolfishly.

Linia grinned back, expression turning speculative. Especially when Zuri came up on Dare's other side and he put his arm around her, too.

"Your party rated monster-slaying companions?" the catgirl asked as she gathered up her armor and padding and stuffed it all into Felicia's arms, then shooed the sulking girl down the street away from them. The page only went a few steps before defiantly stopping once her sister's back was turned, though, sticking out her tongue at Linia's back.

"Yep, this is my party," Dare replied, hugging his lovers closer as he explained to them, "We were talking about the fight with the chimera."

"Wow, your party is a goblin and a dog girl?" Felicia butted in, ignoring her sister's angry look as she drifted closer again. "That's really unusual."

"It is?" Dare gave the mercenaries' own eclectic group a pointed look.

Linia laughed. "Actually yes, it is. Our Commander, Marshal Jind Alor, operates the company by recruiting volunteers from the slave markets. Sign on for twenty years and earn your freedom and a generous retirement stipend, or stay on for even more generous compensation."

"And we're mostly treated as if we're already free as long as we follow orders and don't wander off," Felicia added cheerfully. "All our needs are met and we even get a share of loot, too! That's why freedmen also join us, not just slaves."

The male human rubbed his chin thoughtfully, looking Dare and his companions over. "Speaking of which, would you three be interested? Your share of loot increases by level, and if you're not slaves you can get a generous signing bonus along with the other perks."

Maybe it was a good offer for most, a safer alternative to leveling on your own and for many a better option than slavery. But Dare wasn't in any way tempted.

He wasn't about to sign his freedom away to a fighting company just so he could level more slowly, make less gold, and be in more danger.

Not to mention there was no way in hell he could have a harem as a common mercenary. Unless he could rise to a position of power in the company, unlikely since nepotism tended to be rife in these sorts of organizations, he'd basically be a foot soldier.

No thanks.

"It's worth considering," he said politely.

Linia grinned at his obvious reluctance. "Well anyway you should come drink with us. We just got back from a campaign and we're in the mood to celebrate with some drinking and whoring." She gave him an appraising look. "Or getting to know new drinking buddies a bit better."

That seemed like a pretty clear invitation.

Dare wasn't the only one who caught it, either. "Well you certainly get to know *your* drinking buddies better," Felicia said snidely. "Sometimes more than one at a time."

Linia screeched in fury as the other mercenaries laughed, but before she could descend in wrath on her younger sister the older felid grabbed one of Felicia's big velvety ears. "That's quite enough out of you, young lady," he said sternly as he started ushering the teenaged catgirl down the street. "What would your mother think to hear you talking like that? I promised her I would keep you out of trouble."

Dare grinned as the laughter continued; it was good to see someone was looking out for the girl in the company of rough and rowdy mercenaries.

He turned back to Linia. "You said you could earn your freedom? It's good to hear Bastion allows that . . . Kovana was pretty terrible where slavery was concerned."

She frowned, obviously uncomfortable with the subject. "We're more of a frontier here, struggling to hold back the chaos of the wilds. There's a rough sort of fairness to be found, especially for people who know how to fight and can help keep the monsters at bay."

That made a sort of sense. The Wild West was known for outlaw bands and gunfights in the street, but it was also where a lot of people seeking to escape overcrowding and limited prospects to the east went to try to make something of their lives.

"I think drinks is a great idea," Zuri said, biting back a smile. "We were just talking about how the best part of visiting towns is meeting new friends."

"Great!" Linia said, grinning like the cat that swallowed the canary. Or was it the pussy that swallowed the cock? "I need to clean up and take care of some business in town, but if you stop by the Sally Fourth inn just up the canyon from here in a couple hours, I'll be there."

"Sounds good," Dare said. "It'll give us a chance to complete our business, too."

"Until then, Hunter," the human Spellwarder said as he turned away with his sister to head down the street. "I look forward to hearing more tales. And maybe topping them." The other mercenaries followed him, Linia giving Dare one last lingering look before sauntering after them.

Dare watched the group walk off, watching the petite catgirl's pert little ass and sleek swishing tail as she slinked down the street, as if fully aware of his eyes on her.

She wasn't the only one. "I'm guessing your interest in the mercenaries has something to do with the adorable catgirl?" Pella whispered in a teasing voice. "Are you going to sleep with her?"

He winced, cursing to himself as he watched the preternaturally graceful Linia stumble slightly on flat ground a ways down the street. "That depends on if her hearing is as good as yours," he whispered back wryly.

The catgirl glanced back and smirked at him, and he felt his face flush; well, that answered whether she'd heard or not. Although she looked as if she might still be up for it in spite of a few embarrassing blunders.

He supposed he'd have to see in a few hours when they met at the cheesily named Sally Fourth.

"How did your selling go?" he asked his lovers.

293

"Good!" Pella said, ears perked happily. "We sold everything!"

Zuri was already counting out Dare's share, and he began doing the same for his companions. "I doubt we haggled as well as you could've," she said. "But I did my best. Pella's nose for deceit definitely helped."

The dog girl fondly patted the goblin woman's head. "She's just being modest. She has a real head for the value of things, and never let any vendor get away with a bad deal. Even if it meant walking away."

"Sounds like you two make a good team," Dare said, wrapping his arms around his lovers and kissing them both. He glanced at his sled with the trophies. "Guess that just leaves these albatrosses."

Zuri frowned in confusion. "My stone translated that, but I have no idea what it means."

He felt his cheeks heat. "It was a superstition among sailors of my home. Albatrosses were considered lucky, and any sailor that killed one, even accidentally, had to wear it hanging around his neck for the remainder of the voyage."

"That had to suck," Pella said. "Let's get rid of these heads so we don't have to drag them around like that."

That was the trick. Since the fancy hunting lodge had been a bust, Dare tried the next best location: the Adventurers Guild.

Contrary to his impression of those sorts of guilds from most games or stories on Earth, it wasn't a private organization or even really a proper guild. It was more of a glorified job board and meeting place for adventurers, funded by the baron of Jarn's Holdout.

Conveniently, it was where people went to place notices for quests, put up advertisements for goods and services useful to adventurers, and offer bounties for roaming monsters, bandits, and other menaces. And probably most notably, it was where adventurers went to offer their services to leaders forming parties, swap tales, exchange advice on nearby spawn points, and other related tasks.

There was a school nearby for young adventurers, and retired adventurers could congregate to relive their glory days.

It was a fascinating place, with a lot of interesting and useful options for Dare and his companions. Not to mention being full of adventurers of several races, not just humans. He would've loved to stay longer and see everything it had to offer, maybe share some drinks and swap some tales.

But he was on a clock, and there was a sexy orange dream catgirl waiting for him.

His eagerness might've made him less aggressive in getting the best prize for his trophies. Or maybe it was the fact that while the adventurers all seemed fascinated by the lion and serpent heads, few had the funds or the home to put them in.

Finally a few seasoned veterans who ran the guildhall pooled 10 gold to buy the pair, so they could mount them on the walls of the sprawling common room they were currently standing in. There were already a dozen other trophies hung there, monster skulls and animal heads and even what looked like a small dragon skull. Or maybe a wyvern or some similar beast.

Dare had a feeling he could've gotten twice that for his trophies. Still, he kind of liked the idea of having them hang here where adventurers could admire them. And, again, he was in a hurry.

Zuri and Pella agreed with the deal, on the condition that their names be displayed beneath the trophies as the ones who'd killed the beast, which the veteran adventurers agreed to readily. So Dare exchanged handshakes with the grizzled men and split the gold between his companions.

"All right," Zuri said briskly as they left the guildhall. "Let's get ready for your date."

Dare was a bit bemused by how eager she sounded. Pella was a bit less enthusiastic, but she seemed to look forward to a night of fun and agreed fully with them cleaning up and making themselves presentable.

First things first, since he was done with the sleds he broke them down. Then he used the materials from them and what little leather he had left and made a couple collapsible chairs.

His lovers watched him curiously. "Trade goods?" Pella asked.

"My guess would be gifts," Zuri corrected, grinning. "What every girl loves to receive from the man who wants to mate her."

"Hey, you guys like yours," he protested. They just snickered and he shook his head. "Well I'm going to give them to Linia anyway. I've even got the perfect line."

"I'm sure she'll think it's sweet," Pella said politely, hiding a smile behind her hand.

He shook his head; everyone was a critic.

They found a place in town where they could get running water, a public fountain in a square that connected to the underground river, and Zuri cast Cleanse Target on them. Then they found a private place to change into some clothes she'd sewn for them, dresses for her and Pella and a tunic and breeches for Dare.

Nothing fancy, but they were made from nice cloth and looked presentable.

Last of all came grooming, starting with Pella cutting his hair and giving him a shave. Zuri usually did that for him every week or so, but the dog girl insisted she'd performed that service for her master. And she actually did a pretty professional job, judging by his appearance in the shiny tin mirror the girls had saved for their own use.

He looked less like a vagabond and more like a man ready for a night around town.

The girls took turns brushing each other's hair, including Pella's fluffy tail. Instead of putting the dog girl's golden hair back into a ponytail, Zuri arranged part of it in an intricate braid that swept up the rest and let it flow free down her back.

"You look like a princess," Dare told her, grinning.

Pella blushed. "Stop that," she said, slapping his arm. "I'm the farthest thing from a princess."

"You're more beautiful than one, that's for sure. Both of you are."

The dog girl's tail wagged, a slow smile lighting up her features. "Do you really think so?"

"A man would have to be blind not to see how gorgeous you are." He pulled Pella close with an arm around her waist and kissed her softly, meeting her gaze. "In all our talks before now you've seemed okay with me being with other women, but I wanted to make sure you were okay with me sleeping with Linia, if the opportunity presents itself."

"It will," Zuri said confidently.

His golden-haired lover shifted uncomfortably. "I'm happy with the idea of you having a large harem and sleeping with other women," she said with a warm smile. "Other women deserve to have a chance to see how wonderful you are."

It was Dare's turn to feel his cheeks heat. He noticed she hadn't answered him specifically about the catgirl, but he didn't press that point. "Thank you, Pella. And you too, Zuri," he added, pulling his goblin lover close. "I love you both."

"I love you too," Zuri said, grinning. "Now let's go help you fuck a catgirl!"

The Sally Fourth turned out to be a reasonably large four-storey structure, a bit old and shabby but with clear signs of being carefully cared for. The sign above the door showed a team of mounted adventurers of different classes, obviously dressed for travel, with a lordly looking man in the lead dramatically pointing his sword forward.

Most signs for inns and taverns tended to be cheap and simple, getting the name across without much fuss, but this one looked like a professionally commissioned mural.

The first floor of the inn was one huge common room, with a crowded bar along one entire wall staffed by three bartenders, and half a dozen serving girls running to and fro serving drinks to the rest of the room. The wall behind the long bar was crowded with stacked casks and barrels, and several shelves full of various bottles.

The middle of the floor was crowded with tables, while booths surprisingly similar to what he'd see in a restaurant back home lined two other walls. The final wall was a staircase leading to a surround balcony overlooking the floor, with four other staircases leading up from it along each wall to the rooms on the upper floors.

The place was surprisingly crowded, with all but a few of the tables occupied and only one booth open. And then only because a group of cheerfully singing dwarves had recently vacated it, holding each other up as they staggered towards the door.

They were singing a raucous song about a mermaid lounging in a pool of ale, and all the lascivious things she did with visitors of various races as the pool gradually emptied from them all drinking their fill.

Dare regretted that the dwarves were leaving before he could hear how the song ended. The current verse seemed to involve a dragon (not a dragonkin or one shapeshifted into humanoid form but an actual, full sized dragon, as the song clearly stressed) vigorously satisfying her with a cock half as big as she was.

Not exactly realistic . . . he wondered what Trissela would think of the song.

Much as he would've liked to follow along and keep listening, he wasted no time hurrying over to claim the booth they'd vacated. A group of roughly dressed laborers were also making for it, their expressions turning surly when they saw him and his companions trying to take it. They seemed the sort who'd gladly start a brawl over seats.

But then they seemed to realize that the three adventurers were all much higher level than them, and wisely backed away to take one of the tables instead.

There was a nook along the wall above the booth where they could place their things, and with some stuffing Dare was able to get their weapons and gear into it. Then they settled into the booth; the stuffed leather seats and backrests were comfortable enough, if of dubious cleanliness.

At Zuri's urging, rather than his companions sitting to either side of him Pella cuddled up close while the goblin sat on her other side. "That way Linia can sit by you," she said.

"You really are the perfect wingman," Dare told her. Pella looked confused at the term, but he'd already told his goblin lover what it meant and she giggled in response.

A serving girl came by and Dare ordered a round of drinks, including one for their eagerly awaited new catgirl friend. They put off ordering food until she arrived, although Dare did arrange for a nice room with a bed big enough for four.

The woman, plump and matronly, seemed amused at that, although she promised to make the arrangements and bring him a key. She returned a few minutes later with mugs of ale and the key, giving directions to a room on the top floor, then bustled off leaving Dare and his friends to settle back and enjoy their drinks.

They didn't have to wait long for Linia to arrive; less than five minutes later Dare, who'd been idly looking around the room as he sipped his ale, froze and stared with open admiration as he caught sight of the catgirl descending the stairs.

"Orange dream," he murmured in awe.

Chapter Eighteen
Dinner

Linia's flawless skin had been scrubbed to a rosy glow, soft and smooth as the cream it resembled, and her cheeks were flushed with excitement, large orange eyes looking about eagerly.

As if she knew all about popsicles from Earth and was trying to perfectly match the resemblance, she'd chosen to wear a sleeveless, knee-length light summer dress of the same pale orange. The material looked invitingly soft, and was thin enough that he could see her small, perky nipples poking out, proving she wasn't wearing a bra.

And hinting at her mood as well. That or she felt cold, which was unlikely since the common room was borderline too warm with so many people packing it.

Her pale orange hair fell loose to halfway down her back, brushed until it shone soft and sleek. Her tail's short, soft fur had also been cleaned and brushed, and it was curled up in a playful question mark behind her. Her cute cat ears were raised inquisitively, looking so soft he felt the strong urge to rub them.

Gods, the catgirl was even holding her hands up like little paws again. She was so adorable he wanted to just pick her up and cuddle her and listen to her purr in his arms.

If he hadn't known she was a badass mercenary who cursed like a sailor and openly eye fucked him, he would've thought she was the most sweet, innocent young lady on Collisa.

Linia spotted the three of them in their booth and brightened, waving eagerly and hurrying down the stairs. The eyes of most of the men in the room followed her in open admiration as she wove through the tables, and a few even called out compliments and offers.

She ignored them, reaching the booth and giving Dare a hug as he stood to greet her. Her body was soft and warm, and he could feel her nipples pressing into his chest; he felt his cheeks heat and quickly backed away before he embarrassed himself when she noticed another autonomous response.

By her catlike smile he had a feeling she knew exactly why he'd been so quick to break off the enjoyable contact.

"You're early," she said, grinning. "I had a feline you would be."

Dare blinked for a second, thinking he'd misheard, then groaned. "Seriously, cat puns?"

The catgirl giggled, bopping his chest with a small fist. "Normally they're beneath my dignity, but I'm feeling playful right meow."

Zuri and Pella giggled, and he shook his head in defeat as he struggled not to smile. "Here," he said, handing the adorable woman the two collapsible chairs he'd made. "For you and Felicia." He grinned. "Something to remind her how useless Hunters are."

"Oh," she said, awkwardly taking the collapsed chairs; if you didn't know what they were they'd probably look like some kind of splint, or maybe a rope ladder. Either one a pretty bizarre gift for a potential romantic partner. "Um, thanks?"

He grinned wider. "You're out on campaigns a lot, and I can imagine you'd appreciate having a light, easily transportable chair you can use around a campfire. Here." He took one of the chairs back and showed her how to set it up.

Linia's eyes widened as she settled onto the leather seat, rested her arms on the padded armrests, and pressed her back against the leather backrest. "Wow, it's even pretty comfortable," she said, leather squeaking as she adjusted her position. "Where did you get the pattern for this?"

"He made it himself," Zuri said, expression proud. "It beats dragging over a log or sitting on your pack."

"Beats it? There's no comparison." The catgirl made an admiring sound as she sprawled back, crossing her feet in front of her. "Would you be willing to explain the finer details of the pattern to the Irregulars' crafters for a modest fee? I bet pretty much everyone would like to have one of these."

Dare nodded. "Sure. We can sort it out tomorrow."

"Mmm," Linia said, giving him a lazy grin. "Yeah, we've got stuff we want to do tonight, don't we?" She crossed her legs the other way, the gesture far more suggestive this time. Especially with how the motion shifted her cute little sundress just right to show the briefest flash of innocent white panties.

He felt his face heating. "Drinks?" he asked hastily, sliding back into the booth and motioning to the seat beside him.

She laughed as she folded up the chair and handed both to him to put in the cubby. Then she slipped in to sit close enough to him that her leg brushed lightly against his, an unexpected but welcome sensation.

"Thanks for the chair," she murmured, leaning in to press her pouty little rosebud lips against his cheek in a playful peck. "It's one of the oddest gifts I've ever been given, especially by a man who wants to get between my legs, but also probably one of the most useful and well thought out."

The adorable catgirl bopped his nose playfully and reached for her drink, tone becoming naughty. "I promise I'll think of your handsome face every time I sit on it."

Pella, who'd been taking a sip of her drink, choked at that. Zuri snickered. And of course Dare instantly found himself picturing Linia's sleek orange tail swishing hypnotically in front of his eyes as the petite catgirl ground her crotch against his face.

"So tell me about the Flanker class," he said hastily as he took a gulp of his ale, trying to distract himself from the mental image and the feel of the slender, distinctly feminine form pressed against his side; she could see his crotch from her angle, and she'd noticed immediately if he sprung a massive wood right there in the common room. "I'm not sure I ever gave it more than a glance when I was looking at the classes."

He realized his mistake immediately, that he shouldn't have known her class, and silently cursed herself. Zuri also gave him a sharp look, picking up on the misstep.

But thankfully Linia either didn't notice or didn't care. "Oh that's a shame, the Flanker class is really versatile," she said, taking a deep pull of her drink as her orange tail absently flicked his shoulder. "Especially for melee, it's a popular choice."

"Going by the armor and shield, I'm guessing it's a tank class?"

The catgirl stared at him blankly, and Zuri snickered and answered for him. "It's a word from his homeland. It means someone in the defender role, keeping a monster occupied and taking hits if necessary, as well as the classes that usually fulfill that role."

"Oh," Linia said, nodding her approval. "One syllable and easy to remember, I like that . . . usually it's a mouthful to explain what your role is on the battlefield." She took another gulp. "Flankers are kind of a hybrid, you could say. In a raid or larger scale battle we'd be the ones circling around to engage the enemy from the sides or back, keeping them penned in and catching any stragglers that try to get to our damage dealers, healers, and support roles. We can also do fair damage at need."

Dare nodded thoughtfully. It sounded like an off-tank for a raid, picking up adds and otherwise contributing damage, and in an emergency picking up the boss if the main tank went down.

"Heavier "tank" classes are actually less popular in a lot of parties and for solo leveling," Linia continued, seeming to like the new word. "They're slow and their heavy armor is usually overkill for the incoming damage. Besides, a lot of times regular monsters don't even need anyone standing there taking hits from them, they either die too quickly or can be easily led around."

She grinned and motioned to them. "You guys should know, you don't even have a proper tank class and you beat a party rated monster. That's where hybrid tanks like Flankers shine . . . we're more mobile, and have an easier time moving around to engage multiple monsters if things go wrong or the monsters pull a friend. We can also do more damage, and are cheaper to equip."

"Sounds like we need to find ourselves a Flanker," Dare joked.

The catgirl giggled and playfully batted at his shoulder. "I hope you aren't getting your hopes up about me . . . you'd probably need at least 500 gold to buy out my contract. Anyway I wouldn't leave because I'd be abandoning Felicia and Irawn."

He assumed Irawn was the older felid who'd seemed to have a paternal role to the two girls. "Oh, I wouldn't make any presumptions," he said quickly. Then he grinned. "Although you can't blame me for hoping."

"I guess that's what most hope is, huh?" Her adorable rosebud mouth became even more pouty as she stuck out her lower lip. "Anyway I like the Irregulars. We're more than just hired thugs, and we take care of our own."

Dare could admit he'd be overjoyed if he could convince the adorable catgirl off-tank to join them, both for her role and for the pleasure of her company. But if it wasn't happening, he would just be happy if they could have some fun before they went their separate ways.

The serving girl came back and they ordered food. Linia seemed amused when they only asked for various cuts of meat and dessert. "Anything different you'd like to order?" he asked her with a smile.

She grinned back. "Nope, sounds like exactly what I'd order." She playfully nudged his shoulder. "Lucky you, you've got yourself a harem of carnivores."

"Beats you all ordering salads," Dare joked, thinking of some of his dates back on Earth. Although the joke didn't translate and he only got polite smiles in answer.

Linia kept up the light banter as they waited for their food, then it arrived and they all ate their fill, along with another round of drinks. She laughed easily and often, and even more often found excuses to touch and bump and otherwise flirt with him.

She even managed to brush the back of his hand with her small chest when she reached across the table for a dish. He could feel one of her pointy nipples scraping his knuckles, and they both shivered slightly in enjoyment at the contact.

The catgirl made no secret that she was interested in him, and Dare tried not to be too eager in showing he definitely returned the interest. A difficult task considering everything about her was adorable and sexy, from her cute dress to her soft skin to her delicate face.

Not to mention she smelled incredible.

Pella smelled good, of course, and so did Zuri. But even though they were right next to him he only caught occasional wafts of their pleasant scent. Which wasn't the case with Linia.

With every breath he was treated to subtle hints of orange citrus and vanilla from her, along with a strong undercurrent of feminine musk that made him want to bury his face in her orange cream hair and inhale deeply.

He didn't think it was soap or perfume, since he hadn't noticed it when she'd first sat next to him, which he would've. And also it was too . . . intimate to be soap or perfume. It was the heady scent of pure, raw femininity, brimming with sexual potential.

The catgirl smelled heavenly. So much so that his cock was beginning to stiffen from her scent alone, and every time her thigh brushed against his it twitched eagerly.

"Something wrong?" Linia abruptly asked, thigh brushing his again. "You seem a bit distracted."

Dare felt himself blushing. "It's nothing."

"Oh?" She looked at him, pale orange eyes sparkling. "Are you sure? You know you can tell me."

Something about her tone gave him the feeling she already knew, so he decided to be honest. "I hope you don't mind me saying so, but you smell really good. Like, incredible."

Pressed against his other side Pella made a clearly discontented noise. "Maybe so, but she doesn't have to spray it everywhere," she muttered.

It was the catgirl's turn to blush. "I don't mind," she said with an easy laugh, playfully running her small hand along his arm. "When a catgirl is in heat she begins secreting pheromones in her sweat. She can tempt a mate with a good sense of smell from a mile away, and turn even a human's head from ten feet."

Her hand slipped beneath the table and brushed between his legs, and she smirked as he jumped in surprise and his erection quickly swelled against her fingers. "Closer up, a catgirl can drive a man wild," she purred. "And when we're really horny the pheromones are much stronger."

She squeezed him through his pants and made him jump again. "I should probably also mention that when in heat a catgirl is *always* horny. We become as eager as bunny girls, and you know how they are."

Dare did his best to play it casual, but judging by the smirks on all the girls' faces he completely failed.

Making a rumbling purring noise in her throat, the adorable catgirl began stroking him lazily up and down his entire length. He did his best not to squirm in pleasure as she leaned close to him, sweet orange and vanilla scented breath tickling his ear. "Maybe my heat's hitting me stronger than I've ever felt it," she murmured in his ear, "or maybe it's just that you're that fucking sexy and right now my hand's on the biggest cock I've ever felt, but I don't think I've *ever* been this horny."

Dare's erection lurched beneath her hand, straining against his pants, and he swallowed audibly.

Grinning at provoking that response, Linia abruptly pulled her hand back, raising it to flag down a passing serving girl. "Another round for the table," she called cheerfully, then turned to him with a teasing expression. "Unless you're done drinking and want to find something else to do?"

"Another round," Pella said, then added under her breath, "If I have to smell catgirl arousal all night I want to be good and drunk."

"Don't pretend you don't like it," Linia teased.

The dog girl blushed. "I never said I didn't," she said. "It's the felids themselves who sometimes annoy me."

"I'll, um, go get your drinks," the serving girl said, wisely getting out of there. Dare kind of wished he could do the same as the abrupt shift in mood hit him like a splash of cold water, wilting the previously erotic atmosphere.

"And why is that?" the catgirl asked, some of her friendliness fading. Although she made a point of taking Dare's arm and slipping beneath it, cuddling up to his side.

Pella looked uncomfortable; clearly she didn't want an argument. But she was also honest and straightforward. "You're not loyal."

Linia laughed, looking genuinely relieved, and relaxed. "Oh, that's all. That's fine then."

Dare wasn't quite so cavalier. "Isn't that a bit unfair, Pella?"

"No, no," the catgirl said quickly, a subtle edge to her voice. "She's not completely wrong. Although felids prefer to think of it as free of spirit. Open with affection and just as free to move on. We can be fond of people we leave behind, and even come back to them, but few of us like to be held in a relationship. We're independent like that."

"I'd call it something else," the dog girl muttered, sipping at her beer.

"What, slutty?" Linia said, voice becoming sharper. "Nobody calls bunny girls sluts, and they try to tempt wandering strangers to pin them down and mount them out in the open." She sniffed. "Besides, for someone who throws her lifetime love and affection to the first person who waves a leash at her, pretty much anyone is disloyal and easy with their affections."

Pella made an angry sound in her throat. "That's not fair," she snapped. "We give our devotion to worthy people." She glared at the petite woman. "Or are you saying becoming Dare's and Zuri's mate was foolish, because they're not worthy?"

Dare closed his eyes, feeling his enjoyable night experiencing a catgirl for the first time slipping through his fingers. Which was ironic because throughout her confrontation with the dog girl Linia had pressed closer and closer to him, until she was practically in his lap.

At the same time Pella had been doing the same, and it wouldn't be too much longer before they were both perched on his knees, clawing each other's eyes out.

Then Zuri came to the rescue, insistently tugging on the dog girl's arm. "Pella, will you come with me to the privy?" she asked in a plaintive voice. "I really need to go, but I feel uneasy with all these tall people crowding about."

Whatever Pella's mood, she couldn't refuse a request like that from her friend. She reluctantly allowed herself to be pulled out of the booth.

Zuri looked back and gave him a slightly tense smile, and he smiled back at her gratefully.

"Good riddance," Linia muttered, glaring after the departing dog girl.

Even though Pella was all the way across the noisy room, she still stiffened.

Dare sighed. "I can understand you both have very different ways of viewing the world, and it's going to be hard to agree on some things. But I also believe you're both good people, and you could even be good friends as long as you avoid certain subjects."

"Not so sure about that," the catgirl said lightly; she seemed reluctant to argue with him, probably still hoping to salvage this night.

He hoped the same, but he had to be honest. "You know I like you, Linia, and Pella was the first to drag your different worldviews out in the open and start this disagreement. But she's also one of the best people I've ever met, and I love her. Do you think you could give her a chance?"

"Because if I don't and we keep fighting you'll have to take her side." The petite woman huffed irritably and squirmed out from under his arm, scooting out of the booth. "I need to relieve myself too."

Dare figured that was the last he'd see of the pretty catgirl, and glumly reflected on lost opportunities as the serving girl finally brought their drinks around.

She seemed surprised to find him alone. "No luck with all three of them, huh?" she teased.

He saluted her with his refilled mug. "Apparently women go to the bathroom together even on Collisa."

In spite of the serving girl's graying hair, and the sort of plump body that looked as if she'd borne children, she still blushed slightly. "It's rude to speak of bathing in polite company," she said with a sniff as she walked away.

Right, here a bathroom was an actual room with baths, not a privy.

Dare settled deeper in his seat and sipped his drink, trying to distract himself from his sudden gloom by looking around the room at the various patrons. And he could admit it was interesting to see the different races and styles of clothing, and idly inspect people with his Adventurer's Eye while he waited for his companions to return.

After a few minutes he finally spotted them approaching and sat up, eyes widening.

After his pessimism he was genuinely surprised to see Linia with Zuri and Pella. And shocked to see the catgirl and dog girl with their arms around each other like the best of friends, smiling widely.

A bit too widely; he had the feeling they were putting on a show to put him at ease after their argument. But it looked like *something* had been settled between them, and most of the tension was gone.

"Looks as if you two made up," he observed as they settled back in their seats, passing the new drinks around.

Linia grinned widely. "You could say that." She reached across him to pat Pella's floppy ears. "This sweetheart was just worried you were going to fall in love with me since you're such a big old softy, and I'd break your heart with my faithless catgirl ways."

Her grin widened. "But don't worry, me and Zuri convinced her that you and me both want the same thing . . . an enjoyable time together and an amicable parting, with an agreement to maybe do it again sometime."

Dare blinked. "That was . . . blunt."

The catgirl giggled. "Says the man trying to get in my pants with the help of his beautiful concubines."

"Aww, you think I'm beautiful?" Pella said, tail wagging. "I knew I liked you."

He grinned. "Well I'm glad we're all on the same page. The evening's been going so well, I'd hate to see it end early." He lifted his mug for a gulp.

"So would I," Linia said casually, "especially since Zuri confirmed what I've already found for myself, that you're hung like a bovid."

Dare choked on his drink and almost sprayed it across the table. Which was apparently the response the women had been hoping for, since they all giggled as they sipped from their own mugs.

Well, as long as they were united in laughing at his discomfiture.

He decided to change the subject. Probably not with the most romantic topic, but one he wanted to know more about. "So since we all have a vested interest in other races being able to live free," he began, "what can you tell me about how you live here in Bastion?"

The catgirl sobered. "You mean how I'd live once I leave the Irregulars?" She took another long gulp, as if to give herself time to think. "My people have a village farther north where retired mercenaries and free felids live in peace. I'll probably go there and hope I'm still young enough to have a few kittens. Unless I'm careless and happen to get pregnant before then."

Dare looked at her closely; she seemed awfully casual about that prospect. "What would happen if you did?"

"Oh, the Marshal's surprisingly understanding about that sort of thing." She grinned. "Or at least, he wouldn't skin me and wear my hide as a cloak for it. I'd either get a two year vacation from my contract to have the child and care for it until it weaned, then find a friend to raise it and rejoin the company, or I could keep the child and become a camp follower, adding five years to my contract."

"That does seem pretty reasonable," Zuri said.

Dare had to agree, especially since Collisa didn't seem big on the idea of letting slaves earn their way towards eventually buying their freedom, leaving those poor people with no hope at all. Or at least that was the case in Haraldar.

"Well, a lot of it's probably a morale thing," Linia said, taking another big gulp of ale. "The company has plenty of casters able to cast Prevent Conception, and fucking is a great way to let off some steam. But it's not perfect and I get the feeling the Marshal doesn't want his soldiers keeping it in their pants for fear of punishment for getting knocked up, harming morale in the process."

She smiled around a smaller sip. "Especially since he enjoys fucking as much as the next mercenary, and he's never short of partners from among the ranks. He wouldn't want to have to punish his own lovers because of a careless mistake."

The petite catgirl slammed her mug onto the table loud enough to draw the attention of a passing serving girl, motioning for another round. After she got a responding nod she turned to Dare with a mock scowl. "But do you seriously want to talk about pregnancy, given our plans for tonight?"

He chuckled ruefully. "Good point."

"Right, then." She leaned forward to look at everyone at the table. "Anyone know how to do something entertaining?"

Zuri and Pella both turned to Dare expectantly, and he felt his face heat. "Fine, fine," he said, pulling out a silver coin. "You've probably seen magic, right?"

"Sure," Linia said, smirking as if she was in on the game.

"Okay, I'm going to make this disappear." Dare began rolling the coin across the table in her direction, then slapped the hand that had been holding it on the table hard enough to make Zuri and Pella jump.

He was already reaching for the coin with his other hand, faster than the eye could see thanks to Fleetfoot and using his other hand as a distraction. But to his shock he caught the slightest flash of movement and realized the catgirl's hand was already there, closing around the coin.

He hastily yanked his hand back to not ruin the trick, a blur of motion the only indication Linia had done the same.

"Yay!" Zuri said, clapping. Pella laughed and slapped the table, and both looked at him expectantly, waiting for him to make the coin reappear; they hadn't noticed anything. Although the dog girl was frowning slightly now, as if she sensed something in his expression or scent.

Dare turned to the adorable catgirl with a wry twist of his mouth. "You're quick."

She laughed, rolling the coin across the backs of her fingers. "*I'm* quick? Are you secretly a felid who cut off your ears and tail to fit in among humans?" She shook her head wryly to dismiss her own absurd idea. "I've never seen one of your kind with reflexes like that."

"Wait, what just happened?" Zuri asked, smile faltering as she stared at the coin Linia was playing with.

He shrugged and pulled out more coins, idly juggling them and occasionally making one disappear, then another of a different precious metal take its place. "Turns out our new friend is immune to magic."

"No, you just have to try harder," Linia said, eyes twinkling. "I'd be disappointed if sleight of hand is your only trick." She abruptly tossed the coin to him, and although he fumbled he managed to add it to the ones he was juggling. Her smile widened. "See?"

Pella clapped. "Ooh, juggle them between you! I saw entertainers at one of Master's feasts do that once."

"I'm game if you are," Dare said, starting to toss the coins the catgirl's way as he caught them.

She missed half the coins he tossed, and mistimed throwing the rest back so he fumbled and dropped a few of them in turn. But that didn't stop her lazy smile. "Game? No, we're both hunters, aren't we?"

Hunters or not, their attempts to juggle between each other didn't improve much. Five minutes and too many dropped coins to count later, they concluded that it was harder than it looked. "We'll just have to practice our coordination tonight," Linia concluded as she got to work picking up the coins.

Her tone made it clear what kind of practice she had in mind.

That seemed to be a cue for Zuri and Pella. They exchanged looks, then the dog girl made a show of stretching. "Well, it's getting late and I'm all worn out from dragging a sled full of loot for days," she said. "Can I have the room key, Dare? I'm going to bed."

"Oh." Dare looked at her helplessly as he fished for the key. "You sure?"

"I'm sure." She leaned up and kissed him warmly. "Don't worry, I'm happy to get a good night's sleep. Go have fun."

"I think I'll keep Pella company," Zuri said, taking the dog girl's hand as they both slid out of the booth.

He hesitated, torn. His goblin lover seemed happy to take a backseat so he could enjoy new experiences, as she had his first time with Pella and also when he gave their new lover a bath. But he didn't want to exclude her. "Are you sure?"

Phoenix

"Absolutely." She grinned up at the dog girl. "Maybe I can show Pella some of the ways you showed me to make love with your tongue."

Linia giggled and Dare's cock, already partially stiffened at the prospect of spending the night with the adorable catgirl, became rock hard as he imagined the two beautiful women going down on each other. He almost regretted that he wouldn't be there to see it.

Then he looked at Linia, who was grinning at them all as if she was up for anything, and decided there'd be other opportunities to watch his lovers play.

He had a different pussy to lick tonight.

Zuri cast Prevent Conception on him. "Remember it only lasts six hours, so wake me up if you need a refresh," she said, grinning hugely.

Linia laughed. "If he still needs it after six hours, he'll be the most virile man on Collisa."

The little goblin just smirked at him, and he laughed and hugged her. "I'll wake you up if I need to," he promised. "And if you want to join us . . ."

She just laughed as she and Pella gathered their things and headed upstairs, leaving him in the booth with the sexy catgirl.

Linia wasted no time climbing into his lap, velvety ear rubbing his cheek as she pressed her face to his neck. "Ready to go play?" she asked in a cute little voice, licking along his collar with a small, rough tongue. She pointedly brushed her leg against his raging erection, giggling. "This little guy definitely is."

He smirked as he reached down to run his hands along the soft short fur of her skinny tail, giving it a playful squeeze. "Believe me, there's nothing little about it," he whispered, breath tickling the silky tufts in her ear.

Her entire body shivered, and she made a soft little purring noise as she slipped off his lap, taking his hand and tugging him out of the booth. "Then come show me."

Chapter Nineteen
Orange and Vanilla

Linia's room on the third floor was small and sparsely furnished, without much besides a bed that might fit four if they really crowded.

Of course, that was the only piece of furniture they needed.

The petite catgirl closed and locked the door behind her and stepped into Dare's open arms, slender body pressing against him as he leaned down and kissed her. Her plump little rosebud lips were as soft and perfect as they had looked, filling his head with the sweet taste of orange and vanilla.

His throbbing erection pressed against her stomach as he caressed her back through the thin cloth of her summer dress, his hands making their way down to grab her narrow ass. Her pert globes were a perfect handful, firm and yielding, and she made a noise of enjoyment against his lips as he squeezed.

Then Linia abruptly stepped back, orange eyes dancing. "Now that I've got you to myself," she purred, caressing his chest, "I've been thinking about sitting on your face ever since I brought it up earlier."

Dare's cock twitched. "So have I," he admitted with a grin.

Linia gave him an enigmatic smile. "I know. You've probably been dying to taste this pussy."

He couldn't help but laugh and groan at the same time. "You really get a lot of work out of cat puns, huh?"

She giggled. "What can I say? We like to have fun with our prey." With a playful yowl she pounced, bearing him to the ground beneath her slender weight.

Almost faster than seemed physically possible, the catgirl positioned herself over him and descended. Her light skirt settled around his head like a tent, filling his nose with the heady scent of her arousal as it grew stronger and stronger in the confined space. The thin cloth let in plenty of light to see her slender, shapely legs, the smooth, creamy skin disappearing beneath her innocent white panties.

They were already soaked with Linia's nectar, and he watched greedily as they descended to press against his nose and mouth, smothering him in her blissful ambrosia.

Dare kissed her small, delicate petals through the cloth, tasting the powerful pheromones she released while in heat as a delicious combination of honey, oranges, vanilla, and raw, primal musk. It was such an incredible taste that he eagerly dug his tongue up into her panties, pressing them into her slit as he probed for more of her nectar.

The catgirl giggled and rubbed her crotch lightly up and down against his mouth, and he eagerly reached up to cup her firm, panty-clad cheeks with both hands, the cloth soft and warm flesh beneath yielding just enough for him to give it a good squeeze.

The cloth of her summer dress around him abruptly vanished as Linia lifted it over her head, confirming that aside from her panties she was naked underneath, and tossed it aside. Dare was treated to his mental picture of her sleek pale orange tail waving in front of him, feasting his eyes on all the curves and smooth pale skin along her back.

She was beautiful from behind, and he couldn't wait to see the rest of her.

His orange dream lover seemed to feel the same about him; he felt her hands stroke his straining cock through his pants, then begin deftly untying the laces. She had him free even faster than he could do it himself, and he heard her gasp as she took in the sight.

"Zuri wasn't lying," she murmured in awe, soft hand gently caressing his throbbing erection like a pet, "this is the biggest cock I've ever seen, and I've been with some of the larger races."

Hard not to appreciate a compliment like that. And her obvious excitement made him all the more eager to get his first glimpse of her sweet little pussy.

Dare abandoned his efforts to pleasure Linia through her panties and snaked a finger between her legs, pulling the sopping gusset to one side. He feasted his eyes on the flushed, delicate pink petals, beaded with her dew, and her tiny erect pearl just peeking out from beneath its hood. Farther back was her adorable little pucker, just asking to be played with.

She smelled faintly of soap, overpowered by the intoxicating scent of her arousal. He felt an overwhelming urge to taste her more thoroughly and grabbed her ass with his other hand, pulling her tight to his face and teasing his tongue between her folds as deep as it would go.

"Ooooh," the catgirl purred, back arching. "Keep doing that."

He hadn't planned to stop. He eagerly lapped up the nectar flowing from her pink tunnel, lips lovingly caressing her labia as he probed every inch of her walls his tongue could reach. All the while she squirmed and moaned deliciously against his face.

Dare could've gone on like that for a lot longer, but Linia had other ideas. Her gentle hand stroking his length moved down to stroke his balls instead, and moment later was replaced by her small, rough tongue lapping around his tip. "You like that?" she teased. "I bet I can get you off first."

"Oh gods," he moaned against her lips; she probably wasn't wrong, but he was eager to accept the challenge. "You're on."

If she was going to play that game he could do the same. He pulled away from her glorious hole and began flicking his tongue against her little clit, making her hips jerk involuntarily.

The catgirl retaliated by taking him into her small mouth, pouty lips straining around his girth. She didn't even try to take him down her throat, instead gently sucking on his tip and playing her tongue over the underside. Her warm, wet mouth felt incredible, especially as her free hand began stroking the length of his cock, lubricated by her flowing saliva, while she continued to fondle his balls.

Dare tongued her pearl more aggressively, making her hips jerk. He pulled her tighter against his face and kept up the full court press, and she began mewling in pleasure and sucking him harder.

He wasn't sure which of them lost the game first. All he knew was that as she tensed with a surprisingly loud wail, even muffled by his dick, he grunted and twitched his hips, losing his battle with his onrushing orgasm and releasing into her mouth.

He felt Linia's pussy winking around his tongue, flooding his face with her nectar, and he clutched at her desperately as he rode his own wave, one spurt after another shooting right down her throat. Linia moaned, eagerly swallowing it all.

She was incredible.

Once they finally came down from their peaks she gracefully climbed off him, stripping her soaked panties off and tossing them aside to reveal her in all her glory and finally giving him a view of her from the front.

The adorable catgirl's body was perfectly hairless, creamy skin flawless and smooth. She had small, pert breasts with plump nipples a pale pink almost indistinguishable from her creamy skin, poking out erect and proud.

Her abdomen was smooth and clearly defined, like a supermodel's, leading down to a plump mons and her flushed, glistening slit. Her legs were slender and had perfect lines, leading down to delicate little feet just begging to be sucked on.

She cocked her hip to one side, planting a fist on it, and gave him a feline smile. "Well?" she asked. "You're not the only one eager for a show."

"Right." Blushing a bit at her rapt attention, he peeled off his tunic and skinned out of his pants and underwear.

Linia's eyes hungrily played over him as he set his clothes aside, a small hand between her legs toying with her pink pussy as she made hungry little mewling noises. Dare teasingly struck a pose for her, hands on hips and legs planted far apart, and she giggled.

Although that giggle turned to a gasp as she kept staring at his cock. "Did Zuri cast some sort of enhancement spell on you, Dare?" she asked, rubbing herself faster as her pale cheeks flushed even rosier. "It's, um, not going down."

Dare laughed. "Not a spell, I just have that much stamina." He teasingly rubbed his cock, slick with her saliva. "Ready for round two?"

"Primal ancestor, yes!" she said, bounding onto the bed on her hands and knees. She pressed her face into the covers and lifted her small ass, eagerly presenting herself as her pale orange tail lashed in anticipation.

Her sex glistened between her slender thighs like a peach beaded with dew, and he wanted to just dive in and taste it again. But he wanted something else more.

Stepping forward and positioning himself at her opening, he rubbed her smooth ass with one hand and made her purr. "Ready?"

"Fuck yes," she moaned.

He pressed his tip between her folds, their pink warmth welcoming him, and slowly began to push.

As his head slipped past her tightly stretched lips and entered her soft tunnel, Linia's back arched and she literally caterwauled. In a way that made him wince and look at the room's walls; they didn't look all that soundproof.

"Keep going!" she shouted urgently as he paused. "You know what felid penises do to a catgirl's tender little pussy? Getting stretched to the tearing point by your monster feels like bliss in comparison."

Dare still hesitated; she was awfully tight, and he knew from experience that women needed time to adjust to his size. "Are you sure?"

Linia made a frustrated sound. "Fuck it, I'll get us started then." She slammed her hips back against him, pushing him in deeper until he bottomed out at her cervix, and caterwauled again.

He wasn't sure if the noise was discomfort or pleasure or something in between, but she certainly seemed to be enjoying herself considering she pulled forward and slammed back again.

Dare grit his teeth at the raw pleasure of her tight walls slipping up and down his shaft. Deciding he should forget his reservations and follow her lead, he grabbed her ass and began to thrust in time with her desperate motions.

"Fuuuuck," the catgirl moaned, tail lashing violently. "I needed this after a month in the wilds."

"You're fucking amazing," he gasped back, putting a knee on the bed to get a better angle and slamming in harder.

That was all she needed and her back arched again, face burying so deep in the mattress that it disappeared. Even muffled her caterwaul was still loud, and her tight pussy clenched around his length as she squirted all over his crotch and thighs, filling the room with the heady scent of her arousal.

Dare kept fucking Linia even through her orgasm, slamming into her as she squirted again and again, muffled voice an almost constant wail as she reached even higher peaks.

As for him, the incredible sensation of going hard in this little catgirl was making his balls churn. Even thinking of mathematical equations and baseball and frigid mountain lakes in the dead of winter didn't help, and he prepared to lose the battle and embrace the pleasure of emptying himself inside his adorable lover.

But before he could her tense body went limp, slumping down to rest on the mattress with a few final shuddering quivers.

Dare reluctantly headed off his orgasm at the pass and paused in his thrusting. "Still with me?" he teased.

She raised her adorable round face, flushed and glistening with perspiration, to look up at him. Orange eyes huge and glazed with bliss, she gave him a lazy smile. "That was incredible, but I'm not sure this sore little pussy can handle much more of that until I've had a rest."

Before he had time to be disappointed she dropped her legs to hang over the side of the bed, presenting herself at a different angle. "So I guess it's time to switch to my ass."

Fuuuuck . . . this little catgirl didn't slow down, she just switched gears and accelerated into the turn.

Dare's cock was well lubricated with her saliva and copious arousal, and he was eager to get back to the pleasure he'd just enjoyed. Still, he took his time lining himself up with her tiny little pucker, pushing forward very slowly and gently.

Sure, he might've just been pounding his petite lover as if he meant to break her, but the ass was a whole different ballpark. And while she'd been fully on board with their enthusiastic lovemaking, now that he paused and regained some clarity she looked small and fragile beneath him.

Linia grinned back at him as if guessing his thoughts. "Don't worry, I'm far from a virgin in that hole." She playfully wiggled her narrow rump against his tip. "Go slow, but don't be afraid to keep pushing . . . I can take it."

It wasn't an idle boast, either. As Dare pressed against her delicate rosebud it opened obligingly, far easier than when he'd cleaned Pella's bowels. The petite catgirl was crushingly tight, and as he continued she tensed and grimaced, but she began rumbling contentedly as he pushed in deeper and deeper.

After a minute or so of slow, patient effort he bottomed out with a couple inches to spare and paused for a moment, giving her a chance to adjust. "There we go," she said, panting a bit. "See? Told you I could take that monster like a champ." She wiggled forwards and backwards against his invading cock. "Go ahead."

He pulled back and thrust in again, slowly and gently, while she mewled contentedly, tail lashing. After a few thrusts she began pushing back with every thrust, moving in time with him, until they had a good rhythm going.

Dare lasted a commendable few minutes in her crushingly tight insides. Long enough for Linia to give a delicious moan and ease into a more gentle climax, a fresh flood of nectar flowing down her thighs and her asshole lovingly caressing him.

That was enough for him. He grabbed her narrow ass, bottomed out, and tensed. "Coming," he gasped.

"Go for it," she panted languidly, still in the throes of her milder climax.

With a last twitch of his hips he emptied herself deep in her bowels, spurt after spurt coating her insides.

Finally he collapsed onto his side, pulling her down to spoon with him as his cock twitched a few final times and began to shrink inside her. "Gods, you're fantastic," he said, rubbing her flat tummy and then reaching up to fondle her small breasts and tease her hard nipples.

The catgirl giggled. "You're pretty good yourself," she said contentedly. "But I hope you're not done yet . . . the night's still young."

It certainly was. After fifteen or so minutes of contented cuddling to rest and recover, they cleaned themselves up. Then Dare ate her out for a few minutes to get her going again, luxuriating in her sweet taste, before laying her down on her back and climbing on top of her.

He didn't go as hard and fast as the first time, but he managed to tease a few squirting orgasms out of her before he finally gave in, bottoming out in her core and releasing directly against her cervix.

For the next few hours they alternated between cuddling and running their hands all over each other's bodies, teasing and foreplay, gentle lovemaking, and a few rounds of vigorous fucking. He came in her half a dozen more times, giving equal attention to all her holes. Linia even returned the favor and slipped a finger in his ass on their last go, seeming to know just where to press to tease a powerful orgasm out of him.

Then, finally sated, they cleaned each other one last time and cuddled beneath the covers.

"I kind of wish your concubines could've joined us for this," Linia said contentedly. "It would be fun to play with them, too." She giggled. "I hear canids love licking buttholes."

Dare hadn't heard that and wondered if it was true. He grinned and stroked her soft back. "Maybe we'll find out tomorrow?"

"Definitely." She rubbed her head affectionately against his shoulder, then curled up half on top of him and settled down to sleep, chest rumbling in a contented purr.

He soon joined her.

Epilogue
Triumphant

Dare woke with a start to the sound of a distant commotion filtering in through the open windows, voices talking excitedly and cheering, music playing, even horns blowing.

He opened his eyes to find Linia sprawled atop him like a cat, sleeping peacefully. She was still letting out a cute little rumble as she purred contentedly. The light filtering in through the windows gave her skin a lustrous creamy glow, and she felt as soft and warm as she looked.

She was absolutely adorable and he would've loved to just cuddle with her until she woke up, or maybe even go back to sleep himself. But the tumult outside seemed to be getting louder, sounding for all the world like a parade, and he wanted to check it out.

Dare debated whether to try to slip out from under his catgirl lover or wake her up. He eventually decided that whatever the excitement was, she'd want to know. So he began gently stroking her velvety ears. "Linia," he whispered.

"Go away," she murmured sleepily in a cutesy kitten voice. Her catlike curled fist bopped his nose playfully, while her naked body squirmed against him in a way that made his cock stir. "I'm sleeping right meow."

He couldn't help it, he laughed out loud. "Really?"

The catgirl's eyes opened to slits and she gave him a frosty look. "If you woke me up to get frisky I'm going to throw you out the window. You wore me out last night, and cute little catgirls need their beauty sleep."

Dare shifted out from under her, ignoring her complaints, and stepped over to the window. "Speaking of windows, you have to hear that."

She yawned. "Of course I do. It's probably Haraldar's heroes and their retinue passing through town on their way to the kingdom's border, to finally clear out the overflowing monster spawns in the wild and bring some stability back to Bastion. They were only five or so miles south of town when they stopped to camp last night, which gave people here enough time to gather to watch their arrival."

He felt his pulse quicken at the idea of catching sight of high level adventurers. He'd be able to use his Eye to see their basic stats and combat abilities, for one thing. And it would be awesome to see a hint of the grandness that took place at the pinnacle of society here.

"And you don't want to see that?" he asked.

Linia curled up for all the world like a cat, sleek orange tail looping around to cover her eyes, and pulled the covers up over her head. "I'll be seeing plenty of them . . . the Irregulars are going to be traveling north with their retinue when they set out. We've been hired to scout for them, help secure their forward bases, and keep the spawn points in the territory they claim clear."

Dare whistled. "That's pretty exciting."

"It's a job." She finally poked her head out to grin at him. "Although it might be fun to see if any of the grand heroes or stuffy royal guards are interested in pounding a pussy."

He winced. "Ouch. Just spent the night together and you're already looking for someone better."

The catgirl laughed. "Don't worry, I'd be happy to play with you some more if we cross paths again." Her pale orange eyes sparkled. "Although I'm not done with you yet . . . we still need to wake up your concubines and play with them a bit before it's time to head out."

"After watching the parade?" Dare begged.

She sighed and leapt gracefully out of bed, lithe body soft and inviting in the sunlight. "Fine, but we'd better hurry or we'll miss it."

They quickly dressed and made their way up to his lovers' room. Pella and Zuri met him halfway, having heard the commotion and on their way to find him. Together they all made their way outside and followed the noise to where a huge crowd was gathered on one of the largest streets in town.

Even so, it felt cramped and tight with hundreds of people gathered along its length. Although guards were pressing onlookers back to the walls or even into alleyways to clear the way for an approaching column of riders.

Dare lifted Zuri onto his shoulders so she could see, and he and his lovers pushed their way to a spot where they could watch the event.

On Earth he'd witnessed parades with thousands of people that lasted hours, and gatherings that numbered in the hundreds of thousands or even millions. But that was all on TV, and even the larger parades he'd attended in person didn't feel as regal and vibrant as this.

In his time in Collisa, he hadn't seen anything more grand than a squad of guards trotting down the streets of Kov. He knew that most of the towns he'd visited were small, and he hadn't seen any armies or kingdom capitols yet.

Still, knowing that there were bigger things out there than what he'd seen in his travels didn't prepare him for the breathtaking sight of the procession.

No wonder everyone had come out to witness it, throwing the town into an impromptu festival.

The Royal Guards came first, at the front and back of their procession flying the flag of Haraldar, black with a silver border, in its center the silver emblem of a gauntleted fist clutching the hilt of a broken sword.

Dare counted 50 men and women in their ranks, all at least Level 40 and more than half over 50, wearing matching black and silver livery with the silver fist and broken hilt on their surcoats. There were dozens of combat classes represented in their number, many with different armor and weapons.

Although all the gear looked as if it had been created by the same craftsmen, brilliantly polished and enameled in black and silver. It was all Exceptional quality, and some of the officers wore Master quality pieces.

It easily would've looked sloppy and chaotic to have such a variety of classes and gear, but the guards were ordered in ranks by the armor they wore, and in many cases even the weapon type. For the most part that meant that healers and spellcasters traveled together at the back, with ranged weapon wielders and lightly armored melee in the center, and heavily armored tanks at the front.

Although there were Paladins and Spellshields among the tanks, and Healers and other leather-wearing healing classes among the damage dealers. There were even a few damage dealing classes among the cloth wearers.

The Royal Guards looked ahead with perfect discipline in spite of the cheering crowds, although a few smiled as maidens threw flowers at their feet, or ran forward to tuck brightly colored kerchiefs, gauzy scarves, or what looked suspiciously like undergarments into gaps in their armor. Young girls darted forward too, shyly slipping wreaths of flowers over the hilts of weapons or the tops of shields.

Although as excited as the crowd was to see the elite guards, at the sight of the heroes coming up the street behind them everyone went nuts.

There were fewer of them, 20 or so. Although it was hard to tell for sure since many traveled with small retinues of friends or servants (or slaves). Many of those companions were fellow adventurers, also high level and well geared, although nowhere close to the heroes themselves.

In spite of the chaos of the retinues, however, the heroes stood out. Not only did they have ridiculously ornate looking armor and clothing of only the highest quality, but there was an *aura* that seemed to pulse out from them. Like a regal glow that drew the eye and inspired awe. All were at least Level 50, most 60 or higher, and the elderly woman at their head was Level 66.

Dare saw his first Fabled quality item borne by the elderly heroine, a brilliantly shining staff that was far too fancifully carved to be of any practical use, but pulsing with power. And all the rest of her gear was Master quality. Going by the spells and abilities he could see with his Eye, she could've leveled the town of Jarn's Holdout with only a little effort.

Which shouldn't come as too much of a surprise; before his unseen benefactor sent him to Collisa, she'd told him that spellcasters could become stupidly powerful at the higher levels. At the cost of burning through their mana pool with a handful of spells.

What shocked him the most, though, was the Level 61 Warrior riding just behind the elderly spellcaster, a powerfully built man in his 50s with graying hair.

One of his listed abilities was the Adventurer's Eye.

"Fuck," Dare muttered, easing back behind the corner of the nearest building as the man rode past.

"What?" Zuri, on his shoulders and along for the ride, asked anxiously; Pella and Linia still seemed absorbed by the pageantry.

He didn't dare look himself, but he needed to know. "The Level 61 near the front. Did he notice me? Is he acting different?"

"Why?" she asked, even more anxious.

"He's got the Adventurer's Eye. He can see mine."

"Oh. Shit." She wiggled against him in an indication for him to move. "Okay, I'll check. Get me a bit closer."

Dare leaned forward, and his goblin lover cautiously poked her head around the corner. "The older human, with the sword and shield?"

"Right."

She shook her head. "I don't think he noticed you. He's still riding along, looking around at the crowd smiling and waving." She giggled. "A serving girl just threw him her panties and he's ogling her."

Dare breathed a bit easier. The Adventurer's Eye was rare, and you weren't supposed to get it until at least Level 50. If that Warrior saw a Level 23 hanging around with one of his listed abilities as the Adventurer's Eye, it might be unusual enough that the man would come after him.

Even positive attention could sometimes be a bad thing. Especially since Zuri was technically an escaped slave, even though her master had abandoned her, and Braley might've reneged on giving Pella her freedom.

"He's passed out of sight now," Zuri said. "The other heroes are mostly farther along the street, too, and the camp followers are starting to pass by. The crowd isn't nearly as excited about them."

Not surprising; the poor people probably felt awkward and embarrassed about following at the tail of such august company. And they'd have no other choice but to keep up, since this wasn't actually a parade and they had a long way to go today.

Dare rejoined the other women and they watched the last of the heroes pass out of sight down the street, on their way to continue the long journey north to the kingdom's border. "I expect we'll be seeing them again," he said, "if we end up hunting in the wilds out there before they finish their expedition and head home."

Although I'll either have to get to Level 50 first or steer clear of that Warrior, he added to himself.

"I certainly will be," Linia said, settling back against his chest and affectionately rubbing her head against his shoulder. "We'll probably get the order to head out before too much longer. Although the heroes will no doubt have to meet with the Baron and other town leaders for a formal reception before they pass through, so we've got some time."

"Hmm?" Dare asked, wrapping his arms around her. "You sound like you have some idea of what to do with that time."

"Maybe," she said coyly. "Now that we've seen the grand heroes and all the pageantry, it's still early and I'd like to get back to bed." She twisted around in his arms and looked up at him impishly. "Although not necessarily back to sleep."

Eyes dancing, the catgirl squirmed free of his embrace and looped both arms around Pella's shoulders from behind, nuzzling the taller woman's back. "I still want to play with you cuties."

The dog girl tried to pretend sternness, but her tail thumped the petite catgirl as it began to wag. "Oh yeah?" she asked casually.

"Of course. You're absolutely gorgeous and Zuri is adorable." Linia playfully licked the back of Pella's neck. "Have you ever had a tongue bath?" she purred.

The fluffy golden-furred tail began to wag harder and the dog girl abandoned her nonchalance. "I haven't!" she said eagerly. "But my old master once wanted me to give him one, and he really seemed to enjoy it. I've always wanted to see what it was like."

The catgirl laughed. "I thought you might . . . you strike me as a person who really loves baths of any kind. And I wouldn't mind getting some cleaning from your tongue, either . . . I bet it would feel wonderful to have you slobbering all over me."

She turned Pella's head so they were both looking at Dare and Zuri, and used her cutesy cat voice again. "And I bet between the two of us we can give your lovers the same treatment. Maybe even see if they'd like to try out giving tongue baths too."

He couldn't help but grin, fighting to keep his cock from stiffening in his pants right there on the street at the mental images the petite catgirl was conjuring up. There was no question about whether he'd like to lick three gorgeous girls all over their sexy bodies. Especially Linia with her pheromone-rich sweat.

The fact that they were even offering it, let alone seemed excited about it, felt like a dream come true.

Zuri rubbed her thighs together against his neck, hesitant but clearly intrigued and more than a little aroused. "Goblins don't usually do much with their mouths while mating, but everything Dare and the women we've been with have shown me has been really nice. And a tongue bath sounds . . . amazing."

"Good, because I've heard goblin arousal has a super sexy taste. Stronger pheromones than a catgirl, even, although not as abundant." Linia pulled the tiny woman off Dare's shoulders and into her embrace with Pella, then began ushering the two back towards the inn.

After a few steps she looked over her shoulder to give him a smoky look. "You coming?"

He imagined he would be. Multiple times.

Grinning, he quickly caught up to his lovers and joined their group embrace as they headed inside.

End of Kovana.
The adventures of Dare and his harem
continue in Bastion, third book of the Outsider series.

Thank you for reading Kovana!

I hope you enjoyed reading it as much as I enjoyed writing it. If you feel the book is worthy of support, I'd greatly appreciate it if you'd rate it, or better yet review it, on Amazon, as well as recommend it to anyone you think would also enjoy it.

As a self-published author I flourish with the help of readers who review and recommend my work. Your support helps me continue doing what I love and bringing you more books to enjoy.

About the Author

Aiden Phoenix became an established author
writing stories about the end of the world.
Then Collisa called, a new and exciting world to explore,
and like the characters in his series he was reborn anew there.

Made in the USA
Monee, IL
07 January 2024

51343881R00194